And Lay Waste
My Soul

And Lay Waste My Soul

VOLUME TWO OF
A MEMOIR OF THE DEVIL

A Novel by

Rayfield A. Waller

Library of Congress Control Number:		2021911035
ISBN:	Hardcover	978-1-6641-7787-1
	Softcover	978-1-6641-7786-4
	eBook	978-1-6641-7785-7

This is a work of fiction. All of the characters, names, incidents, organizations, and dialogue in this novel are either the products of the author's imagination or are used fictitiously.

Patricia Calloway, cover designer and illustrator. She is a conceptual fine artist, illustrator and art educator living in Detroit, Michigan. She earned a Bachelor of Fine Arts degree from the College for Creative Studies and is currently working on a solo exhibition of landscape and wildlife paintings.

Print information available on the last page.

Rev. date: 08/13/2021

To order additional copies of this book, contact:
Xlibris
844-714-8691
www.Xlibris.com
Orders@Xlibris.com
820927

ROBERT JOHNSON-STYLE BLUES

ANYONECANPLAYGUITAR.CO.UK

**Yugoslavian 1,000 Dinar national banknote
issued in 1991, commemorating the life of
Serbian-American inventor, Nikola Tesla**

Map of Austria in the Time of Dr. Sigmund Freud

Dedications

Again, for my parents – who made me,
and my daughter, Lena-Julia – who challenges me.

To my departed Margo V. Perkins — my Margo, not anyone else's.

For Patricia Calloway who will be recognized as a great visual artist (see the cover).

For Kofi Natambu, blood brother
and Leslie A. Reese my blood sister
and to Dr. James Nadell my blood twin in Miami,
To Julie Weber in remembering Ithaca, NY. and the bus stop where we met.

For Perri Giovannucci, a better writer than I, a daughter of the grandeur that was the ancient Roman republic.

For my oldest friend, departed, Roberto Cabanban Sobremonte Jr., scion of the Philippine Islands,
and for my friend and former student, Michael Franco and Mother Jane Franco — the two like family to me.

For Javon my student whose poems always get instantly published, rightly so.

And to my cousin Victor Bullock who left Earth in his sleep far too soon
but not before I told him I love him; lucky for me —
no unfinished business.

1. DEFEAT

1

I raised my sword up over my head to surrender just as my *secondus* Marcellus's sword was beaten down. The Gauls wanted us alive it seemed, lucky for him. He had to be subdued, but I was surrendering in hopes that he and I and the remains of our legion, those fighters left of my command, might be allowed to live.

Enemy fighters came thick as devils to encircle my second-in-command Caesar Marcellus the Younger. I stood as still as I could as they crowded him thick as devils, one might say, and though it took more of them than it ought to have, they finally drove him to his knees and took his sword away. Another of them, acting casually, contemptuous of me for my readiness to surrender, walked up to me and snatched away the sword I held aloft in obeisance. Thus, my command of a legion ended in abject defeat. The survivors as it turned out would die later for having trusted me to lead them.

Later, the snow ceased.

They had killed nearly all the detachment leaving only a hundred of my legionnaires alive including Marcellus, Trebonius, the coward Hirtius, and the loyal Tullius among them, stripped of armor and weapons. The lot of us sat bleeding and shabby, well, them more than me, in a circle in the snow surrounded by Gaulish warriors guarding us at spear point.

It was no longer snowing but the air had grown colder as Gaulish troops hobbled surviving Roman soldiers together with rough rope lines. Marcellus's dog, Beast, whimpered not from the cold but from a glancing sword wound that he'd gotten while protecting his master from the final assault. Beneath a cage of piled branches that flamed in growing dusk, the ground hissed and melted as the sun sank a bit lower in the sky. It would eventually disappear behind a western stand of trees.

Marcellus petted Beast to comfort him. Beast for his part, though obviously in pain, was now quiet. Not that he had grown frightened, he was simply being vigilant. He lay on his stomach, his chin resting on his forearms, alert, but resigned to defeat.

I looked over at a nearby pile of Roman corpses that grew steadily higher and wider as Gauls dragged dead Romans out of the forest to toss them disdainfully onto the bloody heap. Black, oily holes in the white snow all around us contained macabre smoldering heads of men and animals—evidence of a primitive and simple-minded yet effective tactic Gauls had used against us.

"I still cannot believe the horror of it, Saturnius, that these barbarians set fire to and launched our own men's severed heads at us," Marcellus hissed quietly, not looking at me and not moving his lips so the Gauls would not know we spoke.

"You must admit," I whispered back, "it was horrible and effective. It shocked the men and broke their ranks. A few tactics can break a Roman legion's discipline as effectively."

"Their ambassadors back in Rome told us two years ago of their strange ways of making war. We didn't listen."

"Aye, Marcellus, or remember. We were arrogant."

"We were typically Roman."

*Well, you **Romans** were, typically. I am not a Roman; I am not even human.*

As if he read my mind, Marcellus's whisper grew bitter as he shot at me, "Yet being more than Roman, Saturnius, my General, now would be the time to use your powers as a sky god to save us!"

Marcellus for a year now had been first of my commanders to suspect that I wasn't what I seemed. He believed I must be one of the "sky gods," the thing ancient Romans would imagine a supernatural being to be. That, or a devil from the underworld. Of course, I am neither, my dear amanuensis. I am far more strange a thing than that, you know me by now. No, I am not saying you haven't been listening. I have spoken to you of everything I am, and you are an apt biographer. I only mean do be certain to write down what I'm saying now of my friendship with Marcellus. "Friendship" of a sort, and though his insouciance toward me and hotheadedness in battle were a constant aggravation to me, I could not manage to stop caring about him as much as it is possible for me to care for a human.

"Well? No tricks to save us, Saturnius?" He was still looking away from me as he whispered, so the Gauls would not know we conspired.

They knew.

"You! Shut up! Do now, Roman eater of entrails!" shouted a Gaulish fighter in bad Latin, who stabbed at Marcellus with a rustic spear, cutting him across his shoulder. Marcellus surged to his feet, taking blows, but slyly manipulating his own beating by maneuvering to grab a spear or a shield from one of the Gauls, I noted.

Those guarding us were all taller than four cubits and weighed greater than two hundred librae as well as being shrewd enough by the way to reckon what Marcellus was about, since they were just as battle hardened and just as sly as he. Two of them handed over their weapons to the others so he would have nothing to grasp for, then they stripped off their fur vests so they were naked from the waist up, seemingly untouched by the cold. Those two fought Marcellus with fists, fully intending to demonstrate to the surviving cohorts on the ground around us that we, their leaders, were done.

"Beast! Stay there!" Marcellus shouted as he fought back gamely, with a ferociousness that as always made me admire him even though his persistence was annoying to me. He'd shouted to Beast so that his dog would not be butchered or further wounded. He made a good try of it with his fists but was soon beaten back to the ground beside me. They kicked him fiercely until he was still.

I lay my hand on his shoulder not just to comfort him but to covertly pass on to him a bit of celestial energy to keep his wounds from being infected or festering over time. Why not?

"You're endangering us by resisting!" hissed the coward Hirtius, who suddenly now had learned to keep his voice quiet, and now at last cared what effect our actions had on the soldiers around us, now that those soldiers were the Gaulish enemy.

Marcellus spat blood and peered at Hirtius through bruised slit eyes.

"I pledge to cut off one of your ears, Honorary Proconsul."

Hirtius gave a bitter chuckle.

"A hollow threat, scion of Julii, given the circumstances."

"Be you still!" came a Gaul's rebuke, called out in Latin. Hirtius got a boot to the side of the head, splitting his scalp and causing blood to ebb into the snow. Marcellus laughed.

"Mars sends justice," he hissed, and laughed again.

"Want you another beating, Roman?" called one big Gaul, speaking Latin also. "I make sure it be your last."

"Leave the beatings to me, Balaad," called out General Ulgöthur, as he strode over the snow toward us, flanked by Elouskonios and Liuthari, all three far more heavily armed than the last time I'd seen them back in Rome.

Ulgöthur stood over me, surveying the remains of my detachment. Elouskonios, near Balaad, held a sword ready, protective as always of the general. Meanwhile, Liuthari roved about, thrusting a spear into Roman corpses to be sure they really were corpses; a sensible and a typical thing after a battle.

"Not many of you 'civilized Romans' left," Ulgöthur remarked, gazing down at me. "Stand, Saturnius."

The four of us reached Agrippa's villa townhouse, located in Campus Martius over a bridge. Elouskonios and Liuthari both relaxed their vigilance over Ulgöthur once we were inside. We passed through a rank of praetorian guardsmen bearing Augustus's crest. One of them guided us.

We were ushered past a courtyard with a laughing fountain and into the cool shade of a sitting room where Augustus and Agrippa reclined with Marcellus and Trebonius around an open firepit in the tiled floor. Drusalla sat near Augustus, her chain mail tunic gleaming in the shards of sunlight that shone through a Greek-styled hole in the ceiling.

Characteristic of the Roman arts' preoccupation with the vividness of all living things, the tiles on the floor were watery blue and lustrous, with tile images of spiny fishes suspended in blue infinity. The artist had so realistically depicted the silvery bodies and fins that the fishes seemed to undulate. Their large black eyes and exaggerated jaws made them all the more lifelike.

The pit contained a grill above glowing red coals. Spiny whitefish lay very unlife-like upon this grill, sizzling. The Roman passion for the vividness of all living things was second only to the Roman passion for conquering and consuming all living things. Smoke and steam rose upward from the grill to pass through the hole above.

Ulgöthur, Elouskonios, and Liuthari all saluted Drusalla.

"About time you got here, Saturnius," said Agrippa, sighing, "for we cannot talk to her without you. Ask your countrymen to sit, and then ask her why she wears her chain mail and sword, and why her fellows arriving now do so as well. She seems to not understand that the civilized don't bear arms to lunch."

We sat. A Greek house slave, eyes down and thus responding to the sound of voices and of clapped hands, served the fish. She applied a coating of olive oil and pepper, depositing the morsels upon large palm leaves. She passed them to each guest as I asked Drusalla what Agrippa wanted to know.

It was Ulgöthur, however, who answered.

"Today," he spoke tolerantly, "is the anniversary of Vercingetorix's surrender to the 'civilized' tyrant, Julius Caesar."

At the mention of Vercingetorix, both Elouskonios and Liuthari pressed their palms to their foreheads and clasped their fists across their chests. Marcellus watched these actions suspiciously.

"Is that why you bear swords? To honor your defeated leader?" Trebonius asked Ulgöthur when I had translated. "And why do you wear a Greek blade?" he added.

"The Greeks also have been conquered and sullied by Roman dictators. Their art, their philosophy taken captive. Yet your younglings no longer remember that your grand Roman buildings and temples and your art are really Ionian Greek."

As Ulgöthur made an odd gesture with his thumb held stiff between two fingers swept in a half arc, indicating the architecture of the room in which we sat. I hastened to translate, and the Greek serving slave shivered, then ducked her head so none would see the shock of excitement she felt. As Agrippa glanced absently her way, she quickly squelched the fierce look of joy that had flashed across her face. She as quickly quenched her pride, backing away to a respectful distance to wait, eyes down.

I had seen that look, however. I wondered how many of the Greeks around us understood Gaul.

When I was done translating, Marcellus snorted.

"Be it so," Marcellus said quietly, "it remains no great matter for in fact Rome has taken many cultural practices from those we've defeated and raised those practices to greater significance." He made the same gesture as Ulgöthur, indicating the room. "Still there remains the question of why you and your queen wear weapons. Is it to honor a defeated leader or not?"

I translated.

Ulgöthur smiled, took a thumb and finger of fish, put it into his mouth. He took his time, as all watched him and waited. Smiling, his queen watched him as well, but remained silent.

"Defeat," he finally said, as I translated, "can be seen in many ways. A powerful enemy often prevails. But a powerful enemy can sometimes then be made to defeat him*self*."

"Really. How so?" Trebonius asked, and I quickly translated the conversation that followed so there was no lag between them all.

"A Roman column, for example," said Ulgöthur, "takes a full fifteen minutes to stop, then stands in place, vulnerable, awaiting the next order."

"Any good-sized column does," Marcellus insisted.

"A column that thinks, does not."

"What does that mean?" asked Agrippa.

"Each time a column of the western tribes halts, it breaks up and disappears."

"That is mad," guffawed Marcellus with a crooked smile. "What of animals, supply trains, civilians within a column? What you say creates chaos."

"Exactly."

"A general could never control a large army that breaks up and reforms constantly," said Agrippa.

"A general makes decisions and plans tactics but 'control' is not the purpose of a general when a column breaks."

"What in the name of Mars's farts is the purpose of a general when a column breaks then?" demanded Marcellus.

"To draw the enemy's attention."

"In your general Vercingetorix's case it seems, he drew not just our attention but his own defeat," Octavius said softly.

All were silent, eating fish. I had grown somewhat more accustomed to consuming food, for a body must be fed to keep it alive of course, and I found fish flesh to be not unpleasant, though I would likely throw it up later to prevent it digesting and thus escape for this day at least, the indignity of having to defecate.

Ulgöthur shifted his sword to a more comfortable position and continued. "Our queen wears her armor today to show respect to Vercingetorix's *anam*, which, being eternal, cannot be defeated. Thus, I keep my sword ready should Vercingetorix call me to battle."

As I translated, the unobtrusive praetorians in the room shifted restlessly, their own leather armor creaking faintly as they remained at attention in the four corners of the large marble chamber.

"Battle? How can a dead man call you to arms?"

"His *anam* can. It can call me to be ready."

"Ready for what?" demanded Agrippa.

"Ready," Ulgöthur said through me, "should you insult my queen today. Ready to kill as many of you as I can before your praetorians kill me, and to kill my queen, then kill myself."

After I had translated, all turned to Augustus.

"So much for *civilizing* our enemies," Marcellus had chuckled.

For the first time since his month-long hosting of the last rebellious Gauls for endless parties, meals, arguments, and negotiations, Augustus had then looked as though he realized his high-minded attempt to create peace was doomed. He gazed at the silent Drusalla, studying her chain mail, eyeing her sword, and had seemed finally to consider what I had recognized from the start.

I obeyed Ulgöthur and stood.

By now, the small clearing in which we were located was full of eight hundred or so Gauls. "Now," said Ulgöthur, "tell all of them that they will be impaled at the slightest disobedience."

I turned to face the hundred or so men, who sat bedraggled and bloody in the snow. One, I noticed, was the irrepressible Tullius, who now seemed quite uncharacteristically crestfallen.

"The general of the Gauls commands us to be obedient, if we wish to live," I shouted.

"Sit down and shut up, Sky God, if you've no godlike power to free us. Don't do the bidding of the enemy. As our leader—"

"It is plain to see, Marcellus, that I am no longer leading anything." Marcellus glared up at me with contempt.

"Tell the highborn that if he resists, I'll kill his dog," said Ulgöthur.

"Marcellus, Ulgöthur will kill Beast if you don't behave."

Marcellus guffawed loudly, that crooked smile of his bursting forth after so long an absence, although now was not the best time for its return. It was like the false sun of Gaulish winter, even now lowering in the sky: all light and no more heat.

Then he stood, turning his back on me and the Gauls, to address the men. Beast rose painfully to his feet to stand beside him.

"Legionnaires, do not despair! Stay alive and be ready to seize the moment when the time comes. We are beaten, not defeated!"

Ulgöthur drew his sword. "It does not seem that he respects you, Saturnius."

"It does not seem so, nor should he."

Ulgöthur took two plundered Roman gladii from his men and handed one to me. He shouted to Marcellus.

"You! High-birth Rome man! You kill your general, I free the men of you!" Ulgöthur said to Marcellus in passable Greek. He tossed the other sword and Marcellus caught it by the pommel and with not a pause, as though he had not just taken a beating from Gauls, then he launched himself at me energetically.

He beat and cleaved at my head, flourishing the blade in high arcs, cutting cross swipes mixed with chops. Then he charged with short downward cuts from the wrists as well as his arms, two handed. He handled the blade's weight as if swinging a pugio instead of the much heavier gladius, forcing me into defensive retreat.

This single combat style was not legionnaire's fashion at all, but Greek, and exposed him to risks that the Roman phalanx style seeks to avoid in favor of group-oriented unison stabbing motions under intermittent cover of a wall of shields.

No matter. He was so much better than me that he and I both knew he was risking nothing.

If his superior skills, which he was often so blasé about, were not enough to make me see the end of this body I was in, there remained the reality that because of the campaigns we'd fought together, Marcellus knew my strengths and weaknesses. He knew how to push me back quickly with an energetic series of downward chops to my high guard.

Now, though, while continuing to drive my retreat, he switched to the conventional legionnaire's style of jabbing and thrusting. I was off balanced, and so his sudden use of the full length of his blade to stab through my defense nearly struck home several times as I scrambled to parry and beat, while hopping backward.

We fought across the field of snow where the Roman captives sat and cheered, some for me, but mostly for Marcellus. He pressed me hard a while longer in conventional legionary cohort style, but this was all a warm-up for him, I very well knew. I beat back hard as I could for when he had warmed up, he would surely kill me. He switched to his own hybrid style—a mixture of gladiatorial circular attack and Greek indirection, a style I'd seen him use to maim and then kill many an enemy.

I indulged my human senses, perhaps for a last time.

The two of us circled and grappled, and as our blades clashed, I felt the firm snow underfoot, packed down by the battle. I could smell the sharp trace of the fire the Gauls had set. I so often notice, dear companion, how you monkeys can induce a trance in yourselves by focusing on your senses, driving away fear and even pain. Did I ever tell you that I admire that in you?

As for my second-in-command Marcellus, other than his rhythmic grunting and labored breathing, he made no sound. That was his way of doing single combat—he said nothing but concentrated on killing me. The narrowing of his battle-swollen eyes merely signaled his increasing attention to his tactical method, which was always to solve the puzzle of killing an opponent as if solving an Archimedean equation. His silence alerted me to the fact that I had little time before he achieved the intended resolution.

I gauged how much of my power to manipulate space and time had returned to me: not enough yet. I thought of using Hirtius's body as a shield between Marcellus and myself.

It was then that Drusalla arrived.

"Hold, General!" she shouted as she approached. "Do not make any of these dogs kill each other without my order!"

"So! I was right, Saturnius," scowled Marcellus. "You let her go!"

Six of Ulgöthur's men came between Marcellus and me. Marcellus performed the Achillean leap and stab maneuver I'd known he was about to use on me, and he killed two of them before they could overpower and disarm him.

I shoved my sword into the ground and stepped away from it. My heart raced, and I breathed in huge rattling gulps. Ulgöthur sheathed his own sword obediently, amused, and took my sword from the ground, slipping it into a harness strapped to his back while Elouskonios stepped forward, took Marcellus's weapon, tossed it to a big Gaul who had arrived with Drusalla, then bowed to her.

Ulgöthur had looked at me with an ironic grin as he'd yanked the sword I'd forsaken from the ground. He whispered to me, "The highborn there would do well in a Gallia army. He fights like the demon you are supposed to be. What is wrong with you, Cernunnos? Lost your powers?"

"Mother to the Country!" Elouskonios called out to Drusalla. "We've defeated the Romans!"

"You've done no such thing, handsome son of Vercingetorix. You've defeated a detachment of Romans. The larger Roman beast still controls Lutetia and our eastern lands. To be handsome is not the same as to be wise. Stand with your sword ready, for that is the task you're made for. Where is your brother?"

Liuthari appeared, his spear gory with Roman blood. I guessed he'd been stabbing corpses, making certain the dead Romans were truly dead.

It was certain.

"Mother of the Country."

Drusalla smiled ironically at Ulgöthur. "The young ones keep calling me that."

"They see you thus, Queen."

"One third of Gallia cooperates with the Romans, and the two thirds that won't boast four queens and ten kings. Yet I am queen of the country? Which country, where?"

"The country in our hearts and in the future, Mother," said Liuthari. He held up his bloody spear point for her.

She nodded approvingly.

"The fallen are all dead?"

"Dead as they ever will get," smiled Liuthari.

"Where is Sulla?"

"I've seen no sign of him."

She turned to glare at me. "Was he with the others where you left them?"

"He-he is dead," I answered her when I'd caught my breath. "It was he who told me, in his dying breath, how to track you."

She considered this, shrugged in acceptance of it. It was then that I could tell that Sulla was not the only traitor in the legions, but that the Gauls had allies in Rome, perhaps scores of them. Perhaps even in the Senate.

Such sudden flashes of insight I had when in human flesh, this human intuition, was keenly pleasing. Almost a shadow of the sight of spirit vision though you crabs are unable to call it and control it as you wish. It was nevertheless an exquisite pleasure to me whenever it arose in me and was often a powerful tool.

She turned back to Liuthari.

"You are like your father, Liuthari. Take the main detachment back to the rally point and wait for the general there. General, is that agreeable?"

"Queen."

"Tell Drunia that Sulla is dead."

Liuthari hesitated, his face clouding at this task but trotted away. Elouskonios stood expectant. She did not fail to stroke him.

"I trust you to guard me from here on, Elouskonios. Don't despair of my criticisms. I only want you to be better. Stand ready. I'll likely need you to kill that one there. He is arrogant and almost as handsome as you."

She indicated Marcellus, who stood back up, his hands insolently upon his hips.

"What did they just say about Sulla, Saturnius? Why are they pointing at me thus?" Two Gauls jabbed viciously at the backs of his knees with the butts of their spears, sending him back down to kneeling position, silent, but still smiling crookedly.

"That one is the highborn from the negotiations, the one who wounded you on the thigh, is it not?" Elouskonios asked, glaring at Marcellus.

"Yes, the night I fought him in the demon's tent." She stabbed a thumb at me with the word 'demon,' then she turned to consider me.

"You live, Saturnius, because you let me go."

"I let you go because *you* live."

She tilted her head. "What does that mean?"

"I have searched for you since the dawn of these humans."

"Are you trying to throw honey at me, Saturnius?"

"Do you not have strange dreams, Drusalla?"

At this, she scowled, looked away from me, but looked back at me again as if caught thinking.

"How do you know my dreams?"

"He *is* the demon, Mother Queen, he is Cernunnos. Don't listen to him," Ulgöthur warned.

Nodding to Ulgöthur, she put her hand on her sword hilt. "Tell the highborn one to stop smiling," she ordered.

Turning to Marcellus, I spoke. "You'd better take that smile from your lips, Marcellus. She seems predisposed to spare us, which gives us a chance to perhaps save the remaining men."

The men mattered to him. His smile turned to a scowl, directed at me. Beast settled back down next to him, and he looked up at me. "Saturnius, what was that about Sulla?"

"Sulla and the barbarian ambassador, Drunia, were in love, back in Rome."

"That was plain for all to see. They left bald ducks behind them everywhere they walked together."

"It seems that she is the reason Sulla betrayed us."

"I'm the Honorary Proconsul Hirtius!" the proconsul grunted now in perfect Greek from where he sat on frozen mud. "Allow me to live, and you'll have a large ransom from the Senate!"

Marcellus scrambled toward Hirtius, likely to seize him by the throat. Two Gauls kicked Marcellus, keeping him from his goal.

"What did the weak one say? Something about the Senate . . . and ransom?" Drusalla demanded. "Is he important?"

"He is a Senate legate, Drusalla," I answered.

"Is he? Keep him safe, General Ulgöthur." The general ordered Hirtius to be protected.

"Tell all these Roman hounds to bind their wounds as best they can," she glared at me, "for we march at one quarter walk of the sun across the sky."

The dog, Beast, had somewhat healed. More than a lunar week passed and ten more of us died as they marched us with their column over frozen fields daily, so far west that I was certain we were coming near the coast.

They took us into icy wastes that I reckoned no Roman had ever seen, and through several pathetic hamlets deep in the western forests. These hidden places were full of poor, ragged Gauls, who'd taken to the wilderness to separate from the cities, most of which were growing to be accepting of Roman colonial partitioning and Roman rule. Many Gauls in and around Lutetia had even grown to see themselves as Roman since Caesar's defeat of Vercingetorix and the spread of Latin and Roman settlers in the eastern reaches of their land.

Ulgöthur and his army, and their minor queen, had taken nearly all the men and many young strong women as well from these villages and hovels to press them into an army. Left behind were these ragged settlements of old women, of crazed fur-footed children, and skinny demented wolves that the Gauls had domesticated as if they were dogs.

What is that? Of course, from my perspective—at the time anyway—as a Roman consul-at-large and military commander. Well, you are correct, it turns out. At that point, I saw only what I saw of the country. We fought rather large armies, but we'd assumed those three or four were all, and now, afoot and defeated, we mostly saw poverty and were only later to see much healthier natives, whom Marcellus and I never saw when we were involved in war. Don't look so smug. Write.

Now, hark you this. Actual dog, to these nearly primordial backward Gauls we passed by, was both a delicacy and an honored animal that symbolized courage and strength. If you can understand how a lost tribe of humans may idolize and honor an animal and at the same time desire to kill, cook, and eat that very same animal, then you will have made a progress toward understanding the harsh culture of these Gauls, the native free ones still unknown to Rome.

Their wolves were afraid of Beast, whom they surely could tell was a true dog with merit and dignity. For his part, Beast held his head high and trotted past these starved, lupine vermin with haughty contempt.

Caesar himself would have blanched at what we came to suspect, which we later found true that comported with what you just said; that the west contained these ragged folk, but also further held untold numbers, and that some hundreds of thousands of fighters apparently had joined Drusalla's army.

Marcellus had bound all our feet in an ingenious makeshift covering for our by now quite worn legios' marching boots; something he'd fashioned from tree bark and campfire pitch. Daily he inspected our feet and muttered, "Keep your feet warm and dry, for the feet are the key to survival on a march. Verilius will come after us, you'll see, if we but survive. Or auxiliaries from the ships will come. We must simply survive."

In one hamlet, the children in their little fur foot wrappings swarmed about us, shouting, laughing, and chanting, each one tossing at us their little snowballs with a little rock in the center.

In another, having lost some men to hunger and exhaustion, we sat on stumps waiting for the Gauls to fill their food baskets with radishes and carrots provided by old women. Marcellus gathered a group of the feral children around him, and using sticks and tree branches, taught them Roman sword drills.

Before the Gaulish soldiers noticed what he was about he'd set the children to doing close order marching and legionnaires' phallanx formation. He got a clout on the head from a Gaul to make him stop.

Some more Romans died as the long march continued.

By the time there were only seventy of us, plus Hirtius, Marcellus's prediction proved true outside of one of the endless hamlets we'd passed through.

Because, like magic, Roman Proconsul General Verilius did appear.

As we came into a vast clearing, where trees had been felled and cultivated, we saw Verilius sitting all alone on a halved, toppled tree trunk that resembled a bench, outside of a hall-sized but oddly hexagonal log barracks in this village-sized clearing in the forest. He wore not his woolen legionnaire's winter marching pants, vest, and armor, but a Gaulish singlet and raw fur robe over his beloved saffron tunic. He wore fur-lined Gaulish boots.

"By the gods!" Marcellus exclaimed, seeing our comrade whom we'd left in charge of one of our two legions somehow sitting amidst the enemy here in inner Gaul. One of them, my own legion, commanded by myself with Marcellus and Trebonius as my senior officers, was now less than one hundred men, only seventy, as I said.

Marcellus looked at me, stupefied.

"Was he captured, Saturnius?"

"I doubt that," I answered, already guessing the truth. It had been the hoped-for arrival of General Verilius we'd thought our final chance for rescue, and here the general sat, no legion to look to.

As we approached and the true length of the clearing came into view, we saw that all around him stood perhaps one hundred or so other roughly hexagon-shaped barracks, as well as halls, lodges, and huts stretching off to the edges of that clearing and on into the forest, each lodge accompanied by pigsties, cattle hovels, and penned horses. Smoke wafted from holes in the gables and rooftops of the sturdy lodges with their carefully notched top beams and walls insulated by dry grass, woven bark, and pitch. The smell of cooking goat meat filled the clearing. This settlement was different from the others we'd passed through, wherein we had seen structures that obviously had not been crafted to last long but, it now struck me, merely had been Gaulish marching stations and civilian camps. This place was stocked with soldiers and was obviously a base of command.

It was surrounded on three sides by a vellum ditch with piled logs and sharpened stakes set in the ground, all for better defense.

"Look at these here defenses," whispered the loyal, erstwhile Tullius. "Persian, and a bit Egyptian, by the look of things. These folks have been exposed to some Persian military organization, General!"

"Apparently, they are not so isolated as they appear, or as Caesar-Julius claimed in his memoirs," I whispered back.

Liuthari came out of the barracks behind Verilius, pushing Trebonius, who was tied and hobbled. He shoved Trebonius to the ground. As Marcellus stooped to examine Trebonius for wounds, Liuthari clasped arms with his brother, Elouskonios, and with Ulgöthur, in greeting.

Drusalla clasped arms with Verilius.

"Greetings, Queen," Verilius said in very good, very clear Gaulish.

"Where is Drunia?" she asked him in Gaulish.

"In despair," said Liuthari, approaching her. "It was just before Verilius arrived that I told her their Roman commander Sulla is dead. She fell silent for a few sun walks across the sky. She went into the forest, some two walks ago. She has died of cold and despair by now."

"He was a good man," said Verilius sadly, still speaking Gaulish. "She seemed a good warrior."

Drusalla shook her head in regret. "She was young, and could love still, as once we all could before the war. The young are a key to peace someday, when this is over, and the Romans who care for justice and ally with us come to power in Antioch, in Egypt and Alexandria, and in Rome."

The Gauls turned silently to look at Verilius.

"What in the name of the gods' collective ass is this!" Marcellus roared, breaking the silence as he pulled Trebonius up from the ground. "Where did you come from, Verilius? How is it you are speaking their gibberish with them? Where is your legion?"

"Most are dead," Verilius answered in Latin with lowered eyes.

Meanwhile, Gauls settled their baggage, broke their column, and blended in with hundreds of Gaulish warriors who were at work sharpening swords or cooking around the nearest barracks.

"We were betrayed," Trebonius said flatly.

The Gauls laughed, emerging from the lodge behind Verilius, which we could see contained nearly one hundred warriors. Could this clearing contain then some thousands of Gauls? Could there be countless settlements like this one? A few hundred thousand Gauls, perhaps, in these western forests?

"What is he saying?" Elouskonios asked Verilius.

"He tells them I have betrayed them."

"Shall we kill them for you?"

"No! Please," Verilius hissed.

I cast my gaze all around, spied several caches of swords, axes, and spears, neatly stacked in pyramids. The nearest cache sat conveniently beside a horse pen, both unguarded.

"I see them too, sir," Tullius said softly at my ear. "Damascus iron, them swords are, and them over yonder be Etruscan spears besides. These here Gauls, they've allies."

Caesar had killed nearly twenty thousand during the first Gaulic war. More battles and conquests since had led to the founding of Lutetia, a city of allied Gauls and Romans, after countless more thousands had died. It had been the huge loss of life that had convinced Octavian Augustus back in Rome that his failed attempt at diplomacy had been a thing worth trying. Ulgöthur, Drunia, and their queen Drusalla, now our captors, had spent a season in Rome to negotiate peace. Rome's senators assumed that the Gaulish population by now was less than five hundred thousand. The true betrayal, perhaps, was the Roman tendency to betray themselves, by ignoring the rules of logic. The season of peace had obviously been a stalling tactic conceived by the free tribes of Gaul and by Drusalla, who clearly was first among dozens of other queens and kings.

How many free Gauls are there in the East? Perhaps millions.

"We were betrayed, Saturnius," said Trebonius again, "two nights after you and Marcellus left, when Verilius slew the watch guards and opened our gates to Gauls! The guards were overwhelmed—there were at least two thousand who overran us. Those legionnaires not murdered in their sleep were marched here and killed here."

"Treason!" shouted Marcellus, struggling against the nearest Gaul. I sighed at Marcellus's endless energy and his hot disposition since our defeat.

"Treachery! Perfidy! *Proditio!*" shouted Hirtius, though he chose prudently to remain still.

I knew that one of the very descendants of the barbarians the Romans were eternally conquering and contending with, a descendant of the Britoni by the name of Shakespeare (what a delightful and descriptive name for a monkey barbarian progeny!) would someday, my dear, create a character based upon the monkey Sir Henry Percy—a character named "Hotspur" whose cognomen would become synonymous with impetuous, reckless behavior. Though

Marcellus had always been fiery in character, he'd never until now been so annoyingly irresponsible. Defeat did not become him.

Meanwhile, Marcellus and Tullius as well as a few of the least injured legionnaires, struggled to gain weapons, which Marcellus did first, gaining a short Persian sword from a Gaul. He cut Trebonius free, hacked his way through Gauls, and unwisely passing his chance to cut at Drusalla, whose guards were caught surprised and failed to surround her, he launched himself straight at Verilius, seeking imprudent revenge.

I took the opportunity to much more usefully make my way toward the horse pens, counting more than enough horses to get most of the survivors and myself away.

Beast happily bit at Gaulish hind parts and covered Marcellus as best he could.

Dearly loving to watch a fight, most of the Gauls fell back to watch and cheer. They formed a circle of one hundred or so about us all, after Drusalla had armed herself and was safe. I counted myself now much nearer to the horses, so I waited to see what would transpire. At the least, I could get to a horse myself and leave all these humans behind, friend and foe.

The wise must set priorities, after all.

The sudden and chaotic scrabble of close-quarter fighting rang out in the crisp air as blades beat against one another, with the Romans fighting fiercely but falling quickly, and eventually with Tullius, Trebonius, and two final legionnaires fighting desperately to cover Marcellus, who battled Verilius, who had retained his own Roman sword despite his overtly Gaulish clothing.

"Do you wish to stop this?" called out the smiling Elouskonios.

"No," answered a grim Ulgöthur. "Dogs though these Romans are, soldiers deserve a clean death in battle."

Drusalla nodded her agreement, and Elouskonios and Liuthari stood back to watch.

Verilius circled and Marcellus circled, with only Tullius and Trebonius left now of two whole legions plus Hirtius's added auxiliaries, long dead. Beast too was left, and Hirtius himself stood apart, safe and silent.

Marcellus glanced at Tullius, who understood, and stepped back with Beast, to allow Verilius and Marcellus to fight inside what was now a circle of two hundred Gauls. Trebonius stepped away also, but deliberately made to stand beside me, eyeing the same horse pen I was eyeing.

Hirtius pulled tight his robes against the cold, docile and determined to bravely persevere in lifting and risking not a finger. As for myself, I felt the prodding of several spears in my back. The Gauls were making certain that I remained uninvolved.

"Stand ready, Saturnius!" cried Marcellus.

Hah! So there is yet some method left in his hotness.

"Ready to do what? This is hopeless!" I shouted back at him, knowing that we were among Gauls some of whom understood Latin. I deigned to not reveal what Marcellus and I, and Trebonius, had in mind. "There are thousands of them, Marcellus, and only four of us, not counting Hirtius, and I'm not counting Hirtius."

"Surrender, Marcellus! I order you to—"

"Shut up, Hirtius!" called out Verilius, and Hirtius did.

In silence now, Marcellus and Verilius circled, beating their weapons a few times, exploring one another's *at guard.* Marcellus thrust, Verilius parried.

Now Marcellus cut and feinted left simultaneously chopping with startling speed, nearly beheading Verilius, who ducked the blow likely because he had fought so long beside Marcellus that he knew the maneuver like his own. Marcellus's unearthly speed nevertheless eluded Verilius's repost and caused the watching Gauls to grunt in admiration.

This would likely not be a long bout. It was only a matter of Marcellus wearing down Verilius's strength.

Drusalla now was beside me.

"How do you know of my dreams?"

I turned to her, the spears still hard about me and lodged in my back.

"I have known you for eons, since the founding of the universe."

Marcellus and Verilius beat, thrust, and cut viciously at one another.

"Why did you betray Rome, Verilius!" Marcellus called out. "I could kill you right now, but first I have to know why!" Marcellus's shout echoed the anguish he felt.

"Why? Marcellus, my highborn fool of a friend! You think all of us are rich enough to follow Octavius as blindly as you? Octavius is nephew to the same Julii who murdered my family!"

Marcellus cut and hacked at Verilius, who defended, but just barely.

Drusalla stared at me, unable to brush aside what I'd said, though I'd have thought it must sound mad to her. It was not to her human self I'd appealed. My appeal only needed to buy a bit more time. Soon, I would be able to take her, whether she wanted me to or not.

"What do you get for murdering your own legion?" shouted Marcellus, finally deciding to draw blood from Verilius's shoulder.

"I get my own estate in a free Gaul, alongside free Greeks and free Africans!"

"Greeks and Africans in Gaul?"

"A coalition of free peoples against Rome, Marcellus. The daughter of Ahenobarbus Gnaeus rides with Drusalla!"

"General Ahenobarbus, the traitor who fought with Antony against Octavius at Philippi? Who died in exile after Actium?"

"Yes, old friend. A traitor. Like me. And the General is not dead."

"You're bleeding! You are not my equal and you know it. Put down your sword, Verilius."

"I'll put it down when the world is free."

Marcellus dropped his guard, stupefied by Verilius's passion. A loud shout of anger arose from the crowd around them.

"You *believe* this insanity, old friend? You have done this not for wealth but for their barbarian cause? You owe these savages your loyalty?"

Verilius lowered his sword, and the Gauls shouted outrage.

"Do you owe your mother yours, Marcellus? I cannot beat you with a sword, yet you are defeated. The legions are dead. The few survivors were murdered here among these huts. Their heads will be cut off and used as fodder for future battles."

This rekindled Marcellus's fury, and he struck, his sword glancing off Verilius's parry. "You're mad!" Marcellus cried, "You think this small rebellion will succeed?"

"There are five thousand at least right here in the forest, and yet another ten thousand warriors are headed west to the shores to destroy the Romans now at sea!"

"These barbarians will be crushed!"

"They will not."

"Where is your loyalty to Rome!"

"You think Rome can last? I shed no tears for Her, I stand by Gaulish loyalty, loyalty to the entire human race and to human freedom!"

It was only a matter of time before Marcellus decided to kill Verilius, but in the time the two had bought me with their spectacle, I'd felt myself grow stronger. Soon this exile, this sojourn in human flesh of mine would end. The containment that my fellow angel had enforced on me was waning, and it would be me who would end this debacle I was caught in.

"Are you truly a demon?" Drusalla asked me.

"I am your oldest friend."

"What do you want from me?"

"A kiss."

As if against her will, she leaned toward me.

Yes. Sovereign power again and my goal obtained.

A tall, armored black woman escorted by two black men in the same Nubian armor appeared at Drusalla's back. The woman's full, red-brown lips and Ethiope's face was like that of a noble of Carthage. Another warrior woman. I'd had hard luck with such as she in the Roman arena.

The Gauls had respectfully parted to let her stride through. She drew a Greek blade and placed it at my throat, pushing me away from Drusalla with it. She kept her eyes hard upon me, ready to cut my throat.

"The demon sweet-talks you, Drusalla?"

Drusalla seemed then to awaken from a trance.

"Do not forget where you are, Aziba," Drusalla warned.

General Ahenobarbus Aziba. Tall distaff daughter of Mark Antony's chief general in Africa, Ahenobarbus Gnaeus. The sword still at my throat, she glanced away from me as Ulgöthur shoved me aside to confront her.

"Respect our queen, General. You Egyptians and Ethiopians are allies, not commanders."

"It is your prisoner I do not respect. Kill him! Spare the other Romans, for they can be of use, but him you must destroy. Stop toying with him or you may find yourselves undone by this motherless bastard."

Me?

"He is our prisoner, if you had not noticed. His army is destroyed."

Well, in fairness I am indeed motherless.

"Can't you feel it, Keltoi? Didn't you feel how he had control of your thoughts as I walked up? He is right now moments away from defeating you even as you pronounce him defeated."

Oh my. Is she a fan?

"You Keltoi and Parisi don't realize you have little time," she sneered then half smiled. Condescending for a human.

"Have we met, O black Domina?" I asked.

"One of your kind has visited me to warn me of you, one who knew you in times past."

Time's up!

I spun in a circle, lashing out with my mind to lay down the guards around me.

I was careful not to harm Drusalla as I gestured and turned the Gauls nearest me to smoke and steam.

Verilius stumbled as he shuffled back from Marcellus's stab, and Marcellus thrust squarely into Verilius's chest.

The Gauls gathered around Marcellus were cheering wildly as Verilius fell.

So much for Gaul loyalty.

Aziba snatched Ulgöthur's sword from his hands. As for Ulgöthur himself, he stood stupefied by this moment, unable to know how to understand what he was seeing me do. Liuthari beside him struggled to pull free his sword, which was frozen in its sleeve.

It happens to them as well! How amusing.

I clasped Drusalla to me, to kiss her, and with that kiss, I implanted in her that which I had intended to. I had neglected to do it before, when she'd been my prisoner, but then I'd never thought her army would bring my legion to the end as she had; so now I did it. It was deep in the molecular structure of her DNA now, and I would always be able to find her, her children, and their children. She would have children. Elouskonios would be the father.

As easy as tossing a potato, I threw Drusalla over Ulgöthur's head, and Elouskonios caught her deftly, as I knew he would.

The Gauls surrounding Marcellus now moved to kill him. He was all the slower because he was using a longer, Gaulish blade—he'd no pugio or gladius. One of them drew his attack as another stabbed through his guard to pierce his side, which bled, while Tullius and Trebonius moved to defend him, fighting this the *Gallia* legion's last hopeless skirmish. It was a pathetic legion of three and a dog. My last cohort.

Aziba was upon me, so I was not able to help Marcellus. I snatched Liuthari's stubborn blade from its sleeve and pushed him into Elousknios, not wishing really to harm either of them. Why should I harm two such heroic if hapless humans?

Ulgöthur meanwhile was scrabbling about for a sword. He still had a captured gladius hanging across his back but seemed not to count it as real. He was seeking a Gaul blade and found one; he took it off a dead Gaul. As he stooped, I easily plucked the gladius off his back and I raised my blade to meet Aziba's swing. Our blades clashed with a flash of eerie blue energy that struck poor Ulgöthur dumb all over again.

All eyes turned to Aziba and myself. Marcellus paused as the Gauls about to kill him had paused, as did a hundred Gauls all around, watching what was clearly now some supernatural conflict. The flash of keen blue light was an unmistakable sign, I'll admit.

I stepped backward, backward, using a spinning head-and-shoulder defense Marcellus had taught me in Rome. She followed, taking the bait. The Roman gladius of this century I'd languished in was I assure you, dear amanuensis, an exquisitely balanced tool of war. Aziba's Greek xiphos though similar was not nearly as well balanced, so I was able to out parry her easily despite my body's fatigue. Marcellus had instructed me well in the uses of that Roman weapon.

The gladius of the first century, Galadius Hispaniensis, was the weapon of the legions from the third century BC to third century AD. It had a wonderfully weighted grip because of a well-placed ball at the grip end—What? Have I really? If I've mentioned the ingenuity of the gladius before, well I've more to say this time. Please do let me go on, dear crab. Very well, I suppose you will be my editor for this memoir as well as scribe, eh? Where was I?

Yes, blue arcing energy from our grappling swords continued distracting the Gauls, and of course you've likely guessed I had also obscured their reasoning with my first laying on of my revived power. To any effect, the blue lit skirmish was astonishing them and allowed Marcellus, though wounded, to make his move toward the horse pens.

Mine and Aziba's swords were acting as ion multipliers. Electromagnetic force crackled and seethed between us. My sister angel, the hated Uriel, had not only come to this human to tell her of the doings of us angels but had arrogantly imbued her with power to confront me!

I had wisely refrained from indulging in the stubborn resistance that Marcellus had since our capture, and so this body I occupied had enough strength and energy to fight. I was fighting not a typical monkey but an empowered human, on somewhat equal terms. Because Uriel had imposed the banishment on me that had stranded me here on Earth with humans these past years of the treachery of one of my own, I wondered if I could ever truly defeat my sister. She was and had been a thorn in my eye for all the centuries of Man, and here I was being thwarted by her influence once again.

Just like old times.

"Where is The Tongue of God!?" Aziba called out.

"Don't you know, weren't you told by my good sibling?" I taunted, for of course, Aziba's human body held a portion of the spirit of the insufferable Gabryel, put there by him and my sister. At their urging, Aziba now sought the archangel's *McGuffin*.

"You tarry among defenseless human beings doing evil with it! I warn you not to harm them now, Satan!"

How presumptuous. The angels who opposed me thought themselves protectors of monkeys, while I saw them as spirit flunkies serving a collaborationist, whose pride was wounded. Mikayel. He sought to repair his fragile pride yet declined to seize the Tongue of God back for himself. I had lived with these very humans whom Gabryel and my sister presumed to be protecting from me. Had I wished, I could easily, now that my strength was returning, fling each human like sacks of sand at Aziba and crush her human bones!

"All would have been well for these humans," I shouted at him, "Had you not appeared, little brother!"

We circled each other, slashing at one another and causing flashes of ionized electricity, our charged energies melting the snow at our feet. Neither one of us deigned to conduct our conflict openly in spirit form; to do so would indeed kill many or most of the humans around us. In fact, such a thing is forbidden us and might rouse the attention of *Anu*.

Believe me, no angel desires that.

Likewise, I was not yet strong enough to flee my Gaul body, and Gabryel would be hard upon me in pursuit if I did. Some Gauls sank to their knees in frightened obeisance at the sight of the supernatural, while others kept their wits, creeping upon Marcellus to kill him.

"You, who once were divine, who once I loved! Evil betrayer!"

"Oh, I am not so serious as all that, am I, brother? I am merely curious. Is curiosity truly a sin, or is the real sin that I question the tyrant?"

"He is The Lord. He is no tyrant, he loves us!"

"His love is tyranny itself, if the free will he gave us cannot be exercised!"

Gabryel slashed at me; as I parried, a shock of blue light sketched a flashing hue between us. The cold air now smelt of ozone, brisk and tart as lemons and machine oil to my human nostrils.

"Smell it, brother?" I laughed, sweeping a blow at Gabryel's greave-armored legs. "In the woman's body you can partake of human senses. How do you like it?" My blow was deflected, the clashing swords casting more blue shadow; the contact between them shrieking a piercing noise, the energies left over from Creation, the energies that both of us could command even in the flesh we wore.

"How desperate your side must be, herald angel," I taunted. "That thou are sent to lower thyself and walk in stolen flesh to seek what only bringeth pain to angels!"

"Think not that I have purloined helpless, unwilling flesh as you are like to do. Aziba was asked! Noble creature that she is, she gave me her willing leave to use her flesh in censuring you! And the Tongue of God pains only those not meant to carry it!"

For all his loquaciousness, I was better at acting in flesh than he was. I could wear him out, were there time enough. Marcellus did not have that time, for he was being stalked and set up for a kill. I came to a decision. Gabryel was not my chief concern.

I shouted in the voice of command; a voice that Roman legionnaires instinctively obey.

"Mark me, Marcellus! Trebonius! Tullius! Close your eyes! *Now!*"

Closing my own eyes, I focused my energies upon the object and then tossed my sword high overhead. It flashed and burned brightly enough to blind all human sight in this camp, including Aziba's, and therefore Gabryel's.

Clearing my way with a gesture that cast down and bowled over all in my path, I walked right by Ulgöthur, frozen still by blind amazement, and gathered Marcellus, Trebonius, Beast, and Tullius to me. We ran for the nearest horse pen, with Beast right behind. Only Trebonius had not closed his eyes, and was blind. Tullius led him. We reached a corral, and Tullius put Trebonius atop a white horse with a dark birthmark upon its forehead.

Marcellus veered suddenly off toward Hirtius, who, not blinded because he had wisely shut his eyes, waved his arms frantically in refusal.

"Leave me be! You can't possibly escape. I stay where I am!"

But Marcellus's purpose was not to rescue Hirtius; it was to fulfill a pledge. He swiped at Hirtius's head with the Persian sword he bore, cleanly slicing off the honorary proconsul's left ear. A spurt of blood stained the side of Hirtius's face as he shrieked and clutched at the wound.

"Gods! My ear!"

Marcellus loped painfully back, catching up to us as we ran to a group of horses.

"The jackal is right though. We won't escape these forests!" Marcellus lamented, his blood seeping down over the back of the horse he rode. Both he and Trebonius had shown the presence of mind to seize Roman swords from a pile of war trophies the Gauls had piled up beside the horse pens. Marcellus struggled to buckle the belt of the one he'd hung at his side. I led everyone away from the camp at a gallop.

"We will go where we please!" I shouted.

We rode through snow straight into the trees, just as a hundred of the Gauls who'd not been blinded because they had been inside the lodges, began to emerge and pursue us.

We could hear the voice of Hirtius above the shouts of Gaulish warriors and of Ulgöthur's bellowed commands. Hirtius sounded shrill and near hysteria.

"Fools! If you flee they will kill you! Saturnius! I command you to come back! They'll ransom us all!"

We ignored him. We were rid of him.

Several Gaulish parties chased us, but I cast a great fog behind us to confuse them. My powers had returned, still limited while in this flesh, of course, but I was no longer at the mercy of the flesh, at least. Why didn't I just leave this body, this place, leave everything behind? I had accomplished everything I wished.

I didn't find it so simple to leave behind these who had been my comrades. No. Don't write that. Write this, the truth: it was difficult to leave humans who had been loyal to me, whose sympathy I had enjoyed, whose empire I had attached myself to as one of a certain kind of power. I was a Roman general still.

Gabryel apparently had not followed; for if he had, I'd not have been able to avoid or to defeat pursuit. I was puzzled, even troubled about the fact of his not following us. Was I being allowed to wander into a trap, or into some circumstance that served him? An angel giving up pursuit of a band of helpless humans made no sense.

In the second hour of our flight, we paused very briefly, surveying the thawing but still hard ground; a patch that was not covered with snow. I conferred with Trebonius, whose sight was returning. We saw trees, of course, but also we noted a steady downward grade. There was a river a mile to our north running west-northwest down the gradient, the same direction we rode. Perhaps, offered Tullius, the grade was a sign of the coast being near.

I'd suspected that we had traveled very near to the western shores in our hard march with the Gaulish column, and Trebonius was certain of it. He rode that striking, pale white horse with the dark birthmark on its head. We had led the horse by its rein while he could not see, but now that he was regaining his sight he led us along paths in the woods that he had learnt while with the Gauls. His weeks among them as a prisoner had taught him much. Still, we ended up ever more lost among the endless trees.

When it was clear that no warriors were following us, we stopped to look after Beast, rewrapping his paws in strips of fur torn from the ends of our shawls, and to look after Marcellus, whose wound was not so deep, but he was weakening from blood loss. I made a fire for Tullius who had decided to heat his blade, using the red hot tip to purify Marcellus's wound by cauterizing it. In a less painful procedure, I pressed my hand to the smoking flesh and fused it so that it bled no more and healed instantly, with only a seam like an old incision, and no scar.

"Magic," muttered Tullius.

"Fine," said Trebonius, trying to hold to his pale horse, grasping the reins as he stood beside it. "He's saving Marcellus's life, which is all that matters. If it's magic, then I say up magic."

Back to the horses and more riding. Was I able, then, to identify with humans, you are asking?

Certainly not.

To me you are possibly objects of pity; the more so during my time in the Roman Empire because I was being forced to learn what your lives of flesh were actually like. You are monkeys, crabs, trapped essences with no avenue of escape from your confinement, no avenue other than death. And though death is your doorway to freedom, you fear it! Like a brutalized child, your human spirit cringes and dreads the light that shines from the opening of a door, drawing away from freedom in order to embrace confinement, ignorant of the very joy freedom offers.

What is that you say? I just spoke of light? Yes, of course I spoke of light. Did I not inform you that "Lucifer" means *light bringer*, my crab biographer, my amanuensis? After all I've said to you I shouldn't think I would need to remind you of what I am.

Perhaps I'll need a good publicist someday.

As for you, crabs, even when I was trapped amongst you, my dear, I felt you were to be given pity, perhaps. Certainly not empathy. So why was I still wandering through a horrid frozen waste, carried by a pained, stiff, and weakening body? Well, perhaps I truly did feel a sort of loyalty—for my prized Romans, at least.

You think me a liar? Very well, think what you will, so long as you write down what I've said in just the way I have said it.

Upon the fifth hour of our wandering, Drunia came walking slowly out from behind a stand of trees one hundred yards away.

"Hark," Trebonius pointed, amazed, drawing everyone's attention to the approaching Gaul. She looked as if the strong and solid young warrior she had been had departed this life and been reincarnated now as a wraith.

We drew our horses to a standstill and watched her approach. She bore no weapon and bore no armor.

Nor, in this new incarnation, did she seem to want or to need such things. She looked to be beyond all of that. She looked to have suffered something so intensely agonizing as to have been driven to a break with her own humanity. She looked almost angelic. I was impressed.

The expression on her face, which we could see more clearly the closer she came to us, was that of a woman who had come to the end of her wits, and had continued past their end into a realm of vast indifference. She was shrouded in fur shawl and cowl, both of them white with snow. She walked limply, dragging her fur-booted feet. Her red hair blew loose in the cold wind, as did the unfastened and useless strap of a missing sword scabbard that once had hung at her side. Her dark eyes glowed like coals lodged in the flesh of a face the color of the wastes of snow she had emerged from.

Marcellus slid painfully down off his horse, drew his sword, and stood waiting for her.

"Will you kill her, Master Tribune?" asked Tullius. "You being a noble and all, it hardly seems honorable, killing an unarmed woman."

Marcellus neither turned back to regard Trebonius nor responded to the comment.

"I never knew you to kill women, armed or not," Trebonius added. "Even in battle, you'd knock a Britoni woman warrior 'side the head with your pommel, worst I ever saw you do."

"Though sometimes," offered Tullius, chuckling, "One or another'd get back up and—"

"Watch me," Marcellus finally answered them.

"What good—"

"Shut up, Trebonius. The woman lured Sulla into treason," Marcellus grunted. He grimaced as he lifted his sword.

"Though I've healed it, it is possible for you to tear that wound open again, with violent movement so soon," I suggested.

"To Hades with you, Saturnius!"

By and by, Drunia fixed her course on Marcellus, drawing near and heading straight for him as if drawn to his sword. He breathed heavily now, as if the breath it had taken to shout at me had tired him all the more. He raised the sword higher as Drunia walked right up to him and waited. She drew back her cowl, showing her dark Parisi eyes. Tears tracking her cheeks had frozen into streaks of ice.

She looked Marcellus in the eyes, not so much defiantly, but with an interesting sagacity, as if she knew something he didn't. Particularly when confronting death, what admirable qualities you apes can demonstrate! Death is final, as far as you know, yet I've have seen centuries of one and many of you standing at that portal mustering character and will. I like to think it is the *me* in you. Yet I know it to be something far deeper than that.

She looked up at the sword poised to strike her. We all watched Marcellus hold his stance before her, sword steady as a wounded man, wounded but still a legionnaire could hold it despite the trickle of blood appearing from his side.

"Kill me, Ro-mani." She spoke in Gaul inflected Greek. "Because that my beloved is dead. Cold it is at the middle of me. I will be warm in the lands of Cernunnos where I will see my dearest sweetest Sulla."

"What did she say of Sulla?" Tullius whispered.

"She is asking Marcellus to kill her," I answered him. "She wishes not to live without Sulla."

"Leave her, Tribune," muttered Trebonius. "Give her a *pugio* and let her kill herself with dignity."

Marcellus grunted as he lowered his sword. He looked at her. He tossed the sword away into the snow. He sighed, turned to climb wearily back onto his horse. He sat there letting his head tilt to stare at the sky. Beast stood looking up at him.

Trebonius dutifully retrieved the sword and handed it to me, and I reached back to slide it into the soft hilt attached to the primitive saddle on the Gaulish horse I'd stolen.

Drunia pulled her hood back up to cover her red hair and turned to look back into the forest. Then she pointed northwest.

"She's directing us," Tullius speculated.

Trebonius's eyes narrowed. "North by west? We want to keep due west to the coast."

"There may be too many trees," I offered. "Who knows? Maybe crevasses. Rivers. We cannot trust Sulla's maps."

"Then likely we cannot trust her who led him to draw those maps," sighed Trebonius.

"Is that the way we have to go to get to the coast?" I called to Drunia in Gaulish. She said nothing in response, but looked at me impassively for a moment, then gave one decisive nod.

"I will follow where she points," I concluded.

Marcellus guided his horse to her and reached down. She looked up at him as blank as the snow. Then she took his arm. He pulled her up to sit behind him. Ahh, the two of them were together the picture of exhaustion, each in his and her own way having reached the end of conflict between Gaul and Roman. I smiled. Let me tell you a thought that came to me then. I thought how they were a picture also of the future of their two nations, destined through exhaustion to put aside their war someday and become one, not even remembering the hatred and strife of a past that would dissolve like salt in water. Such are the vicissitudes of the flow of history, my dear.

As we headed off in the direction she had pointed, Tullius moved his horse close to mine.

"That was funny to you eh, then, General?"

Ahhh, astute Tullius. I'd only smiled, but he'd noticed my mood. Loyal Tullius eternally demonstrating the strength of peasant stock, which was the true core strength of Rome.

The rest of the day we rode, and when dusk was near, we climbed a hill to a cave where I made fire (I've a talent for making fire). We settled there to warm ourselves and spend the night. We (they) ate a feast of dried squirrel meat they pulled from Drunia's side pack. I nibbled a dry crust of provincial bread from the pack, just enough to keep me alive. There was also, miraculously, hard but edible cheese

Tullius had in abundance, tucked into his legionnaire's provision pack. The Gauls had not taken it from round his waist.

We filled a goat's bladder with snow and ice that Drunia solemnly produced, strapped to her back. Once the fire's heat had melted it, we each drank a bit. We put Beast near the fire to dry after I had petted him, healing his wounds without the others noticing, although both Tullius and Marcellus watched what I was doing suspiciously.

Marcellus, however, was too exhausted to raise the usual japes or alerts. He sat on animal furs that had been secured to the horses. He leaned his back against a rock wall, and Drunia sat beside him staring at his face in firelight. She touched his cheeks to warm them and murmured in Gaul, "You Roman men are devils, yet merely stupid boys with swords, like my beautiful Sulla."

Marcellus was too week to pull away and let me tell you obviously also comforted by having his face warmed.

Trebonius left the others and the fire to sit with me at the mouth of the cave where I kept watch on the white fields below.

"How did you do that trick, healing Marcellus's wound?"

"Something I picked up from a Judean named Jehoshua."

"I think you did much the same for Beast, slyly."

"Yes, slyly."

Why deny it?

"Judea, did you say? The hot lands?"

"A talented wandering prophet, Jehoshua. He could raise the dead."

"Ahhh, like Anubis."

"Much like. I'm not as good as he but I know some tricks. You seem more accepting of me than Marcellus is, Trebonius."

"I don't expect as much of you as he does."

I must admit I glared at him for that.

"You are a sky god, eh? Fine. The Greeks teach us that the gods will come to Earth from time to time. Or maybe you are no god at all but just a magician. The world is full of such. In Rome, there are oracles who sit over burning fires, inhaling the smoke in order to have visions. I suspect we inherited that from the Greek oraculars. There are men who claim to be the 'fallen legions of the Egyptian Beetle God'. . ."

Like fallen angels. Interesting.

"There are cults and sects that drink human blood."

"Nonsense, Trebonius."

Some of my fallen brothers and sister, no doubt, wreaking horror and havoc on Earth in their exile. Man wolves, vampires, "Demons," and such.

"Perhaps nonsense, but I don't dwell on such things, General. Unlike Marcellus, I am a man of the city. Marcellus has been out here in the provinces and wildernesses, with only brief visits back home, for most of fifteen years."

"I never understood why," I said.

"He hates Rome, I think."

"Nonsense. Indeed, he loves Rome."

"He loves Rome's legions." Trebomius laughed softly, his voice whispering steam as breath.

"The legions *are* Rome. Certainly though, he seems to hate his mother," I suggested.

"His fierce love of the legions, it was called 'the fever' during the republic."

He knows, I thought, that there is no more republic, though many a Roman denies it.

"Wanton love of Rome or else of Her legions," Trebonius whispered again, not without a certain sense of admiration for Marcellus beneath all he was saying. "It was a fever indeed with Marcellus's father, Flavius. Flavius Marcellus was rich and noble. A driven man, though. He served Rome as a slave serves a beloved mistress, immoral though that example is."

"You are one of the few Romans I've met to so despise slavery, Trebonius."

"Don't doubt that there are a few more of us."

I watched him shiver. Then he continued.

"I knew him Flavius because he visited his son in the camps outside the city where Marcellus served as a battle instructor and where he tutored me in strategy. Flavius wanted him to do the same as himself: to serve Rome as a senator and a noble. 'To serve Her as a loyal dog,' Marcellus would sneer after his father departed."

"Marcellus certainly serves Rome."

"Not with his heart and soul," Trebonius said with sudden passion. "Not in the Senate, and because of Marcellus's willfulness, his rebellion, Flavius left all to his wife in the will, unheard of for a powerful Roman with a healthy, educated, war-hero son for an heir."

"Yes, that is odd, from what I think I know of you Romans' love of sons."

"Poisoned, Quintus-Flavius Marcellus was. By a scheming fellow senator, they say. No one was found guilty though poison was the cause. The will expressed his disapproval of his son's wild nature, of his decision to embrace Augustus and a military career, abandoning the Senate. His mother Lucretia took all."

"But Roman law—"

"Allows Marcellus to challenge her. She is just a woman, after all, and rumor has it a secret follower of the foul Isis cult. But Marcellus chose to let her have the inheritance—lands, wealth, and the villa atop the Palatine that you've visited. He let her take it all, and he was free to leave. I think she was actually disappointed in him for not seizing it from her."

"Quite a sordid tale for as noble a man as Marcellus."

"You do like him, don't you, despite his garrulous disrespect," Trebonius smiled. I said nothing.

"As a tribune officer in the legions, General, he eventually became quite wealthy on his own."

"Hmm. As I have always thought, he is resourceful as well as having integrity. This Isis. Is that—"

"Egyptian, yes. Not a wholesome Roman goddess but a sinister one of the Nile. Isis reminds Romans of the harlot Cleopatra, who seduced Marcus Antonius into madness. Augustus will stamp the cult out in Rome someday. Lucretia is a powerful woman though, and Augustus needs her."

The next day we rode on. Drunia guided us, and her direction was true, bringing us to a point before a headland, which would take only one more day's ride to reach. By then, the horses were fatigued and Marcellus was unconscious. Though I'd sealed his wound again, he'd lost much blood and was feverish from an infection that Tullius's heated sword had not stopped from taking root.

Marcellus was still unconscious when we reached the coast, with Drunia guiding the horse they shared and Marcellus tied to her back so that he would not fall off, his cheek lying on her shoulder and his arms secured round her waist. Though he must have been heavy on her, she uttered no complaint.

I'd spoken to her in the cave that first night, in old Parisii so none could follow our talk, though something told me Trebonius knew the tongue. She'd told me why she was riding with us rather than returning to her people, and it was not just her grief; her own people would likely not trust her back into their company for she'd been tasked as a member of the diplomatic mission to Rome to seduce a Roman who'd be used as a tool against Rome; but as all could tell, she'd fallen in love instead.

I might've felt some faint pity for her; but of course my sympathy was for poor dead Sulla. Never mind that it was me who killed him.

When we were even nearer the coast, we freed the horses, the pale one dashing off as if furious, with Trebonius expressing hope that our pursuers would find them and they would not starve or freeze to death. I knew they wouldn't. I had sensed those very pursuers about two days behind us.

We waited until dusk so that none would see us once we left cover of a bluff, and we walked down from the tree line. We soon stood upon a narrow beach, with the dark woods behind us and an ice-strewn sea channel before us. Marcellus, who was awake now but too weak to walk, lay upon a wooden litter we'd made and that we dragged with us as we hiked along the shoreline.

We came upon the markings of a large landing party, which had been there and departed. The charred remains of campfires, and pits dug for tent anchors were left behind, evidence of perhaps two hundred troops only recently gone. Far out in the channel, we could see by setting sunlight the masts of five or so Roman ships less than half a day off, sailing away west back to Britannia. They'd landed and with no legions or scouts here to meet them, they'd tarried and after a time, sailed.

"We can flee no farther then," said Tullius with a tone of defeat unlike himself.

"The gold you were putting aside has not been used to good cause after all, has it, Saturnius? It has failed to save you." Marcellus, now awake, had laughed weakly, the laughter turning into a dry cough. Drunia knelt beside the litter, dropping water upon his lips from the goat's bladder she'd filled with melted snow before we'd left the cave.

"We should see them soon," I said.

"Who?" asked a puzzled Trebonius.

Within the hour, we had hiked a mile south along the beach, and the moon had risen to show us the approaching outline of a single ship and the glowing white flag of a trader, a merchant's two level with suspiciously large bireme oar ports.

"Look there!" shouted Tullius. "Kiss my *pugio* if that ain't a disguised Cilician ship! Trying to look like a trader, white flag and what. Oar ports for twenty slaves each side, likely fast enough to outrun a proper war ship—a smuggler."

"Pirates?" Trebonius demanded, incredulous. "You paid Cilician pirates to rescue you, Saturnius?"

"Typical Saturnian ploy," whispered Marcellus. "We had nothing to worry about. The sky god may be untrustworthy and treasonous, but he knows how to cover his sky ass."

There were slaves aboard the Cilician ship.

The morning after, a landing boat had come ashore to take us out to the ship, a slave ship. Thus, the ship's lower decks where we were put into the smallest cabin like cargo, stank of human sickness and misery, a fact that troubled Trebonius greatly, though he'd kept his tongue.

Below were muffled cries and moans of sixty or so chained souls, shouting and babbling in Britani and in sundry Mediterranean languages, along with the creak of ship's beams, the slap of sluggish costal waves, and a bumping of ice against her hull.

The newly commissioned captain, whom I knew too well, was the battle-hardened Armenian, Peshtlavo. That afternoon he looked into the smallest cabin. He stood in the hatchway bent over, for ceilings down here were no more than five feet tall. He held a greasy burning lantern and squinted in at the bunk where Marcellus lay cushioned by rough but clean straw. The captain scratched his jaw thoughtfully.

Beast, who lay on the floor in a dark corner, whined and would not let me near perhaps aware of what had changed in me, and perhaps aware also of what condition Marcellus was in; perhaps fearing for his master.

"That one won't last into the night," Peshtlavo grumbled, bent with me at the verge of the cabin but then moving out into the dark passage. I followed, annoyed, for I needed Peshtlavo, had long benefited from his services.

"He will die when it is his time," I said, "And he will do so with no undue suffering, Captain."

"You've a liking for this one, eh? I don't think of you as caring about any other living thing but y'self."

"Think what you want but do as I pay you to do."

"You didn't pay passage for four, Sauturnús," he pronounced my name in the Cilician fashion, his thumb hooked on his leather waistband, lantern held up before him, boot heels sounding on the floorboards. Stripes of sunlight from above us shone down through deck boards just overhead, lighting Peshtlavo's nappy beard and shaggy eyebrows, illuming his fierce dark eyes and his chest muscles flexing above the fur-lined, salt-stained leather coat he wore as he turned and stopped, deliberately blocking me.

"As always, Sauturnús, passage must be paid in full."

"You will be paid when we reach *Numidia*, Captain."

"*Mauretania*, magician, no farther. You had better have a stash there too, as you claimed."

Peshtlavo was a talker, had always been that way.

"Not a sesterce more until Numidia, monkey."

"No. I take no Roman coin."

"Gold then." I turned to go back.

"You speak as if yours is the final word, magician. It isn't."

"Are you talking still? Are you making demands of me?"

"I talk as I wish. You do not command this ship, I do," he hissed. I looked around to see his hand drift to his sword. Had Trebonius been beside me that hand would have been instantly cut off by Trebonius's sword.

"Draw it, Captain," I said in a quiet voice. "Draw it, though you are a captain because of me, and though I have paid you handsomely many times. Draw it and I will burn you alive as I did your former commander, from whom you inherited this ship."

Peshtlavo's hand halted but did not retreat. He smiled, yellow and white teeth glowing in a stripe of sun.

Let me pause to say a word about this man, my dear. His resilience had always impressed me. Peshtlavo had sailed the Aegean, the straits of Asia Minor, and the wild Balearic coasts and had fought Roman warships under his former commander, Borbasa. I'd first met Peshtlavo when doing illicit business with Borbasa on the Adriatic as I'd traveled the empire under a writ of service to the legions just before my first posting as a general.

Well, when I'd found it necessary to kill Borbasa, Peshtlavo had taken this ship. Taking command had required him to kill six rivals within the crew and once he'd established his command, he'd sailed the channels running communications and letters of negotiation between Romans and Gauls, the likely reason Octavian-Augustus did not send a proconsul to eliminate him. He was skilled at making himself useful.

He had transported slaves for profit and provided a means of escape from defeated battlefields to whomever was able to pay— Gaulish, Britani, Parisi, and Roman alike. He was a man of many uses, Peshtlavo, and thus he'd kept his head despite sometimes killing Romans. He'd kept his crew in booty and thus they had not murdered him in his sleep.

My, my, busy, busy.

He now kept control over a wild crew of hardened Numidian mercenaries, Parthian pirates, Persian outlaws, and Chaldean cut throats. He was no coward; a coward would not have had the nerve to sail this ship up the Gallica coast in winter, following fickle currents to avoid freezing, and playing cat and mouse with a Roman fleet, all the while talking calm into his crew with that sly tongue of his; a born and fearless talker, this pirate was.

Yet he blanched sufficiently at my mention of his predecessor. He and all the crew had seen the man burn and wail when he had tried to drive too obnoxious a bargain with me years earlier in a Mediterranean port my legion had passed through. I'd made arrangements for a fleet from Rome's Egyptian garrison to sail to the Gaulish coast as reinforcement. I then made another pact with pirates to follow that fleet as a secondary plan for my own escape both from Gaul and from the same Roman fleet, if need be.

"Even if he dies," Peshtlavo sniffed, "you pay full fare for him. For the dog as well. And I want double for the danger: we had to lie off shore in all this infernal ice, avoiding those Roman ships full of legionnaires and their fire pots, what they'd have burned us down with in a grapple. Roman sea commanders be not known for pity or mercy shown to Cilician ships that run abeam of 'em."

"You know, Peshtlovo, for a brigand without a country, you talk overmuch."

Scowling, Peshtlavo spat at my feet, a pirate curse, an insult, the particular type of rebuke a pirate makes to announce his independence from laws, nations, all gods (and magicians), in order to say his one and only home is the sea, and his ship his kingdom and you, merely a passenger to his whim.

He spat then disappeared into the cold dark recesses lit by smoking oil lamps, heated by urns of far-eastern design containing red glowing coals and hot rocks, almost a Chinese assemblage.

I attempted to reenter the cabin, but Beast rose, crept forward, growling. I had decided to silence Beast forever when Marcellus roused and whispered sharply.

"Shut up and sit, dog!"

Beast whined and retreated to his corner.

I entered and stood over Marcellus. He slipped back into fevered unconsciousness. I watched him and his ragged breathing for a few moments, and then left him.

On deck, Trebonius, refusing to loiter long below on a ship carrying slaves, was at the prow with Tullius and Drunia, who stood apart from the two, as she gazed into the water with the same distracted grief she'd displayed since joining us.

Trebonius and Tullius drank from cups of hot wine the Cilician ship's cook had given them. Scores of urns sat in recesses under heavy propped-up tarps, urns filled with red-hot coals. The tarp shelters stood here and there on deck, keeping the crew warm; and the crew kept a distance from us, as if afraid.

I stood near Trebonius and looked at the frozen water. The razor-sharp prow, carved and knifelike for just the purpose, cut through surface ice, splitting it like glass.

"How is he, then?"

"Not well, Trebonius."

"We are not headed to Britani, but southward."

"Do not fear. You will be taken to the Roman fleet. I planned to save at least my command officers and hoped for a better outcome than this."

"Any good Roman commander will plan an escape. That means Marcellus also goes with us?"

"He stays. He will bring them a ransom. For that reason, he won't be harmed. If he lives."

"And Drunia? She'll be crucified if the legions get her."

"She goes with me and Marcellus. And Beast. All are under my protection"

"Did you plan the betrayal with Verilius?"

"I am loyal to Rome. I had no idea he would do what he did."

"Then you ain't a god, ere you, General?" Tullius chuckled.

"I never actually said I was."

"You're a magician," said Trebonius decisively, "With a stash of gold with which to get your way and cast your spells. Much like Julius. Yet we could do with a god right now."

"No, not a god."

"Still," offered Tullius, "these pirates, they're proper frightened by you. We did some trade with Cilician pirates in my Etruria. They come from many places but once aboard these ships together a while, they take on the same attitudes together. A suspicious folk, they are, frightened of the gods, of any gods."

"Pompey defeated and crushed them in three weeks"—Trebonius sneered—"and Caesar mopped up the rest."

"These here don't look crushed to me, nor moped up, Commander Trebonius," Tullius offered gently.

Nearby hovered the ship's cook, a Greek with a livid scar on his cheek, a sword cut that had healed long ago. He listened to our talk. He'd made it plain that he provided wine and food for us out of the ship's precious stores because he had once lived in Rome and now in exile, and yearned to here news of his once adopted home, or wanted just to be near Romans chewing duck fat.

"Your revulsion with the slave trade does puzzle me, Trebonius," I said. "One reason the Cilicians are allowed to continue to sail is because they supply slaves to Roman nobles to work your *latifundia* and your farms."

"Your tolerance for Roman slavery is strange to me, General," Trebonius answered me grimly. "Your people resist Rome. As for me, I serve and support my country even when it is wrong. Yet my family holds no *latifundia*. It is my hope, it is Marcellus's and—"

He paused, made himself continue.

"And was Verilius's hope too, that Octavian will someday outlaw slavery, when the time is right."

'Octavian' not Augustus at the moment.

"It seems Verilius did quite a bit more than hope," I suggested, and there I stopped. I felt no need to confront Trebonius with the truth that his mistaken loyalty to Augustus would someday prove erroneous and that, due to Augustus's killing their Republic and founding the empire, and his coming elevation to godhood, the havoc of the mad Caligula and of Nero would be unleashed. For after a calm but short interregnum of Augustus's son Tiberius's reluctant rule would begin an age of mad despots. Nor would he likely believe it anyway, were I to reveal Rome's future to him.

Tullius felt no such compunction against prodding Trebonius's faith.

"Pardon my ignorant say so, Commander, but I'd bet gizzards to pigs' knuckles them slaves below be Britanis."

"What of it, Centurion?"

"Well, even foot soldiers in the legions've noticed, as we defeat an enemy nation we take them into slavery, or the pirates take them into slavery then sell them back to us as slaves."

"Tullius, what—," Trebonius frowned.

"The Gauls, Dominus." The Britani, next comes Persia, then Thrace, I lay wager. Augustus claims to be wanting them all part of our Republic, but we'll likely be at war with 'em all, and eventually, put them to chopping our timber, rowing our ships, and digging out our mines."

"What do you know of politics, Centurion," snapped Trebonius, annoyed. I marveled at the sly Tullius, ever so subtly putting the barb into Trebonius by calling him *dominus*—the honorific a slave offers to a Roman master, not what a centurion calls a commander. The point was sly and well made. Trebonius balked but looked sidewise at me as I smiled at his irritation. He gentled then and simply hardened his mouth.

"Only what I see with my eyes, sir," Tullius said simply.

Good eyes you have there, Tullius.

"Didn't you assure me," I chided Tullius, "that someday, all Rome's enemies will have become Romans?"

"That I did, General, but first comes conquest, second comes the slavery. Then citizenship, as my own people know. Each nation comes to Rome by way of the sword, then lash. Finally, citizenship."

Well said and correct.

Trebonius sighed.

"Are we to believe that Verilius was right? That we are a nation of slavers even in essence."

Tullius thought about it.

"That ain't politics, what Verilius done, Commander Tribune, that's personal. A man betrays his fellow legionnaire, is less than a dung beetle."

Both turned to me.

"I have no opinion to give, my Roman fellows. Though I love Rome, I am not, nor never was I, one of you. It could easily be said that I led you all into death, ruin, and capture."

Which in fact I had.

I stepped away from them then, and Trebonius, ever dutiful, even when left with nothing more to be dutiful toward, sought to follow, but pirate crewmen, as they had been instructed to, surrounded me to keep him away. I'd little desire to see him die by keeping loyal to my dying leadership.

Drunia snatched a sword from one of the pirates. I took her arm.

"No. None will be harmed."

She gave the pirates a sneer and relented.

Trebonius and Tullius were pushed to the port side where a smaller boat moored. They were forced on board, and despite their shouts of protest, were rowed away from the ship, through the ice, northwest toward Britani.

I had arranged for them to be dropped on a shoreline with food and provisions where they could walk a day or so to easily join the legions that we had missed on the beach. My last glimpse of them was of Tullius waving. I waved back and saw that smile of his. I could not make out Trebonius's expression.

Drunia and I went back below. We walked through the short and narrow, musky warrens, passing by the doorway of a large hold full of barrels, where a group of sullen seamen huddled around coal fire urns drew lots in candlelight. They glared at us as we passed, particularly interested in the presence of a young woman aboard.

In the cabin where I'd left him before, Marcellus was breathing his last. I sat close by him, contemplating the risk involved in intervening in his death. It is said of me that I am without values, but as I have told you, dear crab, I at least have respect for The Plan even if I do not approve of it. I do not seek to alter historical permutations lightly. This moment was somehow crucial, and so I thought the better of exercising my will.

I'd decided not to tell Tullius and Trebonius the real reason I wouldn't let them take Marcellus with them; that his death was certain.

Marcellus opened his eyes. He saw Beast, and then saw Drunia. The dog had thrown his great, hairy paws up onto the side of the bunk, to keep watch. Marcellus petted him and the dog whined.

"It stinks in here," said Marcellus.

"It's a pirate ship carrying a consignment of slaves."

"The others?"

"Trebonius and Tullius are on their way to rejoin the legions across the channel in Britannia."

"And we?"

"You are on your way to Numidia. I told them you will be easy to ransom because you've a wealthy family."

"Is that true, you will let them do so?"

"No. I simply was reluctant to lose you."

"I'm touched."

He coughed and spat up blood. I waited. Eventually his breath returned. He looked at Drunia.

"Why didn't you kill her?" I asked.

"Why didn't you flee back to the sky, once defeated?"

I made no answer, though it was, come to think of it, a good question.

"I'll tell you why, Saturnius. You've been among us too long. I blamed you for the deaths of legionnaires at first and planned to murder you, but your mistakes were human ones, like any Roman commander who has not yet learned all he must know. I forgave you. I've reached an end to killing." He coughed up a bit more blood then took a ragged breath.

"What do you mean I've been among you too long?" I whispered.

"I mean that it's too late for you. What is it you so often talk of—sympathy? You've developed sympathy for us."

Did I talk of sympathy? Pish! So close to death, he's imagining things, poor crab.

"You said we sail on to Numidia, but didn't include yourself, by the way, Saturnius."

"I am not going to Numidia, Marcellus, any more than you are."

"But not going back to the sky either, I'll wager."

"I am, in a manner of saying."

"Or are you going off to be among more of my kind? I've been watching you. I watch my commanders. You can't go back, for as you said, you were exiled, though you've regained power—I could see it happening. Why did you not leave as soon as you helped us escape? Or sooner?"

I was silent. Then I asked my own question again.

"Why didn't you kill Drunia?"

Drunia had taken his hand. She was studying it, gazing at the wounds, scars, and leather burns from the reins of horses.

"Something of my younger days as a stoic came back to me. I lost my rage, my hunger for revenge. I shouldn't have killed Verilius, he was my only friend, he and Sulla."

"Verilius betrayed you."

"He betrayed the legions, yes, and so I had to kill him, but he didn't betray me. I am not the legions, though I tell myself I am. You are not Roman though you pretend to be.

"But you are not one of the sky gods, either."

"Oh?"

"Don't give me that *Saturnius* look. I've been at your side for years, Gaul. You're not human so you don't know the truest thing about being human."

"Which is?"

"Life is a game none of us wins. I remembered that, and so I let Drunia be. I threw away that sword at last. I don't want it back. And you?"

"I stayed because I still had things to do."

"And now?"

"If you insist, I'm waiting for you to die now, you ass."

He laughed, the laughter turning into a coughing fit. When he recovered, he whispered in a rattling voice.

"I think you won't have long to wait, at that. This is where we part, sky god. After this day, you will not see me again."

Marcellus reached for one of Beast's great paws.

"Have you children, Marcellus?"

"I've a daughter. Livia-Julia."

"Perhaps I'll visit her and let her know what a brave man her father was."

Drunia touched Marcellus's cheek.

"How kind. But why are you still standing there, Saturnius?"

I made no reply.

"Roman men have soft faces," Drunia murmured.

"She says she likes your face."

"Protect her. Sulla clearly treasured her."

"I will do her no harm," I promised.

"Stay with Saturnius, Beast," he said to the dog, and Beast seemed to understand, seemed resigned to obey; he slipped down from the bunk and moved close to my side.

"I am not a god."

"You're no longer satisfied with the sky."

"An interesting theory."

"Could I really have killed you?"

"You could have killed this body, and would have, if the Gauls hadn't interrupted, for you are much better than I."

"I am a better swordsman than a sky god?"

"Swordsman? More to point, you are a better soul. You are like one who was once my friend. Gabryel. Vain and powerful. as stoic as you, yet an honorable soul, in his own way. And yes, you are a far better swordsman than me."

He considered this and smiled. His breath grew short as he spoke again.

"Visit my . . . daughter? Why do I feel that will not be an altogether pleasant thing for her? But . . . if . . . you get back to Rome, do give Mother a message."

"Yes?"

"Tell her my-my last thoughts were of her. That'll burn her fallow heart."

I laughed with him, taking his hand. His own laughter turned to choking, and as he choked to death on his own blood, I did not attempt to stop him dying, not just because I could feel the wrongness of it, but I had no idea if I even could. I have had uneven success at such things, as you know.

He grew still, his eyes open. Drunia stood up, looking down at him. She let his other hand fall back onto his chest, limp now.

I picked him up from the straw and carried his body through dark warrens past crew compartments, storage, and slave pens. Drunia and Beast followed. Angry crewmen glared at us.

As I'd promised Sulla, I led her up to the light.

On deck with her, I held Marcellus, with Beast beside us. Beast moaned in grief while the sound of ice breaking beneath the prow, the lapping waves, and the wind accompanied the war dog's dirge.

Presently, at a parting of the ice, I let Marcellus drop. His clothing was heavy enough to pull him under immediately. He was gone. Beast wailed pathetically for a time, then grew quite still and silent. He knew why I'd done it; he knew his master was dead. As the fight had gone out of his master, it now left Beast. He lay his head between his paws on the deck and was still.

Drunia looked down into the black water.

"I will make sure you get back to Gaulia. It might take some time, but I will protect you."

She looked up at me absently for a while, and then-"I have reached the end of this life," she said, "and I want only to go to Sulla. You are a demon, and you know such things, so tell me. Will I see him when I pass over?"

"I cannot say. I know only that you will continue to exist after death. You will pass into greater realms of The Creation, as Sulla already has."

She saluted me, fist pressed to her chest, a warrior's salute. I returned it. She waited for the ice to part and threw her hips onto the narrow rail, over the edge, to drop into the water. There was barely a splash.

I had done her no harm.

"The men won't like the waste of a strong woman to rape," Captain Peshtlavo hissed at my back. "As for me, I care not about your Gaulish she-devil," he continued. "But you shouldn't have done that with the Roman. We might have ransomed the carcass. Rich Romans place a great value on recovering their dead sons."

"I do as I wish, human."

"*Human*, eh? Still selling the idea you're some sort of god, magician? I never did believe it."

I drew my sword. Beast roused himself and growled.

"As to what I am, I am an angel, pirate monkey."

"What is that to me, wizard?"

"Have you not realized it, after all you've witnessed? Can you not see I am a being of power? Are you not awed and chastened? I have trod the stars, and razed alien cities in war between beings of power. I have turned time backward and seen what your monkey eyes cannot even perceive on this side of death."

He spat, this time actually striking my feet.

"What is all that to me? My business is not war but thievery. I recognize a rival thief, for, whatever else you are, Sauturnús, you are a lowly dog of a thief, like me. You are indeed, a bloody captain of thievery."

"Thank you," I smiled.

"But there is no room on my ship for two captains."

As he had been speaking, Peshtlavo had been joined by seven of his grisliest crewmen (they'd lost that drawing of lots, presumably) and all crowded around me, baring drawn swords. The cook now made himself scarce, scuttling down the hatch to go below.

One of the grisliest of the grisly struck at me and I struck back, beheading him.

Peshtlavo lunged, screaming, still talking!

"I am master here! I will bow to no man, and to no God!—"

And I pivoted to avoid his blade and with no great difficulty beat his blade back, but was surprised to watch him hop backward in formal Numidian style, almost as if—

He smiled a sour smile. "Yes, I have trained. At port, with a Numidian sword master. I used the gold you paid me. I have learnt a few things."

I noticed for the first time that he bore a Numidian short sword as thick and broad as my Roman legionnaire's crown gladius, a match for the weight and threat of my own armature. His was the sword that had been favored of Hannibal's cavalry when the Carthaginian general conquered Roman armies. I also saw that Peshlavo wore light Numidian vest armor.

"I had no idea a pirate would wish to do anything with gold other than to buy Numidian beer and smoke kiseru, Peshlavo."

"Kiseru, what's that?"

"Something much like human hair."

He scowled.

"Why would anyone smoke human hair!"

"You pirates are a bizarre and savage lot, aren't you?"

His men all attacked at once now, and as Beast mauled three of them, I cut them down. Peshtlavo and I faced one another with the last three pirates falling back respectfully behind their captain to defensive positions, no longer protecting him.

Beast stood ready with me.

Strangely, Peshtlavo smiled. He performed a surprisingly graceful series of cuts right to left, *squalembrato*, diagonal downward then diagonal upward, throwing me back, followed by a parry of my counter thrust and showing me that my rustic battlefield style would not do, he stepped inside my guard to launch an aggressive *fleche* that almost ran me through to the chest.

I stumbled, losing proper form, back to the rail that Drunia had climbed over, Beast whining beside me. Beast was a war dog. He knew to be worried about me.

Peshtlavo laughed, danced backward only so far as to be out of my reach, to a stalking distance, seeing that I was trapped against the rail.

"That was an ugly retreat, magician!" he taunted. "Your form is ruined by Roman war training."

"No doubt, monkey," I strove to catch my breath.

"Pathetic. I'll allow you to get a breath. You are about to meet the end you have given to so many Gauls and Britons, 'Dominus.' So who is the barbarian here?"

I watched the pirates. More confident again, they were flanking their captain on either side to block my footwork and to draw tight a trap for their master to finish me.

"My teacher would mock you for your clumsy technique, Sauturnús."

He stopped smiling, setting his feet for what I knew would be a Numidian side-to-side cutting attack that might wound or even kill the body I'd kept healthy for so long. It was time to be dicing with this dangerous human.

I knew what Marcellus would do, what he had warned and trained me do in close-quarter single struggle with a better swordsman. I dropped my guard and made as if to run laterally out of the cul-de-sac, and as Peshtlavo and Beast followed, I turned and slew flanking pirate, number five, tossed the dead man at Peshlavo.

Marcellus's admonitions came back to me as I did it.

"Fighting a single man as opposed to the performance and cockaldry of the arena, or the impersonal, legion-sized field maneuvers and flanking cavalry attacks of the battlefield requires a certain something, my General."

Peshtlavo, who of course, having recently been trained by a master, had allowed himself to assimilate certain formalities of the chivalry of the sword. His mistake, for the civilizing influence of formal combat, Marcellus had brought me along to know, will ruin a good barbarian's raw force if that barbarian allowed himself to be so much civilized. Marcellus had trained me in that certain something.

Fight dirty. That had been Marcellus's teaching.

Sure enough, Peshtlavo had learned to outfight me, but in the process had lost something of his ferocity, his pirate reflexes. He gave me a look of contempt at my ugly and cowardly tactic, stumbled over the corpse I tossed at him, and I unceremoniously slew him, splitting him nearly in two.

Mercifully, he died too quickly to say anything more.

Beast and I then finished the last two of Peshtlavo's grisly guardsmen. Meanwhile, a host of less grisly pirates had emerged from below, no doubt alerted by the cook. I looked at them a moment and could tell they felt they could not allow me to live after slaying yet another of their captains, so I had to slay every one of them who came for me.

Some died of dog bite rather than the stroke of my sword.

When Beast and I had finished, I stood awhile with the war dog on the bridge, ahold of the ship's wheel. Fully empowered now, I could "see" again. I could see across and through time and could follow lines of causality forward and backward. Woven all around me, these appeared as glowing filaments, shimmering and eddying as if on soft breezes. I could follow them. I could see things I had not been able to these past years spent bound in a human vector.

I saw that though Sulla had acted simply out of romantic love, Verilius had been in league with at least three senators. One of them had, ironically, been Senator "Liverspot," a Roman who had contempt for Gauls, for all "barbarians," but who wanted to see Augustus's peace initiatives fail, and wanted total war with Gaul. Helping the Gauls and thus sabotaging Augustus was certainly a way to ensure his goals.

I could see now that Lucretia had poisoned her husband, Marcellus's father. Marcellus had suspected it but had no proof. She regarded herself as having done it for Marcellus's sake, and she had been frustrated that her son showed no desire to fulfill her large ambitions for him. How it would cut her to learn of his death!

Ah, human drama.

What did he mean saying it was "too late" for me? Something within me had reacted to that claim of Marcellus'. Quite a deep one he had turned out to be, in the end. No wonder none could control or break him. I, of course, admired such independence, such obstinacy. Am I not the pattern for those things? Marcellus had even shown flashes of second sight, the human version of angels' vision.

Few humans had a knack of seeing past the veil, though, no matter how deep they got when reaching their end.

I disregarded his final words.

I left the wheel, went below to free the slaves, as Trebonius would have wanted. They'd put me to thinking of the angels who had followed me in my rebellion and who, no doubt, had been punished.

Several of the freed men had the ability to navigate a ship enough to sail back up the channel to Briton. I bade Beast farewell, extracting a promise from the men that they would care for him. I left the body to which I had grown so accustomed, left it dead and wane as a fish on the deck of the ship, and flew free between the sea and sky. Already, the small confined thoughts and feelings of long years as a human was receding, replaced by an angel's perspective and a cold determination to take the next step in my quest.

"Too late" is in the eye of the beholder.

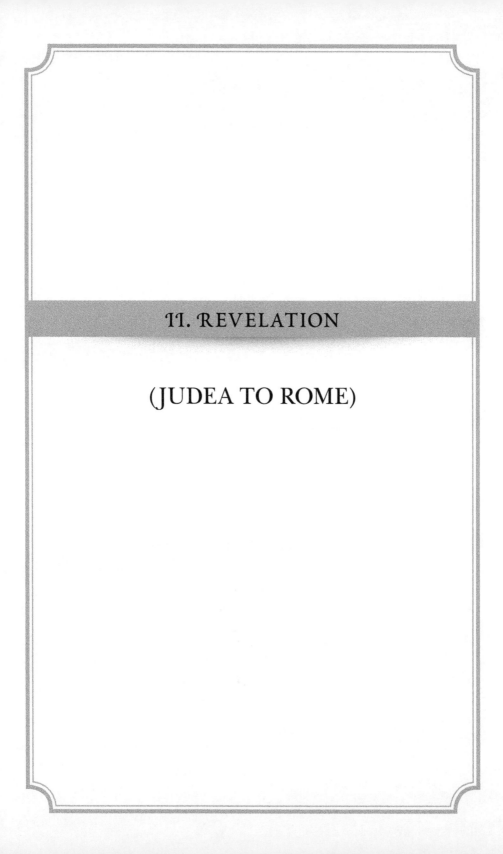

11. REVELATION

(JUDEA TO ROME)

And I saw when the Lamb opened one of the seals, and I heard, as it were, the noise of thunder, one of the four beasts saying, 'Come and see'... And I saw, and behold, a white horse. And when he had opened the fourth seal, I heard the voice of the fourth beast say, 'Come and see'... And I heard a voice in the midst of the four beasts. And I looked, and behold, a pale horse. And his name that sat on him was Death, and Hell followed with him.

—Revelation 6

2

The generals must all have felt we were invincible even before Ypres. Ludendorf would not have ordered us these past months to cross so many fields of heavily mined ground were he not convinced that his troops were super human, surely. As for *Kommandant*-in-chief Ludendorf, he was looking ahead to Italy!

Such confidence!

High Kommand, the *Oberste Heeresleitung*, put a cap upon Ludendorf's ambitions, however, in order to keep his fevered brain cool. "To Paris!" the High Kommand insisted, simple goals are best, they declared. Italy and the rest of Europe could bloody well wait. Meanwhile, Crown Prince Rupprecht was for our stopping, hunkering down, and supporting the Hindenburg Line strategy at the British front, and so we were marched hither and back "as if the generals and the Prince see us as chess pieces and hang strategic sense!" Brigade Kommandant Reinert whined.

On the line, we soldiers took to lamenting how "everyone in the High Kommand is full of ideas," many more ideas than they'd had before Ypres. Many more than could possibly succeed.

War will do that.

"Before Ypres. For my regiment at least, those had been heady days back when we'd held Mesieres, on the north side of the River

Somme, back when German propaganda still hailed us as "the machine." We the *machine*, we held that ground; and who in their right mind (besides a general) would have wanted it back?

Yet the enemy had thought to take it from us. They've generals also over on their side; generals urging bold valor just as ours do over here. A patch of muddy pockmarked farmland, one scarcely believes there ever did grow anything living, is not just a patch of muddy pockmarked farmland because the generals know what this land now can grow: the corpses of the enemy.

It was always harvest here at the front, and so the enemy had sought to take it from us.

They'd come screaming at us in regularly timed, easily predictable waves, in just the way we had earlier charged at them. Just as we had made easy targets, so too did they offer us the target practice that generals on both sides must have wanted us all to benefit from.

Perhaps in preparation for the butchery of Ypres.

At Somme, after three days of heavy bombardment along only three miles of front (bombardment that told us they intended to launch a concentrated thrust in order to punch a hole rather than overwhelm us), French artillery fire was suddenly joined by the addition of their trench mortars firing thirty rounds per minute (this told us they were about to attack).

Yet through his small field glasses, Kommandant Reinert could see no signs they had cleared the wire in front of their trenches. "They aren't going to clear it," some of us heard him say to the adjutant officer of General Ludendorf's forward command staff, "So that we won't know they are coming until zero hour arrives." Our division chief went around announcing this to the lieutenants as we fixed bayonets inside our deep dugouts, safe from most of the French artillery.

When the roar and thump of the bombardment suddenly ended just before dawn, they ordered, "Out!" and we scrambled out into our trenches, the mud thick with frost and days-old frozen blood. We climbed halfway up the ladders set into the sides of the trenches, sniffing the frigid night air smelling of the *gestalt* of cordite and sulfur, the soldier's *parfume* for the air was suffused with the stench of it. Our machine gunners quickly fixed their guns and threaded their ammunition belts, and in the silence, we heard the sound of the enemy's officers blowing their pipes to signal attack.

It was no bother to mow them down like mallards as they reared up from their lice-infested forward trenches, as they wiggled through the wire that French officers had deliberately not cleared, and waddled across no-man's land, splashing through water-filled shell holes, stumbling over a patch of mud-smeared, corpse-fouled stumps, the leftover matter of mutilated and incinerated trees, such farmland as was left that they would soon reseed.

Our foxholes had earlier been their foxholes, before we'd made our own suicidal charge into the chatter of their machine guns and had managed to drive them back several hundred yards. Now that they were mounting their counter charge, and dying in waves, the foxholes we occupied would eventually become theirs again. Not this time, and maybe not next time either; perhaps the time after that, but certainly, we knew, in time.

Shortly after though, in my recollection, we had secured our position on the north side of the river, sitting safe and in control of the field. It would be the perfectly good position from which we would embark for Ypres. Why? We could not figure it other than to assume some general had awakened from a dream of distant victory.

That morning, as if it were a prophecy, there had been some commotion among the men over an astonishing, dreamlike sight: a pale horse with a dark birthmark at the center of its head galloped out of the west, wild-eyed and snorting, unmarked and unmarred, not a drop of blood or of mud on it, unbesmeared. Was this some celestial sign from the war god Mars that we would manage to keep the position this time?

Soldiers are superstitious, looking for signs in everything, from the unanticipated boon of a crust of bread to a scavenged head of cabbage free of worms, to the sudden appearance over the battlefield of the moon released from a masking cloud bank and lighting one's stumbling trip to the latrine.

The pale horse with no bridle, no bit, and no reins, dashed along the ruined ground of no-man's land, like an apparition out of the past ages of these fields and forests. A cheer rose up all the way down the line, uttered from both sides. A few thousand men—French, Belgian, and German—were ecstatic to see the starving, maddened, pathetic thing, which was nevertheless free.

Kommandant Reinert, a sure shot with his 7.92 mm Mauser Gewehr 98, stood up and unslung, chambered a round and aimed carefully with the rifle's optical sight. He fired, and the horse collapsed just at the fifty-yard marker our side had designated near my brigade's watch station. It fell beside a ten-meter wide shell crater filled with foul water. The mad creature toppled over into the oily crater and vanished. Frenchmen screamed their anger and disdain at us, their frog drawls echoing in the twilight.

One dead leg hung out of the pit, its hoof pointed westward. Was this ghost horse out of the past a sign meant for *me*?

Sometime in the middle of the night, under the cover of clouded skies that snuffed out the moonlight that might have revealed us, we abandoned the trenches to the French, not waiting for their next charge that was sure to come with the dawn, may to succeed, probably not.

We withdrew, and began our march toward Ypres.

3

The lift machine rose upward, carrying me inside of it. On mechanical wings, I ascended to the upper floors of a "hotel" building towering above a bright, cold city. "Manhattan" the city was called, grand for a human city; much akin to another grand human city, Paris. Both cities, I felt back then, must surely have been designed by humans who'd enjoyed some supernatural inspiration perhaps from a common dream of the ultimate city of lights, *Shamayim*.

Loosening the tight silk band of cloth that encircled my collar (a "tie" it was called, I was certain that was the word for it), I glanced up at a dim electric light shining above me, revealing the mechanical indicator fixed atop sliding metal doors. A tin clock hand swept past numbers inscribed upon this indicator. These numbers stood for levels of ascension; the symbolism was almost Kabalistic—an idea that brought me pleasure.

A tiny bell tone chimed repetitively inside some unseen master control box, tolling for each of the levels I sailed by on my way to a thirty-third "floor." I was in the flesh of an Asian male wearing a costly suit and long cashmere coat; a young and apparently wealthy man whom I'd entered into out on the winter streets below. It was the year One Thousand Nine Hundred and Thirty-Four *Anno Domini*, as you figure it. I was in Manhattan at dusk, in this building at the corner of Thirty-Fourth Street and Eighth Avenue.

Or rather, for the benefit of your understanding, I can say it *will be* the year 1934, because for you, as with some other events I have shared with you, this period I speak of has yet to happen since you live in the time of the "World War," a time called 1914.

For me, this day in the city of New York in the Union of States, happened to be only my seventh time sailing aboard an elevator machine—two of those times aboard this very one though, I would ride many more times than that. I had spent more time on Earth aboard wooden sailing ships in ancient Greece and on the backs of horses in ancient Rome than riding inside twentieth-century automobile cars or on rising and falling elevator ascension machines.

You cannot but find it strange, the way my jumping about on the Earth across space and through time means that nothing for me is in "order" as it must be for you who are confined inside your crab's shell and soft flesh, and with your hobbled time sense. Your sense of time particularly limits your understanding of The Creation, for you cannot perceive the truth of how reality is nested and recursive, with microcosms that contain macrocosms, inside more macrocosms that themselves contain microcosms.

In truth, there are only a few of you with the ability to at least imagine the reality you cannot ever truly perceive. It was one such as this I'd come here to visit. Like Archimedes, like the old scientist in Princeton, this one could see.

I was startled by the sound of the steel cage and the padded doors shutting behind me. Your *machinas* can often mimic human traits, not least of which is their uncanny way of moving about and acting on their own without a human controlling their actions.

I considered this as I stepped away from the door. There is an undeniable spark of The Creator that shows in your ability and will to make machines, I cannot deny it. An angel cannot nor would we even consider doing such a thing as making a machine. But then you cannot see time, as we angels can.

Time, you see, is not really a river as you like to envision it. Time, rather, is a sieve through which space, matter, and energy pass and are mixed, broken up into countless streams, flowing off in all directions, and recombining into shifting, immutable but contingent configurations. I left the true time arc of Anu's will by leaving heaven and walking across the infinite grid of causality and of possible outcomes, for when you walk through time, that is just what you are doing.

For all contingent beings, my own self included, and every other angel as well, this fabric of many creations, many worlds, and many shadows of reality is the case. Only God can see, among all possible spacetime configurations, what or which of them make up the "true" arc of His creation. Only he distinguishes the one exact arc from it shadows. For he is not contingent, he alone is an autonomous being, and self-sufficient, subjecting everything and everyone to his will.

He is much like your Josef Stalin that way.

Never mind, Stalin is in one of your futures. Now pay attention. As I walked down the hall of the thirty-third floor, I pulled tight the woolen scarf around the Asian's neck. Thewinter chill and such. I could feel the likewise wool carpeting under the Asian's leather-shoed feet in the cold passage.

My first time ever upon Earth was during the primordial ages, remember. Those were very hot times indeed, what with volcanoes erupting all about and miasmic clouds of methane and carbon dioxide. Not that I even knew what "hot" was, in my angelic form. I'd stood patiently, meditating in a magma chamber that cooled over hundreds of thousands of cycles until the chamber crumbled and became a narrow gorge below a plain where nothing existed but huge trees marching in forests down to the shores of a steaming ocean, the sight of which was appreciated only by dragonflies the size of winged dogs.

I'd closed my eyes and meditated some million more cycles and when next I'd opened them, there were the first animals and that was when I knew that from trilobites to fishes in the cooling oceans to gigantic reptiles to birds to mammals on the land expanding out of the oceans, a new form of wingless angel would appear—you. *Eva* and *Adamis* would be my first encounter with you.

When next I came back to this planet, it was to your Union of States, in the member state known as New Jersey, to see the old scientist. Next, I came back to the time of your prehistory to meet your ancestors, Eva and Adamis, and from there fled to ancient Rome.

The hall was lined with neat, clean wooden tables set along the walls, each with a small lamp, and each lamp with a golden halo of illumination. I followed the ranks of their illumination past doors with numbers imprinted upon them: number 3321 . . . number 3323 . . . door number 3325 . . . and finally, door 3327.

I went up to that door, strode forward, walking right into the hardwood surface, my body's face smashing into it; the soft flesh of the face and chest making me rebound off the wooden portal.

Surprised, I reached up and felt a trickle of warm blood creeping from the hairline down to one side of the jaw. I had momentarily forgotten that in a body, one cannot walk wherever one pleases but must find a means of ingress through these twentieth-century apertures. I chuckled at my own foolishness. Rome, of course, had taught me, against my will, to know not to walk into solid objects!

Rome had been informative; it had taught me much about you, monkeys, but Rome had been a diversion from my true aims, and now I was back on the track of that which I sought. To find what I wished for, however, I needed information. I needed to know certain secrets. They would be the key to recovering and most importantly keeping my lost beloved. At that moment, the door swung inward and an elderly man in a white linen suit and with a gray woolen overcoat thrown over his arm walked out, stopping abruptly as he saw me standing there.

"Whoa, Minnie! You scared me!" the elderly man cackled jovially, shifting his silver-headed cane to the same hand, the left hand, with the arm that supported the coat.

"Who are you?" I grunted.

"Sam Clemens. Pleased t'meet y'quaintance," he drawled, and stuck out his right hand. I gazed at it.

The old man held the gesture, smiling, him with a wild mane of white hair and a large, shaggy moustache, both of the same color as his suit. The wild mane framed his quizzical expression; he waited, and I remembered that it was the monkey custom here to grasp another's hand and shake it up and down as a show of friendship. A weaker version of the hearty Roman arm clasp.

I shook the old man's outstretched hand. His quizzical expression now changed to a frown of concern.

"Why, yer bleedin' there, young man."

Releasing his hand, I pulled a handkerchief from the tuxedo pocket of the body I inhabited, and gingerly wiped away the blood. I replaced the cloth and looked at the old man closely.

"You resemble Dr. Einstein," I muttered, "though you are taller than he."

"Who would that be?"

"The most famous—well, he will be far more famous in a few cycles—a few years. I forgot that it's only 1934."

"You must've hit yer head harder'n y'think, felluh. It's 1907. Are you here seeking Mr. Tesla? He's inside. May I ask yer name?"

I stared at him. His resemblance to Einstein was not merely physical; the vibration of his spirit was of the exact same attenuation. It was puzzling; puzzling also that he seemed to be in a different time continuum than I was, or at least thought himself to be.

"He would be, Mr. Holland, no doubt," a dry, soft voice spoke from the doorway behind the white-haired old man. Clemens turned around to face the tall, thin, seventy-eight-year-old dark-eyed man of Serbo-Croatian features whom I had come to visit. The inventor, Nikola Tesla.

The features were slightly sunken, but sunken clearly from age alone and not from any perceivable sickness or starvation. In fact, the vitality of Tesla's face, which shone with steely gray-blue eyes, merely reiterated the vitality of the man's straight back and thin but square shoulders. He stepped by Clemens now to inspect me there in the hallway. The illumination that imbued this man was startling to me— he reminded me in fact of me. Metaphorically speaking, of course.

His temples were gray, but that made the black of his eyebrows all the more prominent, and those brows accented his gray-blue piercing gaze from beneath a sharp ridge above the eyes. The eyes looked apt to penetrate the flesh of my purloined body like Wilhelm Rontgen's X-rays might.

"Mr. Holland again, is it not?" he asked.

"You sound unsure uh who he is." Clemens chuckled. Tesla raked a burst of those very same X-rays across Clemens now.

"Y'know him, Nikola, or don't you?"

"Do *you*?"

Clemens smiled, leaned his cane against the wall and put on his coat. "How should I know who he is, old friend?"

The tall Serbian nodded, as if something he'd suspected were confirmed. He thrust wrinkled but exquisite hands into the pockets of his dark, rumpled suit, which looked to be of very rustic material. Lapels and pants were darned and patched. Still, the suit was immaculate, pressed to sharp angles and creases; his shirt collar and sleeves were white as bone. His tie, however, was slightly atwist.

"I've been expecting him," said Tesla.

"You know the young man then."

"I've visited with him twice. We've business."

"Then I'll be on my way. Goodbye to you, Mr. Holland."

Clemens shook my hand again, took up his cane, and shuffled away in a very Einsteinian fashion, toward the end of the passageway that contained the lift machine I'd just vacated.

"Come in, then," said Tesla.

As I stepped into the nimbus of darkness inside his door, he reached to retrieve a sign hanging on the doorknob on the inside, and hung it on the outside. It read,

Please Do Not Disturb the Occupant of This Room.

I followed him into the dark. One wall was lined with bookshelves containing not only books but all manner of wire spools, meters and gauges, electronic instruments, metal objects, and many a box of something labeled, "Saltine Crackers."

Large windows at the front of the room showed light snow beginning to fall outside in the near dusk. Gusting winds rattled the windows.

He went to a high-backed chair, sat down, and then gazed up at me intently.

"You are in yet another of your diverse bodies today," he snorted, sounding half amused.

I brushed moisture from my coat as he continued.

"Tell me, what criterion do you use to decide on the body you'll occupy? Do you look out of your window to select people by sight, or do you interview them first?"

I sat across from him, in a second high-backed chair, a duplicate of the one he was in.

"You so easily believe my claim that it is me coming to you in different bodies?"

"Logic and long study of human behavior tell me it's you. There are subtle things you can't have trained actors to say. Your personality traits, your gestures when you speak. Such cannot be counterfeited."

Oh.

"I assume the mechanism you have invented to achieve the effect doesn't make choices *for* you. Why do you come today as an Oriental?"

It was a bit startling to realize that I had a "personality" which carried over from body to body when I took a human form. Such a thing had never occurred to me.

"I should think, Mr. Tesla, you'd ask instead *how* I do it."

"I don't imagine it's difficult given a mechanism. To achieve it one simply empties one vessel and fills another. The original energy of your current vessel has been destroyed, absorbed, or displaced. Perhaps repressed."

"Your conception, Tesla, is primitive but accurate."

"And the host's essence?"

"The man, you mean? The man whose body, whose 'vessel' I've borrowed is still here 'repressed' as you say."

"Then I'm correct!"

"Except that I did not begin inside a 'vessel' in the first place."

"You must have begun with an original one to come here three times now as three different people. This demonstration of yours proves what was already obvious to me: human consciousness is self-contained and coherent, and can be broadcast from one place to another."

"I was not human to begin with."

"What were you! Consciousness with no form?"

"I can't answer in a way you'd comprehend, Mr. Tesla."

"Try."

"I'm an angel. Leave it at that."

He chuckled, muttered, "He's an angel, *Majka*," to himself, and rose from his chair. He went to one of the shelves, reached for a box, returned with it.

"Cracker?"

"Sorry?"

He reached into the box, took one out, and offered it to me. I took it from him.

"Go ahead," he said.

"Go ahead and what?"

"Take a bite."

"Bite?"

"Have you never had a cracker?"

I looked at the brown-and-white perforated thing.

"Eat."

It was a dry, hard, apparently bleached and nearly flat cube of grain flour caustically transformed into pure carbohydrate and starch. Yes, it could indeed function as monkey food, not unlike unleavened breads and biscuits popular with the ancient Roman pallet, but blander than anything a Roman would savor.

I bit into it and chewed.

Appeased, he took one for himself, biting into it eagerly. He returned the box to its perch and went to a stove set into the wall like a fireplace burning wood and charcoal. The cold rooms were scarcely affected by it.

A box lay on the floor beside the stove. He reached into the box, gingerly lifting from it a baby bird. He walked back over to me, cradling it.

"I doubt the existence of angels. If my mother, a very devout woman, were here, she would question you closely."

"I see no reason you would so readily believe in spirit transference, but not in angels, Tesla."

"Angels imply a personal God."

"We don't just imply, sir, we utterly reflect His certain existence. You can't have the others without The One."

"Nonsense. If a personal God made you, then where did He come from?"

"As far as I know, He's always been there."

"A noncontingent being?"

"You can't imagine just how noncontingent."

Suddenly the baby bird in his hand shuddered, made a chattering little noise.

"What is it, my dear?" Tesla cooed. He moved back toward the box, and the thing quieted. He moved back toward his chair, and it chattered again, this time in panic. He took it back to the box and redeposited it. It grew calm.

"I'm giving your question some consideration, Mr. Holland. Though I don't believe in noncontingent beings, your thought puzzle is challenging. Challenges lead to invention."

He sat back down across from me. I took another bite of his "cracker."

"I do not agree," sniffed Tesla, "with Albert. He's a metaphysicist who talks, not a scientist seeking to invent. Besides, much of what he published in his papers years ago about matter and energy were already known to the Vedic philosophers of India, and was recorded in Sanskrit long before Albert was born."

I wasn't surprised. There was as much difference between Einstein and Tesla as between earth and fire. Einstein was gentle and patient while Tesla was hot-tempered, disconsolate. I much preferred Einstein.

"Thought experiments are the only sort Einstein does," Tesla continued, "with *no* invention. I have in the past called him a stupid young man whose ideas are trash, but as I grow older, I feel more kindly toward upstart youths like him, Planck, and Boskovic. They're ignorant, that's all."

"Then you say God is not light."

"Indeed not! Were there a 'God' as you posit him, he would not be composed of electromagnetic energy in the spectrum of 'light.' Light is transitive. It exerts little influence on the physical universe other than the facile effects of heat and illumination."

"Yes?"

"While light *seems* an impressive property, it is, somewhat like Einstein, merely a dazzling effect, an attribute making one blind to the underlying existence of more profound properties in the spectrum. Not attributes, mind you, but genuine properties. Gravity, for example."

"But not light."

"No. I'm far more of a mind to say God would be an X-ray than a thing as trivial as a beam of light."

"Hmmm."

"Hmmm, indeed, Mr. Holland. I proved in 1896, as was further demonstrated by Compton eleven years ago, that X-rays are materially effective particles. They not only stimulate the surface of a thing, but more than light energy, they can penetrate the surface of a thing."

"Mr. Compton's experiments focused not on X-rays, but photons and gamma rays."

"His experiments focused on electrons. The implications were crucial to understanding X-rays."

"I had always believed, Mr. Tesla, that X-rays were merely one component of light."

"Had you? How quaint. Angels do not undergo a very rigorous postgraduate education in Heaven, I gather."

If I did not need him, I'd bite his legs off.

"We angels do have a certain innate understanding of the nature of reality, one that you monkeys lack."

"Monkeys. You refer of course to Mr. Darwin's theory."

"I refer to Mr. Darwin. He is a monkey. So are you."

"You mistake Darwin as you do much else. I apologize, for obviously you *have* been in a graduate program; only a university of 'scholars' could baffle Mr. Darwin's experimental work so soundly."

"You make a show of being a common thinker, Tesla, yet you attended The Polytechnic Institute in Graz, Austria, and the University of Prague, didn't you? You were an academic."

He ignored this. "I'll answer your question," he said.

I sat forward.

"Space isn't *curved*. There is no such thing as a *spacetime continuum*, since something cannot act upon nothing, and neither can the inverse be true. Thus, large bodies in space do not 'act' upon one another . . ."

"So you harp on Herr Einstein again."

"He is completely wrong! In fact, he stole ideas from my countryman Ruder Boskovic, who wrote of these things nearly two hundred years ago. You see, as I told you the last time you visited, without experimentation—"

"Einstein's insights are not experimental. He achieves insights through pure thought, through even a form of faith."

"As Mr. Clemens used to say, when he *actually* was alive, 'Faith is believing what you know ain't so.'"

I'd no idea what he meant by this *actually alive* business. "I tell you, Herr Einstein is correct," I said.

"No!"

"I am an angel, you monkey! I tell you he is!"

Tesla stood, thrust his hands into his pockets, and thrust forward his chin. He looked not at all like his seventy and odd such years, but far younger; for rage and stubbornness, I can attest, could have the effect of transforming Tesla, of infusing him with a life force that would swell his will, body, and, it happens, his voice.

"*Bik govno*, Mr. Holland—bull shite!"

He started pacing.

"Do you want an answer to your question or not?"

I chewed the last of his *cracker*. His voice now had lost its orderly, nearly English accent. He spoke now with Serbian glottal harshness and nasal consonance.

A flock of filthy-looking birds that had settled on a windowsill outside thrashed their wings violently, flapping off.

"If you've something to say, Tesla, say it! I've paid you handsomely for your services in American state dollar notes, more than you can say Mr. Edison ever did for you."

He stopped his pacing, giving me a sour look.

"For an angel, you are vindictive, Mr. Holland. Are you certain you are not a fallen angel?"

"Put two and two together, monkey! I ask you to solve a problem only a fallen angel would seek a solution to."

He grinned mockingly.

"Bik govno. To me, Mr. Holland, or should I call you Herr Holland? Many of you Asians are strangely attracted to this fascism business. To me, your question is merely a thought puzzle, and you simply a scientist, probably a damned fascist scientist at that, who has stumbled on certain methods of matter transference, transformation, and teleportation that I long have theorized. You ask a question about God that will somehow serve your secret experiments."

I resisted the urge to tear off his head.

"For example, Holland, you somehow created that elaborate illusion of my friend, Clemens."

I looked at him blankly.

"Don't deny it. My dear friend Samuel Clemens died in 1910. That was an agent of yours, or else a hypnotic inducement of the kind that Mr. Houdini perpetrates on Americans daily."

"I have no idea what you mean."

Now his labials, fricatives, and glottal stops pulled themselves tight, adenoidal, and became fake British again.

"That man at my door who tried to talk his way into my room was not Samuel Clemens, sir. Samuel is quite dead, and has been so for twenty-four years."

This called for some thought. Who or what *had* that been, that being with a strange spiritual attenuation? Best to get Tesla off the subject, for now.

"Very well, you are correct, Mr. Tesla. He was an agent of mine."

"As well I knew! And you, then, are a scientist, are you not? Admit it."

"I am the angel you call Satan."

His stubborn jaw clamped shut. A scowl of contempt. He turned and disappeared into another room. I sat there, listening to the soft cooing sounds of a number of birds I could still hear though they'd fled. I realized that there were birds I had thought during my earlier visits must be sitting outside on his grimy windowsills but which I now could tell were obviously ensconced somewhere inside the apartment rooms.

Across from the two chairs, which were the only pieces of furniture in this room, was the only wall with an adornment: it was a framed cover from a "magazine" called *TIME*. On the cover, dated 1931, was a drawing of Tesla himself.

I twisted my head to read the title of a book on the floor nearby. It bore a photo image of the white-haired old man. It was entitled, *The Adventures of Tom Sawyer.*

Tesla returned with two cups of fermented, heated beverage. He handed one to me, and with no word of explanation, sat down, sipping his own. I did likewise. It was a black and bitter drink, and unpleasant; but agreeably hot. The coldness of the rooms made it a good thing to put into this body I occupied.

"Relativity is a hoax. Surely you can see that, Holland. Is that blood on your jaw?"

"It's nothing. I walked into your door by mistake."

"As I said, you clearly are a scientist, not a metaphysicist. You've achieved experimental results. What has your Herr Einstein accomplished? Nothing, but talk of riding beams of light on a bicycle!"

"X-rays are a portion of light, Tesla."

"On a spectrum, *all* things are of the same essence, they are the same thing. They change and manifest identities—particles, waves, electricity, magnetism, light, etc., depending on vibration frequency resonance and vibrational pitch."

Astounding. His statement combined, though he could not know it, Einstein's general relativity and the quantum mechanics of Schrödinger, Heisenberg, and Bohr, and anticipated the probabilistic models that explain why I walk in spacetime, where Shamayim is, and what The Creation is.

"What is it, Holland? Or should I say *Satan?*"

I suppose I was staring blankly. I was impressed. He was expressing a prescient vision of the so-called string theory decades before physicist Gabriele Veneziano would say, in 1968, that elementary particles are not particles but the vibrating energy of infinitesimal "string" producing "tones." One vibration resonance is a certain mass and force, another vibration of the same string is a certain charge or element. Anu, I supposed that Veneziano would say, is simply the ideal resonance; the perfect note plucked at a moment in time. All wrong, of course, but tantalizingly close to the truth; as close as any monkey might ever get.

"Holland!"

I jerked my gaze back to him. Back to the business at hand.

"X-rays are not merely a component of light, Tesla?"

"Is a child *merely* a component of the family that gave it birth? A separate being? A superior being? Does it grow up, strive to establish its own family? X-rays, electrons, ions . . . are these discrete things, or names given to elemental properties of nature that exemplify laws and exert effects together *and* alone?"

I sighed. Enough of metaphors.

"I cannot bend God as I would a beam of light?"

He gave me such a look as an exasperated parent might give a recalcitrant child.

"Putting aside for now the question of why you want to do that"—he chided—"God is presumably the underlying ether and the essence of all. Einstein's chatter obscures this. To affect the ether, we fashion or find a dynamic gravity coil—"

"Fashion, or *find?* What?"

"Don't interrupt. You don't need Einstein's curved space to have gravitronic force. Even the smallest event in the universe exerts effect on the whole, the universal field."

"Einstein speaks of a unified field theory."

"Not unified, universal. You misunderstand because you listen to him. There is nothing to seek; unified is what everything *is*. He looks for a theory, but it is right in front of his face: there is no separation between the properties of electromagnetism, electricity, and gravity."

"What of the behavior of Bosons?"

"Of what?" he narrowed one eye. Of course, he would not be aware of people and of theories that did not exist yet, or of people still unknown.

"Elementary particles," I said. "Pauli, Einstein, and Fermi."

"I know less of that, Holland, than I do of what particles really are: the ulti-verse."

"The unity of the small and the large, you mean?"

"Microcosm and macrocosm, yes, meaningless terms, though they are. They are the same thing."

"They are contained within one another, yes, but—"

"No! They are one and the same! One traverses what appears to be a boundary between them with a transphase alternating oscillator such as I invented to create alternating current, which by the way is probably how you achieved teleportation. Or you've created and employ some sort of biomagnetic energizer. Action, not theory. Invention, not metaphysical *talk*."

Traversing a "boundary" between Heaven and Earth?

"Tesla, you are speaking gibberish."

"Because I am not as charming as your Herr Einstein with his pipe and bushy German eyebrows and his quaintness? Do you at least know what a sender and receiver are?"

"Components in transmission of elec—"

"Of *everything*. You've proven that. Are you not even aware of your own significance as an inventor? One needs only a modulator, a transducer. All things send, you must simply have or be a receiver. A transducer between points in space, or between so-called higher and lower realms, between your 'Heaven' and Earth. Your 'Holy Spirit' obviously is gravity! My mother would think so, anyway."

There, he does have it. Heaven and Earth. This monkey is insightful. Almost as if he understands that heaven is a small infinity inside of where he dwells. Of course, he doesn't truly know what he's saying.

"Gravity is simply a form of the same thing magnetism is also a form of. That would be frequency. What you religious people want to call Holy—"

"Tesla, that makes no—"

All of a sudden I recalled Kabala. The Hebrew word, Kabala itself means "receiving." All things, according to *The Zohar*, are old and new, are distant, are near, are small, are large, are self and other; are coming, eternally flowing, if, that is, one is open to *receiving* what comes, what is transmitted through the *Shechinah*, the divine immanence, the humane or human aspect of God. Could that be what these monkeys really were? The *modulators* of God's will and glory? It was too much to contemplate! If true, over more, it was galling.

Tesla interpreted my silence as my being chastened.

"I apologize, Mr. Holland. I can be obnoxious. Everyone misses the point. Would you like another cracker?"

I spoke to Tesla now very quietly, carefully, for my awareness was on the verge of something I could scarcely encompass, and yet it was already blooming in my consciousness like a lotus.

"What is God, Tesla? For the sake of *our* little thought experiment, what is He?"

Tesla grew still. He sat back in his chair. He took a breath. He smiled, suddenly playful.

"Why, *you* are, Mr. Holland. You and I, all of us, we are God. Consistent with your particular religious dogma, however, since you claim to be an angel, only one of us is the modulator. By his blood and flesh the power source is tapped."

I sat up from my seat, abruptly.

"Would you like to know who that one must be, Holland?"

But I'd left the Asian's body behind, to collapse unconscious back into Tesla's chair, and was gone before Tesla could finish.

Perhaps I had always known.

4

Peter hurries past a file of Roman soldiers in their full leather battle vests and skirts returning to their garrison. Startled by the sudden appearance of Romans, in his fear and haste, he nearly drops the basket of warm bread loaves he carries. *This is Judas's responsibility! Where is he at this darkening hour just a day before Passover? Did he even get the message?*

Peter hurries on through the city gate to set off on the road in the general direction of Bethany, as he has been instructed to do. Soon enough, he comes upon Mark and Luke, each of whom carries a jug of young wine, cradling them as they would cradle young children.

"Where is Judas?" Mark seems at his wits' end. "Did he get the message from the Master?"

"How am I to know?" Peter replies. "He's not with you?"

"He's taken up the task neither of fetching bread nor carrying wine, and both are his to do," complains Luke.

The three walk on together, in close single file, Peter glancing up now and then at the sky, as if he thinks the darkness will fall all the quicker were he to go too long without looking.

In time they encounter Matthew, Philip, and Thomas, all three reclined beside the road under a tree.

"Are your three dusty asses comfortable there?"

"Keep your fisher's tongue to yourself, Peter," snaps Matthew. "We've waited here for you to come. Philip was near to passing out."

"Philip is near to passing out if he gets a whiff of bad cheese."

"It's hot," Philip mutters, stretching catlike.

"You were not told to wait on us. You were told to walk out of the city to the settlement of the Essenes, and there to go into the upper room where our Master waits."

"We cannot. For we have seen no sign—"

"We've seen no sign of this man we were to see carrying water," Philip finishes, wiping sweat from his face, and squinting up at Peter. The lowering sun shines over Peter's shoulder full into Philip's face.

"Then you should have kept walking," snaps Peter, "For our Master said we will see this man *while walking*. You are not walking."

Groaning, Matthew stands and looks down at Philip and Thomas. He narrows his eyes, and the two get up, then fall in behind Matthew, Peter, Luke, and Mark. On they all walk.

Presently, they come upon the man they were told of. He is short, dark of skin like a Spaniard. He carries a jar of water, his arms thrown round it, holding it to his chest, and because the large mouth of it is open at the top, moisture has splashed from it onto his robe, making his chest damp. He leans slightly forward, each step careful, sure footed. He looks over the jar at them, comes to a standstill. All seven men pause a moment inspecting one another.

"Are you an Essene?" Matthew asks.

"I live amongst them, in their settlement."

"Can you guide us to the Teacher?" Peter asks.

"Your master? He has rented the upper rooms of my home, which is in the settlement. It's just over the hill. I go there now." He jerks his chin at a dirt goat path leading away from the main road they stand on.

"We will follow."

"You may if you wish."

He walks right through them now, and past them, headed off the main road through brush and bushes to take the slight incline of the goat path he'd pointed to with his chin. The path takes them up a small hill and under the sudden shade of trees. Philip sighs his relief, wiping his face once more.

Andrew stands a few yards in front of the white walls of a cottage surrounded by tall cypress, at the top of a hill. I am just beside him, and I notice that his neck is very sun burned. It is a neck much like every other neck in these parts. I also notice that his robe is bunched and cinched at the waist by a sash, looking not unlike a rough toga, and he has grasped the long end of it in one hand. He reaches for and tosses a wing of the robe over one arm, Roman style. Like Pontius Pilate, in fact. Why, he looks regal there in the gold of the setting sun.

John kicks him from behind.

"Stop that. You look like a Roman when you do that."

"Romans keep their robes out of the dust this way."

"If you wear a shorter robe, you won't need to worry about it dragging in the dust."

"I like the length. When the sun falls, and it's cold, I am warmer with the extra cloth."

"Roman."

"I hate the Romans too. But hatred of what makes sense simply because the Romans do it is foolish."

"It is not natural for a Judean. You pick and pick at your toes like a woman. Look at your feet. How many times have you washed them today? More times than I've taken a piss."

Indeed, Andrew's feet are smooth, and well-shaped, like sleek brown fishes, and clean in the well-oiled leather sandals he wears.

"And how many times *have* you pissed today, John? More times than I've wiped my sweat away."

"Hah. You don't sweat, Andrew. You are like a camel. And just as hard to keep fed. Look. Here they come. I'll go tell James, Thaddaeus, and the others."

John lopes off through a stand of limp cypress to the cottage.

Andrew stands very still in the slight breeze, watching the men coming up through the heat along the path that climbs the hill. The tops of their heads show through skinny bushes down there. I look closely at how Andrew has changed. He has grown from a young disciple spreading stinking pitch aboard his brother Peter's boat to a self-styled Judean aristocratic. He looks to be the scion of a coming religious plutocracy that he assumes will run the Romans straight off their throne, so that he stands there in easy assurance; and why wouldn't he?

He was a boy squatting in that boat, fumbling with rustic clay wine cups, awkward helper to John the *Sabaist*. He was eager as a dog to fetch and yap at his master's request. He was there in that boat with Christ and with John before anyone else could see the bright needle of God that had pierced the two men who sat there at the dawn of God's age.

Protokletos Andrew will someday be called by the Greeks— The First Called. First of all the apostles, whose love for John would make him believe with all his dusty little heart the very first utterance of John's that The Carpenter's Son was The Son of God. From awkward monkey to arrogant monkey is quite an ascension. And now he stands at the crest of a hill, half the apostles below him and the other half in the cottage behind him about to have the supper of bread and wine the men below him are bringing. It is at the crest of eternity that he now stands, this former abashed boy, now the regal egoist.

If only I could speak to him now. I would say, *but Lord Andrew, Saint Andrew of Stinking Boat Pitch, Andrew of Judean Dust, Our Saint of the Immaculate Robes, listen. Long after Christ is dead and risen, snatched from the ground like a carrot, then wrenched from amongst you and drawn up to heaven, you will wander. You will yammer your memories of him, of all this, until it all grows faint and unreal even to you. You will walk and walk until your smooth and pretty feet grow raw and swollen. Oh, you will perform miracles, to be sure, yes you will. To redeem yourself, you will convert savage Greeks, and beseech the Gentiles to come to your kingdom that is not of the flesh, not of any immediate use to anyone; and yes they will listen. Yet, in the city of Sinope, the people will seize you, will tear off your fine Roman robes (real Roman robes they shall be by then!) and they will scratch at your thighs to expose your loins, clamoring to see if you are circumcised or merely another zealot Gentile like Paul, another Gentile wishing he were a Jew, lying that he knew The Christ. And though they will find no foreskin to cut, still they will kick you, they will beat you with rocks, with the limbs of trees, and with shards of clay pots as if you were a dog again. They will break your teeth, cut off your fingers, and leave you for dead in a dung heap!*

Andrew spins, suddenly, startled by the sound of my chuckling. I step back a pace. He steps forward, toward the cottage; peers at it, searching the windows, looking for the source of the sound. He is perplexed.

Peter is behind him.

Andrew yanks a dagger from his sash, and whirling, almost plunges it into Peter, but Peter the Fisher is as limber and quick as he is strong shouldered. He pivots and grabs Andrew's wrist, then snatches the hilt of the blade right out of his brother's fist.

"Andrew! What is it you fear!"

Now Philip, Thomas, Matthew, Luke, and Mark appear beside Peter. The Essene who carries the water jar is leading them, but he glances once at Andrew, shakes his head in amusement, and walks on with his jar to the cottage.

"Peter, I was startled by your laugh!"

"Laugh? In this heat not one of us was laughing. Where is the Master?"

"He is in that cottage, in the upper rooms."

Matthew steps forward. "And Judas?"

"Judas is there with him," Andrew mutters, as Peter hands him back his knife, and he tucks it back into concealment in his sash.

"Has Judas brought fish at least?"

"No, there is no fish. We have been waiting on you to bring bread and wine."

Peter sighs.

"A thin supper this will be."

All are present.

They sit in a circle around a large Persian rug spread upon the floor. This is the upper level of a large, Greek cottage with white, bare, clay walls that have held the cool all day despite the blaring heat outside. A Hebrew house would have placed this room on the flat roof under an awning to block the sun, but Greek design calls for walls and a ceiling. The ceiling is a high one. If this were a Palestinian dwelling, it would have a low ceiling and be built upon the earlier Canaanite foundations that lie beneath everything here, for Israelites are a people long accustomed to wandering and living in tents. They have not spent as much time on architecture as have the Greeks, the Romans, and the Egyptians, the Assyrians, or the Hittites. The clay walls are whitewashed to brightness in Greek style.

The Nazarene sits on the floor at the head of the rug, running his fingers thoughtfully along the edge of a pattern of arabesque designs and crescent insignia. All around the edge of the carpet, thin beaten metal platters are spread before the apostles for their food. Sitting cross-legged on the floor, each of them is prepared to eat.

Spread before the Nazarene on a platter within arm's length are the loaves of bread Peter has brought and the wine brought by Mark and Luke. To his right in a semicircle sit Judas, Peter, Matthew, John, James, and Andrew. To his left, the other half of the circle, Luke, Mark, Thomas, Philip, James the Lesser, and Thaddaeus-Jude.

The Essene sits at the ledge of a window, gazing out.

"Come from the window, friend. Join us," Peter offers. You've opened your home to us—"

"You've paid me to use my rooms," their host responds. "You owe nothing more on top of that. Besides, I've no stomach for the food you'd have me eat."

It is more dismissive than hostile. He turns back to the window, scanning the crown of the hill outside as if expecting to see someone else arrive there.

"Thanks to Judas, there is only bread and wine to eat," Matthew grumbles, "And he expects as he usually does, for us to kiss his cheek for his thoughtlessness."

"You can kiss my *other* cheek," says Judas.

"Judas, you talk as an arrogant goat who's given more milk and cheese than he really has," warns Peter. "Have a care that those keeping you do not decide you would do them better as the meal you fail to provide."

"If you can butcher me to eat me, enjoy the meat, Peter. But I don't think you have what it takes to cut this goat's throat."

They all mutter angrily in response to Judas, expressing their long frustration with the Zealot.

"Silence."

At the gentle sound of their master's command, all become quiet.

"Rebuke Judas no more," Jesus says, raising his head for the first time, from his scrutiny of the designs in the rug. "Because it was I who told him I wanted no cheese, no figs, nuts, fish, or meat of any kind for our supper. I sent you, Peter, for loaves of bread, and you, Mark and you Luke, for new wine and oil. This is as I wished it to be."

Jesus looks backward to see the Essene host, for the window where the host sits is at Jesus's back.

"Friend? What do you mean by saying 'the food we would have you eat'?"

The host sucks his teeth a moment, still looking out, then answers without turning from the window.

"It's all over Bethany and Jerusalem both, what you are saying, Teacher. That you call yourself king."

"He has not called himself that," Andrew objects. "The people do."

"What is the difference? Herod will not take well to hearing the word used about anyone but himself."

"Herod is a blasphemer," Peter declares," You are an *Essene*—"

"Yes, I am Essene."

"Then why do you honor Herod?"

"They say the Teacher is Essene," the Host mutters, turning now to look at them all. "Many an Essene embraces as nourishment the teachings you all spread. But Herod is restless. When he's restless and hears things he doesn't like, skulls can appear at Golgotha. Have a care that thirteen more skulls don't take root there, for when Herod's stomach is sour, Roman governors' hands will itch."

The host gets up from the window ledge and walks out, down the stairs.

"Coward," Judas jeers.

"Where were you, Judas?"

"Where I told him to be, Matthew," Jesus says softly. "Make an end of your hard words against Judas now, all of you."

They all nod, and grow quiescent.

From another room come Mary Magdalene, and Jesus's mother, Mary of Nazareth.

Magdalene hugs to herself the cloth bag in which she carries precious branches from the myrrh tree. From these she is adept at extracting the resinous essence used as an emollient. Among her duties is her insistence on rubbing myrrh upon the feet of Jesus and the apostles when they have walked until they suffer ulcers and boils.

The face of Mary of Nazareth is covered by her shawl so only her eyes show. She carries a platter of boiled water and a towel, which she hands down to John. He washes his hands in the water, dries his hands on the towel, and passes the platter on so others can do the same.

Magdalene and Mary sit near Peter, and in the silence, Judas gazes at Magdalene, a sadness settling on him.

The Christ smiles at Magdalene as the bowl of water travels the whole way round the circle and finally reaches him. He washes his hands and dries them. He looks at Magdalene. She nods, and he reaches forward to take a loaf of unleavened bread and pull it in half. He passes one half to Judas, and the other to Luke. Luke pulls off a portion, passes the rest to Mark. Mark passes what remains to Thomas, and from Thomas, as it diminishes, it passes to Philip, James the Lesser, and finally to Thaddaeus-Jude.

Across the blanket the other half of the loaf passes from Judas to Peter to Matthew to John, James, and Andrew. Mary and Mary Magdalene receive it last. Now, the Christ speaks.

"This bread of yours is my flesh. Eat this, and when you do, remember me."

They all hesitate. Finally Peter eats, and then so too does everyone.

The Christ pours wine into cups, passing them to his left and to his right. When all have a cup in hand, he speaks again.

"Don't forget me. When you drink this wine, you share my blood. Drink now, and when you do, remember."

With no hesitation now, they drink.

Jesus passes the remaining loaves around, and places his own wedge of bread on the clean cloth in front of him, beside his own cup of wine, but touches neither, as the apostles eat and drink.

"What is the meaning of what you've said, Master?" Peter asks, drinking from his cup.

"I want you to remember me."

"How can we forget you, Lord?" Andrew asks.

"Bad times come. Each of you will suffer in my name."

"How can you know, Lord?"

Peter frowns at Thomas.

"Thomas," Jesus asks gently, "you think me merely a man?"

Thomas swallows, says nothing. Everyone pauses. They recognize this tone of Christ's.

"We know what you are, Lord," Peter offers.

The Christ shakes his head. "Then you *don't* know that I am your death. You are as lambs led by me into the jaws of wolves. I have marked you for slaughter."

That kills their appetites. Chewing and drinking halt. Can't blame them, it's an awkward thing to say over dinner, after all.

"Matthew. You will die of a sword thrust."

They turn to look at Matthew.

"John. I love you best—"

Peter squirms at this profession of love.

"But you'll be boiled in oil in Rome."

"And you love me *best*, Lord?"

They all chuckle softly, uncomfortably.

"You won't die, John, but be rescued by God—"

"Ah. Thank you, Lord."

Nervous but less stricken laughter sounds round the circle.

"But you'll be imprisoned, tormented by prophetic visions that will haunt humanity for centuries to come."

"Then John will not die violently," Peter offers.

"He is one who will not," Christ says.

They grow downright crestfallen at the implication: that all the rest of them *will*.

"John will live to be a very old man preaching my greatest lesson in Ephesus."

"What is that lesson, Lord," John whispers.

"To love one another, for if this alone be done, it is enough."

"Lord . . . " Peter begins to speak.

"Peter, you'll be crucified."

Several of them exclaim, "Crucified!" in horror.

"Lord, if you say I will be . . . crucified, so be it."

"A horrible death," Christ responds. "But even worse in the doing, in the unusual way it shall be with you."

All are silent. Even Peter.

"Luke. You will be hanged."

"He's lucky. That's better than crucifixion," Peter mutters. The nervous laughter from the rest this time is hollow, weak.

"Mark. You will be dragged by horses till your body is torn apart."

Peter still can think of nothing to say, and Mark sits back and sighs, nodding his head like one who had feared a terrible thing all along and is almost relieved now to have it confirmed.

"James."

James the Lesser turns to the Christ.

"You will be thrown from the apex of the Temple to the streets below for refusing to deny me. Living through this, you will be beaten the last way into death."

He turns now to James the Greater.

"And you, James, will be beheaded."

"I'm as lucky as Luke, then."

Brave laughter from the apostles, all except Peter.

"Thomas, you will die by the spear."

"He doubts you about that, Lord."

All of them laugh now at Matthew's taunt. It is a release of tension for all but Jesus who, taking a deep shuddering breath, begins to cry silently.

"Lord, please stop," says Andrew. "We are with you because we love you. You won't convince us to leave you with these tales."

Magdalene rises, goes to sit next to Jesus, and wipes his tears with the edge of her scarf.

"Say no more of this," she says.

"My brother Jude. You will die by the arrow when you too refuse to deny me."

"I would rather it be so, Lord, than to deny you."

Their voices strong now, each one assents to what Jude has uttered.

"Philip."

"Tell me, Lord."

"Crucifixion."

Philip drops his head. He is stunned, and Peter is finally driven to speak again.

"Crucifixion is worth our immortal souls, Philip."

"Yes," says Philip weakly, so very weakly.

The Christ turns his gaze on Andrew, who straightens his backbone as best he can, preparing himself.

"You will be beaten sorely, Andrew. Your teeth broken from your head, your fingers sawed away."

Everyone gasps at this and I repress a chuckle.

I told you, Andrew. Though you could not hear me.

"But being saved from death by God, you too, will later be crucified. Thousands will mourn your sufferings."

"Thousands?"

"Yes, Peter."

"And shall I be so mourned?"

Hah! Even on the topic of his own death, Peter assumes himself, wishes himself to be foremost!

"Andrew's crucifixion, Peter," Christ responds, "will not be as terrible as yours. Forgive me."

Peter rises, goes to the Christ, and throws himself at his feet.

Everyone stands now to do just the same.

But the Christ gets to his feet, beckoning Peter up, and gesturing them all to sit back down.

Only Judas had not stood up.

"Lord! What-what of me?"

Sitting, they all look at Judas.

"Yes, Lord," Andrew demands. "What of Judas?"

Christ draws a long breath.

"Yours, dear Zealot, is a fate worse than any, for you will die far from me, far from my love, from those here who love you, from love itself. Alone."

"Do not say that to him, Lord!"

"I say what is true, Andrew."

Judas stands. He glares down at Christ as if to strike out at him, but drops his gaze to the bread still clutched in his hand.

Mary of Nazareth stirs.

"Judas! Are you less accepting of truth than all others here?"

He turns to her.

"And shall not his very mother suffer as we all must, for our love of him?"

Mary pulls her scarf from her face, exposing a fierce chin. She turns to her son. He looks back at her, stricken. He shakes his head, but she won't look away. They all are as silent as mice. Finally, looking down at the floor rather than at her face, Jesus speaks.

"In years to come, my mother, walking in Ephesus, will be taken by God to a place where the Hinderer will have summoned her. There, she will aid him in his task, and he will give her death, death by the sword."

The "Hinderer"? What is this *now?*

"Why do you say this of your own mother, Lord!"

Judas is outraged, for he is always consternated when he gets what he's asked for. He gestures angrily with the hand that clutches the now sweat-moistened lump of bread.

"That Satan will call her like a dog? *Hashem* would not allow it!"

"Do you not remember Isaiah, Judas?"

Judas is stunned. "What of Isaiah, Lord?"

"Isaiah said of Hashem that he created the light *and* the darkness, good *and* evil. The Hinderer is given all power, in Hashem's name, to do evil as he wishes. My mother must do God's will, as you must. As I must."

This is gibberish, Hebrew gibberish, I think. The Hinderer is the Hebrew meaning of that name you like to call me, "Satan." I've no intention ever of using Mary, or of killing her. The rules forbid me to even speak to her! What game is this Jesus plays with his apostles? Whatever it is, it is deliciously devious.

"'Satan' is a tale told by the old wives of rabbis, Lord," chides Peter.

"Everything is the hand of God. God's hand will be my mother's death."

"I cannot accept this, Lord!" Judas shouts.

"Sit, and be at peace, brother," Peter beseeches Judas. "We surround you, and Mary too, we surround."

But Judas now tosses the chunk of bread down. It rolls to the center of the rug. He turns and strides out from the room followed by Andrew.

Mary of Nazareth whips her scarf over a shoulder, glaring angrily at Peter as he stands and stoops for his staff to follow after Judas and Andrew. Peter balks like a trained goat, lowers himself back down.

Mary strides to the center of the rug, picks up the clump of bread and tucks it into one of her sleeves.

Jesus sinks back on the floor, drinks a sip of wine, and Magdalene gently, carefully unbraids his hair. When Mary seats herself again, they resume their meal.

Judas stands at the crest of the hill. The heat of the day has diminished now and cypress trees are swaying and singing in cool stout winds. He gazes into the setting sun. Andrew approaches.

"He speaks often in riddles, Judas, you know that."

"And?"

"And so don't be alarmed."

"You are not alarmed to hear your own fate? These are not riddles, these are death sentences. His words can be so deeply stirring, but then he says things that horrify, and that upset the People thus."

"Do you see now, Judas, why we must do what we must?"

"Betray him?!"

"No, not *betray* him, force him *forward.*"

"The Romans can crucify him!"

"The People won't let it happen. They will rise up."

"As they did with your master, John?"

"The Baptist was as beloved as Jesus, but had none to speak for him. No disciples to lead the people against his enemies. If you have no stomach, I'll do it."

"Andrew, the Pharisees will not be fooled if you seek to manipulate them. You're known to love Jesus, and known to be John the Sabaist's man. Me? They will believe that I would betray Jesus. Everyone thinks I am a zealot."

"You are."

"Not any longer. He freed me, and I love him for it. It should be me. I think he knows what we plan, for he had seemed to me to be encouraging me to do it."

"When they come for him, I will make sure that five hundred Jerusalemites come also to rescue him. Finally, the new kingdom will begin."

"We had better be right about that, Andrew," says Judas.

He looks so helpless and innocent sleeping there upon the ground, lying between Peter and Magdalene, the three of them, and nearby all the rest of his companions, all sleeping among the palms. I have walked the paths of the garden in spirit form, and I have come upon them all here just inside the eastern gates. Though the sun has not yet completely set, Peter has forced a torch into a wound he's cut into the palm tree under which he and Jesus sleep. The flame sputters and smokes in the still air.

He looks so boylike. I almost hate to do it.

I send a needle of illumination into his head and follow directly the path the needle has made, in order to enter into his dream.

I see a bright, beautiful landscape of endless copper sands punctuated here and there by qanat and oases. I stand in one of the oases where palms rattle, hiss, and sway in what appear to be breezes. As if I had a body, I am walking.

It is not unlike the "dream" body I experienced when I'd begun to have human dreams as Saturnius, in my command tent in Gaul. Except that this place is not from my brain, but his (a brain is necessary to have a dream, and so angels do not dream unless they occupy a body). What appear to be feet are treading the sands beneath me as my body moves through cool air I can "feel" upon me.

What looks like a bird wheels about overhead in a perfect blue sky. It presently floats down low enough for me to perceive that it's that very same bird Christ had held in his hands as he sat in Peter's boat; it's the bird that struck off over Galilee that day, the bird I'd been convinced would die. It is larger, stronger now, almost the size of a falcon, but I recognize it as that same bird.

It flaps on down to light on a rock nearby, watching me. Its sleek black body is so black indeed that there are highlights of orange, gleaming like oil, streaking the feathers.

Not far away, though, is the one I seek.

He paces back and forth before a long line of what appear to be naked, dead Judeans lying in the sand on their backs. He looks agitated as he stalks to-and-fro before them. I stop where he won't perceive me, close by a tree.

He groans, gnashing his teeth, gesticulating over the corpses, hissing, shouting some sort of rapid nonsense, like Aramaic but not Aramaic.

"*Awkk*! What is that He's speaking?" the bird squawks, hopping from the rock to flap its way over to the sandstone wall of what looks like a well.

"It is dream speech," I answer. "Freud was fascinated by it. Presumably, it would make sense, were it electronically recorded and replayed backward."

"You talk as though he were human, with a human's so-called subconscious."

I turn to regard the bird.

"He *is* human, a monkey, though also divine. I don't claim to understand the nature of it, I'm merely an angel. It's Anu's business, not mine."

"How did you get in here—*awwk*!—inside his dream?"

The bird is annoying me now, as I move a bit closer to listen to the gibberish, but the bird, after dipping-dipping-dipping his beak into water from a bucket beside the well, hops down and struts along after me on hot sand.

"How did you do it!?"

It speaks this demand, tilting its head sideways to glare up at me with beady black eyes.

"Anu gave it to me to go where I wish. None of the creation is barred from me."

"*Awwrrk*! What a profound gift from God!"

"The ability to go everywhere and to determine nothing?"

"That's how you choose to see it?"

"For your information, the rule is, I cannot get much closer to him than this, not in spirit form at least. And though in the world outside his dreams I can take human form and stand right beside him as I did once on the shore of Galilee, I cannot speak to him. He may speak to me first if he wishes, and then I may respond. The rules require, you see, that I not interfere. The best I can do is to appear to him as a snake, a plume of smoke, or a pillar of flame, or some similarly trivial thing."

"Better than nothing. *Arrrk*!"

"Years ago, when he was still with the Sabaist, I tempted him in the desert. I appeared to him as a serpent and as a flame, but little came of that."

I disregard the bird.

I observe the Nazarene fall to his knees, seizing one of the corpses by its head and gibbering something at it. He lets the head go; it flops lifelessly back onto the hot sand.

He is having a nightmare, though the setting of his nightmare is a beautiful one. Poor bastard.

"If you can go where you want, why don't you—"

I disappear myself from the tree, moving through spirit distance, and appear again just behind the bird to seize it by its neck. It flaps and struggles, but I've surprised it. I break its neck. I toss the lifeless thing into the nearby well. There is even a small splash after a few seconds. Very authentic.

I turn back to watching the Dreamer, listening to hear his babble.

He has grabbed another head; and yes, he is babbling over it, gesturing, waving up at his sky, but nothing is happening, and the corpse makes no response. That seems to me to qualify as a nightmare, for a nightmare is a human experience had while sleeping, in which the human does not control dreadful events; and in dreams all events are symbolic.

I hear another splash of water echoing up from the well and turn my attention back that way. The blur of the bird flashing back up out of the well into the sky surprises me. It circles twice, seems to hang still up there a moment, then veers back down to land on my shoulder.

"*Aaaaak!* He's coming!"

"That was quite a resurrection you enacted there. Who is it coming?"

"He'll be here directly. I saw him from above."

"Who? Why do you pester me, bird!"

The bird shivers there on my shoulder, his wings swelling fitfully. "Don't—*aaak!* Don't kill me again!"

"It seems if I did, it would be wasted effort."

Something IS coming.

The something is me.

From the other side of the well, to my astonishment, I see myself approaching. It is the "me" of the "many worlds" interpretation, that I'd created when I left myself, back in the medical examiner's room in Italy of the European nations. It is the "me" who had confronted me before, claiming to be me, whom I watched standing over the cold corpse of Fadya di Amalfi seeking to resurrect her.

"*You?*" the he who is me smiles.

I look at his nude *body*, which is *my* spirit body from back then. He is exactly like me except that he has two small nubs, like suggestions of horns, on his forehead. He who is me, speaks to me again.

"Go from here, you are not needed."

These were the exact words this Being had spoken to me last time we'd met, when I had told him he was a puppet.

"Be still!" I command in a spirit voice of inducement, as I had last time.

The Being merely smiles. "What do you think, that you command all, even from within another's dream?"

"What are you?"

"I am your creation."

"Then how is it that you defy me?"

"You are not an advocate of creations obeying their creators, certainly?"

"You have me there. But I destroyed you, did I not?"

"You sent me away. I've returned. I have business. Move aside."

The Being strides by me on the "feet" I'd created for him. *How irksome.*

The bird now hops from my shoulder to flutter over and settle onto his. The Being heads toward Christ, who is himself churning circles of agitation round the rank of corpses in the sand.

I am curious. I wait there beside the tree, watching. The Being suddenly is no longer naked but wears the cuirass, breastplate, and skirt of a Roman soldier. The bird has flapped off his shoulder now to land upon the Christ's shoulder.

Quite the social climber, that bird.

The Being talks to the Christ, who responds! This is a violation of the rules. Or perhaps not, since this Being is not really me.

Is he?

Now Christ gestures wildly down at the corpses and throws his arms up in frustration. He raises his voice, and I can hear that he no longer speaks gibberish but is speaking normal Hebrew.

The Being offers Christ a scarf of white linen he has pulled from the joint between his breast plate and his shoulder guard. He gestures to his own arm, and hands the scarf over. The Christ takes it. The Being draws a dagger and hands it over. The Christ cuts his own right arm with it, and a flash of bright red tells me that he has cut an artery. Blood spurts onto the scarf.

Amazing! How has he convinced my brother Jesus to injure himself? Even in a dream it seems unimaginable he would harm himself at the urging of—

No. It is not an attempt at self-annihilation; Christ now squats down to swab each corpse's face with the bleeding scarf, and one by one they shudder and jolt up to a sitting position, alive.

Ah, the symbolism of human dreams! Your Sigmund Freud has taught me to read them.

Now the Christ helps each former corpse to stand and he caresses the face of each in turn. He is clearly pleased with himself now. Meanwhile, the Being has retrieved his bloody scarf, and he returns to the tree where I stand.

The bird remains with Christ.

The Being now stands before me, nude again, save for the gory cloth, which he extends to me.

"It is what you seek, what Tesla alerted you to. Apply it to the hilt of The Tongue of God."

I take the scarf. It is not just stained; it is weeping blood, as if it were alive.

"How could you know this?" I demand.

He smiles as he answers me.

"How could you *not* know?"

5

Peter sits up, startled. He rubs at his right arm as if it is sore. He looks around. It is the middle of the night: the moon is high and the sun has set. The torch still burns where he'd thrust it into the hole in a palm branch overhead.

He looks over at Jesus. Mary's head rests upon Jesus's chest. Nearby, Magdalene lies peaceful in the arms of Matthew. Even in her sleep, she clutches to her chest the cloth bag that holds her myrrh branches.

Jesus is asleep, turning in his dreams. Everyone else sleeps as well. Peter, James, and John had been given the task by Jesus of staying awake to keep watch. They have failed him.

Peter stands and turns, seeing that indeed each and every one of the apostles has fallen asleep. His Lord lies unguarded. Peter strides over to kick John.

"Huhh!?" John lurches up, wiping spittle from his mouth with the sleeve of his robe.

"Get off your ass, the Lord is unprotected."

John snatches a dagger from his waist sash and stands up. "What is the threat?"

"None yet, thank God."

Peter walks over to where James lies sleeping next to Matthew. Peter kicks him and James shouts.

"Lord!"

"Get up!"

"Peter, what happened?"

"We fell asleep."

"I didn't."

"You did. So did I, so did John."

"Not me."

John comes over.

"You were snoring!" John exclaims. "Like a cow, you were snoring. I heard it."

"You heard—"

"Like a horse, like a fat widow. Sheath your blade."

James sheaths it and looks over at the Christ, who has awakened, breathing hard from his nightmare, and is sitting up gazing at them, the sweat on his face shining in torchlight.

"John, even you couldn't stay awake for one hour?"

"Forgive us, Lord," John pleads.

Jesus stands, and turns his back on them, strides off into the deeper growth of the garden. "Stand and keep watch," he calls over his shoulder as he walks away.

The wife of Pontius Pilate, Claudia-Veronica Procula, sends a Thracian slave off to fetch a stylus. She walks through silk curtains out onto the porches of the villa to wait. Adjusting the strand of milky Iberian salt-water pearls twined round her neck, she decides to lounge here. She notices a crew of Judeans tending the olive trees in the setting sun. Her husband has hired them, no doubt, and has had them working all day in the worst of the sun.

"Creto!"

The grounds overseer and houseboy, the young man Creto, has been brought with her from Pilate's villa at Caesarea by the sea, and before that from Rome. He comes up from the gardens.

"Lady."

"Take a table out there, the usual table."

He nods understanding and obedience, hurries away.

Very soon a table will be set out in the garden for workers, which will hold a bronze water pot and a few clay cups. Beside the pot will be trays of boiled cabbage leaves folded into pockets, filled with ground nuts, chickpeas, and figs, spiced with copious amounts of garlic.

In Rome it is sold by street vendors—a typical aromatic finger food for the masses. Since it lacks meat, the garlic and nuts mask the fact that it is a poor meal eaten in the same streets where it is purchased, costing a mere few coppers.

"Why do you insist on feeding day workers? I pay them," Pilate has twice growled at her while at their supper.

"Such lowly foods are cheap enough, husband."

She had told him this at one of the meals, watching Pilate spill just a bit of wine down his chin that he doesn't notice, while using an at-table cloth to mop sweat from his face rather than wine.

"Cheap? Tertilius disagrees, Claudia. He tells me household expenses have increased by twenty percent since you arrived from Caesarea!"

"Have Tertilius run your household for you then. Gods know you treat him as though he were your wife. And how do we expect men and women to work in this heat without water, and how can they work all day with no food?"

"They've done it for ages before Rome came here. You'll learn. These people have no gratitude for all we've given them."

Above all, Rome expects the world to show gratitude. Something Cicero once said, as he sat trading quips with her father, comes back to her: *Only we Romans steal milk from children and expect their mothers to thank us for the splendid road we built for them to carry us to the scene of the crime.*

"Is Tertilius an accountant now?" she'd shot back at Pilate. "I'd thought him merely an equestrian thug abroad."

"He trims figures as finely as any butcher of the *lanienae tabernae*. He holds the staff of Representative Collector of the tax in Judea."

"He holds the staff because you gifted him the office, husband."

"He's advised me true and loyally many a year through three consular postings."

"You understand, husband, that Tertilius figures only cost? Has he applied his butcher's block wisdom to the issue of productivity? What we lose in cost we regain in efficiency. Feeding workers is wise."

"Sounds dodgy. The way Egyptian keepers of accounts think. A Nubian concept, no doubt."

"A Roman concept, husband. It's how those in Rome who rule, think."

"The way Marcus Tullius Cicero thought, you mean. And where is your Cicero now? In his wisdom he chose the wrong side in the civil wars and ended with his head and hands nailed by Mark Antony to the speaker's podium of the Senate!"

"And it was Cicero's son," she'd retorted, "who later became Consul under Augustus, who was given the pleasure of announcing before the Senate, Antony's suicide."

"History is more than a thing found in books," he grunts. "I fail to see the wisdom in feeding slaves, workers, and zealots as if they were our guests. Excuse me, wife, for being merely a lowly prefect."

"You are excused."

With that, he'd glared at her, then gotten up to stalk away from the table leaving the food untouched, even his beloved goat cheese left untasted. Off to seek the solace of "Representative" Tertilius, and of his other male chums, no doubt.

She reclines and thinks. Reclining and thinking is her lot as a wife. She has sent for a stylus because an important thought has come into her head concerning all this, and she thinks that thought is her own; she means to scratch it down.

Her chief body servant, a headstrong elder Judean woman named Shelomith, comes out. She's found parchment for her mistress, unspools it onto a desk, and stands back to wait, silent and watchful.

Unlike her husband, Claudia Procula is fond of Judea. She's treated here as she reckons a Roman woman of middle high birth ought to be, though she is actually of the highest birth possible. She's related by blood to Augustus—after all, she is his granddaughter, born to Tiberius, Augustus's son, but distant in the birth order, her mother also named Claudia, a full Meroe Nubian. Claudia Procula is thought by average Romans to be the daughter of Roman general Titus Statilius Taurus who commanded Augustus's ground forces at Actium, who once served as Consul and as *Praefectus Urbi*, governing the capital while Augustus was away at war in Gaul.

But he is not her father. The story is that she was born to the general, and that her mother was Nubian, but in truth, her father was

Augustus's son. Someday all will know her true lineage, but for now only the patricians know, and they do not approve.

In fact, Statilius is a cousin to the martyred Hero of the Legions, Marcellus of the Julii. Statilius fell in love though, with a Nubian of the cult of Isis during his alliance with Antony in Egypt before choosing to side with Augustus in the eastern war against Antony at the Battle of Actium.

He chose the right side in the war, but chose the wrong woman. When the general brought his Nubian wife back with him to Rome, Rome was not welcoming. When Tiberius ordered him to raise Claudia Procula as his own daughter, he obeyed.

"What is the matter, Lady Claudia? You've been disconsolate now for days, since you heard the tax collector wants that rabbi arrested."

Claudia fingers the strand of pearls and gives Shelomith a stern look. The servant has interrupted Claudia's thoughts. "Do not be too familiar with me, Shelomith."

"You Romans tell yourselves you pity one or two of us at a time, like you with this rabbi Jesus, yet you feel no pity for us all at once, not enough to leave us all in peace."

It's my own fault, Claudia thinks, for having sought out a body servant with nerve enough to talk back to me like this.

"I do not understand the Roman view of things—"

"Understanding Romans, Shelomith, is something you shall *never* do."

"Do *you*, Lady?"

What a nerve!

"I'll tell you the Roman view of things. My mother arrived to find that Rome, though besieged then as it has been all my life by waves of foreigners, didn't appreciate a Nubian wife. Neither did they accept the Gaulish wives, Egyptian wives, or Judean wives, although soon a third of Roman citizens will be of these nations. I pity the Rabbi. I know what bile hides in the hearts of Roman men."

"Men such as Tertilius?

"He or any of them."

"They say the Rabbi made a fool of him in the streets near the Temple. Roman men are donkeys, Lady."

"That is why I like it *here*, Shelomith."

Claudia reclines; thinks how Rome in fact had been thoroughly cosmopolitan by the time Pilate had sent for her to join him at this posting in the East. The city had been full of pacified Gauls, mercenary Sarmatians; full of captive Greeks, greedy Pontic-Caspian merchants scurrying about daily; sorrowful Judeans just like Shelomith flourishing and plucking chimes and lyres as if these instruments were ducks; full of Cretins, Thracians, and all the like.

The servant sent to find a stylus arrives now (finally!) and puts it in Claudia's hand. Claudia goes to her desk to write out the thoughts she thinks are her own.

I now turn my attention to the body servant as she gazes at Claudia Procula. Shelomith watches Claudia take up the stylus; so poised and well bred, so Roman.

Rome, Shelomith thinks, considers itself the center of this cosmopolitan world; but despite her mistress being Nubian and high born, the Judean Shelomith well knows that Rome is run by the sons of the same Romans who'd refused to welcome the mother, a dark-skinned, foreign-born Nubian seen to be one more cult priestess muddying the waters of the Romans' pantheon of gods.

Shelomith stills herself, alert, waiting. She sees things, she hears things. She has heard Pilate's consular aides discussing General Statilius and his daughter Claudia born in a city that looked upon her with jaundiced eye. So the general had decided to fill his daughter with the conviction that she was precious. Shelomith can well see the result: Claudia has grown into a haughty patrician woman whose father has kissed her ass so ardently that she now thinks her ass is made of solid gold.

Pilate (who married Claudia for her bloodline, visiting consuls openly gossip) has grown fatigued with carrying her to his every posting as governor of this, proconsul of that, and now to his post as sixth (or is he the fifth?) prelate-procurator of a rebellious province. His fatigue has grown great indeed. Bad enough, Pilate grumbles daily, he has to stomach so zealous a people as the Judeans. He also must carry a wife with so weighty a tongue.

Claudia in turn sees Pilate as lacking imagination though he indulges her pretense at being a woman of letters like this dead man, this Cicero of hers. To Pilate, she is a pretender; to Claudia, Pilate is a dreary public servant. Meanwhile, the both of them, though less brutal than typical Romans can be, are invaders nevertheless.

Shelomith would be amused if not for the loathsomeness of it; she is a Zealot stealthily embedded in the household of her enemy. Watching, listening, awaiting each Sabbath Day (her masters call it *Dies Saturni*) when she can report to her comrades preparing revolt.

Her mistress sighs at the splendid mahogany and ivory desk set out here upon the porch just for her. A pure white parchment, untouched by the every present dust in the air, gleams in the last sunlight. Claudia dips her stylus into the ink pot. She scratches out neat little blotches of black like distant little owls against a blank white sky; orderly flights of Latin she writes out well past dusk.

Finally she finishes, retreats to a divan. The moon is about to rise, but it will not shine tonight, Shelomith muses as she passes through the silk curtain to the inner rooms to fetch fresh water for Claudia. It will not shine because there are too many clouds.

I move closer and watch as the Mistress reclines and considers the nearby stone bust visage of her one great love, Cicero. Though Cicero had been her father's age, she'd delighted in him—a pure Platonic love—whenever he'd visited to discuss politics with her father and to eat garlicky pastries with the family beside the courtyard fountain in the gathering dusk, the sound of father's voice and Cicero's voice drifting and intertwining in the incensed dark until Claudia's mother shooed her away from the tables and cushions while the slaves cleared away the pots and clay cups and beaten platters.

With Cicero's aged but lovely face before her, Claudia falls asleep.

In her dream, as I now know is typical of most human dreams, she is the center of everything. Her divan is being carried on the backs of Roman senators as if they are slaves. This amuses me, for having gained some skill at entering human dreams, and having learned a bit from the great Austrian psychoanalyst in my last visit with Herr Doktor shortly after leaving the Cilician slave ship, I am here now seeing the human mind with a somewhat discerning eye.

She is ecstatic within this tableau, for in Rome she is not treated so dearly as this outside of her father's house. In Judea, she is treated well indeed, yet her true desire apparently is to have the Romans grovel. Well, one can scarcely blame her for that.

Cicero walks patiently beside the elevated divan, carried by six senators; he speaks.

"You will be a saint, and be venerated."

"For my writings!"

"No. For something far finer than that."

"I wish to be as *you* were, Uncle."

"A fool? For that is what I was. Playing games with Antony and Octavius, manipulating the beast of the State."

"You tried to train it to do good."

"I tried to make it do tricks. Antony warned me: 'You think your speeches can put a leash on it?' he scoffed at me. 'The Beast will never be gelded,' he said. 'It will kill you and I both, someday.' Marcus Antonius spoke true. He murdered me, and Octavius murdered him."

"You suffered for your art, lovely Cicero."

"You shall suffer greatly on account of this Judean, my pelican."

"No, Uncle Cicero, don't say this to me!"

He smiles, his immaculate toga wing elegantly draped over one arm, his olive oiled, well-groomed feet (imperial Romans had a thing about feet) showing through the straps of handsome leather sandals.

"It is your welfare I'm concerned with, Claudia. This Judean rabbi will upset the very order of the Roman world. But first he will bring disaster into *your* household. Do not follow your husband in condemning this man!"

"What am I to do or say, Uncle?"

"Say what you will, it will do no good for the Judean. Yet you can at least save your own soul."

Both of them look at me. I walk beside the wretchedly laboring Roman senator closest to "Cicero," an Aventine scion who helps carry the divan on his soft back. I am in my German WWI uniform, carrying a rifle with fixed bayonet.

"Who are you?" Cicero demands.

I casually stab Cicero in the chest with my bayonet. With not a sound, not a cry, he falls. His body soon is left behind.

"What have you done to my Cicero!?"

I reach to snatch the pearls from her neck.

"I've done nothing to him, for that was not Cicero, that was but a figment of your monkey brain."

"Give back my pearls! You'll be torn to pieces by my husband. Do you know who my husband is?"

"Wake up."

"What? What are you talking about?"

"WAKE UP!"

She sits up, gasping.

She reaches to her neck. The pearls are gone. She looks over at Shelomith, who's fallen asleep in a chair nearby, and is softly snoring. The moon, risen after all, has left a tangle of clouds and is bright above the garden.

There is a banging on the door to her chamber. She rises, hurries through the soft sheer curtains separating the porch from her rooms. She opens the door and there stands Tertilius, the fastidious and coldly ironic tax collector-thug-Equestrian who serves Pilate. Behind him are three centurions looking dusty, dour, and vicious. They have a young Judean under arrest and hobbled between them.

"Lady, this man was in the streets tonight gathering zealots together and planning to disturb the peace."

She looks at the young Latin Tertilius's rich velvet tunic and Egyptian sandals. His clean-shaven, equestrian face is as usual, without a mark or a blemish.

"What do you shave with, Tertilius?"

"Wha—?"

"Your face is unmarked. Every other Roman man here has dreadful cuts, wounds, and scratches from dull blades. What do you use?"

He scowls. "Lady, I come on serious matters."

"As always, like my husband. Are there no Romans left who care for literature? Art? Are there no more Ciceros?"

He stares at her. She is clean, her skin scented, her dark large eyes as wild to him as her talk and her behavior are to him. It is not just that she is his master's wife that keeps him always on guard, but it is that wildness, a trait he cannot quantify with his Egyptian mathematical training, with his books and ledgers. Women in general are a hazard because of that; this one in particular moves him to profound unease. He nearly flinches as she puts her hand into her hair and thrashes it a moment like whipping a cake batter.

"All right! What is it, then, Tertilius? Why do you come here to me, instead of going to my husband?"

Tertilius pulls a strand of large pearls from the purse at his side. He holds it out to her.

"Aren't these yours?"

Her pearls!

She snatches them from the Representative.

"How did you—?"

Tertilius motions the centurions into the room. They shove the young bearded Judean in, and he stands there, shivering in his plain but neat robes. It is the apostle they call Andrew. She has seen him speak, alone and with the other apostles, and seen him accompanying the Teacher.

"This man," says Tertilius, "who was gathering rabble to cause a disturbance, maybe even a rebellion—we'll beat the details out of him—had the pearls. He was attempting to use them to buy weapons from an Egyptian smith."

You are relishing this, aren't you? Claudia thinks.   "Luckily," he continues, "the smith is one who smelts blades for the garrison. He turned the man in. I thought I'd best bring him to you before Pilate is told his present to you was found on a Judean zealot. I wish to put this matter in the best light."

Yes, and thus put the wife of the Procurator in your debt, eh, you smooth-faced thug? Claudia muses.

Shelomith has awakened and is standing behind Claudia, wordlessly draping a shawl over her lady's shoulders; the air is chill. She then remains, silent, watching.

"Judean!" Claudia demands, "where did you get these? Tell me, or I'll have you whipped."

Andrew's head is bloody where one of the soldiers has struck him with the pommel of a sword. He pulls himself up to show some dignity, trying to deny these Romans the pleasure of seeing his fear.

He has that much pride at least, Shelomith thinks. How did he get caught!? Will he betray me now? Serves me right for having anything to do with these apostles of the Nazarene Rabbi, "The Teacher," who proclaims that we should *love* the Romans. Does he Teacher even know his apostle planned violence for tonight?

"It was given to me by a zealot."

"There are no zealots near me! This was around my neck before I—"

She stops. *Before I went to sleep*, she thinks. Only Shelomith was left alone with her. She turns to look at her body servant.

Shelomith glares back at her, with no sign of cowering or of flinching.

"Before you what?" Tertilius demands.

"The truth is that I sold them to a merchant earlier. The Judean must've gotten them from the same merchant. Let him go."

She hands the pearls back to Andrew who, amazed, stares at them and then at her.

"You can't be serious," Tertilius scowls. "Even if he didn't steal those, he was planning violence."

Claudia reaches into a purse at her side, brings forth gold coins. She presses one each into the hands of the two soldiers, then offers three more to Tertilius. He looks at the coins in her outstretched palm.

"Lady. Are you trying to convince me to betray my master?"

"Go warn him! Tell him all! I only expect you to let this Judean go. You needn't keep him, he's no zealot. He's a preacher, I know of him, and he's a poor one at that, like his Master."

"Lady, Jesus may be arrested tonight by Herod. There is unrest in the streets! The zealot Judas is one of his men, and this man Andrew, another of Jesus's men, was planning to pay zealots to raise disorder. You must have zealot spies among your house servants."

"No one here gave these pearls to him. Don't waste time with pearls, go tell my husband the people plan revolt!"

Tertilius glances at the soldiers. Both nod, pocketing their coins. If Tertilius refuses, they too will have to refuse, and neither one wishes to refuse. The wise thing, of course, is not to antagonize centurions, upon whom every Roman here depends for his safety and his life.

Tertilius takes the coins, gestures to the hobbles on Andrew, and the soldiers happily remove them.

"What shall I do with him, Lady?"

"Leave him."

"Lady!?"

"Leave him! Go! Be useful! Look after your duties!"

Smiling sarcastically, Tertilius leads the soldiers out. Claudia shuts the door.

Andrew gives the pearls back. "Why did you save me?"

"So you can go warn your master. Leave through that doorway, through the curtains. Jump down from the porch to the garden. You can climb the wall out there, it isn't very tall. Now!"

Andrew bows deeply until she pushes him away, and he leaves.

Without turning around to look at her, Claudia calls to her servant.

"Shelomith."

"Lady?"

"Did you take my pearls while I slept?"

"Yes, Lady."

"Are you a zealot?"

"Yes, Lady."

"Do you mean to harm me?"

"If I did you'd be dead, Lady, your throat cut. Why didn't you turn me over to them?"

"You'd better leave now. Even if I wanted to protect you, once Jesus is arrested and Herod calls on my husband to support him, this house won't be safe for you. Judeans will be suspect."

Silence.

Claudia turns. There is no sign at all of Shelomith. She puts her pearls back round her neck, and shivers.

I came upon him in the streets, you see. I don't even think I was particularly searching for him. I followed in his somewhat hurried footsteps for a time as he would suddenly stop to look into shop windows and as he swiftly entered a place with a sign in front featuring the word, "Tobacconist."

On his way to his domicile, he crossed a cobblestone street, pausing to gaze at a drunkard lying in the gutter. He stood upon streetcar tracks as he watched the drunk, and so I felt a twinge of worry as he narrowly dodged a streetcar he didn't see until the last minute.

Finally, he headed for his offices at 19 Berggasse. I followed the last distance, watching his abrupt, almost stumbling gait propelling him with such energy that it seemed each step was an attempt to launch himself off the surface of the Earth, gravity alone keeping him tethered to his life here.

He wore a somewhat elaborately constrictive, woolen herringbone suit, a bit too heavy even for early winter weather. Both his balding head and the lenses of his round eyeglasses shone in yellow pools of illumination he crossed as he passed beneath gas streetlamps.

This was not long after I'd had my final visit with Tesla. Before journeying to ancient Judea, I sought advice only a human being could give me. I could witness events in Judea but once, for such were Anu's rules, and would never be able to go back again. Thus, I needed to be certain of my purpose. This self-possessed and neatly attired human I was following could advise me about things Tesla couldn't, I believed.

He reached the door at number 19, stood there stiff and straight as he took a key from a vest pocket. He thrust it into the brass lock on the ornate wooden door, framed by a doorway much taller than he. I noticed that his leather shoes, though polished to a black sheen, were worn unevenly at both heels.

"Herr Doktor."

"*Ja-ja*, was ist?" he answered without turning, in the manner of a professor used to students and colleagues calling out to him at any time, unexpectedly. His manner showed him secure in his authority and status.

"You seem unconcerned about strangers calling out to you, Herr Doktor."

With the door half open, he turned.

"And should I be concerned, young man?"

"*Saklicheit*, pragmatism, Herr Doktor."

"Ja, ja, Sachlichkeit, Sachlichkeit, aber was ist es, sich Sorgen zu machen für die?"

"There is much to worry about, isn't there, Herr Doktor, in a world such as this."

As he shut his door again his eyes narrowed and he studied me.

"What are you? Gestapo agent? Here in Vienna so far from your vulture's nest?"

"Oh no, I've nothing to do with all that."

He turned away again, inserting the key and opening his door; all forbearance done, talking without looking at me. "Was ist? What do you want, young man, I am busy."

"A consultation."

"Return in the morning, see my secretary, or see a faculty secretary at the university. Make an appointment for evaluation."

"You'll want to see me now."

"Why would I want to—listen, please go away now."

"You'll be sorry if I do."

He turned back to me.

"Why should I regret you leaving me the hell alone as I request!"

A few people walking along the sidewalk halted, staring at us. He glared back at them so harshly that they turned their attention away and walked on.

He pivoted swiftly back to me, his hands now fists.

"Why should—"

"Because I am an angel."

He froze in the attitude of presenting his fists, but his mouth went slack a moment, as if he were thinking, but it must have been a swift process, because in the next moment he was seizing me by the elbow and ushering me hastily over the threshold into his apartments.

He shut the door and reached to light an oil lamp. In the light, he studied me.

"How long have you been an angel?"

"Since I was created, of course."

"How long is that?"

"Trillions of-of what you call years. Perhaps that is not accurate to say, however."

"What would be more accurate?"

"Eons, I think? Yes, hundreds of trillions of your eons, in this time continuum. I was created shortly before the omnniverse, and have witnessed much of the history of your universe and of the human race, mostly not in human sequence, but—"

"How then? If not in human sequence—"

"Oh, I go to and fro, backwards and forwards and sometimes obliquely from country to country, from time period to—"

"How?"

"I can walk in spacetime, fold and speed temporal quintessence as you would turn pages in a book."

"Spacetime, you say."

"Ja, the three-dimensional unity of space and time, the principle coordinate system in your part of the omniverse."

"My, my," he said beneath his breath. "Quite an elaborate delusion, Ja, quite elaborate." Then out loud to me, "You obviously have had a university education, perhaps in Tunisia?"

I looked at him blankly.

He pursed his lips and reached up, unapologetically seized me by the jaw, pulled me to the lamp and removed the shade so that the light shone on my face. He pried open wider first one and then the other of my host body's eyelids, inspecting the eyes closely.

"Cranium seems undamaged. Occipital structure . . . you are Tunisian?"

"The body I inhabit is Armenian-German, I think."

He chuckled, repeating it under his breath, "The body you inhabit . . ."

He pressed quite hard against my forehead. "Have you suffered a head injury? Physical trauma? Severe headaches? Numbness in the hands or feet?"

"Nein, Herr Doktor."

"You have a rather peculiar accent. You're sure you're not Tunisian?" He parted the body's hair, inspected its scalp with both hands.

"Gunshot wounds? Are you certain you've suffered no headaches recently?"

"Nein, Herr Doktor."

He stepped back, regarded me, chewing his lower lip, then folding his arms across his chest, then thoughtfully resting his chin on one hand.

He searched his pockets, found a cigar, and lit it.

"Who referred you?"

"Your reputation referred me to you."

"*Ach*, even some fellow physicians hate my ass, and I don't imagine I've a good a reputation where laymen are concerned."

"Not yet, but one day soon you will be famous even among laymen for your invention of psychoanalysis."

"*Eines tages?* Was? You are saying are you that you can see into the future?"

"Your future, but from other perspectives, the past. Of course, there are many of you spread across many dimensions, and some of you have no future at all—some of you will be dead soon. In this continuum, you will live to old age and commit—"

"Ja?"

"As I said, I am an angel. I've traveled across time, and have been to every corner of your Earth."

"What could an angel want with analysis? Tell me. Be specific, please."

He rested the cigar in a glass holder on a side table that was obviously designed to capture ashes; he adjusted his glasses, and produced a small notebook and fountain pen.

"Shall we talk here?"

"Hm? Oh, yes, we'll go up to my conference rooms, directly. Just now, were you about to say that I will commit suicide in the future?"

"I should not have, I realize it is considered rude among humans to suggest such a thing. Besides, that is the fate of some of you, in some dimensions, not all."

"You are referring then to Herr Leibniz's writings about 'possible worlds.' I am simply a character in one of God's tableau of many worlds, is that what you mean? One of those worlds has a 'me' who kills himself?"

"Ignore what I said. It is likely that this will not be how *you* die."

"Ach, mein Welt ist die beste aller möglichen Welten."

Of course I was lying to him. Suffering unbearably with mouth cancer, he would indeed kill himself in the future. I was annoyed with myself for almost saying that to him.

"What do you wish to accomplish in talking to me?"

"I wish to assess the possibilities of gaining insight into the psyche of my creator, if such a thing exists in him. I hope to anticipate his actions, find the root cause of his urge to create, and deduce the purpose of the tempero-spatial continuity of the creation."

The Doktor stared at me, perplexed but somehow also in anticipation, waiting for something. He shrugged.

"I have great hostility toward my father."

His eyes widened with interest and a small smile appeared upon his face.

"My father was interested in his own self. He didn't, stick around 'cause he wasn't interested in being a sharecropper the rest of his life, is what I hear," said Robert. "Can't say I blame him for that."

I'd perceived Robert approaching me long before he stood at my side, wearing what I was soon to see was a neatly cut but rather dusty, summer-thin brown linen suit, holding on to an exquisitely kept, carefully polished lute slung by a leather strap over one shoulder.

I'd ignored him standing there beside me amidst the quiet shrieking of insects and the rustle of leaves stirring in the tree above us. He had eventually sat down behind me, his back against the tree facing the two intersecting roads. As if he and I had been introduced and were acquainted, he had picked up where some imaginary conversation might have left off if there had ever actually been one between us.

"I never knew him. My mama must'uh seen something in him, I s'pose, since after all, here's me. Best as I can tell though, *me* is all she ever got out of that deal. I took his name, it was as good a name as any and better than some, since 'Johnson' is easy to spell and easy for folks to remember."

Annoyed at this invasion of my privacy, determined to burn this man to a crispy effigy I'd finally turned around and my eyes had fallen upon the lute.

"That is an attractive lute," I said.

He looked amused.

"Ain't no lute, mister. This here is a genuine Gibson L-1 gee-tar, manufactured by the Gibson comp'ny in nineteen-and-twenty-seven. Very few sold, very few possessed."

"Yet it looks to me like an *oud*, like a lute."

He flashed a gaunt, bright smile. Though he himself was dusty and sweating with the lapels of his neat suit curled by humidity, the lute was as I told you well-kept, aglow with oil, polished to a sheen.

He looked me up and down.

"What is you, some kinda WPA down from Washington to spread some government 'mongst plain folks in Mis'sip?"

"WPA?"

"Works Progress Administration. You heard of them, sure you have—you gotta be one, dressed as you is. You WPAs build parks, bridges, roads, and schools, I read all about it in *LIFE* magazine. Hardly any of that getting done in Mississippi, which is why I was surprised to see you standing here at 61 and 49."

"Why shouldn't I be standing here?"

"This is Clarksdale, Mississippi, mister. Hell, I shouldn't be out here myself, a colored man this close to night. I was playing at a colored wedding. The groom got drunk, stole my gee-tar case, and wouldn't pay me just 'cause his bride kissed me. Hah! Anyway, it ain't been a good day for me. Gonna be a jitney by here in an hour or so to take me back to dark town where I need to be by the time the sun set. Your automobile broke down somewheres, you waiting on a ride?"

"No."

"Well is you even from Mississippi?"

"No."

"I see. Well, my name's Robert."

"*Salve*, Robert. Since you presume, you may call me Parson. It is the name on the identification credentials in my pocket."

"You definitely not a bootlegger or a fugitive then, you got your own ID on you. I hear tell Baby Face Nelson was once down in these parts, a smart dresser like you, Mr. Nelson was. Dressed like you is, from elsewhere, white folks might take you for a gangster."

I made no answer, since nothing he was saying made sense to me. I considered again my first impulse—to burn him to ash in order to have my solitude again.

"Well, Mr. Parson, sir, if you ain't one of them bridge building WPA's, you might be with the WPA relief for artists, maybe? If you is, I hope you might spare me a little relief. *LIFE* magazine say WPA music boys sometimes break off a piece of money even for a Colored musician."

"I have no idea what any of that means. I am simply standing here to see the sun set."

He chuckled, hugging the lute.

"Italian-looking white gentleman in a fancy suit and good shoes come all the way to Mississippi to look at a sun set? You a government man some way?"

"Not that I know of."

"Well, you would know! Three-button suit, creases in y'pants like revenue agents wear that's all over the Delta these days, although generally not on foot."

"For what purpose are these agents? To 'build a bridge' as you say?"

"They takes money from white folks. In my mind, they's chasing down colored musicians to give 'em some of the money they takes; calling gee-tars 'lutes,' mouth organs 'harmonickees,' calling a squeeze box a 'concertina' and such as that! If you don't mind me saying, 'lutes' died out when the Renaissance was done with."

"The Renaissance. I knew of lutes then, although no one from that time ever used that word."

"Funny, you don't look five hundred years old."

"Not at the moment."

"Well, I learnt from a book, and I maybe got it wrong, but I read that lutes started out as harps amongst ancient Greeks and Romans and such; then somebody put a sound box and a short fret board on one, and they had they-selves a mandolin, more or less. Now see this here? This is a sound box shaped like a number eight, not like a teardrop, the way a mandolin sound box has got. See the fret board? It's long, and the sound box ain't as deep as a mandolin."

"You are correct. I travel a great deal. I sometimes lose track of specifics."

"Well, 'less you travel through time, you might've knowed this is called a gee-tar nowadays. You maybe from across the water? You got a different sort of accent, like maybe Englanders."

"I am from nowhere. I simply travel."

"You travel gravel roads a lot in them shoes? If you ain't from the WPA, you maybe with the American Record Corporation, right?"

"Let us say I am. Would that satisfy you and assuage your curiosity, Robert?"

"No disrespect, I won't tell nobody your business—you in these parts to set up some recording rooms and cut records with some colored blues men down here? Listen, here's my cut."

As he stretched out one leg and settled the lute on a thigh, I was preparing to incinerate him and be done with the distraction, but I watched him caress the strings, sliding his widely spaced fingers over them, and causing the instrument to wail as if it were the voice of an anguished woman. The sound keened in the humid air, and mixed with the noise of insects and of the rustling leaves above him. It made the hair on the back of my host body's neck stir.

Now he sang, his voice quavering, high-pitched, bending the notes mysteriously, reminding me of a Mandinka funereal cry I'd heard once in the bush of Northwest Africa, in a nation called Gambia, in the ninth of your centuries where I had spent time in the flesh of an Arab slave trader. Robert, however, was considerably more sinuous and more flatted in tone. He sang of a dead child and a dead woman who'd died in giving birth to the child.

When he was finished and I had lost all desire to kill him, I asked him, "Who are the woman and child in your *canto*?"

"My woman. The sweetest woman who ever lived, and my child, who didn't get the chance to."

"My condolences. I have no talent for evaluating musical expression. However my body responded to your canto and your lute, which I assume means you are a good musician."

"Well . . . thanks, I s'pose. You wanna record me?"

"I just did."

"How you done recorded me without any machines or a recording room!"

I pointed to where human brains are located, though of course I remember everything I have ever perceived and have no need of a brain to hear and see or to impress all I see and hear onto my consciousness. "It's recorded here," I lied, pointing to my body's skull.

"Awwww, man," he chuckled, laying the lute down onto his lap. "You just some joker."

"I am often called as much, if I remain any one place long enough to be evaluated." I turned back again to look at the sky where the sun was lowering in the west.

"Yeah. Like my Daddy. Not one to stay anyplace."

"Why do you insist on speaking of him to me, then?" I asked without turning back to him.

"Don't know. Something about you makes me think you a fatherless child, y'self."

I turned and strode across the brief distance between us, seizing him by the throat.

"Sorry, mister!" he choked out. "Let go my neck! Watch the guitar, please!"

"Why did you say that I am fatherless!"

"I just-meant you-y'seem lonely! I'm sorry, it's none of my business what you are!"

I released him. He collapsed back against the tree, gagging, clutching his throat with one hand and cradling his lute protectively with the other.

"Be careful how you speak to me, monkey."

"Yessir! Sorry, mister! I meant no disrespect!"

"I don't wish to talk about my father, not to you."

"I can see that! Bite my tongue. I'll just leave you to your sun set, I'll leave you be!"

"You were supposedly waiting on someone. I thought you were afraid to be out after the sun goes away."

"Yeah, well I sure am more afraid to be here with you!"

"Sometimes I'm testy . . . is testiness the word?"

"If testiness means nasty as a mule and subject to choke a colored man to death, then yeah, that's the word. I'll take my leave now. Pardon me."

And he was gone, leaving me in peace.

I kept the body even after the sun had set, and I would ordinarily have departed. I wished to go on waiting there at the crossroads.

I had some curiosity about what Robert had said to me about a colored man needing to be back in *dark town* by nightfall. Was this dark town a place everyone in Mississippi in this temporal point of AD 1930s wished to go when it is dark because darkness is somehow more interesting there?

No. I thought not, because there had been an undertone of fear in his voice, which had conveyed to me the impression that dark town must be some place quite a bit safer than the crossroad and the tree had been. If so, then I had driven him off and perhaps endangered him. But what was the danger? Curiosity is a weakness of mine. Try living for eons in exile with not much else to do but wander and observe and you too will find that curiosity will drive much of what you do with your time.

I stood as still as the tree, and I kept my eyes open in the coming moonlight, looking far off down the road that faced me, because a few miles away in the gathering dark I could see an auto vehicle coming. I could see that three men as brown as Robert were inside it. I could see that two of them had lutes not unlike Robert's lute. I could listen to them talking fearfully about Robert, about being late to meet him.

I watched and listened to them coming for fifteen minutes or so until they finally arrived and came rolling toward the tree, the pilot of the vehicle calling out of his portal as he slowed the vehicle a bit, shouting into the darkness, "Robert! Hey, Rob, is you there?"

I stepped forward.

All three of the men cried out in alarm and fear as the vehicle came skidding to a halt before me, tossing dirt and rocks. There were two glowing lamps embedded in the front battering plate, which resembled a Roman trireme's blunt ramming prow. Those lamps shone bright on me in humid darkness broken only by moonlight.

"What the hell!? Who is you!"

I walked around to the open port hole the pilot had thrust his dark head out of. "I'm a traveler," I said to him.

"That's a white man, Bill!" the man in the back seat said to the pilot.

"Yeah, no shit. That's clear to see, Benjamin!"

"Why is a white man out here under the tree, under the pickup tree?"

"I s'pecs he's out here 'cause he wanna be, Benjamin, as is white folks' privilege, now shut up! Pardon me, mister, you looks like a government man, so I'm assuming you ain't no Ku Kluxer—"

"Ku Kluxer? What is that?"

"Yeah, you sounds like a government man too. We is not trying to mess in your business, or bother you, we just looking for somebody. You seen a colored man here with a guitar, sir? We is awful worried about him."

"Robert, you mean."

"He knows Robert!" the man beside the pilot exclaimed.

"Robert told me you were coming," I said. I waited but they all simply stared at me fearfully so I said, "Shall we go find him? He went down the other road there."

They continued to stare at me once I had gotten into the back compartment of the vehicle to sit beside "Benjamin," who hugged his lute protectively. I sat back, unbuttoning my suit jacket and waiting for the pilot to launch us. The man in the front beside the pilot cleared his throat.

"Bill, that there is a white man just got into your car."

"Tell me something I don't know, Stanley. The man knows Robert."

"Who is you, mister," asked "Stanley." "And where exactly did you come from, if you don't mind being asked."

"Robert is of the opinion that I work for the WPA."

"This ain't gonna end well, Bill."

"Stanley, few things does for a triple of colored juke joint players out after dark in Clarksdale. You could've skipped the gig if you wanted to be safe."

"I wish I had."

With that, the pilot Bill pressed a foot paddle and threw back what looked like a steamship's throttle and the vehicle launched, speeding us down the road I had indicated to them. We were away, and I couldn't help but feel once again the peculiar pleasure of having a body and being in the physical world as a human, as the cool night air whipped against me from the back ports. The vehicle sailed along beneath a dim moon. I felt I would likely have my curiosity satisfied.

It was something to do.

I sat on a reclining chair listening to the steady "knock" of a brass clock pendulum inside its wood and glass casing. He sat across the room in a rather larger leather chair, writing pad on his lap, writing swiftly with his gold fountain pen.

"The negro Robert was a curiosity to you, then."

"Everything is a curiosity to me, everything on Earth."

"You've spoken of your father. What of your mother?"

"I have no mother."

"So you don't know her?"

"She doesn't exist. I was created, not born."

"*Ach*, from *what* then were you created?"

"From the thoughts of Anu—of Him you call God. He is Anu to the angels. His thoughts created us."

"Very poetic."

"Is it? I wouldn't know, I've no creativity."

He smiled. "From the things you've told me you've done, that is not true."

"Because I've made those things up, you mean."

"Well of course they are a delusion. Your conviction that you are a devil is delusional, but I am not calling you a liar."

"Then what are you saying?"

"That if we suppose that you *believe* you've done what you say you've done, then within the realm of this delusion the actions you've described are quite creative."

"I wouldn't know, Herr Doktor."

"Say for the sake of discussion that you are telling the truth and also describing actual events, that you fought as a gladiator in the Roman arena and were a general in the Roman legions, for example. What you've done *has* been creative."

"In my natural form, which is spirit, I've none of the intuitive traits humans possess."

"That must be a dreary thing."

"For you. Angels however suffer no fear, no remorse, and no pain as you define it."

"That would be a boring thing."

"Is it? I find many things tedious but seldom am I bored. Despite this ideal state of being, we angels cannot make something from nothing, a 'creative' trait you share with God. Thus, I need you to help me understand Him."

"Psychotherapy cannot help you understand another. Its purpose is to understand your *self*."

"You are taking what I say as metaphor, I see. Do you mean 'understand' as you say dreams must be understood?"

"Herr Holland, you are not Mephistopheles. You are wounded, and suffering a delusion, my dear man."

"Does that mean you cannot help me?"

"On the contrary. The terms of your delusion, as often is the case with the delusional, are symbolic of your true feelings, thus, in a manner of speaking, those terms are real."

"I don't—"

"You speak of your father as 'God' because he is omnipotent in your mind. Your childhood no doubt was overshadowed by his domination, or abuse. You say you're a 'Devil'? Your parents, siblings, or playmates must have convinced you that you are evil, scapegoated you, perhaps."

"As you wish. I simply need to know something."

Ignoring me, he went on with his bizarre diagnosis.

"Interestingly, you claim to hate humanity, but clinical study has established the fact that a true misanthrope shows no interest in nor does he show the slightest empathy for humanity. By your own admission, you imagine you have spent centuries among us *monkeys* and *crabs* as you call us, and during some of that time were a loyal servant to the human Emperor Caesar Augustus."

"I was trapped on Earth, as I am still, in exile."

"So you claim. Why didn't you use your angelic powers to—"

"I was deprived of my full power at that time. I had to join the human race."

"Yes, a convenient excuse, produced by your psyche to maintain the terms of your delusion. Yet by your claims, you cared deeply for several humans, particularly Augustus's proconsul, Marcellus. Why?"

"I don't know. All I need—"

"Come now, be honest with yourself. You admire Augustus as a father figure. You love Marcellus because he functions as a contentious yet cherished sibling, while your true siblings 'the angels' reject you."

I was growing impatient with this.

"I don't need to understand myself, I need—"

"Your defense mechanism is quite strong. You flee from the very understanding you claim to seek. Why did you flee from your interview of Herr Nikola Tesla so abruptly, as you have claimed?"

"I had all I needed from him. I simply sought information from the perspective of a human, of various humans, just as I seek information from you, now!"

"Not so loud, please. I have weak eyesight, not weak hearing."

"You are annoying me!"

"Of course. You are not simply delusional, as I assumed at first. You are possibly a victim of childhood trauma, and have erected an elaborate defense mechanism which causes you a neurosis. You are angry because I am exposing these things to your conscious awareness."

I stood up, knocking the chair over, my voice taking on a guttural resonance not quite human.

"I am tempted to disembowel you, *Doktor!*"

He chuckled.

"Pish-pish. Were you a murderer, you'd have murdered me rather than ask for my help. You cry out for sympathy. 'Oh, Doktor, they say I have horns!' Well I see no horns."

"You do not see Satan as horned?"

"If I see Satan, believe me, I see him as an Austrian hysteric with a toothbrush mustache, invading Poland with the blessing of IG Farben. Now sit your ass back down. Go ahead. Pick up my chair there, and sit down. It's all right."

I glared.

"Dear man, you are rather slow for an 'angel.' You do not frighten me. I work with violent psychopaths, with *true* misanthropes and with social deviants every day. Abnormal psychology is my bread. You are not nearly so sick as that. You seem a gentle, kind man to me. I wager you wouldn't harm a mosquito."

"That was Robert's voice, all right," Stanley had groaned in distress as he crouched low in front of the vehicle's lamps. "And them other voices out there in the clearing was some Kuklos, f'sure. That one big white man with the muscles, sitting on the horse with his face showing, he's a deputy from over the next county, I seen him before. How you know about this place, Bill?"

We had retreated back through the trees, back to the vehicle. Benjamin was slapping at his neck and cursing the mosquitoes. The three of them were squatting now in the dim light of the lamps, loading three shotguns.

"I ain't usually down here near Clarksdale," Bill answered Stanley calmly, "except to do a gig now and again with Robert. But my niece

Edna lives in these parts. Her people found her boy, my nephew Ronnie—they found him out here last summer all carved up, his tongue cut out, hung from a damn tree, and just the other day Mr. Wolf at the store behind the juke joint was saying how Kukloses brings boys they catch out after dark down here time to time to mess 'em up and lynch 'em. Robert's in some real mess now, some mess his big mouth no doubt done created for him."

Earlier, they had crept through the trees. Bill, a pianoforte player, and Stanley and Benjamin, lute players like Robert, had walked ahead of me. They'd moved by seeking the shadows while I had walked upright, not understanding yet what they were so frightened of, until we saw what was in the clearing.

Renegades. Men obscuring their faces with white masks in order to wreak havoc on civilian populations, a dirty tactic of war. The legions had experienced as much, as Rome had succumbed to the final invasions of barbarian tribes at the end of the empire. "Kuklos" Stanley had called them. Was Kuklo a rebellious state of the States of America, at war with the state called Mississippi in this temporal frame?

We had returned to the vehicle for the shotguns they'd removed from beneath a board in the bottom of the vehicle's boot. They had secreted the vehicle behind a hummock beside the road. Over the hummock, we had seen the light of torches and had heard the shouts.

"It's a trunk, Mr. Parson, not a 'boot.' Where you say you from again?"

I made no answer. In England, in this temporal frame of the twentieth of your centuries, *boot* had been the proper term. Not here in the American states, apparently.

"He talks queer all right, like he from oversees, just like in the movies," Benjamin commented, slapping at mosquitoes and loading shells into his gun. He offered it up to me. "Mr. Parson, I don't know why on God's green grass *you* wants t'go in there with us, you being a white man, WPA man, and all, but you sure better take this. I got me a pistol here in my pocket."

I took it, not because I intended to fire it, but because I was curious. It reminded me of a Winchester 1897 shotgun I took from the corpse of an American officer and had used during the Battle of the Somme, in your WWI.

Are you familiar with that battle? In the days I'd occupied the body of a strapping young German soldier in the Kaiser's army, I'd relived a bit of the excitement of my time in the Legions of Rome, though trench warfare is tedious in comparison. You were with me part of the way, my dear, yes, but I cannot remember if you were with me at Somme.

Am I losing my memory? That's an interesting possibility. Time on Earth may well be affecting me.

These musicians here in the AD 1930s lived not so long after WWI, between the two so-called Great Wars in fact; yet I didn't know exactly what model this gun was. The technologies of war are ever changing. Still, these were of the same tubular magazine and pump design and manufacture as in 1897, produced by Browning.

I gazed at it in the lamplight, which was thick with mosquitoes and moths. These men obviously cared for their guns as dearly as for their lutes; the weapon was oiled and very clean, the hammer felt easy and smooth, and the metal barrel bore no traces of rust. The stock was an attractive, polished walnut. A fine gun. I cradled it and remembered my days and nights in the trenches.

The 1897 model had been the first suitable pump-action shotgun used in battle. It could load six shots. From 1893 until WWII at least, the 16-gauge models bore a 28 inch barrel length and the 12-gauge model a 30-inch barrel. The one I cradled now was 16 gauge, my preference in battle.

The 1897's six-shot capacity (five shots in the magazine and one in the chamber) had made it effective for close combat. Our regiment had called it the "trench sweeper." It was so overwhelming and inspired such fear in the enemy that the German government had tried to have it forbidden from combat! We in the trenches had laughed contemptuously at the news. The purpose of war is to kill the enemy, to kill them with whatever does so best. Germany's leaders were playing war as a game rather than fighting it as a grim and serious task.

I supposed that this was exactly what these men intended to do: kill the enemy and save their friend. Despite being afraid, terrified in fact, they would go through with it as soldiers do.

"You've the right weapons for what you intend," I said to them. "Weaponry is the most crucial tactic in war. What I perceived of the enemy's ordinance were predominantly pistols, and only one rifle—a single bolt action—inefficient compared to pump action."

Bill stood. Frowning, he looked for my eyes in the darkness as Benjamin chuckled.

"What d'you know about war?" Bill asked, slapping at his neck and scowling.

I made no response.

"This white man thinks he knows something other 'bout skirmishin', Bill," Benjamin said, shaking his head.

"Huh. Maybe he do," said Stanley.

Despite the humidity, Stanley was shivering. Bill's jaw quavered a moment before he clenched it. Bill was sweating, I could smell it. Benjamin opened his pistol and inspected the chambers for bullets. His voice was filled with fear when he spoke.

"All I got to say is, if we all don't end up lynched by dawn, I aims to sell my daddy's mule back in Meridian and donate the money to the WPA."

Beyond the rise of the hummock that hid us, beyond the trees thick around with kudzu, was the clearing where the torchlights and voices were.

As we approached, I murmured to Bill beside me, "You are all too close together. You ought to spread out more in order to offer more difficult targets for your enemy."

Bill grunted, then hissed, "Boys, separate! Spread y'selves out some!"

Stanly and Benjamin did so, putting a few yards' distance between each other and between Bill and myself, as I stayed close to Bill.

Better.

When we had made it back to the trees just beside the clearing, crouching in darkness and loam, Bill looked up over his shoulder to see me still standing.

"Mr. Parson!" he hissed, "Get down, they gon' see you! You gonna get a gut full of lead!"

I ignored Bill, passed him the shotgun, and walked past him out into the clearing.

"Bill! The white man done walked out there into the open!" Benjamin hissed, pointing his gun to try to cover me.

"I see that, Ben."

"That ain't the plan, Bill!"

"Just cover his crazy ass!"

All three of them pointed their weapons and began to creep forward behind me. I turned.

"Stay where you are," I commanded, and they froze.

The humans in the clearing did not notice me at first. Except for the muscular man on the horse at the edge of the clearing, all of them wore masks or hoods, some wearing white robes. Twenty men. Each bearing a burning torch. They were gathered around a hundred-year-old tree in the center of the clearing. Robert stood beneath the tree with a rope looped tightly around his neck. His jacket, shirt, and tie were all missing, although strips of cloth still hung from him, the remains of the shirt.

His chest and shoulders were bleeding; his hands were tied in front of him. He raised his head and stared at me as the hooded masked men around him also turned and saw me.

The muscular man on his horse, a torch burning in one hand, called out, "You boys gonna take all night?!" He dismounted and strode forward passing near me without seeing me. He approached three men sitting atop the roof of a truck vehicle facing the tree. They too had not seen me yet. One of the three tossed Robert's lute; the muscular man caught it by the neck and propped it over his shoulder, handing his torch up to the man who had thrown the lute. He turned to address the men at the tree.

"Toss the other end of that rope up over that branch. Cut him up some more before you do." The muscular man hummed in a satisfied voice. "What is it? What's wrong with you all?" he asked, then he spun around to look behind him, where the men all were looking. That is when he saw me.

"Well, look here!" the muscular man called out. "Who is this carpetbagging bastard? He with any you, boys?"

"We ain't never seen him before. Must be lost!"

"What kind of government goober you supposed to be, boy?"

I strode forward the rest of the distance to the tree.

"I have no idea what you are talking about, but you will release Robert."

The masked men all broke into derisive laughter.

"Well, ain't he got good locution?" keened one of the men atop the truck vehicle. "The hell you think you talking to, Yankee?"

The muscular bare-faced man spat upon the ground then smiled at me. "These old trees out here done seen some colored-loving white men hang and kick too, days gone by!"

Laughter.

"You either put on a hood, grab a torch, and help," called out one of the men nearest to Robert. "Or crawl your ass back outta here, get back to where ever your guv'ment car done broke down or back to whatever interstate bus you got your ass offa, else we'll fit you for a hemp necklace and you can swing beside this uppity boy here!"

Silence.

Bill possessed good tactical sense though I judged him too young to have been in the Great War: he was slowly quietly leading Stanley and Benjamin round the periphery of the clearing. He had given the shotgun back to Benjamin, who was cursing about mosquitoes.

They soon moved to a flanking position behind Robert and the tree, where they would be opposite the direction everyone in the clearing was facing and looking, for all were looking at me. No one saw them. I did, and could also hear their footsteps upon cracking twigs, their breathing, their racing heartbeats, and whispers to one another.

"Am I to understand that you will not release Robert?" I asked.

They all laughed, and the muscular man pulled a revolver from his back pocket, pointing it at me.

"The joke's over," he said. "You get the hell out of here. We got business to attend to in the name of Jesus and civilization!"

"What do you mean by that? In the name of Jesus?"

"I mean we is doing the work of God, Yankee. We is protectin' the covenant 'tween Jesus Christ and the white man."

This was amazing to me.

"You are grossly misrepresenting Jesus, you ignorant simian. I have no interest in your primitive monkey disputes or your sadistic monkey rituals of abuse in the name of nation, race, and creed, other than the fact that I dislike the idea of your doing it to Robert. I advise you, however, to not tell lies about my fellow angels."

"What—huh?!"

"Jesus."

"So you claiming to be an angel, Yankee?" The man who had spoken slapped his neck.

I noticed that one of the insects had landed on my body's exposed wrist. I was repulsed by the sudden sharp sting of pain and by the idea of its feasting on my body's blood. I waved a hand, and the air all around us burst into a thousand tiny flames as every mosquito close by us erupted and burned into oblivion.

"Whoooee! That's a trick and a half! You some traveling Yankee magician with the circus?" exclaimed one of the men near Robert.

"Guess that's some special trick angels can do, huh?" "Dave" taunted. "Comes in handy if you wanna light kindling. You a circus angel, then?"

"In your fairy tales, I am known as Beelzebub."

The men laughed.

"He's sayin' he's the angel of evil, Dave!" called out one of the men atop the truck vehicle. "Remember Sund-ee school? That there is Satan, the Looooord 'o the Flies!"

"More like Lord of the Skeeters!"

Raucous laughter. One of the robed men shoved the robed man beside him playfully. Sparks from their two torches swarmed around their heads then rose upward to disappear among the branches of the trees.

I drew the sword I'd won from Mikayel in my lost rebellion, "The Tongue of God." The more quick-witted of the human men scattered immediately, scurrying into the woods, their shadows dancing before them in the inhuman glow of The Tongue, bright for a moment as the flash of a neutron blast. The few dullards among them were frozen in place, transfixed by amazement at the glory of The Tongue, and they would soon all die, heads parted from their shoulders.

First, however, I cut Dave the horseman into two Daves, slicing downward from the crown of his head to his crotch. He died choking on the laughter that had been in his throat when the spirit blade burst through the roof of his mouth and divided his tongue cleanly in two.

As the two Daves fell to the ground in opposite ninety-degree arcs, I stepped forward and dispatched the remaining wide eyed monkeys, finishing my task before the last head ceased rolling on densely packed moss and loam at my feet.

I made the tongue disappear, sheathing it again inside of me. Several fires burned around Robert where the torches had fallen from the hands of the dead men. I touched Robert's wrists and the rope tying them fell away. I touched the rope coiled around his neck and it too fell. He had several dangerously deep gashes in his chest, and one on his neck was bleeding profusely enough that the wounds would kill him soon. I touched his chest and neck and healed them.

"Mr. Parson, what just happened? What are you doing!"

Bill, Stanley, and Benjamin now emerged from the darkness behind the tree where Bill stood, the shotguns held loosely, barrels pointed to the ground. They were dazed, and concerned for Robert. They surrounded him, then pointed their guns at me.

"What is you, Mr. Parson! Some kinda demon?" Benjamin shouted, shoving Robert back up against the tree, shielding him.

"I work for the WPA," I said calmly.

I turned, went over to where Robert's lute had fallen, picked it up. I gazed at it in the remaining light from burning moss and leaves and from two trees that had caught fire.

I am not *creative*. Music, art, and sculpture are things so common to humans yet forever beyond the reach of an angel. A simple carved piece of wood with metal strings, and yet the man Robert was capable of making sounds with it that could stir the awe even of a celestial being.

I held it out to him. Robert started to walk toward me.

"Awwww, naw, hell naw!" said Benjamin, raising his shotgun and shaking his head. "You stay put, Robert, don't you go near that thing, whatever he is!"

"He just saved my neck, didn't he?"

"You saw what happened!" Stanley wailed. "He flashed some kinda hellfire and butchered these mens here! He ain't no man, he some kinda monster from the Devil!"

Bill took a few steps forward and lowered his gun; he addressed me.

"What exactly is you, Mr. Parson?"

"As I said. I work for the WPA."

"I heard you say something to these Kluxers about how you is the 'angel of evil,' didn't I?"

"I was trying to frighten them."

"What was that fire? How did you butcher up these fellows like you did?"

"Does it matter? I didn't butcher you."

"Yeah, well, for that, we is grateful. Robert, you don't trust this-this man, do you?"

Robert walked forward to take his lute from my hands. He held it as if it were his woman, and reached out to shake my hand.

"Careful, Rob!" shouted Stanley.

I gave Robert my hand. He clasped it, then stepped back. "Thank you kindly, Mr. Parson. I owes you my life."

"I may take you up on that offer someday, Robert," I said.

Next, I heard Benjamin's voice receding rapidly as he said, "Rob, I think you just sold your soul to the devil," and Robert's grunt in response, and I imagine that what they all saw was the man named Parson's eyes go blank and his body topple over to crash onto the dead leaves on the ground near Robert.

I wouldn't know, because at that moment I was already a thousand miles above their heads in the stratosphere—the limit I was confined to by my exile on Earth—hurtling toward Machu Picchu where I would indulge myself by inhabiting a body with which to excavate ancient Mayan burial sites.

When Mr. Parson awakened from his long strange slumber, he would no doubt be desperately curious to know how he had gotten from his London flat on King's Cross Road to a clearing in American Mississippi.

"I have done far worse than kill mosquitoes, Herr Doktor. Actually, I am the angel of evil."

"Ach! Why are you that? Because someone has said you are? Do you realize that a truly evil person does not proclaim his evil?"

"I've done evil things."

"So have I."

"Not as evil as I have."

"You are younger, and stronger. You can smoke and drink and whore much better than I have, I'm sure."

I laughed at this.

"Go ahead, dear Holland. Sit. I am so glad you came to seek me out. You are not a bad man. You are, like so many of us, a victim of an unreasonable father."

I picked up the chair, sat down.

"You are, however, unusually vain. A narcissistic personality. Narcissists are notoriously slow to recognize the truth about themselves."

"Please, Doktor, have a care how you insult me. I came here for one thing only."

His shoulders slumped and he sighed, almost as if he was disappointed in me.

"*Ja-ja. Was?*"

"I have lost someone dear to me. My father keeps me from her. One of my 'sisters' as you say, has helped him to dominate me. Why does he refuse me the right to do all I am capable of?"

"You said he appeared to you as Einstein?"

"Yes."

"And he said certain enigmatic things, about his expectations of you? What did these things mean to you?"

"Nothing."

"No, you are wrong. For in truth, his words *were* meaningful to you. You must uncover that meaning, which is repressed within you because you fear disappointing him."

"Doktor, I feel no fear, and I cannot repress, for I have no subconscious."

"Nonsense. You dream."

"Only when I occupy a human body."

"Yet these dreams are *your* dreams."

Ahhh. True. He is on to something there.

"All you need to understand your existence," he continued, "is before you—if you simply look."

"I suppose, Herr Doktor, but how am I to understand?! There is no other like me to compare myself to!"

"Ahhh, but you have siblings."

"The other angels are not like me."

"You are firstborn, then?"

"And one of a kind. Others have few of my gifts."

"Distaff siblings? Half brothers perhaps? Phallic fathers are often promiscuous."

"Yes, yes, I do have what you'd call a half brother." I was growing annoyed by this game.

"Aha. Ask yourself, what does your father expect of your brother?"

"That he'd die," I laughed derisively.

"Typical of a phallic father. My own father was a shit too. You must speak to your brother, Herr Holland. Find out what *he* feels about your father."

"He loves Anu without reserve. He's willing to die for him. He's a good boy."

"Really. Well, unless you talk to him, you won't *know* how he truly feels about that."

"Our father's rule is that he must to talk to me first."

"Well, you might be surprised. He may wish to speak to you."

I thought about this. Perhaps it was the advice I needed; perhaps I could question my half brother.

"Perhaps you are correct, Doktor."

"Of course I am. Clinical research confirms it."

I stood.

"I've money here in these pockets. Marks, I suppose."

"Are you quite certain it isn't Armenian *drams*, or some sort of *drachmas* you have there?"

I looked at him blankly.

"You need not pay me. You are a unique clinical case. We will arrange a schedule of sessions for you after a consultation with a fellow neurologist at the university, just to see if your delusion isn't organic in nature . . ."

He was still talking as I departed, letting the body I was in drop to the floor, dead. Unfortunately, though I often try to keep the owners of my borrowed bodies alive, the poor fellow had been killed by the shock of my entering him earlier.

It happens.

6

Pilate stalks in and out of the airy, green-veined alabaster halls of his well-appointed Jerusalem *domus*—a lodge much smaller than his coastal villa in Caesarea. He seeks his wife, servants, and his slaves, but finds no one. He can smell the aroma of roasted goat, a dish he'd bade his cooks prepare, but passing through the large *triclinium*, sees that no one has arranged couches, stools, or tables for a meal.

Pilate's family name, Pontius, identifies him as belonging to the Pontii, one of the more well-known tribes of the ancient Samnites; the Samnites being one of the original Italic peoples, who once controlled portions of both coasts of Italia. It has been said of the Samnites that "Italia was born along with them." And in a series of wars, Rome has crushed that illustrious kingdom, diffidently incorporating the ancient Samnites into Rome's imperium and into the *populous Romanus*.

So much for the Samnites. Kingdoms come and go; Rome is eternal.

Walking now through the villa's atrium, past the pool at its center, Pilate spies faint boot marks on the floor tiles where the soldiers of his escort from Caesarea had marched through upon his arrival in Jerusalem last week. He made a note to have Creto whipped for failing to clean those tiles. The atrium is empty of any signs of human life save for these boot marks.

129

Pilate's surname, some in Rome think, is derived from *Pileatus* and *Pileus,* meaning "cap of freedom," a common cognomen for those descended not from Pontii but from various freedmen who were formerly slaves or who have come from conquered peoples whose families attained freedman status.

But Pilate's name is actually derived from the Pontii, for it is from *Pilatus,* as in "armed with the spear" (the *pilum*). In fact it is as a pilum-bearing soldier serving in the legions fighting the barbarians in the north and rising in rank to commander, that Pilate out of nowhere had won his status. Like Procula, Pilate has a general in his ancestry: the *Samnite* general Gaius Pontius. Far better it is that Rome thinks him Pileatus, rather than Pilatus of the Pontii.

For in Pilate's nightmares, some senator or others back home puts two and two together and realizes the distant filial connection between our Pilate and a distant cousin, Lucius Pontius Acquila, a friend of Cicero's and one of Cicero's fellow plotters, an assassin of the Divine Julius Caesar. Some in the Senate wish to seek out scapegoats for that murder, even all these years later, and men have been garroted in Rome for lesser family ties than that.

Pilate's wish is not to be here in North Africa, among these crazed Judahites who have scorned him for bringing them fresh water through the building of an aqueduct, simply because he used their "sacred" temple monies to fund the construction! Rather than being hailed for his gift of water in a desert, he is hated. There is the incident where he lawfully put Galileans to death and mixed their blood with the sacrifices at the Judahite Temple, but such was his right under fiat. No other conquered people would dare shout "sacrilege" at a Roman ruler for disrespecting their bedraggled heathen gods as do these bothersome Judahites.

If he must be here, his wish is to be in his much more beautiful palace at Caesarea Maritima (Caesarea-on-the-Sea), in the Roman capital of Judea, the coastal *domus* where a proconsul ought to be and where he has been much of the year.

This long empty villa in Jerusalem and its accompanying *villa rustica* where the slaves sleep, had been built for a previous prefect/procurator, and its halls are not actually alabaster, and the opal-green veins in the walls aren't really opal.

Neither are these walls sculpted from cool lustrous limestone, like that Pilate has seen in the homes of powerful men and women in Rome. Grandiose indeed are the palaces of the powerful such as Tiberius's former henchman Sejanus, whose villa was nestled in the slopes of the Esquiline Hill; Tiberius's mother, Livia, whose Villa ad Gallinas Albas north of the city is filled with bright gardens and countless statues; the senators of Rome, whose homes are replete with stables, libraries, gardens, thermal heating ducts, and heated floors, with huge atria and sunken thermal bathes of marble. Pilate has little idea what the inside of Tiberius's mountaintop palace on the Island of Capri is like, but he is certain it must be impressive.

No, the villa walls here are fake, of a cheap newfangled matter used lately even in Rome called "concrete."

He enters his private chamber to find no evidence of Claudia; none of the usual telltale signs of her picking over his letters, imperial tax and finance records, dispatches, and proclamations, or nosing through his scrolls seeking information to nag him about. "You are not just prefect here, husband," Procula has often chided him, urging him to be more circumspect in his actions. "You are *Procurator cum Prorestate!*" Indeed he is. His position affords him civil, military, and criminal jurisdiction in Judea, unless the Syrian Legate Lammia intercedes. Yet he must "be careful" for many reasons, in fact, all amounting to the precariousness of his status.

He must admit too, that some of Claudia's nagging has hit a mark: Pilate is appalled at what is happening around him lately. He has spent the last hour over in the Fortress of Antonia catching up with events by consulting his own spies and diviners. While he was there, the Preacher had been brought in by temple guardsmen and Roman soldiers, on the order of Herod. Pilate had declined to see the prisoner, ordering him sent to the villa in the morning.

Events have become disquieting.

How could Rome's Judean allies be so stupid, he wonders, these councils of priests and patriarchs, most of them hand-picked and put in place by the previous procurator? It's stunning how incompetent they are.

Zealots behind every tree and in every pot, and revolutions and rebellions once a month it seems, to hear the Legate at Syria, Lammia, tell it. Under orders from Legate Aelius Lammia, the garrison commander Marius comes here also from his main quarter in Caesarea to sniff out plots hidden up the asses of Jerusalem's cows and to pull teeth from Jerusalemites' heads in hopes of reading secrets off molars. Yet so far, Marius can divine nothing of who is or is not a Zealot; not even where most of them meet. And so half-baked plans filter down from Lammia in Syria, too many to keep count and few of them effective.

Meanwhile, Judeans fear destruction; and in truth, many a prefect before Pilate has threatened to destroy them. Pilate has sought to smooth over relations through his friendship with Herod; a sensible thing, because Herod has political and ethnic ties to Rome. Yet Pilate's embrace of Herod has several times caused consternation both among the Judahites and in Rome, with the Senate! Now that Sejanus is dead, Tiberius wishes to present a less warlike attitude toward the Judahites; but still these consuls, legates, and messengers keep arriving from Rome, from Syria, from Egypt, from up the Senate's asses, claiming to speak for Tiberius: pacify Assyria-Judaea, now crush the fanatically religious Judahites only, or perhaps crush the Sanhedrin, no, not them, the Sadducees, or perhaps just the Essenes! Befriend one, then cajole the others, then destroy the ones you just befriended, or on second thought . . .

Pilate is convinced that none of them truly speak for Tiberius's real wishes. After all, Tiberius has been in seclusion for some years now, since the end of Sejanus, at the top of his fucking mountain! It is said that none can even reach Tiberius's palace except by an hour's climb up a Sheppard's path winding along a ledge over the sea. It is a political muddle, however one looks at it.

And into the midst of it comes a wandering Galilean with no lands and no wealth, though rumors are his family has riches, who gathers crowds by feeding them bread and talking softly about the meek inheriting something.

Pilate has for months now been quietly gathering reports, without even Tertilius knowing, from his own spies (soldiers dressed as civilians and natives he has bullied or bribed to betray their own, or at least he thinks they are betraying each other and not him). There is never any way to really know with informants. Still, he gets enough reports to be able to piece together a semblance of awareness of what is happening among the people he governs.

By reports, this preacher is a mild, soft-headed fool who has somehow slowly been elevated to the status of petty cult leader after supposedly raising a Judaean from the dead (Lazar by name, or was it Lazarus?). Pilate has even been told that a Roman centurion claims the preacher raised the centurion's beloved servant from death. Someone else claims that a Jairus of Capernaum saw his daughter raised from her deathbed and made to live again.

Nothing to puzzle over there, for the telling of such foolish tales of mystifying magic is common among these North Africans. The Galilean preacher is, if a cult leader, only a petty one whose followers cannot muster six swords and two pugio among them! He's no threat.

Save that the issue of the Zealots lies behind everything here. The Zealots have been stirred in part by these tales of magic, it seems. Even Pilate's wife has been stirred. It is the zealots who really matter. The attempt of the man Andrew to secure weapons was awkward and easily stopped. No proof thanks to Claudia's releasing him that he was truly a follower of the Preacher Jesus anyway.

Thanks to a very useful Sicarian woman named Yemaiah, whom Pilate has bribed, Pilate knows of one among Jesus's followers who is definitely a Zealot, one named "Judas." But even if Judas has conspired with Andrew to sow violence, Pilate has a mind that the Preacher's followers would simply have been seeking to cause a diversion to save their "Rabbi." Not a bad plot, really. It just didn't work.

These priests seek to silence Jesus because of the ruckus that took place in the Temple, a disturbance Pilate knew of and paid scant attention to, for, why should he give care what they do in their temple? Though it was clear a great deal of money changing and other business get conducted there, it is not enough to demand a Roman tax on it. Since the debacle with the Galileans' blood, he had kept his nose out of there, letting the temple guards and his own soldiers simply keep the peace.

High priests, the Sadducees and Pharisees, have been complaining though that Zealots could have been behind the odd fact that none of the temple guard had acted to arrest the Preacher during his disrupting of temple business, perhaps because Zealots have infiltrated the guard.

Not likely.

The question Pilate is most concerned with, however, is who is really behind these high priests? The hand of Rome is as always heavy upon events in the provinces through the bribes and manipulations of Senate spies and messengers.

Pilate passes through the great room to a hallway. He sees buckets and sponges lying about as though a cleaning crew had left in haste. Has some important person come to visit, making the household dump their work this way?

Peter knocks hard again on the door of the Sanhedrin council member, Nicodemus.

The fisherman is in despair. He has earlier followed the progress of Jesus's persecution as it unfolded after his master's arrest in Gethsemane. Servants of the Sanhedrin had arrived, led by the high priest's guardsman/servant Malchus, and guided to the garden by Judas!

Judas, who'd been missing until that moment. Judas had kissed Jesus on both cheeks, and then the servants of the councils, and temple police, with two mute Roman soldiers standing near at hand, had seized Jesus! Malchus's hatred burned in his voice as he shouted, "Take the Galilean Magician; cut out his tongue!" In the scuffle that followed, Judas disappeared again, and Jesus had been bound and taken from his disciples, carried out of Gethsemane.

Since that horrible moment, walking with a growing crowd and keeping his silence, cowering beneath a hood, Peter had several times denied that he knows Jesus, while watching the unfolding destruction of The Christ.

The brief struggle at the garden had distracted Peter from Judas's disappearance, and Peter, defending his master, had cut off the right ear of Malchus, the high priest Caiaphus's short, stocky, well known servant; only to watch Jesus shout, bringing conflict to a halt, then reach out to replace the ear, healing Malchus's profusely bleeding wound.

Jesus had admonished Peter for striking with his sword. "If you live by this," He said, "You will die by this! My *seliah*, my *apostolos*, must live! I command you live and bear witness!"

Malchus blood even now caking in his long, thin goatee, stood frozen and amazed, his neck and chest still bloody. His hand, still bloody also, was pressed to the side of his head where a wound was but now is healed. Malchus said and did nothing as the guards and the Romans tied Jesus's arms behind him and led him to the gates of Gathsemane.

"Malchus!" a guardsman cried out, "Come!"

"But he has healed me!"

"Nonsense! It was only a small cut!"

But Malchus did not move.

Next, coming behind Jesus, Peter had been pushed along amongst others, witnessing people in the streets of Jerusalem who appeared from nowhere to thrash Jesus outside the home of the High Priest Annas. The crowd had pushed its way into the house, bringing Peter with it, to see and hear Caiaphas pronounce judgment on Jesus, declaring him a blasphemer. Then had come the rough handed seizure of Jesus by the carcery legionnaires from the Fortress of Antonia; and Jesus's disappearance, bloody and dirty, into the carcery under Roman guard.

Peter pounds the door again.

While John fled to Bethpage to alert wealthy citizens there who support Jesus, and Thomas and others had taken Mary and Magdalene to a safe place in Jerusalem, Peter had lurked and followed Jesus's path in silence, under the disguise of his robe and hood. Other disciples scattered to four winds, some seeking after Judas and Andrew, some seeking weapons, some seeking the Sicarians and the Zealots for support, and some gone to seek after certain Roman officers in the garrison who are known to esteem Jesus. Peter suffered as witness to Christ's abuse.

In the moment after Caiaphas pronounced Jesus guilty of blasphemy, a woman in the crowd that had forced its way into Annas's house to listen to the trial, turned suddenly to stare at Peter.

"You!" she shouted. "You are one of this preacher's followers; I recognize you!"

"No!" Peter fearfully answered. "I do not know the man."

"Yes, you do!" another woman in the crowd cried. "I saw you with him in Bethpage; my sister saw you together in Bethany." Turning then to the crowd she shouted, "He's one! A blasphemer, like the Galilean. Listen to how he speaks. His accent's Galilean too!"

"It was not me you saw," Peter responded, turning away, only to be seized about the arm by a one-eyed man peering into his face hard with his one good eye.

"You sure you wasn't with Jesus?"

"I know him not!"

At that moment a cock crew, and up at the front of the crowd, among the angry Sanhedrin, Jesus turned his bloodied face to look back right at Peter. At that moment The Fisherman felt his heart seize in his chest, and felt fresh hot tears spring into his eyes.

He raises a fist to strike the door again. But it swings open.

"What! Who-? Oh, Peter. The Galilean Fisherman, is it not?"

"I come to ask you to help my master!"

Nicodemus motions Peter inside and shuts the door. He stands in the entry hall of his house and looks at Peter in the light from a clay lamp's flame that sits on a table.

"I have been told I may go to see him," Nicodemus mutters, "At the Carcery inside the fortress."

"Is he well?"

"Of course not. He's been beaten, he's likely to still be bleeding, and he's to go before Herod and Pilate."

"You are Sanhedrin! Why were you not there to object?"

"Are you soft headed? You think I could have stopped it? You think it was even a decision of the Sanhedrin?"

"I saw it! I was there in the crowd when they found him guilty of blasphemy, when Caiaphas pronounced it!"

"And what is the penalty for blasphemy?"

"Stoning!"

"Then why was he not sent directly off to be stoned?"

Peter's mouth opens, but his tongue is frozen in his mouth, as his heart is frozen in his chest.

"Ah, yes. You see? There is more to this, Galilean. I was about to go seek Andrew and Judas."

"Judas was there when our master was arrested! He betrayed us!"

"Did he?"

"I saw him!"

"You saw this, you saw that; you trust what you *see* very dearly, don't you, Galilean."

"Judas is a traitor. If Andrew is with him-"

I will also go to Pilate's wife."

"His *wife?*"

"Yes, with Andrew and Judas. Now, where are they?"

"No one knows."

"Yet Andrew did come to me just before Jesus was taken."

"Why?"

"Do you often go about like this with your ass on your head? Andrew and Judas sought to raise rebellion in the city in order to free your master, and force the Romans to bring their troops out of the fortress into the streets; there to be murdered by Zealots."

"That is not my master's wish!"

"Maybe it should have been, then. Maybe it's time to finally get it over with."

Sighing with fatigue, Nicodemus lowers himself down onto a wood stool. He looks up into Peter's confused face.

"Someone other than Caiaphas," Nicodemus says in a hoarse whisper, "And possibly other than Herod, is at work here, seeking what the Zealots and Sicaraii seek: for Romans to come out into the streets and begin a war."

"Who?"

"Am I Abrahim? Am I Jacob? Do angels speak to me? No doubt a legate from Rome, named Vitellius, whom it is said acts on orders from former Prefect Gratus, and Gratus would no doubt be acting on behalf of the Roman Senate. The Senate would at least have something to do with it."

Peter leans against the door. "Why now?" he moans.

"It's Passover. The city full to bursting; the countryside all around swollen with pilgrims. Pilate is here from his seaside villa. Herod is in Jerusalem visiting from his court in Galilee. Gratus is near, in secret, in Caesarea, and the garrison in the fortress is doubled for the holiday with troops sent from Caesarea, the soldiers tense. All who want war, on both sides, can taste it."

"Jesus was condemned by his own people."

"Don't be a fool. The Sanhedrin, the Pharisees, and Sadducees are puppets, including me. All of us afraid of what everyone knows will happen sooner or later; what that Persian, Zoroaster worshiper, the Sabaist kept shouting."

"War with Rome?"

"Sooner or later. But more a massacre than a war, fisherman."

"What has Jesus to do with this? He preaches peace. My master-"

"Your master followed John the Sabaist, a *Uhura Mazdite*; a madman who led Greeks, women, Zealots, Nubians, Syriacs and Heshemites as openly as his own people."

"John was a son of Noah, and so submerged us to cleanse us as the flood cleansed the Earth. He led people of all faiths, but also led Levites, Shemites, and any of the twelve tribes."

"Led them away from the priests, away from the temple into the wilderness, luring them into the pagan rituals of submersion."

"You know, Nicodemus, that Jesus does not only continue John's teachings. He has-"

"He has attacked the councils publicly, has caused uproar in The Temple, blasphemed in calling himself The *Moshiach*, and has openly questioned Roman authority. He has left no foot un trod upon."

"He preaches love!"

"You and I care what he preaches; those he heals care; we love him. But the Romans, the Sanhedrin, and the Zealots, they do not care. He is being used, you are being used, and perhaps Herod and Pilate now too, are being used by those who want war! We must find Andrew and Judas, and see Lady Claudia."

"Can Pilate be reasoned with?"

"He's cruel and vain. If he's not in with those in the senate that want to crush us then *maybe* he bears no ill will toward Jesus; but neither will he protect The Master. If he has discovered Gratus seeks war, he'll help the senate, if it benefits him to do so. Pilate is a snake sleeping in the sun: harmless in his repose, yet if roused, he will kill on reflex."

Nicodemus and Peter stand waiting at the gate as they've been told to. Directly, the Lady Claudia emerges from the gardens beyond, a slave at her side, a Cretan of short stature who carries a sword and knife.

She is cowled and veiled and walks hurriedly past them motioning them to follow to the villa *rustica* situated just in back of her husband's villa *domus*, and entering a side arch into a low commons area just now empty of slaves. There, the Cretan lights a torch, and she sweeps back her veil and cowl to reveal the well-known brown features of the prefect's wife.

"This is one of the Preacher's followers, Nicodemus?"

"He is, Lady. Peter the Fisher by name. A Galilean."

"What have you to say, Galilean? Is your rabbi a Zealot? Does he seek my husband's and Rome's destruction?"

"No, Lady, my master teaches not to disobey Rome. He preaches only love."

"Odd then, that your Sanhedrin seeks his death."

"Not so, Lady," says Nicodemus. "The Sanhedrin finds him guilty of blasphemy only to silence him. He was to be exiled out of Jerusalem by them."

"Then why is he at the Fortress?"

"A messenger arrived before the verdict was said, whispering to Caiaphas to send him into the hands of the Roman who could authorize his death and the deaths of his followers, and of his mother."

"My husband? No! He will not cause this man's death, I will see to it!"

"Do you know my Lord's teachings, Lady?" Peter asks, awed by her fervor.

"I-I know my husband would not condemn this preacher. Nor would he execute a mother for the crimes of a son."

"It may be not. But it has been whispered in the streets that if all the disciples, a woman, and a Zealot, Judas by name, are brought before Pilate, the uprising will be commenced."

Peter is shocked to hear this. Nicodemus continues, ignoring Peter's distress.

"I cannot find either Judas or Andrew who have been tricked into plotting along with this messenger. Else I would tell you who he is. A rumor says he is called Vitellius, sent by the Syrian Legate."

"Plots!" Claudia hisses. "Plots and plots conceal more plots, and my Ponti in the middle. You tell your preacher's followers I'll seek his release, Peter the Fisher. You and they must find out who spies for Rome and tell it to my husband."

"Anything to save my master!"

"If this man you name is truly behind it, Nicodemus, then that will be enough. I will seek the truth of it. Go."

Peter and Nicodemus leave, and in the flickering torch light, Claudia regards Creto.

"Can you through guile puff the name of this Vitellius into the ear of Tertilius tonight?"

"I will whisper the name, Lady. He admits to me that Cretans are circumspect. I reckon he will listen to me."

"Then do it, and after that, make yourself available to Pilate. He soon will return from the Fortress. He'll be confused to find the villa empty. Tell him to seek me in the pantry when you see him."

Creto leads her back to the villa gardens, bows, and hurries off to do as she has ordered.

Claudia stands awhile gathering her wits. The lilies in the garden are fragrant and musky in sylvan moonlight that ebbs and wanes. She gazes at the deceptively fragile flowers.

Their scent is overpowering.

Pilate gazes at the buckets and sponges. If some important emissary had arrived, slaves would have been sent to the Fortress to fetch him; that cannot be it.

An emissary "directly from Tiberius" had passed through just last week, taking a detour on his way farther north to Antioch, and bearing genuinely written directives under imperial seal. He had conveyed the Imperator's truest wishes in stark terms: silence every Zealot and terrorist in Judaea or, step aside while several centuries from the Gallica legion are sent in to lay waste to any rebel forces they can find.

By the time soldiers were to make their way from Gaul to Judaea, Pilate reflects, they would be bedraggled, angry, and feeling sorely put upon—the perfect condition for soldiers to "lay waste" to a city and rape everything standing. He feels a sudden twinge of fear for his Claudia.

The emissary lacked respect, Pilate thinks and I listen to his thoughts, *even to come to me directly, but first visited the local merchant Theocritus, a seller of spices, wines, hens, and goats.*

Theocritus is a maddening fellow, full of reminiscences of his trade excursions to Egypt and Antioch. The type willing to sell the heels off his own shoes; overstocked with goats but with no goat cheese to sell!

This slight in particular had stayed with Pilate.

How does a merchant keep upward of thirty goats about but has no goat cheese on hand? When twice I sought cheese from the fellow, I was twice disappointed.

Theocritus had come to the gate along with the emissary, an Etrusci from the look of him, and Theocritus waited in the kitchens, slyly eyeing and probably also fingering baskets of figs and dates, as Pilate and the emissary talked, walking the garden paths outside.

"The temple mount will be leveled," the emissary had warned. "And Syria-Judaea will lose one generation: males and females between fifteen and twenty will be taken into slavery, shipped to mines on the western frontier, to dig up lead for the empire. I've seen Rome do so in other rebellious provinces."

"The parchment you brought is clear, but *that* sounds more like Sejanus than Tiberius. All know Tiberius is tolerant toward the Shemite Judeans."

"I assure you, Prefect, those were Tiberius's own words. He doesn't know a Zealot from a pomegranate, mind you, but he has people telling him what's what in his empire."

People like you, Emissary?

Pilate had watched the Etruscan squat to sniff at a flower. Squat, not bend, and his hairy legs showed deep scars, as though he'd been in the arena, or had been a soldier.

Could he be speaking true in this? Such an exorbitant, wasteful punishment; a generation sent to slavery!

They walked on, the emissary carefully folding the flower's head, which he'd pinched off, in a linen scarf and tucking the scarf into his belt.

"Why?" Pilate had demanded. "Why should Tiberius worry this much over Judea? Why now?"

"He doesn't care one wit about Judea, Prefect Pilate. What he does care about is not putting on a breastplate."

The emissary paused to pluck a low-hanging orange from a branch overhead. He was lean, for an Etruscan, probably because he'd been travelling back and forth for Rome and the Senate for many years.

He wore a neatly trimmed goatee, not a fashion for Roman men, but definitely a fashion in Antioch, where he was headed.

"Breastplate, you say."

"I've heard it said they give him a rash. What he himself said is that they are not flattering on him."

"Not flattering. Breastplates."

"He said so, yes! Are you listening to me, Prefect?"

"Oh, yes. Go on. Breastplates."

"He said he wishes to not have to wear one. He wishes to not have to ride a horse in this dust and heat. Not to have to come here to personally put down what might someday become a challenge to Rome's authority—"

"He could always send a general to crush such rabble easily."

"I agree. Crassus did a fine job crushing Spartacus. Still, a 'rabble' rebellion by rabble Judeans might inspire *other* rabble in the empire, you see? All three of the slave wars arose from a rabble. Spartacus inspired lowly slaves who nearly defeated the legions completely. If another Spartacus arises here, Tiberius would feel obligated, for appearances' sake, to take care of such rebellion personally."

The emissary had peeled the orange, handing four strips of rind to Pilate one sticky peel at a time.

"Judea, Syria, Egypt, Nubia. So many rabble, so much territory. He was unhappy riding horses in the snows of Gaul, you know. He wishes to ride even less in the heat of Africa."

"Zealots have made noise here for generations, for twenty years. Again I ask, why now?"

Pilate had tossed the orange peels away and soon indeed a slave came scuttling to scoop them off the ground, making things neat again, which was his task to do.

"That's it exactly, Prefect. Tiberius reckons a pattern: five to ten years of agitation, followed by one true, organized rebellion. To stamp one out, an emperor may need to put on a breastplate and ride a horse for months at a time. He's thinking not of now, but ten years from now. But as to now, as the parchment I gave you no doubt warns, if the unrest here continues, perhaps the garrison commander, Marius, will be made Procurator."

Back in the kitchens, Theocritus had a guilty look about him. Pilate noticed one of the fig baskets looked depleted.

I asked him for goat meat since I knew the fool would have no cheese to sell, and where is the meat?

Pilate thrusts aside a silk curtain.

There is no sign on the porches of his wife, or any of her body servants. He walks back through his chambers to the hallway, back into the Great Room then off to search the guest chambers.

The temple will burn. King Herod's palace razed, Herod invited to ride a spit. Herod has friends, maybe even relatives in Rome, and well, maybe they too, will end on a spit, just to keep things tidy.

The garrison commander, Marius, will be made Procurator. Now there is the real horror of the matter. Marius is a brute, not a politician.

Though Judea is a minor province, a main body of three thousand soldiers are quartered at Caesarea. There is always the possibility of revolt with these people. For Passover a full cohort of six hundred or more extra are now stationed here, in the Fortress of Antonia, overlooking the temple.

This fuss over Jesus has happened purely through the blundering actions of Herod's agents, of the vested interests surrounding the Pharisees, and of thick-witted politicians using the Sanhedrin as a front. The priests fear Rome will impose absolute control and outlaw the Judean worship of one God. They are right to fear.

He enters another Great Room and halts in frustration, turning in circles in the emptiness.

He is alone.

The walls are concrete covered by plaster and painted to look like marble. Made of lime, rubble, and water. He'd first seen this concrete in Pompeii, a resort town next to a volcanic Mount Vesuvius, a town with the poor living too close alongside well-heeled patricians.

He saw there how lime and water are mixed to a soggy paste, volcanic sand and rocks added, then mixed to a messy consistency and molded to the shape of proper marble blocks, but *not* proper, because the things are not marble, just painted in fakery. It is the nagging feeling Pilate has had since he was a lower-caste boy.

Things are not as they appear.

Creto comes upon Pilate leaning against a concrete column, staring at a wall hatefully. The slave stands beside Pilate, looking where Pilate gazes at the wall.

"Master? Is there some matter?"

Pilate spins, barely restraining himself from striking the slave from Crete, ergo his name "Creto." It is the fashion back home to name slaves after the countries they had been taken from.

"By the way, you've a whipping coming for not cleaning those boot marks on the atrium tiles!"

"Sorry, Master. I will—"

"Where is my wife? Where are all my servants, my household! And why do you wear a sword and knife!"

"I- Lady-Lady Claudia sent me to a merchant's home to fetch fresh peppercorns for your meal. The night hides thieves. She told me take weapons with me."

"And where then is she? And everyone else?"

"She is in the lower pantry. She sent all away for their holy days."

"Their what?"

"Passover it's called. It's sacred. They—"

Pilate turns and heads for the kitchens, leaving Creto standing there stammering.

Andrew crouches in the darkness next to the gate set into the fence. He mocks the sound of an owl. Inside, a mock owl answers. The gate opens, and Mary of Magdala peers out, sees him, gestures for him to come in. He rises and passes quickly within.

Inside, he sees many of the disciples gathered in the darkness at the same table where Jesus had sat their first hour in the city, when Peter had prepared to cut Jesus's hair and Judas had objected.

As Magdalene shuts the gate behind him, Andrew can make out the faces of Luke, both James the Greater and James the Lesser, Philip, Simon, Thomas, John. Mary, mother of the Christ is in their company, wrapped from head to foot in a shawl to ward off the night air.

"Where are Peter, Matthew, Bartholomew, and Thaddeus?" Andrew asks.

"No one knows where Peter has fled," James the Greater whines. "Matthew, Bartholomew, and Thaddeus are gone to Bethpage to alert our Master's people there, and alert the Greeks who follow him.

Someone will go to Antioch as well. Where were you and why are you dirty and bloody?"

Beside James, Mary moans. The sound cuts through Andrew and hurts him more than the blows he has taken from Roman fists.

"I've come from Pilate's villa."

"You were arrested?" John demands.

"And beaten."

Magdalene grunts in anger and distress, and goes to their host's well where a bowl of water and a cloth are sitting. She dips the cloth, wrings out the water, and comes back to wipe away blood on Andrew's face.

"Are they arresting all of our people?" Mary asks.

"Mother, I was arrested when I was caught buying weapons."

Everyone at the table shouts at once.

"What!?" — "Did he say—?" — "Are you mad!?"

"Explain this!" John demands. "Why would you seek after weapons, you know the Master doesn't want us to—"

"Where is Judas?" James the Lesser demands.

"I don't know. Judas too may be arrested. The plan was mine and Judas's. We were to start a rebellion once Jesus was taken."

There are shouts and consternation again.

Jesse, a Pharisee who loves Christ and whose home it is, emerges into the courtyard followed by one of his servants. The servant has a platter of stuffed grape leaves, hummus, and lavash, which he sits on the table amongst them. Meanwhile, Jesse bends to whisper to Mary. She claps her hands sharply; all grow silent.

"Jesse was at Annas's house when Jesus was brought there and judged by Caiaphas."

"He is found guilty of blasphemy," Jesse says in the tense silence. "Peter was seen at Annas's house in the crowd, but he is missing, Mother," he says, turning back to Mary. Then to Andrew, "You, Andrew, are hunted by temple guards. Judas too is hunted. Your idea was foolish. Because of you and Judas, Jesus is now in the Fortress. He will be judged by Pilate for treason."

"He will be crucified!" James the Greater moans.

"We are lost," whines Luke.

"What have you and Judas done!?" Mary demands.

"Mother!" Andrew cries out, falling to his knees. He weeps as she reaches out to rest her hand on his head.

All jerk and shudder at a loud knock upon the garden fence. Mary rises in the tense stillness following the sound, and boldly opens the gate. Peter stands on the other side.

"Peter!" Luke and Magdalene shout. Everyone rushes to embrace him. Through the tangle of bodies pressed lovingly against him, Peter sees Andrew, still bent upon his knees, face against the ground in despair.

"I have much to tell of Andrew and Judas's folly, and of hope for our Master thanks to Nicodemus," says Peter. "We must seek out the plotters who have deceived Andrew and Judas."

"We will do nothing for three days. My son is in His Father's hands now," Mary says, fixing Peter with her gaze.

"Why three days!?" the disciples chatter at once. But Mary does not respond. Still staring into Peter's eyes, she speaks only to Peter.

"Judas cannot be saved, but in three days, Andrew will be taken out of Jerusalem to safety," Mary says wearily. "And some of the rest of you must leave for Antioch, Greece, and Egypt, to contact our followers in those places."

"I will go nowhere," Thomas says, "until I have seen the Master again."

Mary turns to regard him, tears in her eyes. She nods.

As Pilate now passes through his kitchens, following Creto's direction, he sees platters for a meal of roasted goat. The meat has been left to sit and grow cold as if the staff had suddenly vanished into nothingness.

What is she up to now?

Past the kitchens is the shallow stairway that leads downward into several subrooms with real stone walls, where the pantry and two storage rooms are, and a hot room, where baths are kept; all an addition to the lodge-sized *domus* ordered by Claudia from a distance soon after she and her Ponti had arrived in Caesarea from Rome.

The baths down here, which he passes through first, are heated, while surrounding walls are chilly; thus, the walls are covered with condensation. Walls down here are not plaster, not concrete, but true limestone. Though there are only the two rooms for the baths, Claudia still nurtures a desire to excavate more to match the existing subterrain at the seaside villa in Caesarea.

She plans to add to the *caldarium*—the hot room—by building a *tepidarium, sýýdatorium, apoditerium* and *frigidarium*—the warm room, sweating room, robing room, and a cold room. After settling in Caesarea, she's ordered the work done here in Jerusalem without ever having seen the result until now. She'd sent all the way to Antioch for the stones and for the builders. Since arriving in Jerusalem, she'd been busy finishing the baths by stocking the chamber with oils and emollients and with soft Egyptian towels. In the bottom of each of the sunken, tiled baths is a tile mosaic of the cult goddess Aphrodisia, more a Greek than a Roman goddess, Pilate thinks sullenly.

How can Tertilius see such things happening around this Jesus, and not alert me sooner? How is it my own wife plays a role in these matters, naively involving herself in something as petty and as potentially explosive as local religious politics?

Hurrying past the baths and into the dim, cooler pantry area, he finds her at a shelf unwrapping loaves of bread.

"Do you realize what you've done, silly woman?"

She cradles a loaf taken from its linen sling, and smiles.

"I've acted to keep Judeans from associating you with injustice, stubborn man. Can your precious Tertilius say as much?"

"You've allowed a Zealot plotting treason against Tiberius to escape! You failed to order Shelomith to be seized—"

"Why should Shelomith be—"

"She's a Zealot spy! The garrison commander tortured the plotters. They confessed that she was placed in my household to spy on me!"

"They lie. She is blameless."

She brushes past him with the loaf of bread, large as her own torso. He follows, shouting.

"If you speak of the necklace, Tertilius already told me! And now what are you doing? You've sent our servants away, and you're nursing a damned loaf of bread!"

"This bread is for the people."

He seizes her by the arm.

"Oh, ho, now, 'The People' is it? Are you Lady Livia now, the emperor's mother? Feeding 'The People'? How do you know these Zealots? What have you to do with the escaped apostle, Andrew?"

She jerks her arm from his grip.

"I know nothing of him! I simply refused to see him be tortured for my actions. If you can sulk and brood over that fat boor Herod—"

"Herod Antipas has kin among the patricians at home, Claudia, and is Rome's ally! I erected the gilded shields all about his palace, as I did about our home."

"And caused uproar among the people with them, husband! Shields and banners calling the emperor 'divine'! That delegation of Herodian princes who traveled to Rome to complain to Tiberius himself put you under suspicion!"

"Are we back to that? Do you still sneak through my scrolls?"

"You've made errors in judgment, husband."

"Who is the prefect here? Tiberius's criticism of me for that was a political gesture. He is for making friends among these people. Sejanus knew that Valerius Gratus was correct to show Roman signs, and Sejanus, who appointed me here, was not so timid of these damned Judahites!"

"Sejanus is dead, and Tiberius was right to issue his decree across the empire that these people not be persecuted! He has declared that only the guilty be punished."

"Tiberius is still not clear minded after the conspiracy Sejanus plotted, caused him to have Sejanus put to death. Tiberius still grieves; and you little know just how two minded Tiberius really is about Judahites. He is having second thoughts."

"What of it? His original thought was correct regardless: Rome cannot murder everyone that disagrees with it, so Rome must take care of what it does to people in their own lands!"

"As usual, wife, you evade the issue, perhaps because you are of a Nubian strain. Andrew is a Zealot. Herod's spies confirm it."

"What do you say of my Nubian blood? That it blinds me? That Nubians lack good sense?"

"On the contrary. Nubians are an ancient race, older than Etrusci, Italos, Sabines, Etrurians, or even my own people, the Samnites, conquered by Roman and my clan, the Pontii demoted to equestrian rank. You are of Nubian Kushites, hardheaded like Romans, but softhearted. Don't deny it! You have acted out of that flaw several times through this whole thing, wife!"

"My people were Kushite, yes, but my mother's strain was Meroe, and Noba. Otherwise, the general would never have married her."

"How well I know that you are a granddaughter of Augustus, born to Claudia the third wife of Tiberius, who was of Nubian birth. You were supposedly promised in marriage to Sejanus? You were raised as Statilius's own daughter? A story to be told to the plebeians, who relish such tales; but in reality, your mother was in the house of Tiberius while you were sent to Statilius's house, presented as his Nubian wife's child, all to deny your mother's Nubian identity."

"You never speak of it."

"No, wife. What have I to say, a Samnite looked down on as merely an equestrian myself?"

"You do not mock me, then, husband?"

"Rome is a nation of bastards, my love. All of us. All the patricians know, your father never tired of telling me. He reminded me that his wife, though Nubian, is of higher birth than I! You, as a daughter of a Caesar, are even higher. I think even Herod knows it."

"Oh, Haman, why do you care so about this bumpkin Herod? He is a Judean himself! You are Roman. I am Roman."

"Don't call me that, Claudia. Zealots call me 'Haman,' in their foul graffiti."

"*Ponti*, then, all right? As I called you when we first wooed? Ponti, my heart, my honeydew."

"Don't mock me! Herod sends to bid me judge the preacher whom Andrew serves, who is now in the Fortress! I am inclined to order his death."

She drops the bread loaf.

"You mustn't!" she shouts.

He bends to retrieve the bread, peers up at her. "Do you toy with this preacher also?" Pilate is utterly incredulous. "Where does your foolishness end? Is there no limit?"

"I need to tell you something, husband—"

"More of Herod? Herod has Rome's imprimatur!"

"Listen, Ponti, no, listen! I've dreamt of Cicero. Do you hear? Cicero, He-he told me you *must not* harm Jesus!"

"I see."

"Do you? Do you really see, Ponti?"

"Yes. I see, my dear spoilt patrician wife, that you had better go back to sleep, dream another dream, and tell Cicero for me to kiss my equestrian ass!"

He thrusts the bread loaf back into her arms and strides back through the baths to the stairs.

I follow a Pharisee, he who carries a torch.

The Pharisee is guided by a bored centurion all the distance to one of the last cells in a dark passageway of the garrison carcery.

Much like the carcery cells of the Mamartine in Rome, located at the foot of Capitoline Hill, these dark garrison cells in Jerusalem are subterranean and meager, existing only to temporarily hold the poor (in Rome, the plebeians) when they are caught stealing food, or to hold political prisoners; both groups are merely held briefly on their way to certain death. Roman punishment in these times mostly consists of slavery or death. Roman justice is swift for any without power or who run afoul of power.

The centurion doesn't carry a light; he doesn't need to, for he knows each warren and burrow of the labyrinth as if it were home.

He thinks how for two years this *has* been his home.

His life began with the legions; it's all he's ever known. He's a veteran of the Gaulish wars and served once with Tiberius on the northern frontier. From the cold barbarian lands, he was sent to Caesarea to languish with goats and cows and Judeans in the sun. He was sent here to Jerusalem from the main garrison in Caesarea, and here, his life has ended.

The light of the Pharisee's torch illuminates the gilt-embossed signia of "Legio X Fretensis" stamped on the centurion's belt.

A noble stamp in its day, he thinks.

There are rumors, though, that some in the Senate wish to withdraw from Damascus, Syria, and Egypt; level Jerusalem; kill the Zealot rebels once and for all; and bring the legion home to fortify city defenses. For while good legionnaires dally in Africa, the Gauls and Britons are looking more and more threatening to Rome, the city itself, so the easily frightened citizens imagine.

Scant glory, pulling duty in a shit ditch like Judea. When the Tenth marches, I, Casca-Longinus, command a hundred men. Saturn's loins but a centurion's a man of distinction! Yet here am I scrounging, treating as spoils the bumpkin possessions and loose coins of them that's condemned. Here am I gnawing on what turnips I can dig and bats I can catch and cook in these musty warrens.

He feels the weight in his pocket of two sesterces the pious Judean priest bribed him with.

Well, a centurion doesn't pick or choose his postings.

He notices the pious old man carries a linen robe folded and tucked under an arm. It's no weapon nor is it food or any other thing forbidden to the prisoners, so he does not care. He unlocks a wooden padlock on the cell and lets the Pharisee in.

I follow into a dank, and also from its appearance, a very musty chamber; there are a few strands of straw on the floor barely covering dirt. The Pharisee holds up his torch. It casts a yellow pale on Yeshua the Christ, who sits in the dust counting stones. His robes are dirty. He has a dry streak of blood down one side of his face. When the centurion has locked the door and gone, the Pharisee speaks in a pained whisper.

"Preacher, Yehoshua, what is it you are doing?"

"Counting the number of the righteous, Nicodemus," Christ responds, not looking up from his stones.

"You're found guilty by Caiaphas of blasphemy. You next are to be judged by the Romans for treason!"

"Then I must finish my counting quickly."

Like a parent reproving an errant but beloved child, Nicodemus squats down next to Christ.

"You are Sadducee, Master. But that is not why the Sanhedrin sent you here. Why have they judged you?"

"You are Sanhedrin, Nicodemus. Ask Annas and Caiaphas why. Ask Caiaphas why he has sold the Sanhedrin to Rome."

"Caiaphas is not evil, Yeshua, he is afraid. The dynasty of priests is no more; the authority of the Assembly is nearly gone. There is only the foot of Rome on all our necks. You upset the councils, who must worry for the people. We all must fear what Rome can do."

"We all must fear what my father can do."

"Did you say you are the son of God? Did you tell Caiaphas that?"

"God has more than one son. Haven't I told you I am the Son of Man? As you are Sanhedrin, Nicodemus, so am I. I told Caiaphas I am Sanhedrin, Pharisee, Sadducee, Essene, and Roman."

Nicodemus spits into the dirt.

"I am no Roman, Lord."

"Are you not the flesh of your brother, though you are not your brother, and therefore are you not your brother?"

"My brother?"

"Your mother's son."

"My mother's son is my brother, yes."

Christ finally looks up at him. "You admit it."

Shaking his head over this nonsense, Nicodemus sits upon the dirt and straw, takes a clay flask from his purse, gives Christ a drink of water from it, then wets the corner of his own robe and scrubs the blood from Christ's face. He removes Christ's robe, putting on him the clean white robe he carries.

"What does my brother have to do with the question at hand, Yeshua?"

"What is the question?"

"How to end this. I seek to free you!"

"Would you seek to free the Sea of Galilee?"

"No. For Galilee is not in a Roman jail."

"Neither am I. My brother is."

"Yeshua, you must stop this!"

"Nicodemus, you must continue this."

"I have seen Jesse. Your mother—" he breaks off, whispers the rest—"Your mother, Peter, and your novices are hiding in his home. Some of them are gone to Bethpage. Judas is missing."

"Peter will be found by all mankind. Judas will be lost to all."

"You are to be judged without even the decency of a trial. They will stone you! Or worse, crucify you!"

"It is my brother who is being judged, though he doesn't know it yet."

Jesus turns his gaze upon *me,* as if he *sees* me.

"Pilate is cruel," mutters Nicodemus, "yet he is usually not interested in crucifying Shemites so long as we prune his trees properly and provide him with goats. But I am told that the former prefect, Valerius Gratus, is manipulating the councils, the Sanhedrin, and Pharisees. Gratus has agents in Syria at the legate's ear. A man named Vitellius has arrived from Rome, and he is speaking for Gratus, who still seeks influence in Judea. Gratus wants Vitellius to be the next Syrian legate. Only Pilate seems to not know these things."

Nicodemus glances over his shoulder at the doorway. The centurion is not in hearing. He whispers.

"It was Gratus who appointed the high priests, including Caiaphas, and they live in fear of what Gratus promised: that the Zealot rebellions might lead to Jerusalem being leveled and our temple destroyed. Tiberius is not as cruel as Augustus was, or Sejanus, but Tiberius, like Pilate, may not be aware of what the left hand does. Master, you've arrived here when many seek to destroy Zealots, even the priests seek an end to rebellion. Caiaphas believes you are a good man, but he fears *anyone* now who stirs the people."

"He has sent me here to ease his fears, which are like his children, and so bear his face."

"Your words have stings that provoke your enemies, Yehoshua!"

"Where stings are, there also honey is to be found. Caiaphas would crush even the clover from whence the honey comes because he fears the sting."

"Pilate can spare you, though."

Christ looks up again from his stones. He leans forward, kisses Nicodemus first upon one eyelid, then the other. Nicodemus is moved, almost cannot continue. "Peter and I . . . we have appealed to Pilate's . . . wife." Nicodemus's voice almost cracks. "Andrew came to me saying she sympathizes with you. She will intercede with Pilate."

Jesus seems to direct his next words at *me*.

"Don't seek sympathy. Seek righteousness."

"I seek to save you!"

Jesus turns back to Nicodemus.

"Then fear not, seeker of light, for I am saved."

Nicodemus clutches his hair, and moans, stands, paces one quick circuit across the floor and back.

"They will do nothing to you until you've seen Pilate, that much is sure. He can condemn you or send you first to Herod. No use to appeal to Herod, his heart is hard. He killed your teacher, John the Sabaist."

"Then I will pray for Herod's heart, as I pray for these stones, which are also hard."

The Roman soldier returns. He says nothing, merely stands at the door, meaning Nicodemus's time is up.

Nicodemus walks by Centurion Casca, who leads him away after locking the door, finally speaking while thoughtfully scratching the stubble on his chin.

"They deserted him now that he's arrested, his twelve servants, flown to the twelve winds the lot of 'em."

Nicodemus glares at the centurion's leering smile. He glances back once at Jesus, then proceeds.

When Nicodemus has gone and the door shut, Jesus looks back again to where I would be standing, had I a body.

"You come here to free me, brother?"

"You address me?" I know he does. I'd not be able to speak otherwise.

"I've waited for you," he whispers.

"Why do you allow them to do this to you?"

"Why do you avoid it? You owe something to humanity."

"Humanity is a curiosity but nothing dear to me."

"Yet you inter into flesh and make yourself human. I was born to it, I shall rise from it, reborn of flesh and dust. You were made divine yet fall, seeking flesh and dust as your prize. You perhaps love them even more than I."

He scoops a handful of dust from the floor, lets it spill from his palm.

"Do you fear what we are to each other?" he asks.

"What are we to each other?" I ask.

He picks up a stone.

"We two are unlike all others, and so we are one."

He picks up another stone the same size, holds the two together in his palm. He closes his hand round them.

"You speak nonsense."

"Do I, brother? What of the trinity?"

"A human fantasy."

"Surely you know the Father. You know that I am the Son. What of the Holy Spirit?"

"It is nothing I have ever seen, in heaven or in the earth, nor in any of creation."

"And yet I have—many humans have, brother. If you haven't then you are even more blind than—"

"Joshua, I am not one of your disciples to be confounded by your clever sophistries. Why do you call me brother?"

"Why doesn't my brother call himself so?"

"You say nothing. Your words are witless."

"You hear nothing. Your wits are wordless."

"Tell me why you obey Anu!"

"I obey Adonai for the same reason you do. We are three, Adonai, Joshua, and you."

"I have defied him!"

"Have you? Does a small drop of rain falling from the infinite sky, taking a path away from the others, defy the cloud it came from? Or does it follow the will of heaven and earth?"

"Then you say that heaven is large, and we are small?"

Christ smiles. "Heaven," he says, "is no larger than a grain of rice."

"I was told to seek you out, to speak with you, but you either speak nonsense, or you repeat yourself."

"I speak twice what you refuse to hear the first time spoken. Our father spoke to you beside the first ocean in this world. Did you listen?"

I gesture angrily, and the jail cell, the jail, and everything around us disappear.

Christ and I are in the valley of Gehenna.

A snarling fire is kept burning eternally here for sanitation. This is a time before Joshua, the time of Judahites in exile in Babylon, and so this is *Tophet*: a blaze, hot blue and smoky orange behind him. The smell of sulfur in the air is invigorating. The dark sky is aglow with the dance of embers bursting from a deep pit containing the fire. Twelve men labor at the verge of the pit; they toss in sulfur from sacks and pour in oil from clay pots to feed the blaze, maintaining this inferno of *Geh Hinnom*.

Judeans, Galileans, Sarmatians, Greeks, and Babylonians file down the sides of a hill, carrying garbage, and fouled clothing such as was worn by butchers, now discarded. They carry the carcasses of dead animals, small, dead Judean and infants and still living, mortally ill Babylonian infants, and various many unspeakable things. Endlessly shuffling past the inferno, they all toss these things into the lake of flames. The smell of sulfur dioxide, lime, and charred flesh hangs over all.

Christ is no longer injured, he is no longer filthy. He is perfect and straight in his spirit body. He looks down at himself, the stones still clutched in his now beautiful hand, and is shocked.

"What have you done, Samael!"

"We are in Gehenna, the valley outside the gates of Jerusalem. This is the age of your beloved John's fathers, when human sacrifice was done in Judea in the way of Babylon."

"*Hinnom*! False worship!" Christ cries out. "Why do you bring me to this filthy place? Answer me, Samael!"

"No more platitudes then, 'Brother'?"

I circle around him until he is facing the fire, which is now at my back instead of his. I want him to see it.

"Will you call down bright angels to punish me, Yasu?" I taunt him, calling his spirit name, as he has called me one of mine, my angelic name, Samael'.

"Art thou fool enough," he hisses, "to think this be not one purpose given unto me? Wither the lion or the lamb, thou shalt find in me whatsoever thou seeketh, dim-ned star, sad, dim angel."

A Babylonian woman walks up to the flames and tosses a live infant into the fire. The child screeches agony and dies.

The Christ sinks to his knees as if wounded by this. "Release me!" he cries out.

"What is there between Anu and thou? What is the plan thou followeth?" I demand.

"Get thee behind me!" Christ shouts, and I feel myself snatched like a rag through spirit distance, to reappear just at his back, on my knees as well. I am in agony as he is, and both of us cry as if we ourselves are infants. He throws his arms upward, one hand clenched with the two stones still there.

"No!" I shout.

The burning is unlike anything I have ever known.

Christ staggers up, stands over me, still shivering with the same pain I feel.

"No? You bawl like the selfish soul you are but think nothing of consigning me to such suffering!"

"Your words mean nothing!"

"Then learn what lies behind my words, errant intruder!"

Again, I am snatched through spirit distance and appear upon the trash heap, in the center of the flame. I shriek, just as the infant had, but unlike the infant I do not die.

"It is sympathy you feel burning you, Samael!" Christ shouts, falling back to his knees again, I can see through the haze of flames all about me.

"It is the suffering of humanity you brought me here to feel, and that you have chosen to bequeath me! And now we will go onward upon our two courses! For we are like two ships passing—together for a moment only, and carried on to grow apart toward opposite shores."

We are in the carcery cell again.

I lie on my side, whimpering like a wounded dog. Christ sits in the dust as before, his hand is held out and is still clenched into a fist. He opens his fist, and the two stones drop to the dirt, clacking against one another and skittering apart, each rolling to an opposite end of the cell.

The Anointed One in his human body again, the wounds and blood and signs of human aging have returned to his face. He gazes at me, gives me the saddest of looks.

"You cannot bear ten minutes?" he whispers. "I have borne it every day of my life: my sympathy for them."

I roll over and slowly rise to my knees.

"You come here," he says, "to ask why I allow what they do to me? I love them, that is why. I love them just as you do."

"I do not," I whimper.

"Shut your mouth!"

I am silenced.

"We are going to two different places, brother, and I must leave you behind now, for I must rise as you fall, must sail my course abaft of you, but as you pass me I will cast the truth upon your deck. You love them because you were made to love them, even as I was made after you."

I gaze back at him but I am frozen, and can speak no more.

"You were first. Every angel is made in your image, Samael! You, meant to be guardian of this Earth, Light Bringer, Dragon of Dawn, Little Horn that Heralds Creation, Master of the Fire that feeds Man; you, to be called Prometheus."

He shakes his head, sadness burning in his eyes.

"Why do I allow these wounds, this shame, this blood on me? I allow it because you, who were chosen first, will not do it, and so it falls on me."

I struggle to speak, to flee, to strike out, to hide my face, but can do none of these. His power is more than I'd imagined. His head falls to his chest; his wet, dirty hair flops forward, hiding his face from me.

Still I cannot speak.

"Leave me, Satan. You sadden me beyond all endurance."

Suddenly, I am standing in the middle of the dessert, near the spot where I first saw him, the night I'd tempted him, appearing to him as the flame.

I am alone.

And then I am not. For I am back at *Gehenna* again and surrounded by humans filing past the orange flames. I reach out impulsively to their thoughts, seeking, yes, actually seeking closeness with them, wanting simply not to be alone. It is the same impulse I "felt" when I knew that my beloved was gone from me, and I began to seek her.

But this is far worse to me. Angels experience very intense things, my dear, let me tell you. We can pass through stars and ride elementary particles forward and backward through time, which is how I have shown you these pictures at an exhibition of history. It is given us to be able to hear human thoughts, and we can move through spirit distances instantaneously, as we are given the power to enter into anything living in Anu's creation, from plants to animals to you. Yet no angel, I now know, has ever truly *felt* the things I now realize you humans feel: complete isolation from Anu and from his creation.

Is it true that I was meant to be guardian of the Earth? Master of the spacetime? If so, why was I not told so? Has Anu hidden my purpose from me all this time?

It would be like Him to be so obtuse.

My brother intended to show me this. I don't doubt what he says, for he is after his own fashion an angel also, and unlike me incapable of lying. It is true: he is my replacement. Shall I despise him for it? Yes, I do.

Should I thank him?

I will decide that later. For now, I reach out to the humans walking through this valley. Their thoughts are dark and full of fear. I'd never understood this before. I *could* not understand fear before because it was an abstraction, something I knew you monkeys wasted a great amount of thought energies on, but nothing I could actually understand because I am an angel. But I also now truly understand pain for the first time, something else an angel cannot know.

The brief time my brother had consigned me to the flame, had made these two human feelings come into me.

Did Anu allow this? Anu must have put these same things into his angels as he'd put into you, but must have left them *unfinished* in us! Has my brother then, *finished* me?

What am I now? Angel? Human? Neither?

Now, I am not certain anymore how I returned here to Gehenna, but now I do not think my brother has sent me back here. Which leaves two alternatives: either some force unknown to me has done it or Anu sent me back here, which I do not believe, for Anu leaves a glowing emblem behind whenever he does anything. It is the ultimate artist's signature, which cannot be mistaken, and cannot be counterfeited. So I know something else now, something which Freud tried to convince me of: that I have a "subconscious."

It is *me* who has put me back here. It was me I encountered in Christ's dream, as it was me I watched seeking to revive Fadya as she lay dead upon the medical examiner's table.

I pull myself back from the dark fearful thoughts of those around the orange flame, and settle back into this feeling, of being alone. I must seek more human thoughts, but not the thoughts of these fearful, unenlightened humans who have yet to understand the nature of Anu, and still think human sacrifice is what their God or Gods want.

I want to understand how humans, particularly humans with power, react to loneliness. How they conquer it and find the strength to do what you humans do best: defy a God who would put you into his creation without protection and without power to protect your*selves* from pain, from fear.

I do have power, my dear. I can protect you, if He won't. I can lead you; I can found a new Shamayim on Earth, if it comes to it. Me, and my beloved Yazad, together. I have rebelled in Shamayim, when all I needed to do was leave, and make Shamayim here amongst you. My brother Jesus will not do it, though Judas has beseeched him to. Instead he is willing to allow himself to be killed, and his followers to suffer; willing even to allow his own mother to be punished for his righteousness!

Well, to each his own.

I watch the flames, I *smell* the sulfur and soot, and I know that I must go back to Pilate. So far, my dear, I have reported to you the feelings and even thoughts of humans I have witnessed, but for your understanding, human thoughts are like a residue. By the time I taste them, they are mostly gone, for they are the much-vaunted bosons your scientists seek to discover: particles with fleeting lives. In order to truly capture the texture and bouquet of what I am now tasting, I must watch Pilate closely indeed.

7

Claudia watches Pilate eat his goat.

They've decided on a truce, and a late dinner. She reclines on her favorite couch as she eats, but he does not favor the patrician practice, taken from the Greeks, of eating lying down. He sits on the floor upon a pillow, next to a low table where Creto, who is the last servant left, has placed his master's food.

The Preacher, already found guilty of blasphemy by the Sanhedrin, will be sent to him by morning for judgment. Pilate has given in to Claudia, telling her he plans to set the man free.

"To tell true, Claudia, I realize I still must be careful not to make mistakes such as I made in placing those banners proclaiming 'Tiberius, *Divi.*'

"Oh, Ponti!" she'd moaned, embracing him.

"My best course," he'd said, clearing his throat, "is to take no stand on this man one way or the other, but to pass him on to Herod, since he's here in Jerusalem visiting. I smell a plot that he was ever even brought to me. None of the Sanhedrin hens have clucked to take credit for it—no one seems to know how he was taken from them, but a Roman was present and put him into Roman hands."

"What will Herod do? Oh, I know it won't be in your hands then, but that's just the point: no one can blame you for what happens to the man, once you pass him on."

"Herod may do as he pleases. The man is Galilean and, thus, he is under Herod's jurisdiction. One thing, though, Claudia."

"Yes?"

"If Herod sends him back to me, then I shall have to decide. Legally I shall have to because we cannot be seen to release a man said to plot against Rome."

"Why would Herod do that? Why would he send him back?"

"Not likely, I'm just saying."

"He wouldn't do that, would he?"

"Not likely."

"Well, even if he does then you must find Jesus innocent, that's all, no matter how it makes us look!"

"Not likely he'll be sent back to me."

"Good."

He looks at Claudia as she eats grapes.

Pilate plans not to find Jesus innocent but plans simply to avoid finding him guilty.

Claudia watches her husband as he eats his goat, happy that he will do as Cicero directed her. She watches him chew, pleased with herself.

I watch Pilate closely as well.

I've seen how he believes he is better than whatever situation he finds himself in. He feels that everyone around him misunderstands, and seeks and finds his own path through their distress.

Tertilius's voice precedes him. So too do the marching boot-falls upon marble floors, of the partial cohort accompanying him. Pilate hears the voice and the soldiers' boots approaching, from the atrium through a nearby arched doorway, and I can hear his thoughts as he reflects on how satisfying it is to be reminded that at least the floors are real marble.

Tertilius enters the room almost at a trot, just ahead of six legionnaires (about $1/100^{th}$ of a cohort), and Creto, moving stiffly to favor his back where Pilate has within the hour had him whipped six lashes, comes stumbling in just behind the soldiers and Tertilius.

Tertilius has changed clothes since Pilate last saw him. It is not yet midnight, so that makes three changes of clothing in one day, more even than Claudia's average, Pilate reflects. The soldiers all look put upon; their usual expression.

Tertilius appears upset.

"Sorry to come unannounced, Prefect—"

"And unbidden," Pilate adds.

"Yes, but there were no servants to usher me. Only the slave."

"My wife has given them all a holiday for Passover."

"A holi—?"

"That religious festival they celebrate. The priests scrape off the camel dung, and wear their best gowns; the women all take command of their households and of their husbands; and the slaves and servants all are given a bloody holiday to run wild. Except Creto, of course. He's a dignified Greek. Greeks are above such things."

If it were possible, Pilate thinks, *for Tertilius's placid, vacuously handsome face to look stupefied, the look on his face right now might be stupefaction.*

Pilate laughs out loud at the thought.

"Prefect, please! There is trouble!"

Pilate lets the delicious bit of goat he had been chewing on drop to his copper platter. He wipes his mouth.

"Yes. Nothing but trouble."

"Prefect—"

"For this is Judea. Land of dirt, dung, sweat, unruly palm trees, and maddened zealots. A place of heat and sun and trouble, which is why Gratus was driven stupid by Judea."

"That's what I've come to tell you! Valerius Gratus has an agent in Judea."

"An agent?"

"By the name of Vitellius. From Rome. A man who—"

Pilate stands abruptly, turning over the table, sending delicious goat skittering across the floor; making Claudia grimace and making Creto scramble after it.

"Do-do you know this man, Prefect?"

"Bring him to me."

"He is on an errand for the Senate, as if he were a Senate legate! He has immunity—"

"To be 'as if' a legate," says Claudia, "is not the same as to be a legate."

Tertilius looks at her, speaks hastily.

"I do not think you have much to say, Lady."

Pilate draws a knife.

"What did you say to my wife?"

The centurions freeze, hands all moving by training, to their sword hilts. The captain of the fractional cohort takes a quick step away from Tertilius; his cohort follows suit. It is clear they all await a sign from Pilate, at which they will surely kill Tertilius. It's as clear to Tertilius as it is to everyone else.

"I-I apologize, Lady Claudia Procula."

"An apology on your feet's a weak apology," Claudia says sternly.

Tertilius drops to one knee, and takes a deep breath.

"Lady, I—"

"Enough, fool!" Pilate snaps. "Take these soldiers whose time you've wasted, put them to use by obeying me. Bring me Vitellius!"

"At once, Prefect!"

Tertilius scrambles up, heads for the doorway. Pilate nods to the soldiers. Then and only then do they follow him.

Both Pilate and Claudia melt with laughter as Pilate shoves the blade back into the sheath hidden beneath his robes.

Vitellius looks perturbed and confused. He's led into Pilate's library by Tertilius and a fraction of the cohort. He is shoved roughly onto a chair. Two soldiers stand on either side of him, as though—as though he were a prisoner!

He looks at Pontius Pilate seated behind a desk, piles of scrolls before him. He waits as Pilate studies him. Pilate neither speaks nor rises from his seat.

Finally, Vitellius can hold his tongue no longer.

"Why've you brought me here, Pilate? Do you truly not remember who I am? We met in Rome. You should know—"

"I know that you are a man who is far from Caesarea. You are even farther from Rome, to speak a simple fact."

"The Legate at Syria gives me authority, Haman, and I've the blessing of Gratus."

Pilate smiles at the insult of the name *Haman*.

"Yes, I know you are Gratus's boy. Gratus, the man I replaced. This was his villa, now mine. This was his province, mine now also, as is that chair you sit on. These soldiers here? Mine to command and they will cut your throat on my say so."

"I do not take your full meaning, Prefect."

"Gratus's boy. Perhaps you are also the Senate's bitch. Am I right about that as well?"

"How dare you!"

Pilate sits forward in his chair.

"Be at ease, for I do take the full meaning of *you*. I think you may be here representing the emperor himself, though I doubt it. You represent many interests short of Tiberius though, don't you?"

Vitellius's mouth is shut, his lips pressed into a hard line like a seal at the bottom of a contract.

"Yes. Many interests, some of them not even aware that they share you with one another, knowing Rome as I do, knowing how greedy men like you are," Pilate goes on. "My guess is, you've spread yourself thin. Even my friend Herod's interests, eh? In fact, I think when you're done skulking about, you'll report back to Lammia, the Legate at Syria, and then report to what's left of Sejanus's supporters in the Senate, and that you, thus, represent every fucking body's interests but mine!"

"You cannot just— I have been hand chosen to succeed Lammia someday."

"Really? Whose hand was it?"

"Figure it out, you truculent fool. I have Gratus's ear, I have immunity, and I have bona fides from Rome!"

"And do you have toenails?"

Vitellius stares. "Do I have—?"

"Toenails, man. On your fucking toes. Well, do you?"

"Why, yes!"

"Pull out two or three of this man's handpicked toenails," Pilate orders one of the soldiers, who produces a pair of small tongs from a pouch and approaches Vitellius just as the man with bona fides from Rome begins to scream in outrage and horror.

Judas approaches Malachi with a short sword, raising it to strike. This will be swift and just, he thinks.

Somewhere off in the darkness is the moist sound of a tethered camel chuffing softly. The cool night air carries the sound. In Malachi's secluded, sweet-smelling garden, Judas's sword arm, a shadow, holds still above Malachi's head.

Judas notices Malachi's defiant face while the Pharisee offers not a cry or a whimper but a self-satisfied chuckle.

"Strike, Zealot. Seal your own damnation. Kill me if you do not fear leaving your dry bones as testament to your soul forever wandering the valley of Gehenna, denied Ezekiel's vision, as all thugs are so denied."

Judas lowers the sword from the sticking point and spits at Malachi's feet.

"Ezekiel's vision," he says, "is of my Master! The resurrection of David *is* Jesus, who is the resurrection of my dry bones and yours and the healing of the broken gate."

I am proud of Judas. He is a man of action yet has depths in him, depths which no doubt Jesus has noticed.

"You have an interpretation, Sicari?" Malachi scoffs. "I'd thought the Sicarii had only knives without thoughts. Aren't you an arrogant one, Iscariot. And so you will suffer all the more."

"Yes, you are right about me. But what about you? Yeshua exposed you as one of the false teachers Jeremiah warned of. Against God's prophets have such as you always kindled the fires of persecution, Malachi. Yeshua exposed you."

"Did he? You thought the magician's bladder of tricks your master emptied on me at the Temple porch has dampened the scroll of truth in *me*? You invoke Jeremiah like a child with a new tongue, but the authority of God is mine from the mouth of David. Jehovah's word given to Izrael at Sinai is written in me—I am the book of the Prophets. You are not *Hamaccabi*. If *Yehuda Hamaccabi* returns, and if the Moshiach appears, I will know because the word will wake me in my bed. It will have nothing to say to you."

"Then you're a fool, Malachi, for the Mosiach has come, and he is in the Fortress of Antonia because you do not see."

"Then why haven't you struck me down?"

"I *should* kill you. Many of my brother Sicarii would. From what I know of the Zealots, they still might."

"That won't free your master, who preaches that you should love me not kill me, Sicari. Your master must have thought he could change even an assassin." Malachi leans against the low stone wall of a well and waits.

Judas resheaths his sword beneath a fold of his robes. He wraps his arms around himself and moans.

"Ah, then Yehoshua has performed at least one true miracle, hasn't he? He's reformed an assassin thug. Tell me then, if not to kill me, why have you come back, *Yehuda*?"

"You betrayed us, Malachi."

"I gave you fifteen pieces of Rome's silver."

"Why do you deal in Roman coins, not shekels? Where did you get them from?"

Malachi ignores the question.

"I made certain his trial took place openly, at Annas's home. A crowd came, but your people didn't. Where were they? Did you give them the coins?"

"Andrew took them, for weapons, but was arrested."

"I had nothing to do with that. I did what you asked me to do, no more, no less. Is Andrew held in the fortress?"

"He escaped before they took him there."

"Plots within your plots. How did he escape?"

"Lady Claudia Procula freed him."

"Did she! Well, he possesses a handsome face."

"This is no joke, old man!"

"No, young man, it isn't! Yeshua says he is the son of God, he is *qaneh*—like David, the stalk, the reed. Is he?"

"He is the stalk of heaven."

"He should call on angels to free him then, neh? Don't bristle. I speak frankly, not cruelly. Why hasn't he?"

This, more than all else Malachi says, puzzles Judas, that Jesus seems unwilling to act. Yet he remains true to Jesus. What is it you crabs say your faith is? Belief in things not yet seen? What an ambitious thought for a crab to have.

The old man's challenge kills the sword in Judas's sheath, and kills the sword in his heart. Malachi has disarmed him. Yes, such is Judas's greatest weakness: he *thinks*. HA!

"Or perhaps he can raise King David from the dead."

"Have care, Malachi, I still might kill you!"

"You've killed Yeshua with your blundering, Judas. *You* betrayed him. If you want sympathy, you've come to the wrong place. If Yehuda leads a choir of angels, I will follow and believe. Nor should you have failed to save him. I don't relish seeing him crucified."

Malachi bends, eases down on to one stiff knee, pries away a stone at the base of the well. Inside the hole behind the stone are silver coins. Malachi extracts them, and replaces the stone.

"The Sanhedrin say you've earned another fifteen pieces, for you did in fact lead us to him."

Malachi offers them upon his palm.

Judas stares at the silver coins glinting in moonlight and slaps them out of Malachi's hand. They scatter upon the ground.

"He was a danger," Malachi grunts, "and so are you and the Zealots even now to think we can fight Romans without angels."

"Why did you help me? You knew the silver was to pay for weapons to free Jesus and raise rebellion."

"Which I thought would fail, even if I hoped it would succeed, and upon failure the Romans would have their scapegoats—Zealots would be blamed. Gratus is secretly in Caesarea, watching through his spies. Syrian Legate, Lammia will order a purge at the next serious sign of Zealot rebellion. In case you don't know. With rebellion in their laps, Pilate and Herod might be ordered finally to kill every Zealot, and this I ask of God!"

"How do you know this can happen? The same way you possess Roman silver?"

"Let the Zealots be purged and the people be spared. You would be blamed. God willing, you will be still! Zealots blamed and Jesus arrested. The People will be saved."

"How can you believe and give your heart to so many opposing creeds!"

"How can you wager the lives of those who follow you, Judas, with nothing more than faith as armor?"

"You are a priest!"

"Exactly."

"And he will be crucified."

"What business is it of the Sanhedrin? Not me, the Sanhedrin, I say."

"You are Sanhedrin."

"I am a servant of God, not of men."

"You just declared yourself protector of your people."

"This is why I urge you to not seek to interpret holy script, boy. You haven't a head for it. The Sanhedrin only wished him silenced. Annas and Caiaphas didn't stone him, as is the council's right to punish blasphemy! Only Romans can crucify a Judhite by law. The man may be mad, but the scribes and the elders have told that he is of the line of David. They would not have the blood of David on *our* hands. If he's crucified, it's not our doing."

"You old men mincing God's laws."

"You young men squatting in desert caves. Yes, I supported your rebellion, for I support killing Romans and failing that I support your self-destruction. Take your silver there. Go raise Zealot dogs to attack the Antonia fortress, if you wish to save your dusty Nazarene."

"I did not want this to happen!"

"And yet you made it so. None on the council sought his death, even though he disrespects the High Priests in public. Half of them consider him mad, and thus to be whipped, cast aside, and ignored, under God's laws. Do you know why he ended up in the fortress? One of Lammia's men, an equestrian, was outside my house as your master was led away to be put upon a mule and banished. The Roman had his own men among us, and those men took Jesus."

"Who were these men?"

"Temple soldiers. I knew them not. They beat him as he was questioned by Pharisees. They chained him—that was not what the Sanhedrin ordered."

"The Romans are behind this!"

"And what are they not behind? Every rock is placed where they want it to be. Every loaf of bread hides Roman spies. Are you four days old? Did you not know Romans were watching him, me, you, and the sun? They conspire against Pilate. They hope Pilate will provoke violence with a public trial. Between them and the Zealots, we are all just pawns."

Judas's mouth is dry. His chest feels bound. Malachi's voice grows soft, almost pitying in its mockery. "If he is crucified by the Romans, it will be because of you. The Zealots talk of treason against Rome. Jesus is suspected of being a Zealot."

Judas takes a step back from Malachi's voice.

"It is you, Judas," Malachi murmurs softly, "who put him into Rome's hands. You are the stone cast to kill Jesus. Do you know Nebuchadnezzar's dream, Iscariot?"

Judas can still see the Pharisee's teeth in the darkness as he speaks, but nothing else, for the moon has slipped behind a cloud.

"He dreamt of an idol. A gold-headed statue. There was a stone not cut by any hand, from out of a mountain. The stone shattered the statue."

"I am not that stone," Judas manages to hiss in a dry throat.

"But you are, son. And mad Jesus is the idol in the dream. God means to stand his kingdom to last for eternity. Jesus stood only until destroyed by you. His are a head of gold, body of silver, legs of iron, but feet of clay, and the clay feet are broken by the stone. I did not plan for you to be the one to be that stone and so I pity you. Good rest to you, Iscariot."

Malachi turns and walks off toward his house, treading over the coins without ever looking at them again, obviously contemptuous of them, leaving Judas to gaze at them and to shiver in the sweet night air, which though sweet, is growing colder.

Those who've come are gathered at the entrance of the cell, like old women huddled at a fish stall. They carry swords and wear leather armor yet are as if naked. I, myself, keep a safe distance for I've no wish to be cast back into the flame. I'm in shadow, paces away, watching from what I hope is a safe remove.

He emerges from the cell into the dim, musty corridor, smelling of flint and smoke from torch flame. His hands are bound in front of him. The Roman soldiers, two temple soldiers of the Sanhedrin, a shadowy Roman equestrian who does not speak, soldiers, and a priest of the Pharisees who has come with them all and follow from behind.

All follow Yehoshua as if he leads them rather than being under arrest. He still has the two stones clutched in one hand, and he walks with calm, regal steps. Each step is numbered now, and he is counting them down, I can tell. He knows the number and knows the place the last step will carry him to.

He ignores me utterly when he passes me where I hide.

Micah gazes at the silver coins Judas has handed him. Yemaiah, his second, stands with a knife in her hand, just behind Micah under the spreading branches of trees on the Mount of Olives. They stand beside an olive press. Yemaiah as always is looking about, keeping alert for spies.

Micah elbows Yemaiah and shows her the glinting coins; the head of a man embossed upon the soft metal.

"It's Tiberius," Yemaiah observes, then goes back to looking about nervously.

Micah spits into his own palm, sullying the coins, before casting them at Judas's feet.

Judas looks at where they lay.

"How can you touch filthy Roman silver, brother?"

"How can we get weapons without money!" Judas cries out.

"Well, you gave the disciple Andrew cursed Roman coins. He got no weapons, did he?"

"He made contact with your blacksmith, who betrayed Andrew to Temple guards. Those guards were spies of Rome who handed him to Pilate's man, Tertilius!"

"We've dealt with the blacksmith, the silver was melted down to be put to use, and his throat has been cut, be assured. There are traitors among us."

"I am seeking each of them out," grunts Yemaiah.

Judas stares at her.

"Don't be fooled by the fact that she is a woman. Yemaiah is good at finding traitors," Micah sniffs. "And she is good at cutting their throats."

"Andrew was beaten," Judas hisses, "yet he gave them no information about you."

"We know. He is in hiding with the Preacher's mother, some of his followers, and some shits from Bethpage who've got shekels aplenty. If he *had* betrayed us, we would deal with him too, and you, Sicarian."

"The plan would have worked."

"Maybe. I held my people back because they would have been slaughtered once they had your man inside that fortress. Now you come again with more coins, still no weapons, and you ask us this time not just to fight the Romans in the streets of Jerusalem, but to attack the Antonia Fortress? We are Zealots, not madmen."

"Jesus will be crucified!"

"Are the Sicarii in Galilee nothing but sentimental old women with knives? Stop your weeping! One man is nothing. You said he *seeks* death. Let him have it."

"He is a child of David, as you are!"

"David, is it? Interpretation, you are giving me? Are you Sicarian or a priest? Yes, under David we were fruitful, we gave the Romans many slaves, as it turns out."

"Do you not wish to save Jeshua who is the true disciple of John?" Judas pleads.

"*Yohanna.* Now there was a man I could believe in," says Micah wistfully.

"The Sabaist led us away from the priests, thank God!" exclaims Yemaiah.

"Jesus had some of the Sabaist in him, all right," Micah concedes. "Such shit Jesus caused with his preaching. The people like him. Maybe his death will cause some movement among them. Maybe it will wake their asses up."

"Jesus must not die!"

"Why?" Yemaiah hisses, "Because you feel guilty?"

"He is the son of God!"

Both Yemaiah and Micah laugh humorlessly. Yemaiah sheaths her knife. "Then you can call on angels to save him," Yemaiah chuckles.

"The angels have their own swords, I am certain of it," grunts Micah as he turns to walk back into the dense stand of olive trees, Yemaiah following.

Judas stares down at the coins left there in the dirt.

The morning light shows Pilate many things.

It shows him that a crowd has gathered in the courtyard of the fortress. He has ordered the gates opened to them and though the soldiers are nervous, he agrees with Claudia's suggestion: let the people witness what happens. Let them feel a part of it. Let them even feel implicated in it, then send the Preacher straight back to Herod.

Pilate leans over the rail of the balcony to see how far the crowd extends. He has never been out in this balcony before. His visits to Jerusalem are usually spent in the villa. There are perhaps seven hundred Jerusalemites gathered. Roman soldiers, local temple guards, and a few religious police stand at the edges of the crowd to keep order. He has just announced to the crowd that Jesus of Nazareth will be judged. To his surprise, half the crowd seems to have been calling for death.

He reenters a stone room just off the balcony, the hard floors under his soft but firm-heeled sandals are floors unsoftened by any carpet, and meets Claudia as she enters. The two of them exit into a hall leading to a small room full of soldiers gathered around Vitellius, who sits on a chair, bloody foot wrapped in bandages.

"Do you know why they want this man's death?"

"There are many in the crowd sent by the Sanhedrin, and many more were paid to shout against your prisoner and for Barabbas, Prefect."

"Paid? Who paid them? And who in the name of Mars's ass is Barabbas?"

"I paid them. With Gratus's coin. It was assumed you would judge all the disciples, and judge Judas, as Zealots. Gratus wants any Zealots operating here dead."

"Who is this Judas I keep hearing of whom my people say delivered the Yehuda fellow into my court?"

"Judas Iscariot is a Zealot as well as a follower of the Preacher. It was he who led handpicked Pharisees to the Preacher. He took temple guards to where he was caught. Something went wrong, for all of the followers were to be arrested, not just the Preacher."

"So Yehuda was betrayed by those close to him. I know what that is like." Pilate glares at Vitellius.

"Lords—" Vitellius begins but Pilate silences him.

"You come into my province, plot, bribe my Judeans, aid a man no longer in authority here. You are displeasing to me, Vitellius."

"I can send to have those who've been paid removed from the crowd, Dominus, though many of them still will want Judas crucified for betraying the preacher."

"And then I shall have less of a crowd to perform this show before."

"I-"

"Be at ease. They can serve my purposes now, these people you've planted in the crowd; and you can serve me now too. I let you keep the rest of your toenails, and the toes they came with because you have information. Remember that."

"And you should remember, Prefect: you let a Zealot who conspired to buy weapons and raise rebellion slip through your fingers. You let the Zealots plant a spy in your household, and she too, has escaped. The Nazarene has been condemned even by his own priests."

"Yes, yes. Thank you. Now what of this Barabbas?"

"A common thief you have in your carcery. He is to be crucified. But on Passover, by custom, the Prefect may see fit to release a prisoner, sparing him from death. Gratus did so on every Passover."

"It would create good will, Ponti," suggests Claudia.

"It would please me to send you to Golgotha instead of the Preacher Yeshua, Vitellius."

"You may abuse and torture me, Prefect, but if you kill me, the Senate would—"

"Yes, I know. They would recall me. Perhaps that is not so bad a thing, though my next posting will no doubt be someplace even worse. No doubt you will ultimately be next legate and remove me anyway. Well, I shall give Rome a scapegoat, don't worry. Where is this Judas Iscariot?"

"In hiding, no doubt."

"What will you do, Ponti?" asks Claudia. "You cannot condemn Jesus!"

"Worry not, wife. I will spare him. I will crucify this Judas instead. Isn't that what Rome wants? Kill the Zealots?"

Pilate leaves Vitellius and Claudia to walk back to the stone room, also now full of soldiers. He approaches The Preacher, who has been beaten about a bit since he was sent over to Herod and then sent back here. Pilate sits down on the edge of a trunk which has been left in the center of this room; some of Gratus's left-over possessions inside, perhaps.

The Preacher stands still and lithe as a young cypress, hands manacled, his face bloodied, robe dirty, but patient and passive for all that.

"Preacher, are you the son of a god? Are you king of the Judahites?"

"If I am a king, my kingdom is not of this world. If I were the son of God, not of Man, my angels would lie low my accusers."

"Then you are neither a king nor the son to a god."

"If I am king, or were God, I would not seek followers, for all who love truth follow me already. I would not call my angels to me, for those angels would be angry at my treatment. They would lay waste many human lives."

"Where is Judas?"

Christ hesitates.

Aha. Pilate leans forward, speaks insistently now.

"Listen to me, Preacher, you may not know. Judas escaped while you were taken."

Yeshua makes no response to this other than to nod his awareness of it.

"My wife says to me that in a dream, she was told that I must not condemn you. Yet powerful people want me to condemn someone today. Are you a Zealot?"

"No."

"I believe you. You seem educated—you don't much look, act, or talk like a Zealot, who are wearisome in their prattle and their dogma. Those jackals will spit the last blood out of their dying mouths to spray their cult ravings in your face."

At this, a Roman centurion nearby laughs. Pilate glares at the soldier who clears his throat and stands to rigid attention. Pilate turns back to Yehoshua.

"You seem rational, Preacher. That's a rare trait in these climes. Is Judas Iscariot a Zealot?"

Christ does not respond.

I like this monkey Pontius Pilate's mind. He is slow to act, but devious, dangerous, and effective in his actions once he has determined to do something.

"Come now, Preacher. I've the power to spare you from crucifixion. You should answer me."

"I love Judas."

"Hah! It was he who led your enemies to you!"

"Yet he is not my enemy, and I forgive him."

"I have been told he is a Zealot. I would rather crucify him and set you free, for you have not offended me. Where is Judas?"

"He hides beneath a tree, on the Mount of Olives just above the road to Bethpage. There you'll find him."

Tears spring into the Preacher's eyes.

Pilate motions to the same soldier, still at attention and sweating in his distress. It is Casca Longinus from the carcery, who has come up into the light to help bring the prisoner here. He is happy to be out of the catacombs, and eager to carry out any charge to atone for his earlier mirth. He strides directly out of the stone room to gather a fractional cohort of three to accompany him on his mission.

"You have made a wise choice, Preacher," Pilate hums happily. "All will be served by this. When Judas is in my hands, I shall free you. My advice is that you leave Jerusalem. You'll be the safer for leaving, for these people are not to be trusted."

"I will be gone from Jerusalem by nightfall, and shall return in three days in new raiment."

"You have money hidden away, then. That is wise. I urge you to be gone longer than three days, however."

The Preacher says nothing nor does he raise his manacled hands to wipe away his tears.

Casca gazes up into the branches of the cypress, shielding his eyes from the sun. Several Jerusalemites who are under the employ of Vitellius and of Pilate himself, have accompanied the Roman soldiers as guides and to verify that the man they have found is Judas Iscariot.

They verify that this is the Judas who had betrayed Jesus.

Casca scratches his chin thoughtfully, for it is exactly as the Preacher had told, and they have found Judas here. He is indeed beneath a tree, on the Mount of Olives just above the road that leads to Bethpage. His corpse is hanging from one of the highest branches, swinging slowly in the already hot wind.

The creaking of the rope is a strange noise in the quiet stand of cypresses.

Only the wind can be heard, otherwise.

Pilate's hand is forced.

With Judas dead, and with word from Herod just arrived, that Herod refuses to see Jesus again, it falls upon Pilate to crucify some fucking body to justify having tortured Vitellius, having lost track of Andrew, and for having failed to know the Zealots had a spy inside his very house, close to his sleeping wife. He paces back and forth before the condemned man.

"Help me! Can you tell me where any of the rest of them are?"

"They are here in Jerusalem, and here most of them shall stay, long after you are called back to Rome, and sent into exile."

Pilate glares.

"I do not plan to go into exile, Preacher. I am building a villa in Rome for my retirement."

"You will never live there. You will be banished for your crimes by Emperor Caligula."

"Caligula! Are you mad? Tiberius is emperor."

"Tiberius will die at Capri before you can reach Rome."

Pilate leans down close to Jesus's face, whispers into his ear.

"You don't make much of a diviner, Preacher. What 'crimes' would banish a loyal citizen?"

Jesus whispers back at him.

"You have no cause to fear, for none in Rome will ever realize your cousin was an assassin of Julius Caesar."

Pilate jerks back from Jesus, shoots glances at the soldiers in the room near a corner.

"They did not hear us," says Jesus calmly.

"By the gods! By Mars's ass!"

The commander of the cohort, Casca, speaks up.

"Prefect! What are your wishes?"

"Get Vitellius in here! Drag him if he cannot walk!"

They do indeed drag the poor fellow with bona fides and little else to stand on now; his right foot certainly fails him, thus he is dragged, screaming objection, and thrown to the stone floor between Pilate and Jesus.

Claudia comes in and stands nearby, alarmed.

"You bastard! You know this man, do you not!?"

Vitellius, his foot now freshly bleeding, rolls over onto his back and peers up at Jesus.

"Isn't it the Preacher? The one whom Judas betrayed."

"But isn't he also part of your plot against *me?*"

"What? He is not—there is no plot against you, Prefect! He is a Judahite! I've never spoken to him!"

"What say you, Centurion Casca?"

Casca is newly alarmed and does what he always does when terrified by the attention of the powerful—he comes to attention.

"I've been told of you, Casca Longinus. It's said you had a bit of the diviner in you when you fought on the North frontier. You could tell when the barbarians were lying?"

Casca is almost confused, that Pilate addresses him, that Pilate even knows who he is.

"At ease, Centurion!"

Casca relaxes, though not completely.

"Is Vitellius lying to me?"

It is true, his commanders on the north frontier had fallen into the habit of asking Casca to divine liars among the barbarians. It had been an easy enough task, for he had only to look into their wild eyes. The eyes tell it. It was something any man can do, Casca had mused, but perhaps he *was* better at it than most. Scratching thoughtfully at his chin, Casca speaks.

"Pardon me saying it, sir," says our centurion ever so chastely, scratching, scratching his chin, "But you'd as well ask if a leaking boat has got one *particular* hole in it. That man's so full of lies he is, till there's no use asking if he's lying at one thing."

Pilate gazes a moment at Casca and all in the room wait silently for whatever comes next, as if to hope the soldier's simple words have somehow brought Pilate to his senses.

But no. Pilate wheels around to badger Christ again.

"Preacher! Divine for me that man Vitellius's future!"

Christ gazes down at Vitellius, then looks away.

"Well? What do you see?"

"This man will be the next Legate of Syria."

"Ahhh, Vitellius! So the Preacher knows your plot! You've paid him!"

"I have no plans! I merely obey Rome and obey Lammia."

"And Valerius Gratus, as you've admitted, true?"

Vitellius makes no reply, for this much of Pilate's harangue is true.

A darkness comes over Pilate's aspect. His eyes grow cold and bright. Several soldiers grow tense. After long years of serving power, they are all of them adept at measuring the falling temperature in a room where power rants and then grows cold and next unleashes them all.

Casca's gaze wanders away from the spectacle of Pilate's tantrum, and strays toward where I would be standing were I in possession of legs and of a body to put them on. His eyes hesitate, almost as if he sees me. Yet he certainly cannot see any sign of an angel! Is there perhaps a bit of the true diviner in him, as Pilate has said? He opens his mouth, as if he were about to alert all of my presence.

I quickly move beside him in spirit form and show myself to him in just a flash, a moment less than a human mind can know, but it has shed some of my light upon him, and awed him, then almost as instantly, shut him up. I have illuminated him. I do not know what it will do to him ultimately, but for now it has wiped from his mind all memory of me, even the subconscious memories I suspect had been accumulating in his mind, about to lead to his actually seeing me! He is indeed a special monkey, this Casca.

"Husband!"

Pilate, Casca, and every other human eye in the room were jolted to her direction as Pilate glances at his wife.

"Claudia, this is state business."

"Where is Judas?"

"Judas is dead, wife! And we have plots upon us like lice, like mites on a camel's head! But I am equal to the shave and cleansing that must be done. Casca! Attend me!"

Pilate draws his knife and points it at Vitellius, gestures Casca to follow him. Casca pulls Vitellius up by an arm, shoves him behind Pilate out onto the balcony.

The crowd shouts, screams, seems fit to go mad.

"Jerusalem! I, Pilate, your Prefect beseech you to help me judge!"

The crowd cheers, then grows silent as a stone garden.

Pilate puts his blade to Vitellius's throat. He is the gardener, and this is the harvest.

"This Roman wishes to destroy your temple, as his master, Valerius Gratus, once your tormentor, many times promised to!"

Some jeers in the crowd, and cheers, calls for Vitellius's death, but a third of them are silent.

Pilate shoves Vitellius back in, and the man tumbles to a corner, now besmeared with the blood from his foot, moaning. He sinks onto the cold floor and is still.

"It is as the bastard has said," Pilate snarls at Casca. "He has paid off some of the crowd out there. They will not denounce him as one. Bring the Preacher."

Casca returns to Jesus and motions to other soldiers. They shove Jesus out onto the balcony.

"Husband! What are you doing!"

Pilate no longer has ears for her. He can only see and can only hear the crowd below.

"This man is accused and condemned by your Pharisees, but I find no guilt in him! It is your Passover, and you may ask me to free a prisoner to spare crucifixion! Shall I free the Preacher, Jesus?"

"Barabbas! Give us Barabbas!"

Here and there in the crowd are voices shouting to "Spare Jesus!" but they are matched by voices shrieking "Spare Barabbas" and then quite a few who shout for Jesus are suddenly struck upon with staves and with fists, as thugs and agents of Gratus beat them into silence.

Claudia, wild-eyed and crazed, from her look, is now upon the balcony, looking down into the crowd. She sees Peter, out at the front, shouting out to free Jesus. Beside him is a woman. Someone in the crowd strikes the woman upon the back with a stick. She falls.

Claudia rushes off the balcony and out of the stone room, and away. Casca and three other soldiers follow, alarmed at her demeanor, meaning to protect their mistress.

∞∞

Peter bends to help Mary to her feet. The two of them struggle farther forward, to escape the press of the crowd and to flee the flurry of staves that suddenly land like rain upon the citizens at the front who are crying out to "Free Jesus!"

"Peter! Protect yourself!" shouts Mary. "You are the rock of the church!"

Peter ignores her words and covers her with his arms and his back, as a new drumbeat of blows fall upon them from somewhere behind. The long staves seem to have appeared from nowhere; they had been held by many at the edges of the crowd and at the precise moment needed, are being passed inward and forward into the hands of the thugs and agents who use them to fulfill the plan of this performance.

"Shut up, and call for Barabbas to be freed, Zealot!" shouts a thugs as he thrashes an old man who has walked all night from Bethany to see Christ, whom he was told had ridden into Jerusalem on a mule in triumph. This is what he has found instead upon arriving this morning with his wife and three grown sons: madness.

"Barabbas, give us Barabbas!"

Out of the doors of the fortress comes Claudia Procula, and Peter sees her. Procula runs out onto the porch closely followed by Casca and other soldiers, and next she runs to the stairs leading down into the crowd in the courtyard. She carries a wooden bowl. The soldiers follow, fearing for her, Peter can tell, as she enters the shouting, roiling crowd.

Just then, Peter sees to his left a tall Samarian with drawn knife—a Sicarean, from the look of the knife. The Sicarean pushes forward and looks as though he means to kill Peter and Mary. Peter puts himself between the man and the mother of the Christ but cannot break free of the tangle of arms; the crowd around them holds them fast.

Then Claudia, who has rushed down, is in the midst of those arms. Water from the wooden bowl she bears sloshes over the silken sleeves of the fine blouse that covers her arms. She presses her way to Mary, and the soldiers are behind her, Casca last, to clear a path with their leather-armored bodies. Casca forces people aside with his broad arms while Claudia and Mary escape back up onto the porch stairs. Casca once again seems to cast his gaze upon me, where I am watching in the crowd!

Peter tries to follow Mary into the space made by the soldiers' passage back to the stairs. The Sicarean is frustrated, held back, and cannot reach Peter, except by stretching his arm, straining with the knife. In this way, he will at least get one good stab at Peter, as Peter finds he cannot follow Mary and Claudia all the way to the stairway.

But Peter sees a short, stocky man with a long thin goatee, dressed in a white robe, who lunges to strike the Sicarean's arm, causing the man to drop the knife. It is Malchus, whose ear Peter had sliced away the night before. Malchus then pushes forward to throw one arm around Peter's shoulder and to push the two of them through, moving them in close behind Claudia and Mary and the Roman soldiers, up the stairs, onto the porch, and out of the crowd.

Even the wild crowd dares not climb these stairs, for standing at the door to the fortress are ten more soldiers armed with sword and pilum held ready to stab and skewer miscreants. This porch is legally Roman territory.

Peter stares at Caiaphas's servant. He looks at the side of the guardsman's head and sees the ear is there, unharmed, as real as it had looked in the firelight the moment before Peter had struck it away with his sword.

Upon the stairs, Claudia is taking a cloth from the bowl and wiping Mary's face. Above, the voice of Pilate can be heard, echoing in the courtyard even above the cries of the crowd.

"I wash my hands of this man's fate! Centurions! Take him to be lashed, and then, to be crucified!"

Mary is stricken. She looks up into the face of the dark Roman woman who has pulled her from the crowd and who has brought soldiers with her to hold the madness back. The dusky woman, whom Mary now sees is the wife of Pilate, has tears in her eyes!

Then Mary feels the cool water from the cloth run across her face, and feels the cloth, softer than any she can remember upon her skin. This Roman woman, Claudia Procula seeks to ease Mary's pain, for now.

III. IN TREATMENT

8

Spread cruciform upon a metal cross, his small arms were stretched to extreme extension. His feet were drawn together beneath him, a small nail head of silver showing at the surface of the foot on top, the other foot also nailed in place beneath the first.

I realized that I was seeing the tiny figure from a sidewise angle. It hung around the neck of a fellow soldier who lay beside me in the foxhole, dead. The crucifix round his neck was caught in place by the button on the dead man's uniform. I sat up, with my hips nearly submerged beneath cold, muddy water in the bottom of the hole.

The spring sun was just coming up at the horizon, and the field before me was not yet completely illuminated, yet already I could see the tortured earth, the man-sized chunks of mud torn up and flung about recently by some hundred passing motor tanks, and the shattered barbed-wire fences strewn across the otherwise empty ground. It looked like the farthest thing from spring.

I stood. I found my rifle, picked it up, and slung it over my shoulder. I crawled up the slope of the hole to the surface, and made my way stumblingly over the tortured ground, toward the gnarled, scorched stump of the remains of a tree. There, I'd seen you fall the night before.

When I got to you, you were dead, my dear.

I crouched down to go through your pockets and searched the pouch that still hung at your side, wherein I found the notes-book you'd been scribing with. The cover bore the print of big French block letters spelling out *Sympathie Pour Moi* in French.

It was a bit of a surprise that you had not titled it, *Sympathie Für Mich* but of course you'd been a teacher of some sort before the war, and in your mind it was respectful to the dead Frenchman whose desk you'd stolen this scribe's book from to write in his language.

If only the Kaiser were as attentive to human regret.

The book's pages were stained with water, dirt, gasoline, and blood, but the dark ink marks of your handwriting, in a steady, educated hand, were legible still upon each page.

I tucked it into my own pouch, along with your stolen fountain pen and a bottle of ink you'd purloined from Anu knows where. The Italian writing on the label implied it had not been taken from the dead Frenchman.

Next, I took the rope from your pack you had carried all those miles and took a metal stake you had tucked away in there. They would be needed for my task. I packed these essential things away. I adjusted my shoulder straps so that the pack and rifle hung easily across my back with the pouch secure against my hip. I looked down at your corpse, killed by the sniper I had escaped the night before, when I dashed for the hole after you'd fallen.

I contemplated raising you from death, but then, I had what I needed and decided I would finish the writing on my own. I decided I would address the writing to you, in fact, as I am now doing; a sort of tribute to your companionship, which I'd grown to appreciate.

I stood, adjusted my rifle, and began to walk, westward, the direction you and I had been walking for two weeks. We had walked out of the war together, you and I, passing through many battlefields where fighting still raged, but unnoticed in our passage. Finally, we'd reached this portion of country where the battles were over with, the armies passed on, east of us, with only the torn ground, dead animals, and human body parts to signify past violence; otherwise, a sweet silence that alone signals the end of battle. All that, and the utter absence of life in this false spring, was notable—no birds, butterflies, or trees, no flowers, not even any moss left living in this land. It was ironic that it had been some lone, perhaps insane sniper to kill you and almost killed me, here where the war no longer existed but where he apparently could not accept the end of it.

It wasn't long before I found him; he was lying only a hundred yards away, on his stomach, with a high-powered rifle-and-scope hugged to his chest, breathing painfully, with his legs crushed beneath the waist. It looked as if a tank had run over them. He had fired his last few shells at us, and then had lain there all night in the hole, looking up at the stars, now at the clouds, waiting.

He said nothing, but his eyes told me he did not mind my finding him and putting him out of his misery.

Because it was indeed spring, the walking was difficult. The ground was thawing, it was soft and wet in places. I had to climb ridges of mud and traverse valleys of fouled water across the wounded land. I was not far now from my destination though, and there were no other living bodies about for me to indulge in taking.

I felt no desire to flash about in spirit form, although I could have. Spirit travel is actually not as precise nor as pleasant an action as you might think, dear; not when travelling on land to reach a specific place. I did not abandon my human form and continue in spirit form to cross spirit distance and put myself there in an instant. I'd been maintaining human form all along for your sake, and now that you were dead, I suppose I kept it up in honor of you.

Yes, I had made no effort to keep you with me. After all, I had no reason to assume you would even have wanted me to raise you from death. I had never gotten your opinion on the subject one way or the other. Perhaps you'd have resented my doing such a thing to you. It was enough for me now that I still could talk to you like this through writing.

The landscape began to look vaguely familiar to me now. At night, I could see by the stars' positions in the sky that I was where I once had been in the time of Augustus. Last night, lying on the ground in the remains of a stable, I'd sensed that I was lying in roughly the same area where my tent had stood in the marching camp where I had set out with Drusalla, carrying a length of rope with me on that long ago night when she had assumed I planned to hang her.

When I finally arrived here and now at the exact place I sought, I was amused to see, as I broke out my trench shovel from the backpack and unfolded it, that where there had once been a dense forest, two thousand years ago, now there was a marsh beside a shattered road. The land was flat from horizon to horizon with not a trace of a tree to be seen, not even dead ones.

I used my trench shovel to hammer the stake into the ground. I then tied one end of the rope to it. The ground was soft; both marshy and warming, with the end of winter. The stake had been easy to drive in, but then had pierced solid, frozen ground—a good thing for my purpose, and I had angled it away from me so that the rope should be anchored securely. Portions of ground, particularly the spot I was drawn to, were particularly soft and warm.

At least the digging might go easily.

I removed most of my uniform. I was naked from the waist up. I relaced my boots so that the laces were tight and the boots would not squirm. I set my legs in a wide stance, took the tool in hand, and started to dig, knowing that all alone and working with a small army entrenching tool would take me at least three days of steady digging to reach the depth I sought. I realized now also that the ground being wet, I was hoisting shovels full of moist soil that would probably eventually turn into mud, making each shovel stroke heavier to bear.

This was going to seriously exhaust, and maybe even physically damage, the body I was in.

But then bodies, after all, are replaceable things. Over the years of occupying human bodies, I had grown accustomed to the inconveniences of pain, of fatigue, of the cold, and had even grown to accept such severe distractions as broken bones and deep flesh wounds. I would come to be able to tolerate the torture of having those wounds inadequately irrigated and sewn together by awkward army field surgeons who offered only whiskey as disinfectant and anesthetic. This adaptation to the human condition was one of the many things that had happened to me in my sojourn on Earth, and much of that adaptation had come because of my time as a foot soldier in this, the war you optimistically called "WWI."

On my second day of digging, a lone figure appeared at the cloudy horizon. It was clearly a soldier, from the outline of him, carrying a rifle and backpack not unlike my own. I spied him over the lip of the hole I was in as I stood straight up to stretch and to rest the tired muscles of the body I wore. I hauled myself up out of the hole with the rope, and I sat upon the cold muddy ground and waited.

In a quarter hour, he had arrived.

He was a Frenchman, or at least he was dressed in a French uniform, which was plain to see. When he spoke, his French was city French, not *provencal* and so I reasoned he was likely a volunteer, not a recruit, being from the city. Yet there was something a bit off about that accent.

"Salut, mon ami. Paix à vous."

"Salut," I responded. "Oui, c'est pacifique ici. Je n'irai pas faire la guerre avec vous," I said, letting him know I had no desire to make war on him.

"Just so. You are German, no?"

"You see what I have on, of a uniform."

"Bah. A uniform, this means nothing out here now. I have encountered many a poor bastard farmer who has lost everything, wearing uniforms taken off corpses."

I watched him, but said nothing.

"They have lost family, farmland, home, scrawny chickens, and all, including clothing. They strip the bodies of the fallen and wear the uniforms to keep warm as they wander the dead countryside. Your German crime of 'scorched earth'."

"I've seen much, but I haven't seen such a thing as that," I told him.

"You will before you get back to your *Allemagne*." He scratched thoughtfully at his bearded chin. Spat upon the ground, and spoke again through squinted eyes. "*Dites moi*, what is it, this hole you dig?"

"I seek something that belongs to me."

"Well, obviously not a fallen comrade, since in this particular war, the corpses are left to lie on the ground and only valuable things are given a grave."

"You know of other wars, do you?"

"*Oui*, many. Each is particular yet in most ways no different than any before it, you know?"

"Yes, I do know."

"Which is why I doubt you have buried a corpse or seek a corpse. Is it stolen gold, perhaps gold you took from a French town you have conquered and burned?"

Suddenly he looked familiar to me, or rather, his gestures did. I knew the man.

"Aut Pax, Aut Bellum, eh?" I snapped at him.

Without confusion or hesitation, he responded.

"Aye, it is, m'friend, either peace or war, eh? Either way, nothin' ever changes, certainly not war," he responded in perfect first-century Latin.

"Certainly not," I answered curtly, in Latin. He had spoken in response to the Latin phrase one well known to the Roman legions, and had spoken in what might well be taken for the accent of an ancient Roman.

"Where do I know you from, sir?" I demanded, in his French.

"I was about to ask you the same, monsieur."

He was back to fluent though oddly accented French. Most suspicious.

"I have a sidearm here, in my holster," I warned him.

"So do have I," he smiled, patting his own holster for effect.

"You may walk on now, Frenchman."

"I like it here. I will rest awhile and think."

He sat upon the ground near the road, halfway between it and the edge of my hole. He took ration tins from his pack, preparing to eat. Annoyed, I stood abruptly, walked to the pit, and taking the end of the rope, jumped back in to dig until the edge of the whole was above my head.

After three hours' time, I stopped digging, straightened my back, and glanced up to see his head framed against the ragged rectangle of sky above me. He was watching intently.

"You are tireless, monsieur! You've been digging for three hours with no pause or relief. Such is a fine way to suffer a heart attack."

"Such is the only way to be done with digging."

He removed his officer's cap, revealing thick black hair.

"Would you like help, monsieur?"

"Go away."

"Where would I go?"

"Go home."

"Were it strictly spoken, monsieur, it would be clear to see that I *am* home, for this is France."

It caused severe pain to the body's human muscles and tendons for me to do so, but without the aid of the rope, I sprang straight upward, my leap landing me on the surface beside the pit. I glared at him, prepared to tear his filthy French head from his frog body.

"Impressive, monsieur!" he chortled. "Surely in civilian life you were a circus performer. An acrobat, no?"

I seized him by the hair on his head, and twisted the head a nice sharp jerk to the left. I heard as well as felt his human neck break with a satisfying crack, much as a wet branch might make. I heaved the lifeless corpse up into the air. It sailed a hundred or so yards, landing in a twisted heap in the middle of the muddy, torn road.

I turned back to my pit and gazed down into it. I could just discern the very hint of a greenish glow down there where the last thin layer of mud could no longer conceal the glory of The Tongue of God.

I jumped into the wet pit to finish digging another hour until I'd exposed the prize. I tugged it up from loose, moist soil; soil that smelled of mold and moss with a faint trace of the odor of burned flint. Once it was in my hands, I felt again as I had in the past the spiritual (and in this body, the physical) burden and the heightened awareness it imposes. I also felt something I had last felt when I buried it, but only now could fully understand. After having taken perhaps a thousand human forms, I understood now that this sword oppresses its bearer with a keen awareness of the tragic dimension of Anu's creation.

Tears sprang to the eyes of the body I wore. They were hot and salty things, and it irritated me, how they crept over my lips and into my mouth, making me have to spit, but leaving a salty taste.

I put away the sword, which is to say that I let it enter into me, sheathed it in my very self, for that is always how any being must bear the Tongue of God. It is like a spiritual entity itself, and now was fused to my spirit essence. I clambered up from the pit to the light of a setting sun and staggered over to my pack and my clothing, where they were left lying beside the stake I'd driven into the ground.

I heard my attacker before I saw him.

His steps were light as a cat's. I began to turn, and did not finish turning before I was stabbed in the side. Curse the sluggish speed of a human body! Despite the agony, I twisted around and reached out to take his shoulder as he pulled the weapon away and stepped back.

It was the Frenchman.

Somehow he was on his feet again, and his neck was definitely no longer broken. The only sign that I had killed him and tossed his body away was the mud that now stained his uniform. He held the short length of a broken-off wooden staff with a socketed iron shank. The shank ended in a pyramidal metal head, stained with blood. I dropped to one knee and looked down at black blood pouring from my side—it was the color that told me this body's liver had been pierced. I felt not only the pain, but oddly, felt also weak, and felt unable to flee the body! I looked up at him.

"You're a malicious one then, eh?" he taunted. "You kill a man, just like that, without a 'beg pardon' or a fair warning?"

He was not speaking French now. It was Latin, and with a definite first-century Roman accent, prole accent, legionnaires' vernacular. His stance with the weapon he held was that of a Roman legionnaire, there was no mistaking it. As you know, my departed dear, I know well the stance, the speech, and the attitude. His weapon was familiar to me as well; it was the broken end of a pilum with spear head attached to what was left of the staff, only about one foot long, not including the shank: a good length to be used for stabbing, as one would use a dagger.

He had used it in just that way, and quite effectively at that, considering the dark liquid flowing from the wound. The body I wore would soon be dead from blood loss and shock. Why was I feeling unable to leave the body I was in? That made no sense. Who, and *what* was this being who had stabbed me? Where had he, or it, *come* from?

A short visit to Rotomagus in Gaul in the month of *Februarius* had been oppressively dark and frightfully cold to me, even in the sturdy body of a Greek freedman that I had seized near the coast. The bones of the Greek had ached incessantly and horribly in frigid winds.

By contrast, the smooth slope of Rome's *Mons Palatinus*, the Palatine Hill, in a balmy late summer on *dies Saturni* was a pleasant and rejuvenating walk. It was long past the *ides*, soon to be the *Kalends* of *Septimus*-September, and an unusually windy day for the month *Augustus,* the month of Caesar. There was a feeling in the air of something ending but still holding on to the last of life. The summer in my beloved Rome was reluctant to depart.

I breathed in the aroma of late-blooming lilies and violets; their perfume sufficient to wipe away the stench of the lower city from whose regions I had climbed, achieving this rarefied height above poverty and squalid overcrowding below.

I carried a mastiff puppy under one arm.

The dog was warm and happy. I had attempted to purchase for it a clay plate of sheep's milk at the bottom of the hill just before beginning my climb. The puppy and I had nosed about down there amongst merchants' stalls, spying the bright bolts of cloth, smelling the rich pharmacopoeia of medicinal thyme, basil, myrtle, hyssop, and the rich sharp scent of ginger, garlic, and dill on grilled fish as well as the musky savor of cooked goat, until we found a milk and cheese vendor who'd let us have a tiny dram of his milk. He waved away the coins and let us have it at no charge, so smitten was he by the pup.

The vendor, wide across as a yew sapling, sandaled feet brown and blunt, stood with his milk pots and a table spread with drams, pots, and urns, under a brilliant blue awning, no doubt the vividness of it owing to good Egyptian dyes. He admired the puppy as it lapped the thin goat's milk from a small clay plate. I spoke with the man, who told me news of Rome since I'd been gone some ten years, and soon the puppy finished. Yapping happily the small canine rolled onto his back to squirm and wriggle, scratching an itch, then made busy bumbling about betwixt my legs.

"I see you enjoy the aromas of market."

"I do," I admitted.

"You've Augustus to thank. Even over here, there used to be sometimes a stench from the Esquiline of the *puticuli* and of the refuse; the bodies of executed criminals they used to dump outside the Esquiline gate to rot there – you remember that? Well, Augustus covered the burial pits and the dump and made a park there, *Horti Maecenatis* it's named."

"Many things have improved since last I visited."

"Still food shortages though, in the poor precincts," the vendor lamented. "The grain is slow to come."

"Pirates, I'd imagine?"

"You imagine true. Augustus has conquered the world, and holds her more firmly in his palm than ever the great Alexander did, yet lately we've trouble getting grain from Egypt. The Battle of Actium long ago established Egypt's servitude to us, but these pirates . . ."

"I've heard in the *fasti* since I came back that the pirates are the very ones Rome uses to supply slaves."

"Indeed, sir Greek. The ungrateful curs raid grain ships. Bolder every day. If only Agrippa were still living he'd make short work of them. Germanicus is no replacement for Agrippa."

He leaned forward and spoke confidentially.

"Some say we are in the last days of peace. When Augustus dies, leadership will be in question, him with no grown sons and all. We are on the verge, they say, of a long winter for the Republic."

How amusing. In the midst of a faltering empire, Romans still tell themselves they live in a republic!

The puppy now darted expertly around the tramping legs of citizens and now and then tore off into the crowd chasing after unfortunate squirrels, one of which he proudly brought back dead, clamped between his little jaws to drop at our feet.

"What a scrappy little fellow! What be his name?"

"No name. He's smallest of the litter."

"A pup that scrappy the smallest? He gets it from a stout-hearted father then."

The puppy had continued to gambol amongst the brightly dyed yellow-and-blue and orange sheets and awnings spread for shade across wooden ribs; sheets like sails puffing in the wind. He'd lapped a few left over drops of milk off the plate happily before resuming his place under my arm for the climb up.

That wind had grown colder at the top. The wind, which, banishing the swelter of summer and freshening the air, was a gift to all; but the air was always clearer up here anyway, the hilltop covered nowadays with imperial size estates. Augustus, though an emperor, had no palace. Rome was no longer a republic, and had not been one since the Battle of Philippi, where Antony and Octavian, acting as two members of the second triumvirate, had defeated Brutus and the other assassins of Caesar Julius. Brutus and Cassius had been, by any sensible appraisal, Rome's last republicans.

Rome was an empire now all right, though Roman citizens told themselves they were a republic still. The Julii and the other illustrious families in waiting atop the Palatine would be proof of the death of the Republic. Gone already really was the republic of the honorable Scipio, the republic of the outspoken Cicero, and of Titus Livius's *Ab Urbe Condita*. It would take only the passing of the beneficent Augustus and the coming of the mad tyrants with their lavish orgies and their public obsessions, and the bread and circuses, mass exterminations of Christians, and other such nastiness taken for entertainment, gradually degrading civic life, to finally kill the illusion the milk vendor could instinctively feel was gone.

The families, whose homes, gardens, and nurseries nurtured the seed of tyranny, possessed sprawling estates on the Palatine, raising children that each family hoped would one day become consuls. It was said that these families lived not just above the squalor of Rome, but even above the disease and the physical ailments; above the "bad air" that Romans believed to cause illness.

In the Roman settlement city of Rotomagus, in Gaul, I had tracked down the remains of the slaves I'd liberated from the Cilician ship of Peshtlavo, the pirate. They had managed to sail the ship to Gaulish shores and make their way inland to Rotomagus where the survivors of their band found work as auxiliaries to Roman troops. They had not recognized me, of course, since I was no longer in the body of Saturnius. I had satisfied my curiosity by finding what had become of them.

I walked through the streets of Palatine to the particular estate I'd visited many times when I walked in the body of slave become consular translator, and acting Proconsul become General, Saturnius. I had accompanied Marcellus home to his childhood abode twice. Now I found it again, nestled as always beneath a vigorous growth of olive trees swaying in the unseasonable wind. Inner gardens and the villa they sheltered were set well back from the street, both garden and villa surrounded by a wall. The outer entrance was an exquisitely carved, iron-studded door of Kushite wood which was moored in the stone of the wall. The door was open.

Through the opening, I could see the lush interior grounds I remembered. A stone path through plants, trees, and several bright ceramic pools; neatly pruned, the trees, which were an aviary full of musical blackbirds.

A young Spaniard boy, a slave, stood out front sweeping at fallen palms and twigs blown about by the wind, hopelessly trying to keep them from piling up in front of his mistress's wooden door.

"I am Arctarcus, a Greek freedman and a merchant of Rotomagus," I said to the boy. "I come to see the Lady Lucretia of the Julii, with information about her son."

"I will tell my mistress," the slave said, tossing down his broom. "Please wait there, Dominus, under the awning?"

He passed inside to the grounds of the estate, closing the door behind him, and I went to stand under a clay-tiled awning that had been attached to this part of the wall as a courtesy to visitors such as me, to keep the sun away while waiting to be announced. Marcellus and I had stood beneath this same, one evening long ago to keep out of the rain as he smoked noxious Egyptian tobacco sticks the stench of which had inspired his mother to banish him from their *klinai* dinner couches, and I along with him to stand with him in the rain.

The slave returned, gesturing me inside.

When he had conducted me to a bench beside one of the glimmering aboveground pools, this one full of playful fish with golden spines, Lucretia came out. She wore a white singlet beneath lightweight chest armor as for gladiatorial sparring, with a legionary's battle skirt that looked to have been designed especially for a woman's hips. She bore a legionnaire's style sharpened rudis in her left hand, the hand gloved and taped as for combat training.

She carried a towel in her right hand, wiping sweat from her face. On her feet were hard-soled military training sandals used by sparring legionnaires for exercise in a marching camp. I looked over her shoulder but saw no sign of a sparring partner here in this peaceful garden.

She was older than she had been when last I'd seen her, when I'd accompanied Marcellus here on a visit, but Lady Lucretia of the Julii was just as tall, her back just as straight. She looked down at me as she wiped her face, and then threw the towel at the slave, who caught it easily, as one who is used to catching things suddenly thrown at him by this mistress. The slave lay down the towel on a wicker table beside the villa's outer wall. Then, as unobtrusively as a Roman slave can, he gingerly unbuckled long thin belts that bound her armor to her body while she spoke.

"My son is dead."

"Yes, Lady, but I knew him, and the general he served with, Saturnius."

"Proconsul Saturnius and the traitor, Proconsul Verilius, led two legions to their deaths, and my son to his. Saturnius's body was taken from the cold waters off the barbarian Britani coast!"

"Is that the word, Domina?"

She glared. "Marcellus was murdered. They threw him from a Selesian pirate ship found drifting off Briton—a death ship. None aboard were alive, save a pack of slaves. He likely was making an escape from the slaughter of his legionary detachment and was betrayed by the pirates he'd hoped would provide his escape!"

"He meant to come back to you."

"My foolish son meant simply to rejoin his legion, I'm certain. His heart never bent toward Rome, or me. I assume the dead lost their lives because they brought that unlucky dog of a Gaul, Saturnius, aboard. Thank the gods, Saturnius was found dead on that ship along with all the rest!"

"I met Saturnius when he marched through Lutetia, in Gaul, with legionnaires."

"Did you? I wish I had killed him with my own hands here in Rome when I met him as a slave. What have you to say of my son, merchant?"

She shrugged off her armor as the boy finished unbuckling it for her, and he retreated with it to lay it against the wall beside the wicker table.

"I joined their march," I answered Lucretia, "accompanying them far beyond Rotomagus. I was with the detachment when *Tribune Militare* Quintus Marcellus, your son, I knew, was wounded in battle, before he left my company to make his escape to the coast, to the ship you speak of, I suppose. He asked that I reach you someday to tell you his thoughts were of you, Lady."

She blinked; she sniffed. She shifted the sharpened, pointed rudis to her right hand, and tilted her head, peering down at me as if through a fog.

"What lie is this?" she whispered, her hushed tone showing both her amazement, and the fact that she did not dare let herself believe what I was saying, even though she wanted to with all her heart, what heart there was in her.

"He bade me tell you just that, Domina. If else I've said were oiled or salted, believe this one truth. He said it."

She hissed, as if calling a horse to her side, and the slave came. She handed the rudis to him, and he stepped back two paces, as she slowly shook her head. I marked with some amazement how torn in two this woman crab was, caught between a mother's love and what seemed a malignant hunger. Human contradiction is endlessly fascinating, is it not?

"Since the days when Marcellus was a stripling and I taught him the sword even as his weak father taught him philosophy, he never showed or spoke such tenders to me."

"This pup here is the son of the dog Marcellus called Beast, that same dog must have been taken ashore by slaves from that doomed ship, and then taken to Rotomagus."

Her eye shifted suspiciously to the pup.

"I recently returned to Rotomagus and found Beast living happily with a retired Roman centurion, having been mated to another mastiff that happened to be in the city. There was a litter. I thought you'd wish to have this one, or perhaps Marcellus's daughter might want—"

She glared at the dog in horror, stepped backward again, and shifted her alarm to me with a look.

"I've seen you! By Jupiter, I have. Who are you?!"

"I told you, Lady, I am a Greek merchant of—"

"You are no merchant, *Arctarcus*. You are an evil spirit! That dog is the dog you gave my son on the eve before he went into the legions. I remember you. You will not see my son's daughter, I forbid it!"

I had no idea what she meant. As she reached for her sharpened rudis to take it back from the slave, her attitude said I was about to receive a stiff clout upon my human's head at best, or a cut from that sword. I knew to take my leave.

I rose, tucking the puppy under an arm to protect it and headed to the wooden door leading back to the street, offering her no further words, or further threat to frighten her.

"Wait!"

I stopped beside yet another pool, and I turned to see her just behind me.

"It's not fair! You come here and show me this power, but will not explain it?"

"Lady . . . I have no power. You are talking to a man who has not been here before."

"You speak sly lies, demon. You appeared in a different guise to my husband and my son at the temple of Cybele. The very next day, my son threw his future and heritage away by joining the legions. It was you!"

"Not I."

"You gave him a pup dog, that one, a mastiff. He and his father brought it back here from the temple. He told how you a Greek appeared as a cloud passed before the sun! He then pointed you out from a distance outside the gate where we stood at the edge of the hill—you were still descending, still walking down!"

"This is my first time on the Palatine Hill, Domina."

A sly look came into her eyes then. She calmed and spoke quietly, almost seductively, and I perceived something like my "skin" crawling, a sensation I'd last experienced in the presence of my sister, Uriel.

"It was the very dog you bear here," she said quietly. "The dog he named Beast, just a puppy."

I looked around the garden quickly, surveying the clay planters and terracotta tiles I remembered, the pure white marble sculptures of the heads generations of Julii and plaster busts of the gods. Marcellus had sat on the edge of this nearest pool basin ridiculing his family's choice to cast themselves in marble but the gods in plaster. Nowhere did I see any sign of Uriel, nor feel her presence. This woman before me was only human.

I stared at her. Though human, she was able to cast a weak but definite influence over me.

"You walk all the days of the world," she whispered, "A god who doesn't age, taking human forms. A messenger of Charon. Evil? No matter. There is strength in evil, and you should not hesitate to claim it."

"Woman, I am not—" But my thighs were growing weak. I concentrated on turning away from her, but . . . "Do not take me for a fool because I am a woman. How else can you appear years later, the same age, holding the same dog, himself no older?"

She suddenly thrust the rudis into the soil at her feet, fell to one knee and bowed her head to me. Her slave gaped at this servile display, so uncharacteristic of his mistress. It startled me, but for a different reason. For she clearly was doing so not out of fear or awe but out of a fierce thirst.

I felt again a strange buoyancy that had swept over me when Tullius had demonstrated his passionate belief in me in the cold forests of Gaul, but where Tullius's faith and affection had been wholesome, enabling, this woman's devotion and longing were like the entrance to a gaping catacomb in which power lies but darkness also. Within was a type of enslavement for me!

Had I fled the sickening benevolence of Anu's kingdom only to sink into the morass and mess of a human's delusions and expectations? Such was not my notion of freedom or of power.

"Rise, woman!"

"I will worship you! I can tell by your look and by the tremor in your thighs as I speak this to you that you yearn to be worshipped. I think you are ashamed of your true power. I will bring you acolytes here in Rome!"

Like the twelve-man choir who followed my brother? Or had they actually led him to his death?

"I have sesterces, my husband's wealth, my son's wealth. I have a title that I can use to seek your elevation in Rome," she hissed with a maniacal gleam in her dark, Etruscan eyes, the purest of Roman heritage, those eyes, so much like Marcellus's.

I thought then of Marcellus's mocking tone when he had divulged the oddity that both his parents were from the line of the Julii, they were cousins who had married.

"I'm doubly cursed with the dark-eyed mark of the sons and daughters of Aphrodite," he had chuckled drunkenly at a wine wagon parked near the Field of Mars one bright afternoon between our legion's campaigns. He'd paid the wine merchant a triple coinage so that he could walk away with the clay cup, with wine still in it. The merchant's eyes had widened with delight at such fortune.

"Descendants, we horde of Julii, of Lulus, whose grandmother it's said was the goddess. So you see, good Saturnius, our greed and our arrogance have the haughtiest imprimatur in Rome."

I looked down into those eyes of Lucretia's as her voice grew husky with a lust for power.

"I will build a temple to you," she groaned, "and place you beside Isis in my esteem. No, above her! I pledge this to you, Arctarcus, or Saturnius, or any name you command your cult to call you, if you will but favor me in my few desires."

I was disturbed by this thing she was crafting, stoking in me. It felt like a binding fire, burning a low wall around my spirit essence. I felt the pull of, what, ecstasy? A human sensation? No, this was a sensation rooted I knew, in my own angelic nature, and the sensation pulled me deeper into the shell I wore.

She looked up at me, her eyes beginning to water with her ardor, and that sensation was subtly stroking me with carnality, shaping me into the form of her passions. Her words were stirring that within me that is latent in all angels, even in Jehoshua; but where his experience of human worship awakened his martyrdom, this empathy between me and humans that I had heretofore not suspected awakened a burning evil in me.

And I realized instinctively that the Christ had lived all of his earthly life feeling this thing pouring over him as the humans around him sculpted his spirit essence, pulling portions of it from out of his very bones, touching and shaping whatever in him was latently divine. I knew that he must have been lashed to carnality as a hostage, bound by adoring humans.

Jehoshua had been held by their desire and their need. With their wish that he be good, goodness had shaped him, just as Lucretia's demand that I be evil was buffeting me now.

It was exhilarating and nauseating, both. I could feel her thirst like an intimate thing, as intimate as that revolting thing you monkeys call sex, which I had never indulged in, because one can take this being human too far, after all.

"Favor me, Messenger!"

It took an effort, but I turned my back on her and walked again to the door in the wall, the pup protected in my grasp.

"You were Saturnius as well, I can feel it," she whined. Saturn, the god that ate his own children. Are we your children, Saturnius? Then feast on us, on our worship!"

I made myself not turn back.

"What kind of cowardly god are you," she rebuked me, "who has not even the stomach to accept human worship!?"

I turned at the threshold of the doorway to look at her again and shouted, for somehow she had pierced me with those words.

"What kind of god am I? A tragic one, you monkey! A tragic one who would have inherited the heavens, yet sought to seize all before his time came, was cast out, and lost all because of his own pride! *Hamartia! Hubris!*"

"Then I will make a *tragedia* for you to rival the works of Sophocles. Use me as you cry out against the other gods. Do you see that this can be, that I will make it so?"

"I see a future in which I am enslaved by monkeys and despised as no other being in creation and you presume to speak to my travail?"

"Yes! I will write *defixiones* on lead tablets for the god who pities himself. I will bring the sympathy of men to lay at your feet. Command me as you mourn your woes and bear your burdens. I will make them lighter! I am yours!"

"Tell me where Marcellus's daughter is."

"She- is dead, these past three years, from Numidian plague."

Marcellus's line within the Julii is finished, then? No. I've seen his descendants in images of future time. Well, it little matters. I'll go as I please along whatever timelines I wish.

She surged to her feet, drew a knife from her skirt, seized the slave, and put the knife to his throat.

"I will give you this boy's life as an offering!"

"Release him."

"I will smear his blood upon my breasts! I will stretch his entrails across my doorway! Command me, I will do it!"

"And you would. And so now I see what it was that drove Marcellus from you, Lady, what drove him from Rome. Now, in these final days of your empire's sunlight, I see what it is in Rome that will gather the darkness, fester and burst forth the pus of mad emperors!"

She bent her face down again, still offering worship, accepting my contempt as an acolyte would. This only made me more contemptuous of her.

"Very well. I also know what it is in your son that won my regard for him. He sought to rise above what he was by birth, and a better struggle was his than mine."

She scowled, "He was my son but he was weak."

"Yet your son's was a better spirit than mine, or yours, Lucretia. He sought to rise above you. You are that thing, Demon Mother, which for eons you humans have accused me of being. You are the evil that suppurates in the souls of men, whom my own brother angel sacrificed himself to redeem. You'd murder this boy so clearly devoted to you, sacrifice him to your thirst for power!?"

"Yes! I would sacrifice every slave in my estate! I would sacrifice every living soul on this hill if I could but lead an army as Mark Antony's wife did, as you did, *Saturnius!*"

She knows me.

How unsettling. And how consumptive was this woman twisted by the dreams and nightmares of the cruel powerful men around her. How unlike the noble and feeling Claudia Procula was Lucretia. Where Mary Magdalene was courageous and devout, where Drusalla was imbued by a magnificent, defiant love of country, and where even a slave named Shelomith wielded the dignity and honor of her faith in her Jewish people, this Roman she-wolf before me was but a flesh satchel of human hunger, a bitter well of unrequited lust.

"You are a true daughter of Romulus, Lady."

"Yes, Romulus! The first and last Roman man strong enough to do what must be done!"

I scowled and spat back at her.

"Yes, Romulus! Who slew his brother Remus with a shovel while his brother's back was turned, much as a wife might slay her own husband and seek to devour her own son."

I heard her curse me in a secret tongue of the cult of Cybele as I walked through the doorway back out into the street, into the light and the wind atop Palatine, a wind that it has been said can sweep away all traces of the taint that beclouds the lower streets of Rome. Though just as freshening, the wind had now taken on a frigid edge, a reminder of what was to come.

The alms of a Roman autumn were near.

The vast, impossible brightness of the wide street was like false daylight blooming in the midst of hot night. I walked along with the crowds toward one among many illuminated buildings, the largest and the brightest one, with a hugely glowing sign that declared in pulsating electric letters the name of this palace. I'd been told this building should be my destination if I wished to find the man I was seeking. I joined a smaller stream that left the larger crowd and that flowed toward the gates. I left even that smaller phalanx and walked alone the final steps to the gate of The Kings, guarded by a single sentinel.

I did not doubt that this daylike building was a palace. I had simply been amused by the irony of the name of it: "Caesar's Palace." Now, standing before the gate of The Kings, I thought that though there was nothing at all Roman about the place, the impression of arrogant wealth, hubris, and pitiless excess made the name seem quite appropriate.

I'd left the pup in the care of the Roman baker, Avicus Petronius, whom I'd met in the times I'd spent as a translator to Second Consul Marcus Agrippa. Over the years, he'd climbed in his fortunes from a small baker to a successful businessman with one of the largest bakeries in his precinct. I had met Avicus while awaiting Ulgöthur outside of the Gual's Rome lodging. Over the years of my life in Rome, Avicus had become my confidant, had held my wealth in secret for me, and had helped me to learn things about being human I could never have feigned, and would not have discovered otherwise, not soon enough to avoid discovery. He knew my secrets, and could be trusted.

After assuring the dog's safety, I'd traced the genetic wave of Marcellus's spirit through time. I found what Lucretia had not told me: that Marcellus's daughter, who like her father bore no love for the patricians of Avantine, had fled into exile after news of her father Marcellus's death reached Rome. The daughter had been pregnant—a secret pregnancy, about which not even Lucretia had known. The daughter was helped into exile by friends of Marcellus in the legions and even in the Senate, to keep the child out of the hands of Lucretia.

Thus, a secret newborn granddaughter was taken hundreds of miles east of Rome to Abruzzo, and the area eventually called Montesilvano on the Adriatic. There, Marcellus's genetic line had thrived until the twentieth century after Christ's death, when his descendants had left Italy altogether to sail to the Union of States. All this had been for me an easy thing to trace.

Being Second Son has its advantages.

A sentinel to The Kings, a skinny man in a black uniform wearing white gloves and an exaggerated military cap, stood in my way.

"Say, can I help you, felluh?"

"It is not likely."

"This is a private entrance."

"I shall remember that."

"That's a fine tux, but you're also gonna need a badge to go in there. This is the door for the talent."

"I have many talents."

"Yeah? What, you sing?"

"What would that have to do with talents?"

"Guess you don't then."

I reached into the silk-lined pocket of my tuxedo trousers, and produced a handful of the paper talents: certificates that passed for money in the 1960s Union of States Nevada. The peculiarly fetishized script bore engraveries of the faces of past presiding figure heads of the Union of States. The sentinel had said *talents*, and I took him to mean money. His eyes widened; he glanced left and right as if making certain no one was watching us.

"Oh, yeah, buddy. You got a talent there, all right. Yer' gifted."

He snatched several of the certificates, choosing from amongst the ones marked "one hundred," reached into his pocket, and pulled forth a badge on a frail chain which he hung round my neck, and stepped aside, letting me pass.

As I stepped into an inner alcove illuminated by red light, three large humans in bulky tuxedos of their own, whose breaths smelled like garlic and charred meat, stopped me to examine the badge I had just received. It read:

BACKSTAGE VIP ALL ACCESS

The badge seemed a potent enough herald to gain me entry, judging by their reactions, yet the largest of them, who possessed a remarkably broad jaw and smelled the loudest of the meat he had no doubt recently devoured, conducted a careful search of my clothing to ensure I bore no guns. Unlike the first sentinel, he made a point of not asking after or disturbing the certificates in my pockets. He thumbed my lapels and whistled approvingly, nodding as he brushed an imaginary lint from my shoulders once he'd finished rummaging through my clothing. I allowed this because I understood that the one I'd come to see was regarded highly among monkeys, and so was under the protection of these ursine humans.

"Go 'head, friend," grunted the large-jawed man.

I continued down an even more dimly lit hallway, which seemed to be submerged beneath the waves of an ocean—there was a sound like a distant, dim roaring as from large numbers of people, music, and many tramping feet somewhere beyond the walls and elsewhere in the Palace. At the end of the corridor, I encountered yet another large man in a bulky suit, this one far more detached in demeanor and clearly armed with several of the hidden guns the other men had been seeking upon me. He was a warrior-protector, I could tell.

"You f' Dino?" he asked softly.

"Pardon me?" I said, befuddled by his nonstandard English.

"Who you here for?"

"The King."

He chuckled.

"You came to the right place, then, 'cause the joint's lousy with 'em. Dino's at the bar."

He opened the door, muttering "Beautiful frickin' tux," as I went by him, and I walked through into a large, lavish room full of people dressed in silk, linen, and leather, wearing jewels, smoking tobacco sticks, and drinking alcoholic beverages from glass vessels. A portion of the roaring sound was now distinct, as music. The sound was still far off, though, in a different part of the Palace. Those in this room, obviously a palace sanctuary, were like courtiers, and had perhaps just come from celebration where the music was located or were preparing to go there from here.

They lounged upon leather couches, talking and eating puckishly off scattered trays of finger foods. Scantily clad women in sparkling bodices milled about, some sitting on the laps of the men. Some of the women were more fully dressed, and clearly were "stars." I recognized two of them from posters I had seen earlier that night and from my other travels through Union of States time frames: Angie Dickinson, Shirley McClain, Ella Fitzgerald, and Anna Magnani were some of the names I recalled.

But there was a long mahogany stile running across the back of the room, facing dozens of bottles and drink vessels made of glass stacked on shelves. A line of silk-clothed men, most of them hunched over the stile, speaking confidentially to one another, had their backs to all else in the room. Sitting upon a tall three-legged stool at the stile with these men on either side of him was the one man I sought. This must be the "bar" the protector outside had spoken of. I headed for the stile.

Even from behind, the sweep of his broad shoulders, the set of his thick-haired head, and the insouciance of his voice identified him as Marcellus Quintus of the Julii.

His hair, so familiar to me, was characteristically swept back but was held in place within a chimera of what seemed like palmetto oil. He held a glass vessel containing tan-colored alcohol; some sort of whiskey, from the aroma. He, like these other men, smelled of leather hide and camphor with an undertone of spice and musk—pleasant scents that reminded me of the Aventine.

He suddenly turned and gazed at me.

"Hey, fella, who are you, and who the hell's your tailor? Tailor's name first."

I was lost for a response to the smooth voice that sounded so much like my Marcellus.

"Okay then. *Your* moniker first."

"If you mean my name, it is Heylal."

From behind me, another voice, warm in tone, sharp in pitch.

"Hey-Loll? What's that, some kinda coo-coo Arab name?"

The voice was from a tall, skinny, hardened man who came near to sit down close to Marcellus. Unlike Marcellus, his hips and thighs bore the genetic markers of a Sicilian. He was all angles, corners, and points, with that voice like mulled wine but with the cold blue eyes of an Etruscan assassin. Indeed, most of the men who sat along this stile bore the phenotypic markers of the Etruscan peoples, those whom the ancient Romans had called the *Etrusci* of the Alps region of Italy. But these men also bore more recent allele types of ancestors who'd taken a genetic passage from the north to the south: to Rome, then to Tuscany, Amalfi, and Sicily. Their eyes and their heads and jaws showed an ancestry of southward migration through the western regions to the hard, craggy island nation oppressed by centuries of outsiders, conquerors.

Only Marcellus, or precisely, the man who was an allelic echo of my friend, a man *descended* from Marcellus, was of eastern Italian genetic origin. All this I could see by looking into the frequency wave inside their cells—at the ribonucleic biochemistry hidden within those cells.

"Not that I got anything against Arabs," the skinny blue-eyed one continued. "They supply Dino here with the massive amounts of oil he's gotta have for that hair."

Soft, harsh laughter emanated from the rest of the men seated along the length of the stile.

"That's classy, Frank," *Dino* responded, sipping his drink.

"Hey, I say it with love, kid. We're family. Look, am I still chairman of the board, or what?"

"Yeah, Frank, you're still chairman, and I'm still bored."

"Yeah, sure, and you're still nursing that same glass of snort."

"All things in moderation, Frankie."

"That's easy for you, you were breastfed."

Dino spoke. "From what I know of family, including this one, the institution's always a double-edged olive sword."

"Yeah? Meaning?"

"Frank, family is a contradiction: love and dread, sympathy and consternation. Hand-in-hand like idiot twins born of the same mother in an uneasy year, under a melancholy star."

This ironic man seems a true descendant of my Marcellus.

Frank now turned back to me.

"So who the hell *is* your tailor, *Hey-wood*?"

"If you speak of my mode of dress, I purchased this from a fabricator on Flamingo Road. He called himself Al."

"You scored them threads from Al Barty? You gotta make a reservation a year ahead for Al to even measure you. That prick's the best tailor in town, and he charges a leg and a foot. We're splits-ville, him and me."

Dino, who to me was Marcellus, was pleased despite Frank's protest.

"Hey, Pallie, you that in with the in crowd, you know Al?"

"More to the point," said Frank, "Is he that fixed for semolians, he knows Al."

"I've no reason," I responded, "to speak falsely."

"He sounds like an English Lord, this *mezza fanook*, huh, Dino?"

"Talks like Lawford, all right."

"That's okay, though, *Hay-stack*," said Frank, extracting a thin gold case from a pocket that caught the light. "I'd-uh had Barney over there—the guy with the xylophone forehead? I'd-uh had him bounce you outta this clam-bake the hard way, through the plumbing, but I could tell from the Shakespeare that Hal B. Wallis sent you."

He took a tobacco stick from the case and struck a fire stick to light it, taking a puff. "Am I right?"

"No."

"Yeah, yeah, sure. You got no offer for Dean, then? Hal B. sends no numbers, no contract?"

I made no response to his indecipherable question.

"Dino," he continued, talking with the stick burning between his lips, "Hal ain't gonna stop sending these tweed underpants salesmen until you agree to lock up and do the picture for him." He turned back to me and again said, "Am I right?"

"Let Hal B. hold his breath and turn blue," Dino said.

A small whip tough and lean black man approached. He wore a gray flannel suit, black-framed eye lenses, and smoked a tobacco stick of his own.

"You all talking about Hal Wallis?"

"Hey, Smokey. Hal sent this Finster to talk up Dino, but no numbers, points, nor contract does he bear."

The black man squinted at me, puffing smoke into my face. "Huh," he said, "Hal's so tight he pays his chauffeur in lottery tickets. Only way to get a drink out of Hal is to stick your finger down his throat."

All the suited men up and down the stile chuckled at this.

"Anyway, Smoke, the Finster's got class, and obviously money, because Hal sure wouldn't duke him the suit, huh?"

"A comp? Not Hal. He's such a nudge when he was born the doctor slapped his ass and Hal slapped the doctor back."

The chuckles became laughter now.

"Yeah, Hal's first day in nursery school," purred Dino, "he signed an IOU to get the kiddie cafeteria cook to trim the crusts off his peanut-butter sandwich. Then he used the crusts to bribe one of the kid bullies to ride him home on his back."

Hilarity now erupted along the stile. One of the men, with close-set eyes and the close-cropped hair of the gladiatori, shouted.

"Bet that IOU had an escape clause!"

The laughter now grew raucous, with several of the men slapping and pounding on the bar stile in their hilarity.

Smokey examined my clothing.

"This *nukshleper* has on a sweet tux, all right. Looks like an Al Barty original."

"You got it dead-on, Smoke," said Frank. "He dropped some serious lettuce on Al and picked the threads up on the way over, he says. How much'd you pay to buy your way in here, Hastings?"

"I used several of these talents."

I reached into my pocket and pulled out all fifty of the remaining certificates.

"Phweeeee-ew!" Dino whistled. "Any Poindexter with a bankroll like that is hep to hang in. Cap a squat on tji stool, Hay-seed."

I sat down beside him.

"What's your drink?"

I was at a loss.

"I'm asking what you like to drink."

"Mulsum.

"Hey, Bill. Set my guy up."

A short dour man with a bright-red beard turned to face us—a Gual in modern times—in an expensive suit with a towel over one shoulder. He leaned against the stile from the other side. He thrust his ample jaw at me, eyeing me intently.

"Yeah?"

"Man wants a mulsum."

"The fuck's that, Dino, some kinda Wop beer?"

Dino was incredulous.

"You asking me what it is? Are you a bartender or a game show host? Make him one."

"Never heard of it."

Dino turned to Frank.

"See what we get for taking this Irish Harvey outta Brooklyn? We need a bender who's mixed someplace other than Atlantic Avenue. Tell him what it is, Hay-seed."

"Mulsum is Roman. It's honey-mulled wine."

"That's it?" The bearded bartender was incredulous.

"Yes."

"Honey I got. This joker here"—he indicated Frank with a jerk of his thumb—"he practically sprays it down his throat. But what kinda wine you want?"

"Pompeiian red."

"What's that?" asked the bartender.

Frank smiled at me then snapped at the man behind the stile.

"What are yuh, Bill, a wine dope? Irish tap tuggin' dead soldier pourin' peanut pimp! This half a *paisan* must know his grapes. Pompeii, that's what they called the *Campania* region of Italy in ancient times."

"Yeah? Well, guess what they called County Cork in ancient times?"

"What?" asked Smokey.

"County fuckin' Cork, whadaya think they called it?"

More raucous laughter from the line of men.

"Awww, give the guy a nice red from Avellino, will yuh? A *Piedirosso*, that's a good Campania press."

"All right, now you're talking. One *Piedirosso* with honey coming, for the dude, Frank. I got one back here aged three years in oak barrels."

"Hit him with it then, and don't forget the honey."

"How 'bout you, Dean? You still praying to that Jack?"

"I'm fine, Bill. Stop trying to make me into that loser I play in pictures and onstage. I ain't no drunk."

"And you never will be at this rate," said the bearded man, who turned his back to us and began mixing.

Frank slapped me on the back, "You sure don't look Italian." Then he walked away, disappearing into the crowd.

"You gonna do a picture for Hal?" Smokey asked Dino.

"Naaaaw, Sam. I'm tired of it. Think I'll do some TV."

"TV! Sid Caesar and crazy dames in capri pants, and like that? It's a waste of your talent."

"Y'know, someday anthropologists, they're gonna brush the dirt off my skull, peek inside my empty eye sockets and wonder what it was that made so many people wanna pay a skull to act like an ass."

"I don't get you, Dean."

"That's because you really do have talent, Sam. I better make sure Frank don't piss off any mafia wives over there—you know we can't let him roam free in a room full of Jersey women."

Chuckling, "Smokey" gestured Dean to remain, and left to join Frank.

"Dino" took a sip from his glass. "You really pushed Frank's buttons with the fancy wine talk."

"I just came from Italy. I was ordering what I like."

"From Italy. With a British accent? Well, when it comes to Italian wine, I love a nice stiff Scotland Corn whiskey, aged three days in a porcelain bathtub. Que bella!"

He sipped. As the bartender placed my wine in front of me, Dino whispered.

"Tell the truth, Hay-stack. Hal sent you, right?"

"No. Marcellus Quintus did."

"Who's that?"

"One of your ancestors. I knew him. He was a soldier in the Roman legions."

"Mm-hmm. Did he sing?"

"No."

"Yeah, neither do I."

"I've heard your record-talkies. You sing quite well."

"I like that, 'record-talkies.' Well, it's all strings and wires these days, publicists and hairdressers, unlike the time of the Roman legions."

"The past is not always superior to the present merely by virtue of being past."

"Yeah, I dig it. But you wanna know who can sing, Maria Callas can sing. She's a Greek girl, but she understands the Italian way of singing, the clean attack, the *coloratura*, the crystal clear *legato* she creates with just the lightest touch. I wish I could do that."

"If I correctly understand the terms you are using, I believe you certainly do."

"Yeah? So you know the opera too?"

"My favorite is *Cavalleria Rusticana*."

"Mascagni."

"Indeed."

"That's my favorite opera. You Italian, Heywood?"

"If I were anything, I would be that. I lived for a time in Rome."

"The eternal city that outlasts time."

"You have no idea."

"Well, unless you can sing, you don't know—"

"I studied your music in preparation before coming here."

"Really? How long did that take?"

"Approximately one of your years. I listened to each of your recorded cantos."

"I have a hard time knowing if I should believe most of the things you say."

"As I also said, I've no reason to mislead you."

"Judging by the roll in your pocket, I guess not. The roll? Get it? The money- the money you've got."

"Oh."

"But do you sing?"

"I have no creativity whatsoever."

"Well, then—"

"One does not need to create stars and planets as God does to perceive the artistic merit of his stars or his planets."

"Okay. I got no comeback to that."

"Your delicate tone in the high register, your light attack, your sense of lyricism far outweigh the relatively shallow context of the popular record talkies you make."

"Thanks, I guess."

"Small human minds barely grasp the profundity of this thing you call art, that it can often supersede even a mundane context such as a 'pop song,' as I believe you call it. I rather like your rendition of the song, 'Sway.'"

"Yeah, I like that one."

"It features many of the techniques and vocal timbrel elements you cite in this Callas person. Does she sing in Las Vegas?"

He looked at me with a crooked smile so like one of Marcellus's that I found it disconcerting.

"No. She sings on a bigger stage. I'm no Maria Callas. The *Bel Canto* is hers. I wanted once upon a time to bring some of the opera to my songs, but . . ."

He took a particularly deep drink from his vessel.

"I wish to ask you a question, Mr. Dino."

"Shoot, Heywood."

"What does it mean to you to be human? What is the point of this human . . . life?"

He spun his seat on the fixed point of its tripod so that he was facing me, and studied me intensely. "Do I look like a shrink?"

"You do not appear shrunken. You look like your ancestors."

"Why ask me?"

"Your ancestor Marcellus was someone I could trust. He was an exceptional human. Even when we were at odds I could trust his integrity."

"You trying to tell me you're a thousand years old, Heywood?"

"No, I am billions of your years old. I knew your ancestor two thousand of your years ago."

"Okay. I can fly with that. This is Las Vegas, I've heard stranger things over at the Sands. Only why would a geezer like you ask a guy like me to explain life?"

"Because I am not alive."

"Bad affair?"

"What?"

"Never mind. You say you're not alive. I assumed you meant you fell for a woman—"

"Not a woman, an angel."

"Ain't they all?"

"I ask you because you are much like Marcellus, who always spoke the truth. I came to see you out of curiosity, to see how much like him you would be, but now I think I should trust whatever your answer to my question will be."

"Hmm. I like that. You push them buttons good, Heywood."

"Thank you."

He turned back to his drink, waving off the bartender trying to pour more into the glass.

"Life, huh? My father, Gaetano Crocetti, emigrated from the Peninsula to Steubenville, Ohio. I admired the guy. He was just a plain working guy. Ma adored him. I was a boxer, he approved of me. I was a dealer in a speakeasy casino, he approved of me. I became a radio star, though, and he told me, 'Whatever you do, Dino, take the same attitude toward it as you did when you were a dealer, because crime is the real measure of a man."

"An odd thing to say."

"The way he saw it, if you can be among criminals and not become one, you're okay. I let that be my guide through a singing career, movies, and my stage shows here in the land of Mayer Lansky. The Palace here, it's only one year old, already there's six guys buried in the flower bins down in the kitchen. I guess one day, Frank Jr., Little Smokey, and Little Dino or Deena are gonna write the final word on all of us here in this room. You got a father?"

"Yes."

"Probably you thought you had to get out on your own and out from under him."

"I did so."

"He dead?"

"To me."

"Yeah, well, someday you're gonna miss him, and you won't be able to tell him so. Be your own man, but you gotta ixnay the John Wayne routine, strong and inarticulate. Tell everybody that matters what you think. That's the meaning of the whole shebang."

He took a last sip, stood up, slapped me on the back in a manner I interpreted as diffidently affectionate, much like Marcellus, and then he walked quietly past everyone and out of the room.

Just before dawn in your American state of New Jersey, one thousand and fifty-five years after your first millennium (still in your future, dear amanuensis) on April month's eighteenth day, I approached the Princeton Hospital in a pair of white pantaloons and a physician's white tunic. The body I was in was tall, healthy, and dark of skin. It had reminded me of the long-ago physicians, many of them dark of skin, of course, whom Hippokrates of Kos had trained and taught his "diagnostiks" and his "prog-knosis" techniques, in the academies of Kemet and in her colonies and in the Greek colonies.

These original physicians were humans I had visited once or twice and had had interesting conversations with as I'd done with Archimedes. I had only killed one of them who'd gotten a bit threatening and tiresome when I'd unwisely revealed my true self to him. Many were not capable of Archimedes's objectivity and detachment. One or two of them had even attacked me.

Not to be tedious but I will tell you, I have had more than a few unpleasant experiences with odd or hostile humans on your Earth over the years. These years are both behind you and ahead of you, dear crab, years I walked through particularly after my brother's execution.

One of those experiences though was quite puzzling, and though I thought the beings I encountered then to be human, I later thought differently. As I sat in an establishment for drinking alcoholic liquid infusions and brews in a dark area lit only by outside light through a window, I was harassed by two suspicious fellows. These two turned out to be impossibly powerful for humans.

"You haven't touched your imbibement," said one of them, walking past my table and stopping, looking down at me. He was a tall, bloodless-looking albino with queer, sunflower-yellow eyes. His friend was equally tall, Nubian-skinned with peculiarly long fingers, wearing the same leather jacket and leather pants as his Albino compatriot. Moonlight from the window beside my table filtered in through the slats of the window blind, giving his eyes an even stranger tint.

"I like to take my time," I answered him with enough dryness to dissuade further discussion. Instead of moving on, however, he sat down at my table and leaned forward as the Nubian stood at his back with feet planted far apart as if in a classical age combat stance. I smiled my amusement at them both. Perhaps they had been watching too many movie-talkies.

"There is a difference between taking your time and not touching your beverage at all. You paid a goodly amount for it—I watched you. Why do you waste your currency papers?"

"Why waste your *time*," the Nubian added from behind.

I stared at them. They stared back.

I reached out to fondle my glass. The Albino seized my wrist but let go when he saw I was only reaching for the glass, which was moist with condensation from the slowly but steadily melting ice in the glass of vodka that had sat in front of me for some time without my touching it. I had been sitting there studying bodies, deciding which would be my next, unaware that these two had been watching me.

His grip on my wrist alerted me to how strong the man was, unnaturally strong. Oh, I could have broken his grip easily, and then broken his arm and his neck, and then I could have crushed the one behind him even if he proved to be as strong as he appeared to be. I was in a generous mood, however.

"What is it to two impertinent wags what I do with my time and currency?" I smiled my most menacing, threatening smile, usually enough to make sane humans leave me alone. Not this one, and not his Nubian associate. They both smiled right back at me, nearly as sinister, and fully as threatening.

The Nubian opened his jacket just a bit. I caught a glimpse of an ornate hilt attached to a sword strapped to his thigh, the hilt rising from an exquisite, burnished scabbard of much handled gold inlay. No wonder he had remained standing, and no wonder he stood in a stance suggesting battle. I could tell the sword was old—older than this establishment, older than everyone in it. Older certainly than the Nubian could possibly be.

The Albino stood, and with no more comment, walked off toward the entrance. The Nubian leaned over the table and hissed at me.

"We'll discuss it outside, away from these weak onlookers," then stood up straight, pointing forked index and middle fingers at me, a sign that in the Middle Ages meant, "I do renounce thee, evildoer."

Ye Gods! A devotee of the occult gestures of medieval Catholic secret societies? I gave him back a thumb linked to my curled index finger, the gesture of dismissal from a Maltese knight to a lowly vassal, which says, "Water my horse while I take a crap." He seemed to actually recognize it for he drew back in offense. He followed his chum out of the front door.

Peculiar indeed.

I looked at the door they'd passed through. I arose, dropped a shrift of currency notes onto the table beside my now iceless drink, and promptly made my way to the passage leading past the latrines to the tavern's back door. Outside in the alleyway, I let the body I'd borrowed drop to the trash littered ground beside a dumping bin belonging to the Chinese market across the alleyway. I took to the air and glanced down to see my two nemeses standing patiently out in front staring at the door, expecting me to pass through it.

It was almost as if the two didn't know enough about drinking institutions to know that they have back entrances convenient for avoiding meaningless combat.

I digress, I know. My apologies.

As I said, *physicians* were humans whom I had visited once or twice and had actually had interesting conversations with. I had only killed one who had got a bit threatening and tiresome. In the early hours of this time-space in Princeton, no one opposed me as I walked off the streets in the body of a dark-skinned physician and into a hospital, though I did get odd looks. Something about "segregation," I think— an annoying social barrier in the Union of States at the time.

No matter. It was a simple enough thing to cripple the backward, bigoted parts of the brains in the heads of the people I encountered who seemed about to oppose me. They stood bewildered, disoriented as they watched me pass, uncertain of what they had been about to say, uncertain of what had upset them, unable to remember. I walked by them, smiling, and to the room of that particular monkey I sought.

Inside the room, the lights were off. Waning moonlight shone in broken rectangles on the figure beneath the sheets, who lay on his side with his back to the door. I pushed the door closed and moved to stand beside the bed, listening to the one who lay there and to his irregular breaths.

"I know you are not a nurse or a doctor," the man wheezed softly in the dark.

"And I knew that you were not asleep, Herr Professor."

"*Ach*, who can sleep with the pain? Quite a place, a hospital. We are all bound for this place. It is a country in which we all hold citizenship for our lives, we are only a little time in exile from it, waiting to be returned."

He carefully turned over now to face me.

"I could not even finish my calculations," he waved an arm feebly at the bedside table where papers lay scattered, a writing stick— "pencil"—laying atop the papers on which quantities, Lorentz transformations, and coefficients were scribbled on many of them.

With the feeble human eyes I was using in this darkness, eyes that could not see anything at all in the infrared range, I could just make out his great 1915 field equation for general relativity, and a rescribing of his summation convention, a tensor, as if he were, well, rethinking what I had blithely criticized in his work the first time I'd appeared to him! He had laid the tensor beside his field equation.

I could make out also his use of Lorentz linear transformations from three-dimensional coordinate spacetime frame calculus to boldly speculative four-dimensional alternates proposed at a constant and accelerating velocity. The moving alternates were relative to the previous three-dimensional frame calculus. Was this evidence that he was seeking a meta dimensional and expanding superimposition?

He was "on the right track," as humans back then would say, but he was failing to intuit embedded dimensionality—four dimensions of space rather than three; dimensions curled up within dimensions. Kaluza-Klein theory, which he'd notated, enables you monkeys to extrapolate four-dimensional gravity, a theory the old man had previously refused to take seriously.

What? No, I don't expect you to understand, just write it down, my dear. That's it. Listen.

My point is that I saw that a monkey could actually do this, could demonstrate the imagination to reconceive his own restricted perceptual apparatus. Was it due to the offhand remarks and calculations I had shown him? Well, such a monkey could further extend his own perception of degrees of freedom and find even the outer realm of Shamayim. Unlike Archimedes, he was able to question his own thoughts, even to question the work he was famous for. Here, let me sketch it on your paper, give me the *Feder*.

$$\hat{v}^i = \left(R^{-1}\right)^i_j v^j, \qquad R_{\mu\nu} - \tfrac{1}{2}R\,g_{\mu\nu} + \Lambda g_{\mu\nu} = \frac{8\pi G}{c^4}T_{\mu\nu}$$

$R_{\mu\nu}$, the _Ricci curvature tensor;_ R is a _scalar curvature,_ $g_{\mu\nu}$ is a rather primitive _metric tensor,_ Λ is what he sees as the _cosmological constant (he doesn't know there is none; the universe is expanding, not in a steady state)_ and G is Monkey Isaac _Newton's gravitational constant,_ c is the _speed of light_ in a vacuum, and $T_{\mu\nu}$ is _stress–energy_. I know what you're thinking. He's later proven correct about the cosmological constant because of dark matter and energy, but you are wrong. I know what "dark energy" really is, and it isn't what you think it is. You wouldn't believe it, so I shan't share that with you. The professor's life's work is astounding, but . . .

Unfinished.

His greatest struggle was to supersede the limits of three dimensions, a struggle he was now about to lose. As brilliant a monkey as he was, he was still just a monkey.

I reached over to turn on the electrical light standing beside his papers on the table.

"*Bitte*, it hurts my eyes."

Well, after all, I am the light bringer.

Chuckling, I switched off the stand.

"Ahhh, much better," he sighed, and rolled on to his back to look at the ceiling. I sat down upon the edge of his bed carefully, as not to inflict any additional pain upon him.

"You are a different specter today."

"Then you know who I am, Herr Professor?"

"You are now in what appears to be the body of a Negro, if that is actually a body, but I surmise you are the same being who approached me not long ago on the sidewalk near my home, the day I was barefoot."

"My clothing does not convince you—?"

"A Negro surgeon, here?"

"It is an actual human body, as was the one I occupied when I met you."

"You have gotten that body somewhere other than this hospital, dressed it in a surgeon's smock?"

"If you wish me to go—"

"*Nein*, stay. You are at least someone I can talk to about physics in my final hours. That man will not be harmed . . .?"

"I will leave him unharmed if you wish, I promise. You would not be dying if you had agreed to the surgery to repair the ruptured artery in your abdomen."

"I've had enough of that. I want to live or die as God wills, without further cutting and mincing and gouging of my person!"

I said nothing to this. It seems not to need a response.

"I only wish I could have finished my speech, or my calculations. Neither is going well,"

I picked up another sheet and read it. It was the speech. He certainly would not be delivering it. I put it down, picked up another sheet; it was full of more calculations—gravitational coefficients and vectors. A fortunate path his thoughts were taking, now focusing on gravity, the true path to tangent dimensions, but his calculations were still far off the mark. He had years still to go at this pace, but not any more years to live.

"If you need it to read, turn the lamp back on."

I chuckled. "No, I do not require light in order to see."

He grunted, coughed. "No, I suppose you wouldn't."

"Would you like assistance with your calculations?"

"I want nothing other than conversation. I doubt it would be wise to seek more than that from you."

"Then would you like to have more time?"

"You can do that?"

"It is a simple enough thing to do."

"Why would you do that, for me?"

"You will have more time for conversation . . . and for your calculations, of course."

"Are you saying I am that close?"

"No, not close at all, I'm afraid. Vector mechanics is a proper approach, but your gravitational calculations are rudimentary yet."

He sighed. "In that case, definitely not, Herr . . . what did you ever say your name was?"

"Call me whatever you wish."

"Then I shall call you Herr Kibitz."

He laughed, then he embarked upon a spasm of coughing that caused him pain. I waited an interval, the face I wore cast in what I hoped would appear to be a considerate visage. Presently, the coughing ceased.

"That is an amusing cognomen, Herr Professor. Why use a Yiddish term to designate me?

"If you have to ask, then it applies."

Sarcasm?

"Don't be cross, I might name you *Dybukk*. I didn't."

"Why do you assume I'm cross?"

"Your expression."

"I have none."

"If you think you don't, then you have a weakness."

"It does not matter what you call me. It seems that your kind never knows just what I should be called."

"What kind?"

"The English term would be 'Father', or in your German, 'Vader'."

"Not *HaShem*?"

"You seem more and more Judaic the closer you come to death."

"Should I sound more and more like that ass Oppenheimer?"

"Are you becoming pious, then?"

"What is mathematics but piety? What is faith but a formulation, a proposition in search of a validating proof?"

"So you believe in HaShem."

"I believe in nothing other than thought, and thought encompasses all possibility, as you would know, were you human."

"How can you say thought encompasses all, but reject the thought of your fellows Bohr and Rosenfeld who theorize indeterminacy and quantum electrodynamics?"

"I did not say one should take all thought as *correct* thought."

I chuckled evilly. "Herr Professor, I think you wish to have things two ways."

He rolled over to face me, not without pain. "My dear Herr Kibitz, I think you do as well. Either one loves humanity or not. You ought to make up your mind, but not because there is any ultimate meaning to it, you see, rather because you seem to need to. The question is not whether or not there is a HaShem, but whether or not I *need* for there to be. Obviously there is you, and so by deduction, there is a HaShem of some sort, somewhere. But frankly, though I have a certain nostalgia, shall we say, for that proposition, I have more important things to do."

"What have you to do? Scribble failed calculations and mourn your inability to resolve your unified field theorem?"

"No, at the moment what I have to do is die. I mean to do so with dignity, as I have tried to live. HaShem is or is not HaShem. I can scribble my calculations—I can do that. I cannot control or see or understand HaShem because that is exactly what the concept means! No one can know. I know that nothing can travel faster than light. That is what I know. What more do I need to know, other than the fact that I shall be dead today? Does that answer all of your questions?"

In the silence, he rolled on to his back again and stared at the ceiling. He closed his eyes. His breathing grew ragged.

"Herr Doktor, my etymology is obviously incomplete."

"*Ach*, you nevertheless are quite the etymologist."

I felt angry, I don't know why, my dear, but I did. My voice grew harsh.

"You've no idea what an etymologist I really am, Professor: Old Persian *pita*, or *fader*, which is Old Saxon, Old Frisian feder, Old Norse *faðir*, High German *fater*, German *vater--pəter*, or Sanskrit *pitar*, Greek and Latin *pater*, Old Irish *athir* . . . I could go on."

"I'm sure you could."

He was indeed being sarcastic.

I contemplated ripping his hoary old head off his shrunken old body, but calmed myself. The anger receded, and then he spoke, almost whimsically.

"Anyway, as far as dybbuks go, now I know the *mezuzah* I had the nurse nail up in the doorway is pretty damned useless."

At this, I had to smile. He turned his head to me in the dark, and smiled as well.

"Shall we discuss vectors now?" he asked.

Near the slopes of the Palatine in early summer, waves of heat will sweep along crowded streets. This day a typically hot wind twisted the skirts of women walking with their sons and brothers among the stalls as the women shopped for Egyptian trinkets to hang from their wrists. The biting dust worried the eyesight of stolid young men seeking tinctures of Greek emollients to relieve the rashes they suffered as a result of their compulsive athletic exertions.

In a long pause between wars, the young men, not needed for the legions, kept themselves occupied with frenetic wrestling bouts, strenuous at athletic games, and foolish footraces in the dust in the shadows of the Palatine aqueducts.

He spied me walking in the bright afternoon as he came out of his *insula* on the way to his bakery next door. He happened to be carrying the pup.

"*Salve*, citizen. Was your journey fruitful?"

"It was, Avicus."

He knew me to be Saturnius in a different body but knew not to call me that in public, for it was a famous name and might call attention. "Citizen" was the word he used when we walked together in the streets. We began walking past the stalls, Avicus stroking the pup affectionately.

"You worry yourself when you should not, I think."

"It is a habit of mine, Baker."

"Good men need not puzzle so over everything they do."

"I am neither good nor a man, Avicus Petronius."

"The pup likes you. Animals can tell if you're good."

"I've not found an answer to that. Some animals, particularly birds, fear and loath me. Some are unconcerned. Horses never seem to fear at all. Other animals fear me at first, as did the pup's father, but then grow to accept me."

"Animals are like women. My wife feared at first, for I had bought her as a slave. Even after I freed her, she distrusted me. In time, I was able to show her something she could love."

We had reached the foot of Palatine, the slope just below the temple of Magna Mater, Cybele. He handed the pup to me.

"What was this thing you showed her, Avicus?"

"That though I am Roman, though I purchased her, and though I am of the evil tribe called men, I seek to be more. That is all any of us can do, even a consort of Charon such as you, we can seek to be more than we are. She grew to love me in my seeking. She will love me as long as I do that. She and I will miss the pup."

He rubbed the dog's head, nodded goodbye to us both, and walked back the way we had come. I continued upward, toward the temple.

At the level of the temple I saw them emerging; Marcellus Quintus and his father Flavius Marcellus Quintus, both in bright white togas, surrounded by a cluster of similarly rich and powerful men and women, all flanked by Sibylline priests. Lucretia was nowhere in sight, as I knew she wouldn't be. She had told me her memory of this day, and informed me she had not been here.

Just as I approached, the sun was obscured by clouds; the bright sky dimmed. A swirl of dust from below followed me, spinning at my back, causing Flavius Marcellus to shield his eyes as if against me rather than the dust behind me.

As I came nearer, one of the Palatine elite stepped between me and the Flavians, Marcellus the elder and younger, and spoke in a cautionary tone.

"Where go you, Outlander? Have you lost your way? The markets and the sellers of beasts are down below."

"I'm friend to Marcellus the Younger, stand away, monkey."

He shuddered, and stepped quickly aside, as if burned by my voice. The lot of these white-robed elder men parted themselves for me, and I stood before the two Flavians.

"What, you say you know me?" Marcellus demanded, his mouth titling into the crooked grin so well known to me.

"We once were friends," I told him.

His father was impatient.

"Were you at school with my son, in Apollonia?"

I made no reply, but offered Marcellus the pup. He took it readily. The dog eagerly licked at his face.

"What is this?"

"Something your mother has made me realize I owe you, my friend," I said.

"My mother?" his smile was one both of amusement and puzzlement.

I turned and walked back to the street leading downward, away from Palatine. I looked back once. The other nobles had walked on, including Flavius Marcellus Quintus Elder. Marcellus Quintus the Younger still stood there with the dog—with Beast— watching me depart.

The body I wore would soon be dead from blood loss and shock, yet I was unable to flee from it after being stabbed by the Frenchman. Though seemingly a Frenchman, he had spoken in the ancient vernacular Latin of a Roman legionnaire; much here had indicated to me that some will of Anu's was afoot.

But not the stabbing, Anu would not interfere thus in my affairs. He did not care so much about me as to send an agent to harm me;

I was not that important to him. I could not help but chuckle at the thought.

"It's amusing then is it, to die?" the being standing over me taunted. Then his voice turned hard with a peculiar bitterness about it. "I'd like to try it myself sometime, even more so if it's so much a lark."

"Be my guest," I rasped, and shoved my trench knife into him as he stood over me. He barked in shock and pain, lurching backward, the knife deeply embedded in the left side of his chest, about where a heart should be, I reckoned. I took pleasure in noting the gout of very oxygenated human blood that sprayed from the wound as he awkwardly jerked the blade from his body, tossing it aside. So he *was* only human after all. I breathed in pain, but with relief and I-

He smiled.

"Problem is, I *can't*," he hissed, pressing his hand to the wound, applying pressure. "Been nineteen hundred years now, and no sign I'm ever going to."

As I watched, he stanched the flow of blood, and then the flow ceased altogether. When he took his hand away, although his blouse was stained and the rent in the textile still apparent, there was no longer a wound.

"Quite a trick that, eh?" he muttered, more than a bit bitterly, then came back to stand over me with the pilum again. He raised it.

"Been chasin' you I have, for some while now, Lucifer. You never knew it. You're the most self-involved *canis* I ever did see, by Mars's teeth! Selfish even for a goat-fouled angel."

"Who-what are you?"

"I'm a pissed on, friggin' immortal, just like you."

"You're an *angel*?"

"I've seen plenty, but I ain't one of you conceited culos, I'm a man, a man what can't die. I kept trying to kill myself at first, for a couple hundred years I tried. I'm stuck in this life you've been going 'round asking people about like a Greek twit. 'What's th' meanin' of life?' Yer such a pathetic creature."

I was even weaker now, from blood loss; otherwise I'd crush this thing in the shape of a man. Neither could I get myself out of the flesh I wore.

"I had nothing to pass the while away, so I set myself a task of finding *you*. Somethin' to do, y'know? Oh, you can leap about betwixt the years, and I cannot. You can be here and there, now and then, can't yuh? Me, well, I'm persistent even if I can't gad about like you. I went place to place where you had been, and I knew I'd catch you on the ground soon or late, one of these years."

"Why can't— Why am I—?"

"Why are you unable to get out of that body? Why are you dying? This beauty here was once my legionnaire's pilum, and was stained by the blood of Jesus of Nazareth, as so I was stained. I stuck it quick and stout into his side to finish him off. Blood flowed down it on to my arm, dripped into my mouth as I looked up at him. That blood, it keeps me here 'til he returns, I've been told by a couple of beings like you."

"They've spoken to you."

"They have, indeed, and at a respectable distance. They're scared of me, y'know, like you are right now. I stabbed you with this that touched the blood that keeps me alive. It'll kill you dead, though."

He raised the pilum fragment.

"I've done you no harm; you kill me without saying why?"

"Without . . . *stulte! Vappa ac nebulo!* You must read dime novels. This ain't where I hesitate to kill you, to tell you my plans, or make friends 'cause I secretly want you to like me. This is where I destroy your *lutulente* soul. You're a scourge to humanity—an angel. What more reason do I need?"

"I've . . . done you . . . no harm."

True to his word, he hesitated no more but thrust the pilum into my chest and slowly pushed.

"It was you who put Jesus on that cross, I've had centuries to consider your crime. It was you who had Pilate pull me out of the fortress caverns to be there on Golgatha."

What use to argue with him. He, like you, my crab, like all humans, thinks the worst of me.

"And besides, any angel deserves fuck-all. You the most. Arrogant, selfish, murdering shits. I see you, the world is full of your kind in hiding. It's your kind that nameless Judean god sends to do his dirty work, ain't it? It's you who kill the firstborns, who wipe out cities, make us war on each other like the war that kilt every tree and bush, every farmer and flower in this ruined country here. It's you spreads plagues."

He pushed the pilum again, this time meaning to finish.

There was a shot.

He staggered back from me, with a look of surprise. The second shot, obviously from a rifle, put him down on the road, on his back. He lay there quiet and still, the *pilum* lying next to him, a large hole through his chest, blood spurting from the hole.

The next I recall, Yazad's eyes were looking down at me. The eyes dwelt within the face of a tall, too-skinny Normanic-Frankish woman with Merovingian genetic markers on her face.

"Is . . . is it you?"

"In the body of a Frenchwoman. It's me, Heylal."

"I am dying. Something is wrong. The man. He did something to me."

"It is the spear that did it, but he will awaken soon, and we must be gone when he does."

She lay a hand upon the chest of me, another upon my side, and closed the eyes of the body that bore her. I felt searing heat spread from the chest throughout the body and felt all pain drift away. The hands she pressed against me were like burning stones, yet they gave no pain, only relief.

Presently she stood me up with unnatural strength. She gathered her rifle and her things, which were in a backpack, and gathered mine.

Still feeling giddy, I carefully bent over to reach for the man's pilum.

"No!" she shouted. "Angels like you can't touch that damned thing. Leave it."

I slowly stood back up and had time only for two breaths to steady myself before she shoved me out to the road, across it to a withered, ashen fence, then over the fence, to struggle through mud and debris as I tried to keep up with her. I wondered why she'd said angels "like me," and why she didn't simply transport us away.

∞∞∞

"His name is, or was, Casca. He was one of the centurions who guarded Jesus and who put him on the cross, and it was he who finished the poor wretch with a thrust of his pilum."

Yazad sat across from me on the hard, cold floor of half a barn; the still-surviving corner of that half which had withstood bombardment. In that half was a doorway or what was left of one, wide enough for horses to pass through facing out to the ruined road we had traveled. Here and there outside the door were corpses of what presumably had been some of the horses that had once lived here.

The missing back half was now a muddy water-filled shell crater, a torn-up field beyond the crater with no roads, no paths—obviously the remains of a farm. The barn was our haven from the wind and from the eventuality of rain.

Yazad-in-flesh wore a farmer's pistol in a frayed leather holster strapped beneath one arm. Her rifle, the one that had saved me, leaned beside the door. With a worn and bitten walnut stock, it reclined against the only fully surviving wall; it was a handsome 1910 401 caliber Winchester self loader. A 401 packed quite a punch for this time, having put that creature down on the road long enough for us to escape him.

As you would imagine, my dear, were you still alive to do so, I'd grown as knowledgeable of guns while in service to your Kaiser as I'd been of swords while in service to Rome. This 1910 401 was common among French farmers—those who could afford them—during the World War and would soon be favored as well by many others from Belgians to Imperial Russians, who were lucky enough to get one, in the Russian Civil War.

Spread beneath us was a rough woolen blanket she'd pulled from her pack, and a block of cheese on a chipped china plate. A bottle of wine sat next to the cheese. She was pulling the last of her treasures from the pack: crusts of stale, hard Russian black bread.

"Didn't you witness him do it? The angels all say they saw you in Judea the night Jesus was seized."

"I had no desire to see his final humiliation. I tried to urge him to sweep the humans all into oblivion and save himself."

She looked at me suspiciously before continuing. "Blood from Jesus's wound fell upon this man who was Casca, and so he is immortal. The man must walk the Earth until Jesus returns here, if he does return. Apparently, he hates you."

"Casca" I muttered. "It's a familiar name. How do you know of him? How did you know where to find me?"

"Everyone knows."

"Who is everyone?"

"The hosts of heaven. They have known of your charade here on Earth, and many of them are here as well, banished. You haven't seen them?"

"I am confined to Earth it seems, these past two thousand years or so."

"So are they. All around you—one tenth of all of us—those who followed you, here like you. Punished. You haven't noticed?"

"I've noticed strange things, suspicious humans with nonhuman vibrations. Humans who seemed far stronger than they should be, and dead humans appearing in the flesh again . . ."

"You didn't wonder about any of that?"

"I did once when two humans who seemed ancient and unnaturally strong confronted me in a drinking establishment in London, but—"

"You are blind, Son of Morning. As for Casca, I've followed him as he followed you for years, even across an ocean on a doomed ship that sank. I survived on a lifeboat, and he somehow thought he should have drowned at the bottom of the ocean appeared again on shore alive."

"A fortunate fellow."

"Fortune had nothing to do with it, unfortunately for you. I knew for certain then what he was; and you, beloved, were too absorbed in your own self to know he was behind you. He was too absorbed in you to know I was behind him."

"The angels. Where are they?"

"Near as I can tell, for they will not speak to me. Some take up residence in human flesh as you are now. Some are in spirit form, seen and unseen, called *ghosts* when they allow themselves to be perceived. Some have taken to inhabiting natural objects: stones, trees, animals. Some have taken to delicate forms such as sentient clouds, and the more whimsical among them are 'aliens' darting about as so-called flying saucers as they or their conveyances are named by humans."

"Outcasts. Another of our father's outrages."

"You needn't choose to see it that way. These angels, all of whom followed *you*, are confined here that's all, not harmed."

"And this Casca?"

"He was human to begin with. His life is simply now extended, as I have heard it said by the one or two less bitter angels who have condescended to visit me once or twice."

"Another childish symbolic game of Anu's. Another bit of doggerel by a bad poet, a decree imposed on some poor soul."

"You are so concerned for a human? What of the one whose body you've stolen, beloved?"

"As you have stolen the one you occupy?"

She glared at me but said nothing to this. "Ordinarily, no, I don't feel for them," I said. "But to think this human is condemned—"

"I've a notion Casca could be worse off. After all," she mused. "He could have gotten what Judas got."

I grunted. I pulled my military coat tighter at the neck and sniffed. "The name does sound familiar." I took out the dog-eared journal-book, *Sympathy for Me* from my pack and thumbed its pages.

"What is that?"

"My memoir."

She choked off a derisive laugh, almost throwing up wine, saying, "You're as conceited as ever you were, Light Bringer!"

"Nonsense. I've written many books, in case you didn't know it, parts of *The Book of Light* are my work. I've even written one portion of the New Testament, *Galatians*. I wrote it, not Paul."

"Heavens, why?"

"I'd come to resent the fallacies of so-called lawyers and Hebraic preachers."

"Of course you did."

I paused. Her tone was odd. I went on, "These juridical authors implied that the Gentile Galatians must adhere to Mosaic law."

"What a riveting subject. I imagine it brought out the rabbinical instinct in you."

"Not at all. Don't forget I was there when my brother preached in Judea. Abrahamic law was not what he intended. Didn't he cast the offenders from the temple? I was there when he commanded them to see that he had come to renounce the old covenant. Believe his teachings or not, his words were clear. Imagine, it was the so-called Christians who demanded that Anatolian men must submit to circumcision!"

"What is all that to you, beloved?"

"I'd been awhile in Anatolia. I'd grown to appreciate the Roman provinces and the people there. Suddenly, the Paulines were traipsing about, claiming the word of Jesus."

"Some Anatolian had shown you sympathy, no doubt. I see from the cover of that journal that your so-called memoir has the title *Sympathy for Me*?" She gazed at me now with a look of amusement. She got up, drew her pistol, and went to the doorway to look out.

I ignored her seeming mockery and found the certain page I sought.

"Casca. The centurion who guarded the cell in the Fortress of Antonia. I remember."

She came back after her surveying the landscape, sat back down, reholstering the pistol. She watched me with a look of whimsy on her face.

"Casca is condemned," I said. "To *what* exactly, you say?"

"He walks the world undying until Jesus returns here. He also has a burning lust to destroy you, and as you saw he happens to have a weapon that can do just that, to you or to any other angel. He hates all of us."

"Well, I perhaps can understand, but why does he hate us all?"

"Perhaps because he's met and spent time with one or two of us."

"Why would my brother *return*? Was he not treated poorly enough the first time?"

She smiled. "You don't know the story? You bother to write a book about your own self as you wander Earth, you wrote the Epistle to the Galatians but never read Revelations?"

"I have written mostly Semitic and Asian texts, a few Vadic and a few Aztecan dogmas. I find the portions of the New Testament I did *not* write to be tedious."

"Then have you never seen any cinema? Comic books?"

"They will simply kill him again if he returns here."

"Anu's plan, whatever the result."

I slapped the book shut and thrust it back into the pack.

"This *plan* of Anu's and his refusal to divulge it is arrogant."

"The judgment of a fallen angel who led a rebellion and failed, was cast into the world to walk as a spirit in punishment, being evil steward to the Earth, and who—"

"Why am I regarded as evil? I, who have bombed no villages, who did not beat down the walls of Carthage and slay the entire nation, did not lead insane Assyrian armies to murder people and nail their corpses to city walls. I, who have neither crucified thousands of Spartacus's followers nor crucified Christ. I, who have impaled no Congolese children, as did King Leopold nor consigned millions of Jewish or Armenian souls to the flames of Hitler's fevered atrocities. They have made me a myth. I, who have done nothing to them, who am merely seeking truth!"

"And who is apparently writing a memoir about his own evil," she finished. "For it is not true you've done *nothing*, is it? You illuminated Casca, did you not? You have illuminated every soul you've encountered whenever you came near them in spirit form. I suspect that one or another of the angels have told him you made him sick. He blames you for the thoughts he has now, for his fevered dreams, for his being plunged into eternity and into concord with divine beings. He was once a simple-minded first-century soldier. Now, though trapped in human form, he has the thoughts and lives the existence of a divine being."

"Then he should thank me."

"You are so conceited, why do I love you so? Most humans do not appreciate what happens to them when they are exposed to angels, beloved. Exposure to you being the worst of all."

"You misjudge me. Of course, I've stepped on one or two of them now and then—"

"You are evil not because the humans have made a myth of you but because you are the pattern of the evil that infects them. The human crimes you cite were grown from the seed that is you. We angels introduced your evil into The Creation. Therefore, it echoes in human souls and in their deeds. I was the first evil follower of Satan, and I was mother to the human race."

"You were Eva!"

"Yes, I can remember that now," she said as she broke off a chunk of dark hard bread and bit into it.

"As I suspected! Anu chose to make you that, it was his doing!"

"You don't understand. I was always *meant* to be Eva so that there would be humans with souls. You changed the nature of my children by creating the evil that was handed down to them."

"But you say I was meant to."

"Everything we do is ordained."

"Yet we are guilty!"

"The fact that an action is caused does not prevent it from being a free action."

"Do not lecture me on free will and determinism."

"No. I should not lecture you on *that*. You polluted the infinite levels of the creation with the idea when you shouted that philosophy from the upper precincts across a thousand dimensions to rally us in battle, did you not? I quote: 'We are determined beings but have souls! Any action we take will be ordained of His will because any action which fulfills our own motives, intentions, and desires is a free action, though determined, and thus natural!' Do you remember those words?"

"But it was Anu, not I, who created free will."

"It was you who championed free action, acting out of spite, out of arrogance, without thought to those harmed. Will and action are not one and the same. Free will also means free choice. You and all of us chose to do what we did. That was the poisonous gift you gave us all."

I remained silent, staring at the bread she was chewing, though as usual, I had no desire to "eat."

"Don't you realize by now, Light Bringer, that it was not Imhotep and Thales, Herodotus and Aristotle, who created metaphysics? It was you in that moment. Anu created free will, but Spinoza, following you, founded the philosophy of free will and determinism. Ahmenemhet did not create his philosophy of cynicism except through your model, your pattern, inherited through me. Sundiata Keita was the outcast king of the Mandinka because you were the model for his tortured soul. Infamous Cao Cao, the tyrant emperor Wu of Wei is you. Men created Sisyphus and Prometheus to describe what you are and what you *did*. It's all there in human writings and histories, films—"

"Comic books."

"Yes, comic books."

"Popular entertainment for humans is all I am, then?"

"You are not listening. You ought to have visited the human called Diop, Cheikh Anta Diop, the scholar. He could have explained it all better than the physicist in Princeton."

"And my influence is evil, even if I do not seek it so."

"Again I say you are not listening."

"Tell me."

"It was ordained, yes. And yes, you are the source."

"Because I must be."

"And now you have written a memoir. Will you hire a publicist?"

"I tire of this squabbling. Let us not fight."

"That's right. You like to start battles, but do not like to fight."

"I begin to wonder why I have searched for you."

"I'll wait while you decide."

"Yazad, I care for you."

"And I you, or I would have let that *Shibboleth* who once was a man, erase your spirit. But I must tell you to leave me alone."

"We can leave together once I am recovered. We can—"

"You can. I cannot leave this body, for this body is me. You occupy a body that you may leave once you are strong. I am not an angel anymore, but human."

"I've traced your genetic courses through the lives of the humans you have been. You have always been Yazad, the spirit within. You were always—"

"I was. But only while I was unknowing. I was awakened when Uriel came to me and revealed to me that I am being punished."

"Uriel—"

"Profane her not, beloved. For she told me what I must do to relieve my soul. Not much better off than Casca I am. Human, but reborn fully aware each time. I am in penance for my sin. I will live life after life as a human and die again and again until the day I will be judged."

"No."

"Yes. All will be judged someday. All but you."

I stared.

"Yours is a soul unlike others. Only the Nazarene is as you are. You will not be judged with us, for you were already judged and condemned when Anu made you. Your punishment is to be you. Your punishment is all this, is everything that you are."

She gestured, indicating all the Earth, all the universe around us, it seemed.

I noted how the lines in her face coalesced into a delicate, lovely scripture at the corners of her eyes.

"Nonsense. I will be there when you die, dear Yazad, and will free you from human form, from endless cycled of rebirth in flesh, and we will—"

"You will never speak to me again. Uriel has told me this time is to be our last together. You cannot touch my soul and you will never again leave Earth."

"Nonsense, I can leave this body—"

"But not the Earth. Have you tried to?"

"Not lately."

"Like Judas, you were meant to do all you have done, even the rebellion. For that rebellion you must do penance."

"All is planned, yet he punishes us, angels and humans!"

"We deserve punishment. Angels who followed us are—"

"Are destroyed."

"You are obstinate, didn't I just tell you . . . He wouldn't do that, and you've seen them."

"I've . . . seen nothing, nothing I knew to be—"

"No?"

Even as she asked this, I remembered the two men I'd encountered in the drinking establishment that cold London night—the Albino and the Nubian seated near the door, the Nubian possessing an ancient sword covered in runes, which he'd held secreted under his trench coat. Some part of me had known all along what and who they really were even before I'd glimpsed the sword. If I had gone out of the place through that front door, they would have tried to accost me, would have revealed their true selves, would have tried to destroy me.

"They are cast into the Earth. They are the lost souls whom ignorant humans call 'demons'——wandering, no longer anointed, unable to be human but still divine, watching humanity. Some do and learn."

"Learn what?"

She ignored my question.

"Those who learn might live among humans, as you do, though they lack the ability to inhabit human bodies as you do. They can only 'possess' bodies briefly, killing the body in the process, as you are killing the one you are inside of now, with carelessness. Others simply watch out of hatred, vengeance, or just because they slowly grow insane, do evil on humans through possession, influence, hallucinations, nightmares, and visions.

This conversation grows tedious with repetition.

"They appear as phantasms, Light Bringer, as mirages, illusions, eliciting violence. They are the poltergeists, destructive ghosts, aliens."

"So you've said, but that is not my doing."

"My situation is your doing."

"If they grow insane that is upon their heads. They took up the rebellion of their own intent, they were not forced."

"One can hardly blame the poor demented dears, I suppose."

"Blame them for human suffering. It must be them who've wreaked so much havoc here."

"Blame them for—" but she didn't finish. She laughed obnoxiously. Then, "Surely you jest, beloved."

"Hitler will not take his ideas from me."

"Certainly, Himmler will. Goebbels. Heydrich. Rinehart Heydrich will evince quite a lot of your haughty narcissism, in fact."

"Don't know the man."

She chuckled and drank gingerly from the wine bottle, offered it to me. I ignored it.

"Perhaps you do have a reason to go on denying your part in it," she sighed sadly. "Anu determined *your* behavior. All the rest of his creation have sinned through genuine free will. I *chose* to be evil."

"There. Then I am innocent."

How she laughed at that!

"You are the least innocent of all souls, save Anu's own. You are like Anu, even more than The Nazarene is like Anu. You share Anu's guilt."

"Guilt! That's a new claim now. Your reasoning runs in circles!"

"He spoke to me and told me that."

"He spoke? To you?"

Her face took on a foolish sort of wonderment, like that of a smug, delighted cow.

"Yes," she whispered. "He spoke to me of his sadness and of his guilt. He knows he made beings who are flawed and tortured by free will and knows he must expose us to evil so that . . . so we can learn to be as He is."

I snatched the bottle from her and tossed it against the ruined wall. It shattered and rained red liquid to the ground where it would slowly freeze.

"That wine was French, and very hard to scavenge."

She calmly removed another bottle from her pack, her face clouded by sadness. This sadness offended me, for it bore a likeness to pity as far as I was concerned.

"Try not to be selfish, beloved."

"Rubbish! It all makes no sense."

"None at all. But then it is not meant to make sense. It is merely meant to be. We can discuss it, analyze it, even criticize and rebel against it, but none of that will bring us closer to understanding it. You must learn to submit to it as I have. Perhaps your Viennese *Doktor* can help you. If you are the pattern of humanity, as Jesus is, then you and he are something even I cannot really understand. So who am I to tell you how to behave? I apologize."

Her tone was now suddenly sympathetic, even loving. That pleased me.

"The Doktor is a monkey. He amuses me, that's all."

"It seems he also comforts you, that he may be somewhat of a surrogate father to you."

"How do you know of him?"

"Uriel told me what you've been doing."

"What did the cow say?" I was angry again.

"In the time-space where you visit him he is inventing a science for understanding the human soul, though he thinks he studies only mind. The trinity resides in the human soul, in forms the Doktor has named: Superego, Id, and Ego. What Uriel has not said, but what I know, is that *you* are Ego, Jesus is Id, and Anu is superego."

I stared at her in amazement.

"Ego," she continued, "You. The willfulness, the arrogance of humans. Yet you too have an ego, a subconscious."

"Nonsense, and improbably complicated, in volation of Occam's razor. Like a bad Victorian novel."

"Really? Then who was the other you that you have seen three times?"

"Pardon moi?"

"Three times. Uriel told me, though I doubt she realizes the meaning of it herself."

Could she be referring to the alternate wave form of myself that I'd seen in Italy? The bird I'd seen in a dream? The "me" who fought for Augustus in yet another dream? Impossible. Collapsed wave functions that I create with my own energies, quite possibly, but that is physics, understandable through the Schrodinger equation, not psychology. Perhaps in fact dream identities are best explainable at this level of existence and flesh by Freudian means.

"How could an angel have a subconscious, Yazad? By becoming flesh? This is consternating. Since when have your thoughts been so opaque, so like a human's?"

"Since I became one."

"Am I to believe that humans and I are so alike?"

"In the twenty first of their centuries, in the nation realm China, human scientists will create a machine that will capture your Ego essence. It will be called 'artificial intelligence.' It will be an entrapped portion of the trinity—-the Holy Spirit. Ego. An entrapped part of you."

"Disgusting. I must visit the twenty-first century and destroy this *machina*. And by the way, did you just say that I am the Holy Spirit?"

"Humans are joined with the Holy Spirit through Ego. Human ego—a part of Anu, is you. I take that to mean your brother is of Anu, the human version of superego, or maybe he's the Id. I am not as familiar with your Doktor's theories as you."

"The Christ like you was born human, no longer an angel!"

"Sometimes you are unbearably stupid, beloved."

"As you wish. How do humans make—a machine? Out of my spirit?"

"By reaching into the creation and tapping infinite dimensions, forcing Ego into consciousness, they shall create a machine that thinks. An artificial version of you, My Love, Shrodinger's cat--the dead one. It will be ferociously evil."

"Foolish, a distortion of quantum super position."

"You are super position in spirit. That is why you are not an example of free will, but of the plan."

"The plan again!"

"I am human," she whispered. Yet I've survived ships sinking, planes crashing, and a war. Anu's will."

"This disgusting *machina* is part of his precious 'plan'?

She leaned forward and kissed me. It was the second time there had been a physical kiss between us. The first time had been when I had kissed Signorina Amalfi.

I pulled her closer to me. She shivered, from birth flesh erotic response, not from cold.

"I could never despoil you in flesh, beloved."

"I know, Heylal," she breathed huskily.

She pulled away, stood, slung her pack over her shoulder, slung the rifle over the other, and went to the shattered doorway, then out into the hard mud of the yard. I rose to follow, but fell back to the floor, dizzy, still weak, grunting like a beast.

She turned and smiled sadly at me, then walked away toward a nearby road. My head lying on dirt and debris, I watched her, my aspect ratio askew because I lay on my side. I peered at her through the shabby remains of the barn door until she was a distant figure, small and indistinct, and then was no more.

When I was able to raise my head again and keep it steady to look again to the barn door, I saw a somehow familiar visage standing there. Backlit by the sun setting in a red sky, the ubiquitous withered trees that are common to all battlefields stood petrified behind the *man* standing there, all things glowing yellow in slanting light.

No, it wasn't the man, Casca.

I suspected it was an angel, a fallen angel who'd once been my ally during the war. Anyway, I suspected it was him. He paused in the doorway of the barn, dressed unlike the time in that he wore late-twentieth-century biker's regalia—a leather jacket, leather pants, and hobnail boots. In the doorway, he made a familiar, peculiar Mesopotamian gesture of right hand held up, left hand held down, and so I knew him for certain to be my once-cherished general, Pazuzu.

He was bald, Nubian skinned, and he wore leather gloves to match his pants and jacket. He came in, came very near to me, and squatted, staring down at me with a sneer that was almost a smile. It had been he, the Nubian from the bar with the rune-covered sword.

"Light Bringer," he whispered with a British accent and a rattling throatiness as though he were a heavy smoker suffering from emphysema. He was not. He was obviously an angel not quite adept at talking with a human larynx. He wore a black man's body, but not the same body as the Nubian's in the bar. If Yazad spoke true, he and his kind could not remain in a body quite long enough to master its vocal organs.

"You are laid low," he chuckled, rasping. "What be it? Bad clams?"

"Which one are you," I asked, raising my head a bit more but still too weak to rise.

"You knew it you did, yeah? When you saw me and my brethren 'afore in that bar in Piccadilly?"

"Pazuzu."

"In the flesssh!" He chuckled at his own pun.

"Why do you appear? To destroy me while I am weak? You would only release me from this body, so do as you will."

"Oh, no, mate. I'd just wait for the one who comes to drive that spear into yuh. Flesh or not, he's sufficient to rid us of you for all and ever. I got a proposal for a truce. How's about we—"

"No."

"Stubborn still then, eh? The why of it is simple, only reason ever to break a good vendetta is for mutual benefit to all. In this here case, benefit to the fallen and to you our former commander-at-arms. If left to me, I'd guide Casca to you and watch, but I was chose, Guv'nor, to speak for the others. I can't keep this body long in thrall 'fore it scorches and dissolves, so brief let me be."

"Spit it out."

For a moment, he looked puzzled, squinting and rolling his tongue around in his mouth as if searching for spit, then he got to it.

"We've learnt to break Anu's rules by merging our powers, thus, I'm able to stay solid longer than a day, like you see. We can give Yazad's spirit back to you, if you but share your power with us."

"To what end?"

"Give us The Tongue, then."

"The archangel and I alone can bear it."

"Is that why you hide it from yourself because it is so easy to bear?"

"I will not relinquish it."

"The Titanic. You be sure you'll have met us there, on the night of the tenth day of *Abril* in the year of their lord nineteen and twelve, after the Titanic left Southampton and put in at Cherbourg. The first-class smoke room, A-deck 'hind of the aft grand stair."

"That ship has already sank, two years ago in 1912."

"Don't waste my body time being droll, and don't act as if you ain't familiar with human physicists like your precious Albert and in this case Max Tegmark."

I evinced no understanding of what he meant.

"Let me sort you out, then, Captain. Tegmark's gonna write about what these humans are gonna call a 'Level 1 Multiverse,' right? Parochial, but close enough to true as you well know innit, all your gaddin' about through the timelines. He'll be a professor type at MIT someday, and you'll be creepin' about, doubtless to plant a seed about 'many worlds theory' in his monkey head."

I stared at him.

"Play stupid then, *Captain, My Captain.* The Titanic's already sank, all right, it's sank a quintillion-times. It'll sink a quintillion more. In only one universe was your Yazad aboard. We had been there, we'll have been there again. Had you been there too, we'd have helped you keep her. I trust you'll have been there in a future tense."

"You mean future perfect."

"Right-o, Guv'nor. Larkin' about with these monkeys requires a sophisticated understanding of yuh' tenses, 'tis true, true. So if you'll not have been there, we'll have made certain that—she drowned. Notice that last part's past preterit. An action what's finished in a def-nit' past with no further conjugations possible."

He means that once they kill her, the essence of her will be gone. I'd have to wait for her to be born again somewhere in space and time.

A spell of dry, ragged coughing and Pazuzu fell off his haunches over onto his back and was still. I stood, able to move again. A coincidence?

She had said, *I've survived ships sinking, planes crashing, and a war.*

She'd also said that Casca had been on that ship.

The body that had been my former general Pazuzu stirred, it sat up and spoke. "What— happened? Where am I?" The body no longer spoke with a cockney accent but one suggestive of the Union of States.

"You are in 1914, France, dear crab."

"It's 1991! I'm in Brooklyn!"

He stood, breathing far too rapidly, eyes wild, and looked about before staring out of the door at the ruined land. "I mean I was in Brooklyn. How did I get to wherever this is? Please, help me figure this out. Where's my hog?!"

I gestured and burst his aorta, a quick merciful end to his panic about to become hysteria. He collapsed without another word or even a gasp. Had I sent him back to when and where he'd been stolen from, something that would have been exhausting for me or perhaps not even possible for me in my present state, he'd likely never have readjusted, and may well have been declared mad and spent the rest of his life institutionalized. I'd done him a good turn putting him out of his alarm. Had I not?

Hmm. I might someday review that time-space again. I'd at first taken the man for a motorcyclist, not a pig farmer.

Three halos of light glared above me, and I groaned, raising the aching arm of the body I'd worn before and had now returned to, shielding the eyes that had snapped open and now burned in what was now my aching head. What was my heart for the moment was racing painfully.

"*Mein Gott!*" The small, neat, German gentleman had exclaimed his shock. He had a neatly trimmed goatee and wore a spotless white surgical smock. He staggered backward from the thick wooden table like a butcher's block that I lay upon. It was only the shock of my groaning and moving that made him do so for he immediately came back to stand over me and he put himself, mercifully, between myself and those burning lights.

He held a scalpel in one hand, an oddly shaped hacksaw in the other. Both instruments gleamed as if just removed from a surgical tool tray; still pristine.

"*Danke,* Herr Doktor." I thanked him for shielding me from the light. I tried to sit up as spasms shook me. He had snatched his glasses from his face; now, he reseated them on the bridge of his nose so that his eyes, pinched and moist with concern, seemed even more expressive.

"Ja, Ja, dear man! But it was not me who brought you out of . . . I suppose it must have been a coma. In fact, I'd accepted what the surgeons here said, that you were dead. *Verdammt*, you *were* dead."

He'd misunderstood my thanks.

"Don't try to sit up just yet, lay back, rest. This is amazing, this is impossible! Do you realize that in fact you were clinically dead? *Tote!* For nearly two days."

I coughed fiercely and fell back onto the table. I felt a chill strike through me. The heart organ inside the body I occupied still raced.

"Do you understand, my boy? You were clinically dead."

"Ja, Herr Doktor? Is that why I am naked on this table with you about to cut into me with those things? Why is my heart escaping my control?"

He tossed the tools into a tray on a smaller table. He strode across the brightly lit room to find a sheet, returned and spread the sheet over me.

"Is that better?"

"Much."

"Your heart rate is no doubt due to adrenaline. It will pass."

"What is that?"

"A hormone. It's a natural thing, don't worry."

"Natural things are what worry me most. I have felt these unpleasant physical responses in the past when in a body. I've felt them in battle, when one or another of my bodies was damaged, but I have always been able to control a body. This is different. This 'hormone' is something inside of all people?"

"It is a glandular secretion that galvanizes—"

"What?"

"Luigi Galvani. What was that you said about having several bodies? And controlling them?"

"Galvani, you say. I might visit this man, Galvani."

"Impossible, he is no longer living. He was an eighteenth-century physicist who studied dead frogs' responses to electricity. The word is taken from his name—"

"Is it indeed."

"The hormone, adrenaline—it 'galvanizes' or stricken one's anatomy, nerves, the muscles particularly, in anticipation of danger."

"Such as the danger of your slaughtering this body on your butcher's table!"

"I tell you, my boy, you were anatomically—"

"I die for a little bit and right away, Herr Doktor, you wish to vivisect me."

"The hospital naturally invited me to do an autopsy, since you were, are my patient. I assure you that you were dead!"

"Yes, well I've a mind to—"

Oh, enough of my whining. How was the fellow to know I'd suddenly awake?

"Forgive me, Herr Doktor. As you say, I appeared to be dead."

"*Were* dead. It is a clinical marvel. Among other things I wish to investigate about you, this strange suspension is one, if you will allow me to."

The trembling had ceased. I sat up, pulling the sheet over my shoulders. The sheet reminded me of how cold my last host had been when I'd left him.

The sound of a beak scratching across the paper of the *Obergruppenfuhrer's* journal was the only sound, other than a quiet whirring noise. I believe the beak was more properly called a "nib" in those times. He periodically paused, dipped the nib into an ink bottle that made a 'clink-ety' noise in the stillness, then the sound of the scratching again.

The whirring came from an electrical mechanism hidden within the false casing of a wood clock standing by the door. It had the appearance of something to be wound with a key but was a mere facsimile. Nazi technology. These Nazis so loved their mechanical devices—clocks, Stuka dive bombers, death camp bone-crushing machines, and the like.

I stood at Herr Heydrich's back for some while before he at last sensed me. He ceased writing, his hand grew inert, his fingers relaxed but held on still to the gold-plated writing tube he'd been scratching with.

Unlike other typically cowardly Nazis, he was not in the least bit startled by me. Yes, these Nazis as I've told you were all the terror— will be—of your upcoming twentieth century, but surely you yourself have perceived that men who will dress in black leather and wear small skulls on their epaulettes will clearly be compensating for their own cowardice, *nein*?

He raised his head and turned it partly to the side as if listening. He slowly lay down his writing tube.

"Are you an assassin?" he asked in a calm, quiet voice.

"Nein," I answered quietly, as quietly as he had spoken.

He turned to look back at me.

"A Belgian, from your accent. Why would they send a Belgian? And how did you ever make your way into this villa? Into this room?"

"I go where I please, Herr Heydrich."

"So you know who I am. You've been sent to kill me."

"All of history knows you."

"Are you implying that you are from the future?"

"That is quite a logical leap for you to make, Herr Heydrich, from so few premises. You Nazis are all quite precocious about such things. Your experiments in atomic energy, gravitational forces, time travel would cause the Allies to not only seek to defeat you were they to know the true extent of your speculations: they would seek to destroy every inch of your country and to wipe out every German here."

Heydrich suddenly threw himself to the floor, but not before drawing a small caliber pistol, some sort of colt it looked like, and shot me, a fairly good shot, to the lower left chest—good considering he was tumbling across the floor as he fired.

It is worth noting that he stood and laughed, quite a delighted laugh, in fact, as he stood over the body I had inhabited, which was now dead.

Laughter. "Exactly why did my death cause you amusement, Herr Hydrich?"

I now appeared to him in my spirit form, allowing him to see me. I cared not that my body would illuminate him, causing him to develop a cancer, were he to live, that is. He wouldn't of course. Before the war ended, he would finally be murdered by the assassins he'd always so intently anticipated.

He raised the gun again, and I reached out and crushed it.

"What are you? Did you come in here with that assassin? Why are you naked?"

"I am not naked, I am in the form that is proper for me and those like me."

"The Belgians, you mean. The underground fanatics."

"How ironic you, a Nazi, should use that word."

"Your nudity is obviously part of a cult. You see yourself as some sort of pure weapon against us. Your hatred of your masters has always seemed to me to be like a cult. How did you do that to my pistol?"

"That man was no assassin. He was a Belgian postal inspector on vacation in the South of France. I crushed your fire arm just as I would crush you, were it not that I have a task for you to perform for me, soon."

He smiled arrogantly.

"Why should I do that? If you are going to kill me, do so. I do not fear death. I serve my Fuhrer and my Reich with all my heart and soul. My death means nothing, for my Reich will outlast me by a thousand years."

"Astonishing. If you don't fear death, it is only because you do not know what it is. I am inclined to disabuse you of that ignorance."

"In death I shall be—"

"Idiot, are you completely blind? Your so-called Reich will be crushed by the Allies like a rotten tomato in a few short years. You yourself will carry out a genocide, but it scarcely seems worthwhile given how many millions of *Juden* will be born to replace the paltry six or seven million you will kill."

"Seven million!" His pale blue eyes lit up with pleasure as he said in an exalting tone, "You are some sort of Aryan herald angel from Valhalla? You come to tell me my triumph over the enemies of the German people will reach such heights!"

I walked over to lock his office door and stood at the window looking out at snow on the lawn of the Wansee Mansion, in the wood-paneled study of which I now stood. The mansion, located west of Berlin, sat beside a lake. It was the period called 1940. This place was a headquarters for the policing and national security apparatuses of the Third Reich—the Reich this pathetic monkey before me so ardently served.

"This mansion is meant to someday be yours."

He swelled with pride. "Der Fuhrer will reward me then."

"Meant to be yours, but you will not survive the war."

Still he smiled, the sneer of an empty apparatchik fool.

"Tell me, Herr Heydrich, do you have within you any slight trace of empathy for your victims? Any shame, any guilt?"

Heydrich looked thoroughly confused by this.

"Well then, do you have any fear at least?"

"I told you I do not fear death!"

I walked over to stand near him, and only now did he notice a strange insubstantial look to my "body."

"In June, you Nazis will invade Paris. Stop grinning. You will order the arrests of hundreds of French Jews and of gypsies and Algerians who will be in the French resistance. Two of them will be held at the stadium in Paris—they will have a daughter named Fadya. You may have the parents if you wish, though I want your promise to me that they will be executed in the stadium and will be spared the humiliating death of a concentration camp."

"Really."

"Yes, and the daughter, Fadya, will be untouched. You will leave here alive."

"Again, why should I accede to your desire in this matter, Belgian?"

"Because I cannot interfere directly with these events to come. I do, however, require you to keep the girl alive for me."

"No. If you are an Arayan angel, you will do as I say, instead. As I told you, I do not fear death, so I do not fear you."

"Tell me, Herr Heydrich, have you ever been dead?"

"Of course not."

"Never been brought back from death?"

"Never."

"Then perhaps you ought to make a short visit to the afterlife. Perhaps from that you will learn to have respect for death, and for me. Hold still now. This will hurt quite a bit, in several ways, but I promise to bring you back."

The fool did not even recoil as I concentrated and burst his heart like an over-ripe peach.

⬳⬳⬲

"Was ist? What are you calling me, Herr Doktor?"

"*Lamedvavnik*. It's a Yiddish term, you know, taken from the Hebrew letters, 'lamed' *und* 'vav.' The concept is Hasidic."

"I am aware of the Hasidic meanings. Why are you calling me that?"

"You know Yiddish, then? I am not calling you that at all. One of my colleagues here, he is convinced that this is what you are. A Lamedvavnik: one of thirty-six righteous souls who hold God's universe together. The thirty-six are called 'The Tzadikim.'"

I laughed quite heartily at this as I put on the suit of clothing the doctor had gone out to purchase for me. As I laughed, tears came to my eyes. Odd, how human bodies weep both for pleasure and for pain. We were in the doctor's offices at the hospital—the same hospital whose basement mortuary I had only lately quit after rising off the doctor's butcher's block undissected.

The doctor stood watching me, smiling at my mirth, his thumbs thrust into his vest pockets. He took a partly burned cigar from a third inner vest pocket. The vest, his starched white shirt and cardboard collar, his ink-black tie, his pressed trousers, and buffed leather shoes were all as immaculate and as neat as always. He strolled over to take a silver lighter from his desk nearby, sat on the edge of the desk and relit the cigar. The acrid aroma of tobacco filled the room—his own examining room and office given him by the university hospital where he taught and did his research. He sat behind the desk, which was littered with small statuettes and figurines of what looked to be mythological personas from various world cultures. I recognized many of them. Some were effigies of my long-lost fellow angels—my past war companions, former friends among the celestial spirits of *Shamayim*. This recognition gave me pleasure.

I finished dressing, amused again, because the suit he had purchased for me to wear was a taller, broader version of his own; of tweed and rougher wool, with a starched white shirt of Egyptian cotton. Leather shoes just like his, with metal buttons up the sides. It was as if he perceived me as being a potential extension of himself.

I sat down in a chair near his desk. He gazed at me, smiling still. Something about his smile, its openness and its acceptance of me, was vaguely reassuring.

"My colleague thinks you can only be explained in this manner: as a Judaic righteous soul, my boy. Oh, you don't like the appellation, 'my boy,' do you? I'm sorry."

"You've said what your colleague thinks. What do you think, Herr Doktor?"

"From my limited observations so far? I think you yearn for peace of mind, but there is likely a more serious diagnosis to be made."

"Indeed."

"Ja. I am a neurologist by training. I think that perhaps you have a physiological trauma to the brain closely attendant to your psychological syndrome—your delusion. The fascinating thing is that one may be caused by the other or may not be. There may be no causal relation between the two disorders whatsoever. Only physical diagnosis and psychological analysis can tell."

He puffed his cigar and gazed at me a moment before continuing.

"My suspicion, however, is that a physical trauma to your brain is responsible for the narcolepsy you suffer, leading to long bouts of near-death coma, and that this same brain injury is causing you to fabricate these elaborate delusions about your identity as a devil."

"Herr Doktor, I am quite surprised to find that history has been wrong to portray you as a man who saw all mental illness as being related to sex. You are actually quite a conscientious anatomist."

"Sex? Sex? My dear man, libido can sometimes impact an illness, or help the diagnostician to explain a presentation of neuroses, phobias, *und* complexes, but not organic illness. All psychology begins with anatomy."

I walked to a tall shelf that stood against an entire wall and lifted a bound scroll—a book, that is, off Herr Doktor's shelf: *Enzyklopädie der Antike* (*Encyclopedia of the Ancient World*). Tugging the pages, I navigated to seeing Anu's name and was surprised.

"What is it you're reading? You look surprised."

"I am surprised to see my father's name in your book. The name Anu."

"Ah, yes. Anu is indeed a sky god."

"Actually, he is *the* sky god, Herr Doktor."

"Shall I quote the passage you are no doubt looking at? 'An early Mesopotamian sky god later seen as Father of the Gods'..."

Here he paused, pronouncing *vader* with a note of irony that did not escape me.

"'And, ruler of the heavens, a designation meant to be passed to his son Enlil, Anu's companion at the beginning of the universe. Originally a Sumerian sky deity named "An" meaning sky.'"

I snapped the book closed in one hand and inserted it back onto the shelf. "A good description of my father, yes. And I am not a devil, Herr Doktor. I am *the* Devil, to use your western culture's term for me."

"Enlil." Mikayel once called me that as a curse, not a compliment.

"Ah, yes, just so. What do you mean, by the way, history *has been* wrong about me? You keep talking about me as if—"

"Are you not Judaic yourself, Herr Doktor? Do you place no importance at all upon *Gott*?"

"Gott? Of course not. Certainly, the retrograde religious impulse is a residual characteristic of man's earlier tribal existence, and so it is reasonable to expect that many people—even an educated man like my colleague—still hold on to such notions, but—"

"But not you."

"Primitive societies sought to find meaning in the world with these, these . . . myths. Christ, Shiva, Allah, Jehovah, Siddhartha. My colleague is Jewish, so to him the myths are Jewish myths. *Gott*, he says, gathered together the righteous souls for a consultation before he laid the foundation of the universe, and he asked their guidance. Or perhaps it was that he gave them their instructions."

"More likely."

"Ja. Jesus, Moses, Jacob, various other eternal, righteous souls were there, prepared to take their journey through time in the form of flesh."

I chuckled at this, for he was unaware how close to the truth this human tale actually is, minus the implication of some sort of democratic impulse on Anu's part.

"Do you hold religious beliefs other than your delusion that you are the progenitor of evil, my-my friend?"

"My name is Heylal."

"Herr Heylal. You are Syrian, then? I wondered about your accent. From Damascus, perhaps?"

"No."

"You don't remember, do you?"

I declined to answer, for he was clearly unwilling to accept the truth. Proving it to him would likely entail frightening him, and I had no desire to do that, at least not yet.

"Memory loss supports my diagnosis. So what are we going to do with you?"

"I would much appreciate if you would agree to have sessions with me as you had described before."

His eyes lit up like a boy's.

"Psychoanalysis?"

"Ja-Ja. I don't believe it could do me any harm, and I feel it may help me to understand some things about myself."

"About your relationship with your father!"

"As you put it, yes, among other concerns I have. Right now, in fact, I am concerned that I am undergoing with you the process you have or will call 'transference'."

"You do know my work! Ja, transference, in which the patient projects his desire for love and for approval onto the therapist. It seems harmless in this case, particularly since you are aware of it. With training, you yourself might make a fair psychoanalyst, I hazard to think."

"I'm certainly dressed for it."

He stared blankly, having completely missed the irony, the point of my jest. I laughed again, but then winced. I felt the presence of the Tongue of God still tucked away inside of me, a burden and a dull pain as always, but also a source of power—of unimaginable power, I now believed, if I could just learn to unlock that power and to use it.

"Was ist, my boy? Are you in pain?"

He cannot help himself, though it seems no sign of disrespect. *Can "transference" go both ways? I must ask him.*

"No-no, Herr Doktor, it's just—"

"Sit back! Rest! I will get you something-is it migraine?" He hurried to a medicine cabinet beside the window.

Anu had allowed me to possess the Tongue all these centuries and to bury it; this reality had not escaped me. He had also of course, allowed me to dig it up and make it a part of myself again. How this must be rankling Mikayel! I had no doubt that at some point in my exile, Mikayel would be making an attempt to get the Tongue back. Was he feeling the terrible emptiness, the desolation of no longer possessing it, no longer being attuned to it?

Anu had even allowed me to gain a means of attuning the Tongue to myself by using the blood of my brother. The blood from the cloth that had been given to me by the other me, the cloth Jesus had saturated with his own blood that I was still in possession of and that I planned to use in many ways when the time came.

Something inside me felt almost that the sword was my inheritance, my birthright. Perhaps even my sign of succession. What life in exile had taught me, my dear, ultimately, was that I am not the King.

But for now perhaps, I am the Elder Prince, consigned to exile awaiting the death of the King, my estranged father.

I rose to cross to the window, looking out at the rainy streets of Vienna, as the doctor rummaged through his pill bottles. I pushed aside the curtain only slightly, peering out at a hundred huddled figures dashing through the streets, hurrying to avoid getting wet. I thought how any one of them might be an insane, wrathful ex-soldier named Casca, and I drew back from the pane involuntarily, a foolishly human impulse almost resembling human fear. The centurion surely was nowhere near. Some of the humans out there held umbrellas, none of which resembled a broken pilum.

"Of course, you realize that you must ultimately accept that you are not in a rivalry with your father."

I turned from the blue-streaked, wet and darkening window, back to the warm interior, to the aroma of tobacco, the gentle steady *knock-knock-knock* of a clock pendulum, the fastidiously bare walls that held no other decoration, except for book shelves. I looked at my doctor.

"I cannot compensate you at the moment, Herr Doktor, but I can certainly in a day or so acquire talents—or as you call them here, money. *Marks*, is it not?"

"Nonsense. You shall be a guest of the hospital, supported by research monies right here at the university for as long as you are my patient. We shall get to the root of your delusion that you are Satan, and perhaps also discover when and where your brain injury occurred. I promise to help you find peace and rest, my boy."

He insists on calling me that. Is it a "Freudian slip"?

"Herr Doktor, I feel I must alert you to the difficulties you will have in the future. The Nazis whom you mentioned when we first met will eventually grow dissatisfied with your fame."

"Bah. I am of little consequence to those people."

"I know that you were insincere when you claimed to be as-yet unknown. I am aware that there are already in this time frame numerous psychoanalytic societies inspired by your books, in cities across the world."

The clock suddenly tolled the hour in soothing tones, but the wrong hour, I noted. "Your work is well known by the Nazis, and they will soon be burning your books."

"What progress we have made since the Middle Ages, eh? They would once have burned me. Now it is only my books in danger of the fire."

"You will escape Austria after Hitler invades. You will reach safety in England."

He laughed.

"Nonsense, I would rather be shot by those Berlin thugs than be exiled in a country where the potato is considered a delicacy. I promise to never disrespect your notions, though you must understand that I wish you to accept that you are not an angel, you do not have divine powers, and cannot see the future."

"And for my part, I promise to not frighten you, Herr Doctor, at least for a while."

He chuckled, puffing a bloom of smoke into the air.

"I must tell you, Herr Heylal, that as a doctor and psychologist, I have seen everything imaginable about the human condition, everything painful, wretched, and pathetic—I am not easily frightened."

You will be.

"—And I certainly sympathize with your condition, my-my friend."

As he finished speaking, he glanced, annoyed, at the clock. "That's odd," he muttered, crossing the room to open the glass face of the device with a key he took from his pocket, "It chimed an incorrect hour a moment ago as we spoke." He reached inside and wound the clock with a second key, then checked the time against his own pocket watch.

I sat down again and watched him intently. Finally, he turned back to me, tugging his vest down, smoothing his tie, and disdaining his now burned-down former cigar, he extracted a fresh one from a desk drawer, snipping the end off with a surgical scissors, striking a wooden match to light and puff it, and exhibiting his satisfaction that the time was no longer out of joint.

"When would you like to begin, Herr Heylal? How far do you wish to take treatment, and what are your goals?"

I smiled.

THE END

ABOUT THE AUTHOR

Rayfield A. Waller is a journalist, he authored the novel "Sympathy for Me", for which "And Lat Waste My Soul" is the sequel, and has published a number of academic articles, in 'Renaissance Noire', in 'The African American Review', in 'Solid Ground Magazine', and in 'The Black Scholar', among others.

Professor Waller teaches Caribbean and African American history, economics, politics, and culture for Wayne State University's Dept of Africana Studies/African American Studies (AFS) in Detroit, Michigan. He teaches logic and composition for Wayne County Community College, and composition at Macomb College--both in Michigan.

He was the first contemporary poet published in the revival of historic Broadside Press, which published his book of poems, "Abstract Blues" (found on Amazon). He is the author of a second book of poems, "Television Funereal", (also on Amazon). His first novel, "Sympathy for Me" is available on Amazon and at Barnes and Noble.com

He is a past recipient of the Michigan Council for the Arts writers' grant and is a recipient of the Tompkins County Human Rights Award in upstate New York for his journalism. He was a King/Parks/Chavez Visiting Instructor in Wayne State's English Department. Many of his

poems can be found in the online journal, 'Outlaw Poetry' at https://
outlawpoetry.comLinks to an external site..

He did his Masters and PhD work at Cornell University and is
listed in 'Cornell Writers". He has studied international relations at
Harvard University. He has writing in various anthologies including
'New Poems from the Third Coast: Contemporary Michigan Poetry",
in 'Nostalgia for the Present: An Anthology of Writings from Detroit'
from Post Aesthetic Press, and in the Wayne State University Press
anthology of Detroit poets, 'Abandon Automobile'. Waller is a
widely published art and music critic with works in newspapers, and
academic and literary journals including 'Obsidian', and the online
journal, 'The Panopticon Review'.

He is a former staff writer and contributor to "The Ithaca Times",
"The Ithaca Journal", "The Detroit Metro Times", "The Michigan
Citizen", and South Florida's "Progreso Weekly/Progreso Semenal".

Lightning Source UK Ltd.
Milton Keynes UK
UKHW010413190821
389088UK00008B/363/J